THE LEAVENWORTH CASE

By Anna Katherine Green

BOOK I. THE PROBLEM

I. "A GREAT CASE"
> "A deed of dreadful note."
> —Macbeth.

I had been a junior partner in the firm of Veeley, Carr & Raymond, attorneys and counsellors at law, for about a year, when one morning, in the temporary absence of both Mr. Veeley and Mr. Carr, there came into our office a young man whose whole appearance was so indicative of haste and agitation that I involuntarily rose at his approach and impetuously inquired:

"What is the matter? You have no bad news to tell, I hope."

"I have come to see Mr. Veeley; is he in?"

"No," I replied; "he was unexpectedly called away this morning to Washington; cannot be home before to-morrow; but if you will make your business known to me——"

"To you, sir?" he repeated, turning a very cold but steady eye on mine; then, seeming to be satisfied with his scrutiny, continued, "There is no reason why I shouldn't; my business is no secret. I came to inform him that Mr. Leavenworth is dead."

"Mr. Leavenworth!" I exclaimed, falling back a step. Mr. Leavenworth was an old client of our firm, to say nothing of his being the particular friend of Mr. Veeley.

"Yes, murdered; shot through the head by some unknown person while sitting at his library table."

"Shot! murdered!" I could scarcely believe my ears.

"How? when?" I gasped.

"Last night. At least, so we suppose. He was not found till this morning. I am Mr. Leavenworth's private secretary," he explained, "and live in the family. It was a dreadful shock," he went on, "especially to the ladies."

"Dreadful!" I repeated. "Mr. Veeley will be overwhelmed by it."

"They are all alone," he continued in a low businesslike way I afterwards found to be inseparable from the man; "the Misses Leavenworth, I mean—Mr. Leavenworth's nieces; and as an inquest is to be held there to-day it is deemed proper for them to have some one present capable of advising them. As Mr. Veeley was their uncle's best friend, they naturally sent me for him; but he being absent I am at a loss what to do or where to go."

"I am a stranger to the ladies," was my hesitating reply, "but if I can be of any assistance to them, my respect for their uncle is such——"

The expression of the secretary's eye stopped me. Without seeming to wander from my face, its pupil had suddenly dilated till it appeared to embrace my whole person with its scope.

"I don't know," he finally remarked, a slight frown, testifying to the fact that he

3

was not altogether pleased with the turn affairs were taking. "Perhaps it would be best. The ladies must not be left alone——"

"Say no more; I will go." And, sitting down, I despatched a hurried message to Mr. Veeley, after which, and the few other preparations necessary, I accompanied the secretary to the street.

"Now," said I, "tell me all you know of this frightful affair."

"All I know? A few words will do that. I left him last night sitting as usual at his library table, and found him this morning, seated in the same place, almost in the same position, but with a bullet-hole in his head as large as the end of my little finger."

"Dead?"

"Stone-dead."

"Horrible!" I exclaimed. Then, after a moment, "Could it have been a suicide?"

"No. The pistol with which the deed was committed is not to be found."

"But if it was a murder, there must have been some motive. Mr. Leavenworth was too benevolent a man to have enemies, and if robbery was intended——"

"There was no robbery. There is nothing missing," he again interrupted. "The whole affair is a mystery."

"A mystery?"

"An utter mystery."

Turning, I looked at my informant curiously. The inmate of a house in which a mysterious murder had occurred was rather an interesting object. But the good-featured and yet totally unimpressive countenance of the man beside me offered but little basis for even the wildest imagination to work upon, and, glancing almost immediately away, I asked:

"Are the ladies very much overcome?"

He took at least a half-dozen steps before replying.

"It would be unnatural if they were not." And whether it was the expression of his face at the time, or the nature of the reply itself, I felt that in speaking of these ladies to this uninteresting, self-possessed secretary of the late Mr. Leavenworth, I was somehow treading upon dangerous ground. As I had heard they were very accomplished women, I was not altogether pleased at this discovery. It was, therefore, with a certain consciousness of relief I saw a Fifth Avenue stage approach.

"We will defer our conversation," said I. "Here's the stage."

But, once seated within it, we soon discovered that all intercourse upon such a subject was impossible. Employing the time, therefore, in running over in my mind what I knew of Mr. Leavenworth, I found that my knowledge was limited to the bare fact of his being a retired merchant of great wealth and fine social position who, in default of possessing children of his own, had taken into his home two nieces, one of whom had already been declared his heiress. To be sure, I had heard Mr. Veeley speak of his eccentricities, giving as an instance this very fact of his making a will in favor of one niece to the utter exclusion of the other; but of his habits of life and connection with the world at large, I knew little or nothing.

4

There was a great crowd in front of the house when we arrived there, and I had barely time to observe that it was a corner dwelling of unusual depth when I was seized by the throng and carried quite to the foot of the broad stone steps. Extricating myself, though with some difficulty, owing to the importunities of a bootblack and butcher-boy, who seemed to think that by clinging to my arms they might succeed in smuggling themselves into the house, I mounted the steps and, finding the secretary, by some unaccountable good fortune, close to my side, hurriedly rang the bell. Immediately the door opened, and a face I recognized as that of one of our city detectives appeared in the gap.

"Mr. Gryce!" I exclaimed.

"The same," he replied. "Come in, Mr. Raymond." And drawing us quietly into the house, he shut the door with a grim smile on the disappointed crowd without. "I trust you are not surprised to see me here," said he, holding out his hand, with a side glance at my companion.

"No," I returned. Then, with a vague idea that I ought to introduce the young man at my side, continued: "This is Mr. ———, Mr. ———, —excuse me, but I do not know your name," I said inquiringly to my companion. "The private secretary of the late Mr. Leavenworth," I hastened to add.

"Oh," he returned, "the secretary! The coroner has been asking for you, sir."

"The coroner is here, then?"

"Yes; the jury have just gone up-stairs to view the body; would you like to follow them?"

"No, it is not necessary. I have merely come in the hope of being of some assistance to the young ladies. Mr. Veeley is away."

"And you thought the opportunity too good to be lost," he went on; "just so. Still, now that you are here, and as the case promises to be a marked one, I should think that, as a rising young lawyer, you would wish to make yourself acquainted with it in all its details. But follow your own judgment."

I made an effort and overcame my repugnance. "I will go," said I.

"Very well, then, follow me."

But just as I set foot on the stairs I heard the jury descending, so, drawing back with Mr. Gryce into a recess between the reception room and the parlor, I had time to remark:

"The young man says it could not have been the work of a burglar."

"Indeed!" fixing his eye on a door-knob near by.

"That nothing has been found missing—"

"And that the fastenings to the house were all found secure this morning; just so."

"He did not tell me that. In that case"—and I shuddered—"the murderer must have been in the house all night."

Mr. Gryce smiled darkly at the door-knob.

"It has a dreadful look!" I exclaimed.

Mr. Gryce immediately frowned at the door-knob.

And here let me say that Mr. Gryce, the detective, was not the thin, wiry individual with the piercing eye you are doubtless expecting to see. On the

5

contrary, Mr. Gryce was a portly, comfortable personage with an eye that never pierced, that did not even rest on *you*. If it rested anywhere, it was always on some insignificant object in the vicinity, some vase, inkstand, book, or button. These things he would seem to take into his confidence, make the repositories of his conclusions; but as for you—you might as well be the steeple on Trinity Church, for all connection you ever appeared to have with him or his thoughts. At present, then, Mr. Gryce was, as I have already suggested, on intimate terms with the door-knob.

"A dreadful look," I repeated.

His eye shifted to the button on my sleeve.

"Come," he said, "the coast is clear at last."

Leading the way, he mounted the stairs, but stopped on the upper landing. "Mr. Raymond," said he, "I am not in the habit of talking much about the secrets of my profession, but in this case everything depends upon getting the right clue at the start. We have no common villainy to deal with here; genius has been at work. Now sometimes an absolutely uninitiated mind will intuitively catch at something which the most highly trained intellect will miss. If such a thing should occur, remember that I am your man. Don't go round talking, but come to me. For this is going to be a great case, mind you, a great case. Now, come on."

"But the ladies?"

"They are in the rooms above; in grief, of course, but tolerably composed for all that, I hear." And advancing to a door, he pushed it open and beckoned me in.

All was dark for a moment, but presently, my eyes becoming accustomed to the place, I saw that we were in the library.

"It was here he was found," said he; "in this room and upon this very spot." And advancing, he laid his hand on the end of a large baize-covered table that, together with its attendant chairs, occupied the centre of the room. "You see for yourself that it is directly opposite this door," and, crossing the floor, he paused in front of the threshold of a narrow passageway, opening into a room beyond. "As the murdered man was discovered sitting in this chair, and consequently with his back towards the passageway, the assassin must have advanced through the doorway to deliver his shot, pausing, let us say, about here." And Mr. Gryce planted his feet firmly upon a certain spot in the carpet, about a foot from the threshold before mentioned.

"But—" I hastened to interpose.

"There is no room for 'but,'" he cried. "We have studied the situation." And without deigning to dilate upon the subject, he turned immediately about and, stepping swiftly before me, led the way into the passage named. "Wine closet, clothes closet, washing apparatus, towel-rack," he explained, waving his hand from side to side as we hurried through, finishing with "Mr. Leavenworth's private apartment," as that room of comfortable aspect opened upon us.

Mr. Leavenworth's private apartment! It was here then that *it* ought to be, the horrible, blood-curdling *it* that yesterday was a living, breathing man. Advancing to the bed that was hung with heavy curtains, I raised my hand to put them back, when Mr. Gryce, drawing them from my clasp, disclosed lying upon the pillow a

6

cold, calm face looking so natural I involuntarily started.

"His death was too sudden to distort the features," he remarked, turning the head to one side in a way to make visible a ghastly wound in the back of the cranium. "Such a hole as that sends a man out of the world without much notice. The surgeon will convince you it could never have been inflicted by himself. It is a case of deliberate murder."

Horrified, I drew hastily back, when my glance fell upon a door situated directly opposite me in the side of the wall towards the hall. It appeared to be the only outlet from the room, with the exception of the passage through which we had entered, and I could not help wondering if it was through this door the assassin had entered on his roundabout course to the library. But Mr. Gryce, seemingly observant of my glance, though his own was fixed upon the chandelier, made haste to remark, as if in reply to the inquiry in my face:

"Found locked on the inside; may have come that way and may not; we don't pretend to say."

Observing now that the bed was undisturbed in its arrangement, I remarked, "He had not retired, then?"

"No; the tragedy must be ten hours old. Time for the murderer to have studied the situation and provided for all contingencies."

"The murderer? Whom do you suspect?" I whispered.

He looked impassively at the ring on my finger.

"Every one and nobody. It is not for me to suspect, but to detect." And dropping the curtain into its former position he led me from the room.

The coroner's inquest being now in session, I felt a strong desire to be present, so, requesting Mr. Gryce to inform the ladies that Mr. Veeley was absent from town, and that I had come as his substitute, to render them any assistance they might require on so melancholy an occasion, I proceeded to the large parlor below, and took my seat among the various persons there assembled.

II. THE CORONER'S INQUEST

"The baby figure of the giant mass
Of things to come."
—Troilus and Cressida.

FOR a few minutes I sat dazed by the sudden flood of light greeting me from the many open windows; then, as the strongly contrasting features of the scene before me began to impress themselves upon my consciousness, I found myself experiencing something of the same sensation of double personality which years before had followed an enforced use of ether. As at that time, I appeared to be living two lives at once: in two distinct places, with two separate sets of incidents going on; so now I seemed to be divided between two irreconcilable trains of thought; the gorgeous house, its elaborate furnishing, the little glimpses of yesterday's life, as seen in the open piano, with its sheet of music held in place by a lady's fan, occupying my attention fully as much as the aspect of the throng of incongruous and impatient people huddled about me.

Perhaps one reason of this lay in the extraordinary splendor of the room I was in; the glow of satin, glitter of bronze, and glimmer of marble meeting the eye at every turn. But I am rather inclined to think it was mainly due to the force and eloquence of a certain picture which confronted me from the opposite wall. A sweet picture—sweet enough and poetic enough to have been conceived by the most idealistic of artists: simple, too—the vision of a young flaxen-haired, blue-eyed coquette, dressed in the costume of the First Empire, standing in a wood-path, looking back over her shoulder at some one following—yet with such a dash of something not altogether saint-like in the corners of her meek eyes and baby-like lips, that it impressed me with the individuality of life. Had it not been for the open dress, with its waist almost beneath the armpits, the hair cut short on the forehead, and the perfection of the neck and shoulders, I should have taken it for a literal portrait of one of the ladies of the house. As it was, I could not rid myself of the idea that one, if not both, of Mr. Leavenworth's nieces looked down upon me from the eyes of this entrancing blonde with the beckoning glance and forbidding hand. So vividly did this fancy impress me that I half shuddered as I looked, wondering if this sweet creature did not know what had occurred in this house since the happy yesterday; and if so, how she could stand there smiling so invitingly,—when suddenly I became aware that I had been watching the little crowd of men about me with as complete an absorption as if nothing else in the room had attracted my attention; that the face of the coroner, sternly intelligent and attentive, was as distinctly imprinted upon my mind as that of this lovely picture, or the clearer-cut and more noble features of the sculptured Psyche, shining in mellow beauty from the crimson-hung window at his right; yes, even that the various countenances of the jurymen clustered before me, commonplace and insignificant as most of them were; the trembling forms of the excited servants crowded into a far corner; and the still more disagreeable aspect of the pale-faced, seedy reporter, seated at a small table and writing with a ghoul-like avidity that made my flesh creep, were each and all as fixed an element in the remarkable scene before me as the splendor of the surroundings which made their presence such a nightmare of discord and unreality.

I have spoken of the coroner. As fortune would have it, he was no stranger to me. I had not only seen him before, but had held frequent conversation with him; in fact, knew him. His name was Hammond, and he was universally regarded as a man of more than ordinary acuteness, fully capable of conducting an important examination, with the necessary skill and address. Interested as I was, or rather was likely to be, in this particular inquiry, I could not but congratulate myself upon our good fortune in having so intelligent a coroner.

As for his jurymen, they were, as I have intimated, very much like all other bodies of a similar character. Picked up at random from the streets, but from such streets as the Fifth and Sixth Avenues, they presented much the same appearance of average intelligence and refinement as might be seen in the chance occupants of one of our city stages. Indeed, I marked but one amongst them all who seemed to take any interest in the inquiry as an inquiry; all the rest appearing to be

8

actuated in the fulfilment of their duty by the commoner instincts of pity and indignation.

Dr. Maynard, the well-known surgeon of Thirty-sixth Street, was the first witness called. His testimony concerned the nature of the wound found in the murdered man's head. As some of the facts presented by him are likely to prove of importance to us in our narrative, I will proceed to give a synopsis of what he said.

Prefacing his remarks with some account of himself, and the manner in which he had been summoned to the house by one of the servants, he went on to state that, upon his arrival, he found the deceased lying on a bed in the second-story front room, with the blood clotted about a pistol-wound in the back of the head; having evidently been carried there from the adjoining apartment some hours after death. It was the only wound discovered on the body, and having probed it, he had found and extracted the bullet which he now handed to the jury. It was lying in the brain, having entered at the base of the skull, passed obliquely upward, and at once struck the *medulla oblongata,* causing instant death. The fact of the ball having entered the brain in this peculiar manner he deemed worthy of note, since it would produce not only instantaneous death, but an utterly motionless one. Further, from the position of the bullet-hole and the direction taken by the bullet, it was manifestly impossible that the shot should have been fired by the man himself, even if the condition of the hair about the wound did not completely demonstrate the fact that the shot was fired from a point some three or four feet distant. Still further, considering the angle at which the bullet had entered the skull, it was evident that the deceased must not only have been seated at the time, a fact about which there could be no dispute, but he must also have been engaged in some occupation which drew his head forward. For, in order that a ball should enter the head of a man sitting erect at the angle seen here, of 45 degrees, it would be necessary, not only for the pistol to be held very low down, but in a peculiar position; while if the head had been bent forward, as in the act of writing, a man holding a pistol naturally with the elbow bent, might very easily fire a ball into the brain at the angle observed.

Upon being questioned in regard to the bodily health of Mr. Leavenworth, he replied that the deceased appeared to have been in good condition at the time of his death, but that, not being his attendant physician, he could not speak conclusively upon the subject without further examination; and, to the remark of a juryman, observed that he had not seen pistol or weapon lying upon the floor, or, indeed, anywhere else in either of the above-mentioned rooms.

I might as well add here what he afterwards stated, that from the position of the table, the chair, and the door behind it, the murderer, in order to satisfy all the conditions imposed by the situation, must have stood upon, or just within, the threshold of the passageway leading into the room beyond. Also, that as the ball was small, and from a rifled barrel, and thus especially liable to deflections while passing through bones and integuments, it seemed to him evident that the victim had made no effort to raise or turn his head when advanced upon by his destroyer; the fearful conclusion being that the footstep was an accustomed one,

9

and the presence of its possessor in the room either known or expected.

The physician's testimony being ended, the coroner picked up the bullet which had been laid on the table before him, and for a moment rolled it contemplatively between his fingers; then, drawing a pencil from his pocket, hastily scrawled a line or two on a piece of paper and, calling an officer to his side, delivered some command in a low tone. The officer, taking up the slip, looked at it for an instant knowingly, then catching up his hat left the room. Another moment, and the front door closed on him, and a wild halloo from the crowd of urchins without told of his appearance in the street. Sitting where I did, I had a full view of the corner. Looking out, I saw the officer stop there, hail a cab, hastily enter it, and disappear in the direction of Broadway.

III. FACTS AND DEDUCTIONS

"Confusion now hath made his master-piece;
Most sacrilegious murder hath broke ope
The Lord's anointed temple, and stolen thence
The life of the building."
—Macbeth.

TURNING my attention back into the room where I was, I found the coroner consulting a memorandum through a very impressive pair of gold eye-glasses.

"Is the butler here?" he asked.

Immediately there was a stir among the group of servants in the corner, and an intelligent-looking, though somewhat pompous, Irishman stepped out from their midst and confronted the jury. "Ah," thought I to myself, as my glance encountered his precise whiskers, steady eye, and respectfully attentive, though by no means humble, expression, "here is a model servant, who is likely to prove a model witness." And I was not mistaken; Thomas, the butler, was in all respects one in a thousand—and he knew it.

The coroner, upon whom, as upon all others in the room, he seemed to have made the like favorable impression, proceeded without hesitation to interrogate him.

"Your name, I am told, is Thomas Dougherty?"

"Yes, sir."

"Well, Thomas, how long have you been employed in your present situation?"

"It must be a matter of two years now, sir."

"You are the person who first discovered the body of Mr. Leavenworth?"

"Yes, sir; I and Mr. Harwell."

"And who is Mr. Harwell?"

"Mr. Harwell is Mr. Leavenworth's private secretary, sir; the one who did his writing."

"Very good. Now at what time of the day or night did you make this discovery?"

"It was early, sir; early this morning, about eight."

10

"And where?"

"In the library, sir, off Mr. Leavenworth's bedroom. We had forced our way in, feeling anxious about his not coming to breakfast."

"You forced your way in; the door was locked, then?"

"Yes, sir."

"On the inside?"

"That I cannot tell; there was no key in the door."

"Where was Mr. Leavenworth lying when you first found him?"

"He was not lying, sir. He was seated at the large table in the centre of his room, his back to the bedroom door, leaning forward, his head on his hands."

"How was he dressed?"

"In his dinner suit, sir, just as he came from the table last night."

"Were there any evidences in the room that a struggle had taken place?"

"No, sir."

"Any pistol on the floor or table?"

"No, sir?"

"Any reason to suppose that robbery had been attempted?"

"No, sir. Mr. Leavenworth's watch and purse were both in his pockets."

Being asked to mention who were in the house at the time of the discovery, he replied, "The young ladies, Miss Mary Leavenworth and Miss Eleanore, Mr. Harwell, Kate the cook, Molly the upstairs girl, and myself."

"The usual members of the household?"

"Yes, sir."

"Now tell me whose duty it is to close up the house at night."

"Mine, sir."

"Did you secure it as usual, last night?"

"I did, sir."

"Who unfastened it this morning?"

"I, sir."

"How did you find it?"

"Just as I left it."

"What, not a window open nor a door unlocked?"

"No, sir."

By this time you could have heard a pin drop. The certainty that the murderer, whoever he was, had not left the house, at least till after it was opened in the morning, seemed to weigh upon all minds. Forewarned as I had been of the fact, I could not but feel a certain degree of emotion at having it thus brought before me; and, moving so as to bring the butler's face within view, searched it for some secret token that he had spoken thus emphatically in order to cover up some failure of duty on his own part. But it was unmoved in its candor, and sustained the concentrated gaze of all in the room like a rock.

Being now asked when he had last seen Mr. Leavenworth alive, he replied, "At dinner last night."

"He was, however, seen later by some of you?"

"Yes, sir; Mr. Harwell says he saw him as late as half-past ten in the evening."

11

"What room do you occupy in this house?"

"A little one on the basement floor."

"And where do the other members of the household sleep?"

"Mostly on the third floor, sir; the ladies in the large back rooms, and Mr. Harwell in the little one in front. The girls sleep above."

"There was no one on the same floor with Mr. Leavenworth?"

"No, sir."

"At what hour did you go to bed?"

"Well, I should say about eleven."

"Did you hear any noise in the house either before or after that time, that you remember?"

"No, sir."

"So that the discovery you made this morning was a surprise to you?"

"Yes, sir."

Requested now to give a more detailed account of that discovery, he went on to say it was not till Mr. Leavenworth failed to come to his breakfast at the call of the bell that any suspicion arose in the house that all was not right. Even then they waited some little time before doing anything, but as minute after minute went by and he did not come, Miss Eleanore grew anxious, and finally left the room saying she would go and see what was the matter, but soon returned looking very much frightened, saying she had knocked at her uncle's door, and had even called to him, but could get no answer. At which Mr. Harwell and himself had gone up and together tried both doors, and, finding them locked, burst open that of the library, when they came upon Mr. Leavenworth, as he had already said, sitting at the table, dead.

"And the ladies?"

"Oh, they followed us up and came into the room and Miss Eleanore fainted away."

"And the other one,—Miss Mary, I believe they call her?"

"I don't remember anything about her; I was so busy fetching water to restore Miss Eleanore, I didn't notice."

"Well, how long was it before Mr. Leavenworth was carried into the next room?"

"Almost immediate, as soon as Miss Eleanore recovered, and that was as soon as ever the water touched her lips."

"Who proposed that the body should be carried from the spot?"

"She, sir. As soon as ever she stood up she went over to it and looked at it and shuddered, and then calling Mr. Harwell and me, bade us carry him in and lay him on the bed and go for the doctor, which we did."

"Wait a moment; did she go with you when you went into the other room?"

"No, sir."

"What did she do?"

"She stayed by the library table."

"What doing?"

"I couldn't see; her back was to me."

"How long did she stay there?"

"She was gone when we came back."

"Gone from the table?"

"Gone from the room."

"Humph! when did you see her again?"

"In a minute. She came in at the library door as we went out."

"Anything in her hand?"

"Not as I see."

"Did you miss anything from the table?"

"I never thought to look, sir. The table was nothing to me. I was only thinking of going for the doctor, though I knew it was of no use."

"Whom did you leave in the room when you went out?"

"The cook, sir, and Molly, sir, and Miss Eleanore."

"Not Miss Mary?"

"No, sir."

"Very well. Have the jury any questions to put to this man?"

A movement at once took place in that profound body.

"I should like to ask a few," exclaimed a weazen-faced, excitable little man whom I had before noticed shifting in his seat in a restless manner strongly suggestive of an intense but hitherto repressed desire to interrupt the proceedings.

"Very well, sir," returned Thomas.

But the juryman stopping to draw a deep breath, a large and decidedly pompous man who sat at his right hand seized the opportunity to inquire in a round, listen-to-me sort of voice:

"You say you have been in the family for two years. Was it what you might call a united family?"

"United?"

"Affectionate, you know,—on good terms with each other." And the juryman lifted the very long and heavy watch-chain that hung across his vest as if that as well as himself had a right to a suitable and well-considered reply.

The butler, impressed perhaps by his manner, glanced uneasily around. "Yes, sir, so far as I know."

"The young ladies were attached to their uncle?"

"O yes, sir."

"And to each other?"

"Well, yes, I suppose so; it's not for me to say."

"You suppose so. Have you any reason to think otherwise?" And he doubled the watch-chain about his fingers as if he would double its attention as well as his own.

Thomas hesitated a moment. But just as his interlocutor was about to repeat his question, he drew himself up into a rather stiff and formal attitude and replied:

"Well, sir, no."

The juryman, for all his self-assertion, seemed to respect the reticence of a servant who declined to give his opinion in regard to such a matter, and drawing

13

complacently back, signified with a wave of his hand that he had no more to say.

Immediately the excitable little man, before mentioned, slipped forward to the edge of his chair and asked, this time without hesitation: "At what time did you unfasten the house this morning?"

"About six, sir."

"Now, could any one leave the house after that time without your knowledge?"

Thomas glanced a trifle uneasily at his' fellow-servants, but answered up promptly and as if without reserve;

"I don't think it would be possible for anybody to leave this house after six in the morning without either myself or the cook's knowing of it. Folks don't jump from second-story windows in broad daylight, and as to leaving by the doors, the front door closes with such a slam all the house can hear it from top to bottom, and as for the back-door, no one that goes out of that can get clear of the yard without going by the kitchen window, and no one can go by our kitchen window without the cook's a-seeing of them, that I can just swear to." And he cast a half-quizzing, half-malicious look at the round, red-faced individual in question, strongly suggestive of late and unforgotten bickerings over the kitchen coffee-urn and castor.

This reply, which was of a nature calculated to deepen the forebodings which had already settled upon the minds of those present, produced a visible effect. The house found locked, and no one seen to leave it! Evidently, then, we had not far to look for the assassin.

Shifting on his chair with increased fervor, if I may so speak, the juryman glanced sharply around. But perceiving the renewed interest in the faces about him, declined to weaken the effect of the last admission, by any further questions. Settling, therefore, comfortably back, he left the field open for any other juror who might choose to press the inquiry. But no one seeming to be ready to do this, Thomas in his turn evinced impatience, and at last, looking respectfully around, inquired:

"Would any other gentleman like to ask me anything?"

No one replying, he threw a hurried glance of relief towards the servants at his side, then, while each one marvelled at the sudden change that had taken place in his countenance, withdrew with an eager alacrity and evident satisfaction for which I could not at the moment account.

But the next witness proving to be none other than my acquaintance of the morning, Mr. Harwell, I soon forgot both Thomas and the doubts his last movement had awakened, in the interest which the examination of so important a person as the secretary and right-hand man of Mr. Leavenworth was likely to create.

Advancing with the calm and determined air of one who realized that life and death itself might hang upon his words, Mr. Harwell took his stand before the jury with a degree of dignity not only highly prepossessing in itself, but to me, who had not been over and above pleased with him in our first interview, admirable and surprising. Lacking, as I have said, any distinctive quality of face or form agreeable or otherwise—being what you might call in appearance a negative

14

sort of person, his pale, regular features, dark, well-smoothed hair and simple whiskers, all belonging to a recognized type and very commonplace—there was still visible, on this occasion at least, a certain self-possession in his carriage, which went far towards making up for the want of impressiveness in his countenance and expression. Not that even this was in any way remarkable. Indeed, there was nothing remarkable about the man, any more than there is about a thousand others you meet every day on Broadway, unless you except the look of concentration and solemnity which pervaded his whole person; a solemnity which at this time would not have been noticeable, perhaps, if it had not appeared to be the habitual expression of one who in his short life had seen more of sorrow than joy, less of pleasure than care and anxiety.

The coroner, to whom his appearance one way or the other seemed to be a matter of no moment, addressed him immediately and without reserve:

"Your name?"

"James Trueman Harwell."

"Your business?"

"I have occupied the position of private secretary and amanuensis to Mr. Leavenworth for the past eight months."

"You are the person who last saw Mr. Leavenworth alive, are you not?"

The young man raised his head with a haughty gesture which well-nigh transfigured it.

"Certainly not, as I am not the man who killed him."

This answer, which seemed to introduce something akin to levity or badinage into an examination the seriousness of which we were all beginning to realize, produced an immediate revulsion of feeling toward the man who, in face of facts revealed and to be revealed, could so lightly make use of it. A hum of disapproval swept through the room, and in that one remark, James Harwell lost all that he had previously won by the self-possession of his bearing and the unflinching regard of his eye. He seemed himself to realize this, for he lifted his head still higher, though his general aspect remained unchanged.

"I mean," the coroner exclaimed, evidently nettled that the young man had been able to draw such a conclusion from his words, "that you were the last one to see him previous to his assassination by some unknown individual?"

The secretary folded his arms, whether to hide a certain tremble which had seized him, or by that simple action to gain time for a moment's further thought, I could not then determine. "Sir," he replied at length, "I cannot answer yes or no to that question. In all probability I was the last to see him in good health and spirits, but in a house as large as this I cannot be sure of even so simple a fact as that." Then, observing the unsatisfied look on the faces around, added slowly, "It is my business to see him late."

"Your business? Oh, as his secretary, I suppose?"

He gravely nodded.

"Mr. Harwell," the coroner went on, "the office of private secretary in this country is not a common one. Will you explain to us what your duties were in that capacity; in short, what use Mr. Leavenworth had for such an assistant and how he employed you?"

"Certainly. Mr. Leavenworth was, as you perhaps know, a man of great wealth. Connected with various societies, clubs, institutions, etc., besides being known far and near as a giving man, he was accustomed every day of his life to receive numerous letters, begging and otherwise, which it was my business to open and answer, his private correspondence always bearing a mark upon it which distinguished it from the rest. But this was not all I was expected to do. Having in his early life been engaged in the tea-trade, he had made more than one voyage to China, and was consequently much interested in the question of international communication between that country and our own. Thinking that in his various visits there, he had learned much which, if known to the American people, would conduce to our better understanding of the nation, its peculiarities, and the best manner of dealing with it, he has been engaged for some time in writing a book on the subject, which same it has been my business for the last eight months to assist him in preparing, by writing at his dictation three hours out of the twenty-four, the last hour being commonly taken from the evening, say from half-past nine to half-past ten, Mr. Leavenworth being a very methodical man and accustomed to regulate his own life and that of those about him with almost mathematical precision."

"You say you were accustomed to write at his dictation evenings? Did you do this as usual last evening?"

"I did, sir."

"What can you tell us of his manner and appearance at the time? Were they in any way unusual?"

A frown crossed the secretary's brow.

"As he probably had no premonition of his doom, why should there have been any change in his manner?"

This giving the coroner an opportunity to revenge himself for his discomfiture of a moment before, he said somewhat severely:

"It is the business of a witness to answer questions, not to put them."

The secretary flushed and the account stood even.

"Very well, then, sir; if Mr. Leavenworth felt any forebodings of his end, he did not reveal them to me. On the contrary, he seemed to be more absorbed in his work than usual. One of the last words he said to me was, 'In a month we will have this book in press, eh, Trueman?' I remember this particularly, as he was filling his wine-glass at the time. He always drank one glass of wine before retiring, it being my duty to bring the decanter of sherry from the closet the last thing before leaving him. I was standing with my hand on the knob of the hall-door, but advanced as he said this and replied, 'I hope so, indeed, Mr. Leavenworth.' 'Then join me in drinking a glass of sherry,' said he, motioning me to procure another glass from the closet. I did so, and he poured me out the wine with his own hand. I am not especially fond of sherry, but the occasion was a pleasant one and I drained my glass. I remember being slightly ashamed of doing so, for Mr. Leavenworth set his down half full. It was half full when we found him this morning."

16

Do what he would, and being a reserved man he appeared anxious to control his emotion, the horror of his first shock seemed to overwhelm him here. Pulling his handkerchief from his pocket, he wiped his forehead. "Gentlemen, that is the last action of Mr. Leavenworth I ever saw. As he set the glass down on the table, I said good-night to him and left the room."

The coroner, with a characteristic imperviousness to all expressions of emotion, leaned back and surveyed the young man with a scrutinizing glance. "And where did you go then?" he asked.

"To my own room."

"Did you meet anybody on the way?"

"No, sir."

"Hear any thing or see anything unusual?"

The secretary's voice fell a trifle. "No, sir."

"Mr. Harwell, think again. Are you ready to swear that you neither met anybody, heard anybody, nor saw anything which lingers yet in your memory as unusual?"

His face grew quite distressed. Twice he opened his lips to speak, and as often closed them without doing so. At last, with an effort, he replied:

"I saw one thing, a little thing, too slight to mention, but it was unusual, and I could not help thinking of it when you spoke."

"What was it?"

"Only a door half open."

"Whose door?"

"Miss Eleanore Leavenworth's." His voice was almost a whisper now.

"Where were you when you observed this fact?"

"I cannot say exactly. Probably at my own door, as I did not stop on the way. If this frightful occurrence had not taken place I should never have thought of it again."

"When you went into your room did you close your door?"

"I did, sir."

"How soon did you retire?"

"Immediately."

"Did you hear nothing before you fell asleep?"

Again that indefinable hesitation.

"Barely nothing."

"Not a footstep in the hall?"

"I might have heard a footstep."

"Did you?"

"I cannot swear I did."

"Do you think you did?"

"Yes, I think I did. To tell the whole: I remember hearing, just as I was falling into a doze, a rustle and a footstep in the hall; but it made no impression upon me, and I dropped asleep."

"Well?"

"Some time later I woke, woke suddenly, as if something had startled me, but what, a noise or move, I cannot say. I remember rising up in my bed and looking around, but hearing nothing further, soon yielded to the drowsiness which possessed me and fell into a deep sleep. I did not wake again till morning."

Here requested to relate how and when he became acquainted with the fact of the murder, he substantiated, in all particulars, the account of the matter already given by the butler; which subject being exhausted, the coroner went on to ask if he had noted the condition of the library table after the body had been removed.

"Somewhat; yes, sir."

"What was on it?"

"The usual properties, sir, books, paper, a pen with the ink dried on it, besides the decanter and the wineglass from which he drank the night before."

"Nothing more?"

"I remember nothing more."

"In regard to that decanter and glass," broke in the juryman of the watch and chain, "did you not say that the latter was found in the same condition in which you saw it at the time you left Mr. Leavenworth sitting in his library?"

"Yes, sir, very much."

"Yet he was in the habit of drinking a full glass?"

"Yes, sir."

"An interruption must then have ensued very close upon your departure, Mr. Harwell."

A cold bluish pallor suddenly broke out upon the young man's face. He started, and for a moment looked as if struck by some horrible thought. "That does not follow, sir," he articulated with some difficulty. "Mr. Leavenworth might—" but suddenly stopped, as if too much distressed to proceed.

"Go on, Mr. Harwell, let us hear what you have to say."

"There is nothing," he returned faintly, as if battling with some strong emotion.

As he had not been answering a question, only volunteering an explanation, the coroner let it pass; but I saw more than one pair of eyes roll suspiciously from side to side, as if many there felt that some sort of clue had been offered them in this man's emotion. The coroner, ignoring in his easy way both the emotion and the universal excitement it had produced, now proceeded to ask: "Do you know whether the key to the library was in its place when you left the room last night?"

"No, sir; I did not notice."

"The presumption is, it was?"

"I suppose so."

"At all events, the door was locked in the morning, and the key gone?"

"Yes, sir."

"Then whoever committed this murder locked the door on passing out, and took away the key?"

"It would seem so."

The coroner turning, faced the jury with an earnest look. "Gentlemen," said he, "there seems to be a mystery in regard to this key which must be looked into."

Immediately a universal murmur swept through the room, testifying to the acquiescence of all present. The little juryman hastily rising proposed that an instant search should be made for it; but the coroner, turning upon him with what

18

I should denominate as a quelling look, decided that the inquest should proceed in the usual manner, till the verbal testimony was all in.

"Then allow me to ask a question," again volunteered the irrepressible. "Mr. Harwell, we are told that upon the breaking in of the library door this morning, Mr. Leavenworth's two nieces followed you into the room."

"One of them, sir, Miss Eleanore."

"Is Miss Eleanore the one who is said to be Mr. Leavenworth's sole heiress?" the coroner here interposed.

"No, sir, that is Miss Mary."

"That she gave orders," pursued the juryman, "for the removal of the body into the further room?"

"Yes, sir."

"And that you obeyed her by helping to carry it in?"

"Yes, sir."

"Now, in thus passing through the rooms, did you observe anything to lead you to form a suspicion of the murderer?"

The secretary shook his head. "I have no suspicion," he emphatically said.

Somehow, I did not believe him. Whether it was the tone of his voice, the clutch of his hand on his sleeve—and the hand will often reveal more than the countenance—I felt that this man was not to be relied upon in making this assertion.

"I should like to ask Mr. Harwell a question," said a juryman who had not yet spoken. "We have had a detailed account of what looks like the discovery of a murdered man. Now, murder is never committed without some motive. Does the secretary know whether Mr. Leavenworth had any secret enemy?"

"I do not."

"Every one in the house seemed to be on good terms with him?"

"Yes, sir," with a little quaver of dissent in the assertion, however.

"Not a shadow lay between him and any other member of his household, so far as you know?"

"I am not ready to say that," he returned, quite distressed. "A shadow is a very slight thing. There might have been a shadow———"

"Between him and whom?"

A long hesitation. "One of his nieces, sir."

"Which one?"

Again that defiant lift of the head. "Miss Eleanore."

"How long has this shadow been observable?"

"I cannot say."

"You do not know the cause?"

"I do not."

"Nor the extent of the feeling?"

"No, sir."

"You open Mr. Leavenworth's letters?"

"I do."

"Has there been anything in his correspondence of late calculated to throw any light upon this deed?"

It actually seemed as if he never would answer. Was he simply pondering over his reply, or was the man turned to stone?

"Mr. Harwell, did you hear the juryman?" inquired the coroner.

"Yes, sir; I was thinking."

"Very well, now answer."

"Sir," he replied, turning and looking the juryman full in the face, and in that way revealing his unguarded left hand to my gaze, "I have opened Mr. Leavenworth's letters as usual for the last two weeks, and I can think of nothing in them bearing in the least upon this tragedy."

The man lied; I knew it instantly. The clenched hand pausing irresolute, then making up its mind to go through with the lie firmly, was enough for me.

"Mr. Harwell, this is undoubtedly true according to your judgment," said the coroner; "but Mr. Leavenworth's correspondence will have to be searched for all that."

"Of course," he replied carelessly; "that is only right."

This remark ended Mr. Harwell's examination for the time. As he sat down I made note of four things.

That Mr. Harwell himself, for some reason not given, was conscious of a suspicion which he was anxious to suppress even from his own mind.

That a woman was in some way connected with it, a rustle as well as a footstep having been heard by him on the stairs.

That a letter had arrived at the house, which if found would be likely to throw some light upon this subject.

That Eleanore Leavenworth's name came with difficulty from his lips; this evidently unimpressible man, manifesting more or less emotion whenever he was called upon to utter it.

IV. A CUTS

"Something is rotten in the State of Denmark."
Hamlet.

THE cook of the establishment being now called, that portly, ruddy-faced individual stepped forward with alacrity, displaying upon her good-humored countenance such an expression of mingled eagerness and anxiety that more than one person present found it difficult to restrain a smile at her appearance. Observing this and taking it as a compliment, being a woman as well as a cook, she immediately dropped a curtsey, and opening her lips was about to speak, when the coroner, rising impatiently in his seat, took the word from her mouth by saying sternly:

"Your name?"

"Katherine Malone, sir."

"Well, Katherine, how long have you been in Mr. Leavenworth's service?"

"Shure, it is a good twelvemonth now, sir, since I came, on Mrs. Wilson's ricommindation, to that very front door, and——"

"Never mind the front door, but tell us why you left this Mrs. Wilson?"

"Shure, and it was she as left me, being as she went sailing to the ould country the same day when on her recommendation I came to this very front door—"

"Well, well; no matter about that. You have been in Mr. Leavenworth's family a year?"

"Yes, sir."

"And liked it? found him a good master?"

"Och, sir, niver have I found a better, worse luck to the villain as killed him. He was that free and ginerous, sir, that many 's the time I have said to Hannah—" She stopped, with a sudden comical gasp of terror, looking at her fellow-servants like one who had incautiously made a slip. The coroner, observing this, inquired hastily:

"Hannah? Who is Hannah?"

The cook, drawing her roly-poly figure up into some sort of shape in her efforts to appear unconcerned, exclaimed boldly: "She? Oh, only the ladies' maid, sir."

"But I don't see any one here answering to that description. You didn't speak of any one by the name of Hannah, as belonging to the house," said he, turning to Thomas.

"No, sir," the latter replied, with a bow and a sidelong look at the red-cheeked girl at his side. "You asked me who were in the house at the time the murder was discovered, and I told you."

"Oh," cried the coroner, satirically; "used to police courts, I see." Then, turning back to the cook, who had all this while been rolling her eyes in a vague fright about the room, inquired, "And where is this Hannah?"

"Shure, sir, she's gone."

"How long since?"

The cook caught her breath hysterically. "Since last night."

"What time last night?"

"Troth, sir, and I don't know. I don't know anything about it."

"Was she dismissed?"

"Not as I knows on; her clothes is here."

"Oh, her clothes are here. At what hour did you miss her?"

"I didn't miss her. She was here last night, and she isn't here this morning, and so I says she 's gone."

"Humph!" cried the coroner, casting a slow glance down the room, while every one present looked as if a door had suddenly opened in a closed wall.

"Where did this girl sleep?"

The cook, who had been fumbling uneasily with her apron, looked up.

"Shure, we all sleeps at the top of the house, sir."

"In one room?"

Slowly. "Yes, sir."

"Did she come up to the room last night?"

"Yes, sir."

"At what hour?"

21

"Shure, it was ten when we all came up. I heard the clock a-striking."

"Did you observe anything unusual in her appearance?"

"She had a toothache, sir."

"Oh, a toothache; what, then? Tell me all she did."

But at this the cook broke into tears and wails.

"Shure, she didn't do nothing, sir. It wasn't her, sir, as did anything; don't you believe it. Hannah is a good girl, and honest, sir, as ever you see. I am ready to swear on the Book as how she never put her hand to the lock of his door. What should she for? She only went down to Miss Eleanore for some toothache-drops, her face was paining her that awful; and oh, sir——"

"There, there," interrupted the coroner, "I am not accusing Hannah of anything. I only asked you what she did after she reached your room. She went downstairs, you say. How long after you went up?"

"Troth, sir, I couldn't tell; but Molly says——"

"Never mind what Molly says. *You* didn't see her go down?"

"No, sir."

"Nor see her come back?"

"No, sir."

"Nor see her this morning?"

"No, sir; how could I when she 's gone?"

"But you did see, last night, that she seemed to be suffering with toothache?"

"Yes, sir."

"Very well; now tell me how and when you first became acquainted with the fact of Mr. Leavenworth's death."

But her replies to this question, while over-garrulous, contained but little information; and seeing this, the coroner was on the point of dismissing her, when the little juror, remembering an admission she had made, of having seen Miss Eleanore Leavenworth coming out of the library door a few minutes after Mr. Leavenworth's body had been carried into the next room, asked if her mistress had anything in her hand at the time.

"I don't know, sir. Faith!" she suddenly exclaimed, "I believe she did have a piece of paper. I recollect, now, seeing her put it in her pocket."

The next witness was Molly, the upstairs girl.

Molly O'Flanagan, as she called herself, was a rosy-cheeked, black-haired, pert girl of about eighteen, who under ordinary circumstances would have found herself able to answer, with a due degree of smartness, any question which might have been addressed to her. But fright will sometimes cower the stoutest heart, and Molly, standing before the coroner at this juncture, presented anything but a reckless appearance, her naturally rosy cheeks blanching at the first word addressed to her, and her head falling forward on her breast in a confusion too genuine to be dissembled and too transparent to be misunderstood.

As her testimony related mostly to Hannah, and what she knew of her, and her remarkable disappearance, I shall confine myself to a mere synopsis of it.

As far as she, Molly, knew, Hannah was what she had given herself out to be, an uneducated girl of Irish extraction, who had come from the country to act as

22

lady's-maid and seamstress to the two Misses Leavenworth. She had been in the family for some time; before Molly herself, in fact; and though by nature remarkably reticent, refusing to tell anything about herself or her past life, she had managed to become a great favorite with all in the house. But she was of a melancholy nature and fond of brooding, often getting up nights to sit and think in the dark: "as if she was a lady!" exclaimed Molly.

This habit being a singular one for a girl in her station, an attempt was made to win from the witness further particulars in regard to it. But Molly, with a toss of her head, confined herself to the one statement. She used to get up nights and sit in the window, and that was all she knew about it.

Drawn away from this topic, during the consideration of which, a little of the sharpness of Molly's disposition had asserted itself, she went on to state, in connection with the events of the past night, that Hannah had been ill for two days or more with a swelled face; that it grew so bad after they had gone upstairs, the night before, that she got out of bed, and dressing herself—Molly was closely questioned here, but insisted upon the fact that Hannah had fully dressed herself, even to arranging her collar and ribbon—lighted a candle, and made known her intention of going down to Miss Eleanore for aid.

"Why Miss Eleanore?" a juryman here asked.

"Oh, she is the one who always gives out medicines and such like to the servants."

Urged to proceed, she went on to state that she had already told all she knew about it. Hannah did not come back, nor was she to be found in the house at breakfast time.

"You say she took a candle with her," said the coroner. "Was it in a candlestick?"

"No, sir; loose like."

"Why did she take a candle? Does not Mr. Leavenworth burn gas in his halls?"

"Yes, sir; but we put the gas out as we go up, and Hannah is afraid of the dark."

"If she took a candle, it must be lying somewhere about the house. Now, has anybody seen a stray candle?"

"Not as I knows on, sir."

"Is *this* it?" exclaimed a voice over my shoulder.

It was Mr. Gryce, and he was holding up into view a half-burned paraffine candle.

"Yes, sir; lor', where did you find it?"

"In the grass of the carriage yard, half-way from the kitchen door to the street," he quietly returned.

Sensation. A clue, then, at last! Something had been found which seemed to connect this mysterious murder with the outside world. Instantly the backdoor assumed the chief position of interest. The candle found lying in the yard seemed to prove, not only that Hannah had left the house shortly after descending from her room, but had left it by the backdoor, which we now remembered was only a few steps from the iron gate opening into the side street. But Thomas, being recalled, repeated his assertion that not only the back-door, but all the lower windows of the house, had been found by him securely locked and bolted at six

23

o'clock that morning. Inevitable conclusion—some one had locked and bolted them after the girl. Who? Alas, that had now become the very serious and momentous question.

V. EXPERT TESTIMONY

"And often-times, to win us to our harm,
The instruments of darkness tell us truths;
Win us with honest trifles, to betray us
In deepest consequence."

Macbeth.

IN the midst of the universal gloom thus awakened there came a sharp ring at the bell. Instantly all eyes turned toward the parlor door, just as it slowly opened, and the officer who had been sent off so mysteriously by the coroner an hour before entered, in company with a young man, whose sleek appearance, intelligent eye, and general air of trustworthiness, seemed to proclaim him to be, what in fact he was, the confidential clerk of a responsible mercantile house.

Advancing without apparent embarrassment, though each and every eye in the room was fixed upon him with lively curiosity, he made a slight bow to the coroner.

"You have sent for a man from Bohn & Co.," he said.

Strong and immediate excitement. Bohn & Co. was the well-known pistol and ammunition store of —— Broadway.

"Yes, sir," returned the coroner. "We have here a bullet, which we must ask you to examine, You are fully acquainted with all matters connected with your business?"

The young man, merely elevating an expressive eyebrow, took the bullet carelessly in his hand.

"Can you tell us from what make of pistol that was delivered?"

The young man rolled it slowly round between his thumb and forefinger, and then laid it down. "It is a No. 32 ball, usually sold with the small pistol made by Smith & Wesson."

"A small pistol!" exclaimed the butler, jumping up from his seat. "Master used to keep a little pistol in his stand drawer. I have often seen it. We all knew about it."

Great and irrepressible excitement, especially among the servants. "That's so!" I heard a heavy voice exclaim. "I saw it once myself—master was cleaning it." It was the cook who spoke.

"In his stand drawer?" the coroner inquired.

"Yes, sir; at the head of his bed."

An officer was sent to examine the stand drawer. In a few moments he returned, bringing a small pistol which he laid down on the coroner's table, saying, "Here it is."

24

Immediately, every one sprang to his feet, but the coroner, handing it over to the clerk from Bonn's, inquired if that was the make before mentioned. Without hesitation he replied, "Yes, Smith & Wesson; you can see for yourself," and he proceeded to examine it.

"Where did you find this pistol?" asked the coroner of the officer.

"In the top drawer of a shaving table standing near the head of Mr. Leavenworth's bed. It was lying in a velvet case together with a box of cartridges, one of which I bring as a sample," and he laid it down beside the bullet.

"Was the drawer locked?"

"Yes, sir; but the key was not taken out."

Interest had now reached its climax. A universal cry swept through the room, "Is it loaded?"

The coroner, frowning on the assembly, with a look of great dignity, remarked:

"I was about to ask that question myself, but first I must request order."

An immediate calm followed. Every one was too much interested to interpose any obstacle in the way of gratifying his curiosity.

"Now, sir!" exclaimed the coroner.

The clerk from Bonn's, taking out the cylinder, held it up. "There are seven chambers here, and they are all loaded."

A murmur of disappointment followed this assertion.

"But," he quietly added after a momentary examination of the face of the cylinder, "they have not all been loaded long. A bullet has been recently shot from one of these chambers."

"How do you know?" cried one of the jury.

"How do I know? Sir," said he, turning to the coroner, "will you be kind enough to examine the condition of this pistol?" and he handed it over to that gentleman. "Look first at the barrel; it is clean and bright, and shows no evidence of a bullet having passed out of it very lately; that is because it has been cleaned. But now, observe the face of the cylinder: what do you see there?"

"I see a faint line of smut near one of the chambers."

"Just so; show it to the gentlemen."

It was immediately handed down.

"That faint line of smut, on the edge of one of the chambers, is the telltale, sirs. A bullet passing out always leaves smut behind. The man who fired this, remembering the fact, cleaned the barrel, but forgot the cylinder." And stepping aside he folded his arms.

"Jerusalem!" spoke out a rough, hearty voice, "isn't that wonderful!" This exclamation came from a countryman who had stepped in from the street, and now stood agape in the doorway.

It was a rude but not altogether unwelcome interruption. A smile passed round the room, and both men and women breathed more easily. Order being at last restored, the officer was requested to describe the position of the stand, and its distance from the library table.

"The library table is in one room, and the stand in another. To reach the former from the latter, one would be obliged to cross Mr. Leavenworth's bedroom in a

25

diagonal direction, pass through the passageway separating that one apartment from the other, and——"

"Wait a moment; how does this table stand in regard to the door which leads from the bedroom into the hall?"

"One might enter that door, pass directly round the foot of the bed to the stand, procure the pistol, and cross half-way over to the passage-way, without being seen by any one sitting or standing in the library beyond."

"Holy Virgin!" exclaimed the horrified cook, throwing her apron over her head as if to shut out some dreadful vision. "Hannah niver would have the pluck for that; niver, niver!" But Mr. Gryce, laying a heavy hand on the woman, forced her back into her seat, reproving and calming her at the same time, with a dexterity marvellous to behold. "I beg your pardons," she cried deprecatingly to those around; "but it niver was Hannah, niver!"

The clerk from Bohn's here being dismissed, those assembled took the opportunity of making some change in their position, after which, the name of Mr. Harwell was again called. That person rose with manifest reluctance. Evidently the preceding testimony had either upset some theory of his, or indubitably strengthened some unwelcome suspicion.

"Mr. Harwell," the coroner began, "we are told of the existence of a pistol belonging to Mr. Leavenworth, and upon searching, we discover it in his room. Did you know of his possessing such an instrument?"

"I did."

"Was it a fact generally known in the house?"

"So it would seem."

"How was that? Was he in the habit of leaving it around where any one could see it?"

"I cannot say; I can only acquaint you with the manner in which I myself became aware of its existence."

"Very well, do so."

"We were once talking about firearms. I have some taste that way, and have always been anxious to possess a pocket-pistol. Saying something of the kind to him one day, he rose from his seat and, fetching me this, showed it to me."

"How long ago was this?"

"Some few months since."

"He has owned this pistol, then, for some time?"

"Yes, sir."

"Is that the only occasion upon which you have ever seen it?"

"No, sir,"—the secretary blushed—"I have seen it once since."

"When?"

"About three weeks ago."

"Under what circumstances?"

The secretary dropped his head, a certain drawn look making itself suddenly visible on his countenance.

"Will you not excuse me, gentlemen?" he asked, after a moment's hesitation.

"It is impossible," returned the coroner.

26

His face grew even more pallid and deprecatory. "I am obliged to introduce the name of a lady," he hesitatingly declared.

"We are very sorry," remarked the coroner.

The young man turned fiercely upon him, and I could not help wondering that I had ever thought him commonplace. "Of Miss Eleanore Leavenworth!" he cried.

At that name, so uttered, every one started but Mr. Gryce; he was engaged in holding a close and confidential confab with his finger-tips, and did not appear to notice.

"Surely it is contrary to the rules of decorum and the respect we all feel for the lady herself to introduce her name into this discussion," continued Mr. Harwell. But the coroner still insisting upon an answer, he refolded his arms (a movement indicative of resolution with him), and began in a low, forced tone to say:

"It is only this, gentlemen. One afternoon, about three weeks since, I had occasion to go to the library at an unusual hour. Crossing over to the mantel-piece for the purpose of procuring a penknife which I had carelessly left there in the morning, I heard a noise in the adjoining room. Knowing that Mr. Leavenworth was out, and supposing the ladies to be out also, I took the liberty of ascertaining who the intruder was; when what was my astonishment to come upon Miss Eleanore Leavenworth, standing at the side of her uncle's bed, with his pistol in her hand. Confused at my indiscretion, I attempted to escape without being observed; but in vain, for just as I was crossing the threshold, she turned and, calling me by name, requested me to explain the pistol to her. Gentlemen, in order to do so, I was obliged to take it in my hand; and that, sirs, is the only other occasion upon which I ever saw or handled the pistol of Mr. Leavenworth." Drooping his head, he waited in indescribable agitation for the next question.

"She asked you to explain the pistol to her; what do you mean by that?"

"I mean," he faintly continued, catching his breath in a vain effort to appear calm, "how to load, aim, and fire it."

A flash of awakened feeling shot across the faces of all present. Even the coroner showed sudden signs of emotion, and sat staring at the bowed form and pale countenance of the man before him, with a peculiar look of surprised compassion, which could not fail of producing its effect, not only upon the young man himself, but upon all who saw him.

"Mr. Harwell," he at length inquired, "have you anything to add to the statement you have just made?"

The secretary sadly shook his head.

"Mr. Gryce," I here whispered, clutching that person by the arm and dragging him down to my side; "assure me, I entreat you——" but he would not let me finish.

"The coroner is about to ask for the young ladies," he quickly interposed. "If you desire to fulfil your duty towards them, be ready, that's all."

Fulfil my duty! The simple words recalled me to myself. What had I been thinking of; was I mad? With nothing more terrible in mind than a tender picture of the lovely cousins bowed in anguish over the remains of one who had been as dear as a father to them, I slowly rose, and upon demand being made for Miss Mary and Miss Eleanore Leavenworth, advanced and said that, as a friend of the

27

family—a petty lie, which I hope will not be laid up against me—I begged the privilege of going for the ladies and escorting them down.

Instantly a dozen eyes flashed upon me, and I experienced the embarrassment of one who, by some unexpected word or action, has drawn upon himself the concentrated attention of a whole room.

But the permission sought being almost immediately accorded, I was speedily enabled to withdraw from my rather trying position, finding myself, almost before I knew it, in the hall, my face aflame, my heart beating with excitement, and these words of Mr. Gryce ringing in my ears: "Third floor, rear room, first door at the head of the stairs. You will find the young ladies expecting you."

VI. SIDE-LIGHTS

"Oh! she has beauty might ensnare
A conqueror's soul, and make him leave his crown
At random, to be scuffled for by slaves."

       OTWAY.

THIRD floor, rear room, first door at the head of the stairs! What was I about to encounter there?

Mounting the lower flight, and shuddering by the library wall, which to my troubled fancy seemed written all over with horrible suggestions, I took my way slowly up-stairs, revolving in my mind many things, among which an admonition uttered long ago by my mother occupied a prominent place.

"My son, remember that a woman with a secret may be a fascinating study, but she can never be a safe, nor even satisfactory, companion."

A wise saw, no doubt, but totally inapplicable to the present situation; yet it continued to haunt me till the sight of the door to which I had been directed put every other thought to flight save that I was about to meet the stricken nieces of a brutally murdered man.

Pausing only long enough on the threshold to compose myself for the interview, I lifted my hand to knock, when a rich, clear voice rose from within, and I heard distinctly uttered these astounding words: "I do not accuse your hand, though I know of none other which would or could have done this deed; but your heart, your head, your will, these I do and must accuse, in my secret mind at least; and it is well that you should know it!"

Struck with horror, I staggered back, my hands to my ears, when a touch fell on my arm, and turning, I saw Mr. Gryce standing close beside me, with his finger on his lip, and the last flickering shadow of a flying emotion fading from his steady, almost compassionate countenance.

"Come, come," he exclaimed; "I see you don't begin to know what kind of a world you are living in. Rouse yourself; remember they are waiting down below."

"But who is it? Who was it that spoke?"

"That we shall soon see." And without waiting to meet, much less answer, my

28

appealing look, he struck his hand against the door, and flung it wide open.

Instantly a flush of lovely color burst upon us. Blue curtains, blue carpets, blue walls. It was like a glimpse of heavenly azure in a spot where only darkness and gloom were to be expected. Fascinated by the sight, I stepped impetuously forward, but instantly paused again, overcome and impressed by the exquisite picture I saw before me.

Seated in an easy chair of embroidered satin, but rousing from her half-recumbent position, like one who was in the act of launching a powerful invective, I beheld a glorious woman. Fair, frail, proud, delicate; looking like a lily in the thick creamy-tinted wrapper that alternately clung to and swayed from her finely moulded figure; with her forehead, crowned with the palest of pale tresses, lifted and flashing with power; one quivering hand clasping the arm of her chair, the other outstretched and pointing toward some distant object in the room,—her whole appearance was so startling, so extraordinary, that I held my breath in surprise, actually for the moment doubting if it were a living woman I beheld, or some famous pythoness conjured up from ancient story, to express in one tremendous gesture the supreme indignation of outraged womanhood.

"Miss Mary Leavenworth," whispered that ever present voice over my shoulder.

Ah! Mary Leavenworth! What a relief came with this name. This beautiful creature, then, was not the Eleanore who could load, aim, and fire a pistol. Turning my head, I followed the guiding of that uplifted hand, now frozen into its place by a new emotion: the emotion of being interrupted in the midst of a direful and pregnant revelation, and saw—but, no, here description fails me! Eleanore Leavenworth must be painted by other hands than mine. I could sit half the day and dilate upon the subtle grace, the pale magnificence, the perfection of form and feature which make Mary Leavenworth the wonder of all who behold her; but Eleanore—I could as soon paint the beatings of my own heart. Beguiling, terrible, grand, pathetic, that face of faces flashed upon my gaze, and instantly the moonlight loveliness of her cousin faded from my memory, and I saw only Eleanore—only Eleanore from that moment on forever.

When my glance first fell upon her, she was standing by the side of a small table, with her face turned toward her cousin, and her two hands resting, the one upon her breast, the other on the table, in an attitude of antagonism. But before the sudden pang which shot through me at the sight of her beauty had subsided, her head had turned, her gaze had encountered mine; all the horror of the situation had burst upon her, and, instead of a haughty woman, drawn up to receive and trample upon the insinuations of another, I beheld, alas! a trembling, panting human creature, conscious that a sword hung above her head, and without a word to say why it should not fall and slay her.

It was a pitiable change; a heart-rending revelation! I turned from it as from a confession. But just then, her cousin, who had apparently regained her self-possession at the first betrayal of emotion on the part of the other, stepped forward and, holding out her hand, inquired:

"Is not this Mr. Raymond? How kind of you, sir. And you?" turning to Mr. Gryce; "you have come to tell us we are wanted below, is it not so?"

29

It was the voice I had heard through the door, but modulated to a sweet, winning, almost caressing tone.

Glancing hastily at Mr. Gryce, I looked to see how he was affected by it. Evidently much, for the bow with which he greeted her words was lower than ordinary, and the smile with which he met her earnest look both deprecatory and reassuring. His glance did not embrace her cousin, though her eyes were fixed upon his face with an inquiry in their depths more agonizing than the utterance of any cry would have been. Knowing Mr. Gryce as I did, I felt that nothing could promise worse, or be more significant, than this transparent disregard of one who seemed to fill the room with her terror. And, struck with pity, I forgot that Mary Leavenworth had spoken, forgot her very presence in fact, and, turning hastily away, took one step toward her cousin, when Mr. Gryce's hand falling on my arm stopped me.

"Miss Leavenworth speaks," said he.

Recalled to myself, I turned my back upon what had so interested me even while it repelled, and forcing myself to make some sort of reply to the fair creature before me, offered my arm and led her toward the door.

Immediately the pale, proud countenance of Mary Leavenworth softened almost to the point of smiling;—and here let me say, there never was a woman who could smile and not smile like Mary Leavenworth. Looking in my face, with a frank and sweet appeal in her eyes, she murmured:

"You are very good. I do feel the need of support; the occasion is so horrible, and my cousin there,"—here a little gleam of alarm flickered into her eyes—"is so very strange to-day."

"Humph!" thought I to myself; "where is the grand indignant pythoness, with the unspeakable wrath and menace in her countenance, whom I saw when I first entered the room?" Could it be that she was trying to beguile us from our conjectures, by making light of her former expressions? Or was it possible she deceived herself so far as to believe us unimpressed by the weighty accusation overheard by us at a moment so critical?

But Eleanore Leavenworth, leaning on the arm of the detective, soon absorbed all my attention. She had regained by this time her self-possession, also, but not so entirely as her cousin. Her step faltered as she endeavored to walk, and the hand which rested on his arm trembled like a leaf. "Would to God I had never entered this house," said I to myself. And yet, before the exclamation was half uttered, I became conscious of a secret rebellion against the thought; an emotion, shall I say, of thankfulness that it had been myself rather than another who had been allowed to break in upon their privacy, overhear that significant remark, and, shall I acknowledge it, follow Mr. Gryce and the trembling, swaying figure of Eleanore Leavenworth down-stairs. Not that I felt the least relenting in my soul towards guilt. Crime had never looked so black; revenge, selfishness, hatred, cupidity, never seemed more loathsome; and yet—but why enter into the consideration of my feelings at that time. They cannot be of interest; besides, who can fathom the depths of his own soul, or untangle for others the secret cords of revulsion and attraction which are, and ever have been, a mystery and wonder to himself?

30

Enough that, supporting upon my arm the half-fainting form of one woman, but with my attention, and interest devoted to another, I descended the stairs of the Leavenworth mansion, and re-entered the dreaded presence of those inquisitors of the law who had been so impatiently awaiting us.

As I once more crossed that threshold, and faced the eager countenances of those I had left so short a time before, I felt as if ages had elapsed in the interval; so much can be experienced by the human soul in the short space of a few over-weighted moments.

VII. MARY LEAVENWORTH
"For this relief much thanks."
Hamlet.

HAVE you ever observed the effect of the sunlight bursting suddenly upon the earth from behind a mass of heavily surcharged clouds? If so, you can have some idea of the sensation produced in that room by the entrance of these two beautiful ladies. Possessed of a loveliness which would have been conspicuous in all places and under all circumstances, Mary, at least, if not her less striking, though by no means less interesting cousin, could never have entered any assemblage without drawing to herself the wondering attention of all present. But, heralded as here, by the most fearful of tragedies, what could you expect from a collection of men such as I have already described, but overmastering wonder and incredulous admiration? Nothing, perhaps, and yet at the first murmuring sound of amazement and satisfaction, I felt my soul recoil in disgust.

Making haste to seat my now trembling companion in the most retired spot I could find, I looked around for her cousin. But Eleanore Leavenworth, weak as she had appeared in the interview above, showed at this moment neither hesitation nor embarrassment. Advancing upon the arm of the detective, whose suddenly assumed air of persuasion in the presence of the jury was anything but reassuring, she stood for an instant gazing calmly upon the scene before her. Then bowing to the coroner with a grace and condescension which seemed at once to place him on the footing of a politely endured intruder in this home of elegance, she took the seat which her own servants hastened to procure for her, with an ease and dignity that rather recalled the triumphs of the drawing-room than the self-consciousness of a scene such as that in which we found ourselves. Palpable acting, though this was, it was not without its effect. Instantly the murmurs ceased, the obtrusive glances fell, and something like a forced respect made itself visible upon the countenances of all present. Even I, impressed as I had been by her very different demeanor in the room above, experienced a sensation of relief; and was more than startled when, upon turning to the lady at my side, I beheld her eyes riveted upon her cousin with an inquiry in their depths that was anything but encouraging. Fearful of the effect this look might have upon those about us, I hastily seized her hand which, clenched and unconscious, hung over the edge of her chair, and was about to beseech her to have care, when her name, called in a slow, impressive way by the coroner, roused her from her abstraction. Hurriedly withdrawing her gaze from her cousin, she lifted her face to the jury, and I saw a gleam pass over it which brought back my early fancy of the pythoness. But it passed, and it was with an expression of great modesty she settled herself to respond to the demand of the coroner and answer the first few opening inquiries.

But what can express the anxiety of that moment to me? Gentle as she now appeared, she was capable of great wrath, as I knew. Was she going to reiterate her suspicions here? Did she hate as well as mistrust her cousin? Would she dare assert in this presence, and before the world, what she found it so easy to utter in the privacy of her own room and the hearing of the one person concerned? Did she wish to? Her own countenance gave me no clue to her intentions, and, in my anxiety, I turned once more to look at Eleanore. But she, in a dread and apprehension I could easily understand, had recoiled at the first intimation that her cousin was to speak, and now sat with her face covered from sight, by hands blanched to an almost deathly whiteness.

The testimony of Mary Leavenworth was short. After some few questions, mostly referring to her position in the house and her connection with its deceased master, she was asked to relate what she knew of the murder itself, and of its discovery by her cousin and the servants.

Lifting up a brow that seemed never to have known till now the shadow of care or trouble, and a voice that, whilst low and womanly, rang like a bell through the room, she replied:

"You ask me, gentlemen, a question which I cannot answer of my own personal knowledge. I know nothing of this murder, nor of its discovery, save what has come to me through the lips of others."

My heart gave a bound of relief, and I saw Eleanore Leavenworth's hands drop from her brow like stone, while a flickering gleam as of hope fled over her face, and then died away like sunlight leaving marble.

"For, strange as it may seem to you," Mary earnestly continued, the shadow of a past horror revisiting her countenance, "I did not enter the room where my uncle lay. I did not even think of doing so; my only impulse was to fly from what was so horrible and heartrending. But Eleanore went in, and she can tell you——"

"We will question Miss Eleanore Leavenworth later," interrupted the coroner, but very gently for him. Evidently the grace and elegance of this beautiful woman were making their impression. "What we want to know is what *you* saw. You say you cannot tell us of anything that passed in the room at the time of the discovery?"

"No, sir."

"Only what occurred in the hall?"

"Nothing occurred in the hall," she innocently remarked.

"Did not the servants pass in from the hall, and your cousin come out there after her revival from her fainting fit?"

Mary Leavenworth's violet eyes opened wonderingly.

"Yes, sir; but that was nothing."

"You remember, however, her coming into the hall?"

"Yes, sir."

"With a paper in her hand?"

"Paper?" and she wheeled suddenly and looked at her cousin. "Did you have a paper, Eleanore?"

The moment was intense. Eleanore Leavenworth, who at the first mention of the word paper had started perceptibly, rose to her feet at this naive appeal, and opening her lips, seemed about to speak, when the coroner, with a strict sense of what was regular, lifted his hand with decision, and said:

"You need not ask your cousin, Miss; but let us hear what you have to say yourself."

Immediately, Eleanore Leavenworth sank back, a pink spot breaking out on either cheek; while a slight murmur testified to the disappointment of those in the room, who were more anxious to have their curiosity gratified than the forms of law adhered to.

Satisfied with having done his duty, and disposed to be easy with so charming a witness, the coroner repeated his question. "Tell us, if you please, if you saw any such thing in her hand?"

"I? Oh, no, no; I saw nothing."

Being now questioned in relation to the events of the previous night, she had no new light to throw upon the subject. She acknowledged her uncle to have been a little reserved at dinner, but no more so than at previous times when annoyed by some business anxiety.

Asked if she had seen her uncle again that evening, she said no, that she had been detained in her room. That the sight of him, sitting in his seat at the head of the table, was the very last remembrance she had of him.

There was something so touching, so forlorn, and yet so unobtrusive, in this simple recollection of hers, that a look of sympathy passed slowly around the room.

I even detected Mr. Gryce softening towards the inkstand. But Eleanore Leavenworth sat unmoved.

"Was your uncle on ill terms with any one?" was now asked. "Had he valuable papers or secret sums of money in his possession?"

To all these inquiries she returned an equal negative.

"Has your uncle met any stranger lately, or received any important letter during the last few weeks, which might seem in any way to throw light upon this mystery?"

There was the slightest perceptible hesitation in her voice, as she replied: "No, not to my knowledge; I don't know of any such." But here, stealing a side glance at Eleanore, she evidently saw something that reassured her, for she hastened to add:

"I believe I may go further than that, and meet your question with a positive no. My uncle was in the habit of confiding in me, and I should have known if anything of importance to him had occurred."

Questioned in regard to Hannah, she gave that person the best of characters; knew of nothing which could have led either to her strange disappearance, or to

33

her connection with crime. Could not say whether she kept any company, or had any visitors; only knew that no one with any such pretensions came to the house. Finally, when asked when she had last seen the pistol which Mr. Leavenworth always kept in his stand drawer, she returned, not since the day he bought it; Eleanore, and not herself, having the charge of her uncle's apartments.

It was the only thing she had said which, even to a mind freighted like mine, would seem to point to any private doubt or secret suspicion; and this, uttered in the careless manner in which it was, would have passed without comment if Eleanore herself had not directed at that moment a very much aroused and inquiring look upon the speaker.

But it was time for the inquisitive juror to make himself heard again. Edging to the brink of the chair, he drew in his breath, with a vague awe of Mary's beauty, almost ludicrous to see, and asked if she had properly considered what she had just said.

"I hope, sir, I consider all I am called upon to say at such a time as this," was her earnest reply.

The little juror drew back, and I looked to see her examination terminate, when suddenly his ponderous colleague of the watch-chain, catching the young lady's eye, inquired:

"Miss Leavenworth, did your uncle ever make a will?"

Instantly every man in the room was in arms, and even she could not prevent the slow blush of injured pride from springing to her cheek. But her answer was given firmly, and without any show of resentment.

"Yes, sir," she returned simply.

"More than one?"

"I never heard of but one."

"Are you acquainted with the contents of that will?"

"I am. He made no secret of his intentions to any one."

The juryman lifted his eye-glass and looked at her. Her grace was little to him, or her beauty or her elegance. "Perhaps, then, you can tell me who is the one most likely to be benefited by his death?"

The brutality of this question was too marked to pass unchallenged. Not a man in that room, myself included, but frowned with sudden disapprobation. But Mary Leavenworth, drawing herself up, looked her interlocutor calmly in the face, and restrained herself to say:

"I know who would be the greatest losers by it. The children he took to his bosom in their helplessness and sorrow; the young girls he enshrined with the halo of his love and protection, when love and protection were what their immaturity most demanded; the women who looked to him for guidance when childhood and youth were passed—these, sir, these are the ones to whom his death is a loss, in comparison to which all others which may hereafter befall them must ever seem trivial and unimportant."

It was a noble reply to the basest of insinuations, and the juryman drew back rebuked; but here another of them, one who had not spoken before, but whose appearance was not only superior to the rest, but also almost imposing in its

34

gravity, leaned from his seat and in a solemn voice said:

"Miss Leavenworth, the human mind cannot help forming impressions. Now have you, with or without reason, felt at any time conscious of a suspicion pointing towards any one person as the murderer of your uncle?"

It was a frightful moment. To me and to one other, I am sure it was not only frightful, but agonizing. Would her courage fail? would her determination to shield her cousin remain firm in the face of duty and at the call of probity? I dared not hope it.

But Mary Leavenworth, rising to her feet, looked judge and jury calmly in the face, and, without raising her voice, giving it an indescribably clear and sharp intonation, replied:

"No; I have neither suspicion nor reason for any. The assassin of my uncle is not only entirely unknown to, but completely unsuspected by, me."

It was like the removal of a stifling pressure. Amid a universal outgoing of the breath, Mary Leavenworth stood aside and Eleanore was called in her place.

VIII. CIRCUMSTANTIAL EVIDENCE

"O dark, dark, dark!"

AND now that the interest was at its height, that the veil which shrouded this horrible tragedy seemed about to be lifted, if not entirely withdrawn, I felt a desire to fly the scene, to leave the spot, to know no more. Not that I was conscious of any particular fear of this woman betraying herself. The cold steadiness of her now fixed and impassive countenance was sufficient warranty in itself against the possibility of any such catastrophe. But if, indeed, the suspicions of her cousin were the offspring, not only of hatred, but of knowledge; if that face of beauty was in truth only a mask, and Eleanore Leavenworth was what the words of her cousin, and her own after behavior would seem to imply, how could I bear to sit there and see the frightful serpent of deceit and sin evolve itself from the bosom of this white rose! And yet, such is the fascination of uncertainty that, although I saw something of my own feelings reflected in the countenances of many about me, not a man in all that assemblage showed any disposition to depart, I least of all.

The coroner, upon whom the blonde loveliness of Mary had impressed itself to Eleanor's apparent detriment, was the only one in the room who showed himself unaffected at this moment. Turning toward the witness with a look which, while respectful, had a touch of austerity in it, he began:

"You have been an intimate of Mr. Leavenworth's family from childhood, they tell me, Miss Leavenworth?"

"From my tenth year," was her quiet reply.

It was the first time I had heard her voice, and it surprised me; it was so like, and yet so unlike, that of her cousin. Similar in tone, it lacked its expressiveness, if I may so speak; sounding without vibration on the ear, and ceasing without an echo.

"Since that time you have been treated like a daughter, they tell me?"

"Yes, sir, like a daughter, indeed; he was more than a father to both of us."

"You and Miss Mary Leavenworth are cousins, I believe. When did she enter the family?"

"At the same time I did. Our respective parents were victims of the same disaster. If it had not been for our uncle, we should have been thrown, children as we were, upon the world. But he"—here she paused, her firm lips breaking into a half tremble—"but he, in the goodness of his heart, adopted us into his family, and gave us what we had both lost, a father and a home."

"You say he was a father to you as well as to your cousin—that he adopted you. Do you mean by that, that he not only surrounded you with present luxury, but gave you to understand that the same should be secured to you after his death; in short, that he intended to leave any portion of his property to you?"

"No, sir; I was given to understand, from the first, that his property would be bequeathed by will to my cousin."

"Your cousin was no more nearly related to him than yourself, Miss Leavenworth; did he never give you any reason for this evident partiality?"

"None but his pleasure, sir."

Her answers up to this point had been so straightforward and satisfactory that a gradual confidence seemed to be taking the place of the rather uneasy doubts which had from the first circled about this woman's name and person. But at this admission, uttered as it was in a calm, unimpassioned voice, not only the jury, but myself, who had so much truer reason for distrusting her, felt that actual suspicion in her case must be very much shaken before the utter lack of motive which this reply so clearly betokened.

Meanwhile the coroner continued: "If your uncle was as kind to you as you say, you must have become very much attached to him?"

"Yes, sir," her mouth taking a sudden determined curve.

"His death, then, must have been a great shock to you?"

"Very, very great."

"Enough of itself to make you faint away, as they tell me you did, at the first glimpse you had of his body?"

"Enough, quite."

"And yet you seemed to be prepared for it?"

"Prepared?"

"The servants say you were much agitated at finding your uncle did not make his appearance at the breakfast table."

"The servants!" her tongue seemed to cleave to the roof of her mouth; she could hardly speak.

"That when you returned from his room you were very pale."

Was she beginning to realize that there was some doubt, if not actual suspicion, in the mind of the man who could assail her with questions like these? I had not seen her so agitated since that one memorable instant up in her room. But her mistrust, if she felt any, did not long betray itself. Calming herself by a great effort, she replied, with a quiet gesture—

"That is not so strange. My uncle was a very methodical man; the least change in

36

his habits would be likely to awaken our apprehensions."

"You were alarmed, then?"

"To a certain extent I was."

"Miss Leavenworth, who is in the habit of overseeing the regulation of your uncle's private apartments?"

"I am, sir."

"You are doubtless, then, acquainted with a certain stand in his room containing a drawer?"

"Yes, sir."

"How long is it since you had occasion to go to this drawer?"

"Yesterday," visibly trembling at the admission.

"At what time?"

"Near noon, I should judge."

"Was the pistol he was accustomed to keep there in its place at the time?"

"I presume so; I did not observe."

"Did you turn the key upon closing the drawer?"

"I did."

"Take it out?"

"No, sir."

"Miss Leavenworth, that pistol, as you have perhaps observed, lies on the table before you. Will you look at it?" And lifting it up into view, he held it towards her.

If he had meant to startle her by the sudden action, he amply succeeded. At the first sight of the murderous weapon she shrank back, and a horrified, but quickly suppressed shriek, burst from her lips. "Oh, no, no!" she moaned, flinging out her hands before her.

"I must insist upon your looking at it, Miss Leavenworth," pursued the coroner. "When it was found just now, all the chambers were loaded."

Instantly the agonized look left her countenance. "Oh, then—" She did not finish, but put out her hand for the weapon.

But the coroner, looking at her steadily, continued: "It has been lately fired off, for all that. The hand that cleaned the barrel forgot the cartridge-chamber, Miss Leavenworth."

She did not shriek again, but a hopeless, helpless look slowly settled over her face, and she seemed about to sink; but like a flash the reaction came, and lifting her head with a steady, grand action I have never seen equalled, she exclaimed, "Very well, what then?"

The coroner laid the pistol down; men and women glanced at each other; every one seemed to hesitate to proceed. I heard a tremulous sigh at my side, and, turning, beheld Mary Leavenworth staring at her cousin with a startled flush on her cheek, as if she began to recognize that the public, as well as herself, detected something in this woman, calling for explanation.

At last the coroner summoned up courage to continue.

"You ask me, Miss Leavenworth, upon the evidence given, what then? Your question obliges me to say that no burglar, no hired assassin, would have used this pistol for a murderous purpose, and then taken the pains, not only to clean it, but to reload it, and lock it up again in the drawer from which he had taken it."

She did not reply to this; but I saw Mr. Gryce make a note of it with that peculiar emphatic nod of his.

"Nor," he went on, even more gravely, "would it be possible for any one who was not accustomed to pass in and out of Mr. Leavenworth's room at all hours, to enter his door so late at night, procure this pistol from its place of concealment, traverse his apartment, and advance as closely upon him as the facts show to have been necessary, without causing him at least to turn his head to one side; which, in consideration of the doctor's testimony, we cannot believe he did."

It was a frightful suggestion, and we looked to see Eleanore Leavenworth recoil. But that expression of outraged feeling was left for her cousin to exhibit. Starting indignantly from her seat, Mary cast one hurried glance around her, and opened her lips to speak; but Eleanore, slightly turning, motioned her to have patience, and replied in a cold and calculating voice: "You are not sure, sir, that this *was* done. If my uncle, for some purpose of his own, had fired the pistol off yesterday, let us say—which is surely possible, if not probable—the like results would be observed, and the same conclusions drawn."

"Miss Leavenworth," the coroner went on, "the ball has been extracted from your uncle's head!"

"Ah!"

"It corresponds with those in the cartridges found in his stand drawer, and is of the number used with this pistol."

Her head fell forward on her hands; her eyes sought the floor; her whole attitude expressed disheartenment. Seeing it, the coroner grew still more grave.

"Miss Leavenworth," said he, "I have now some questions to put you concerning last night. Where did you spend the evening?"

"Alone, in my own room."

"You, however, saw your uncle or your cousin during the course of it?"

"No, sir; I saw no one after leaving the dinner table—except Thomas," she added, after a moment's pause.

"And how came you to see him?"

"He came to bring me the card of a gentleman who called."

"May I ask the name of the gentleman?"

"The name on the card was Mr. Le Roy Robbins."

The matter seemed trivial; but the sudden start given by the lady at my side made me remember it.

"Miss Leavenworth, when seated in your room, are you in the habit of leaving your door open?"

A startled look at this, quickly suppressed. "Not in the habit; no, sir."

"Why did you leave it open last night?"

"I was feeling warm."

"No other reason?"

"I can give no other."

"When did you close it?"

"Upon retiring."

38

"Was that before or after the servants went up?"

"After."

"Did you hear Mr. Harwell when he left the library and ascended to his room?"

"I did, sir."

"How much longer did you leave your door open after that?"

"I—I—a few minutes—a—I cannot say," she added, hurriedly.

"Cannot say? Why? Do you forget?"

"I forget just how long after Mr. Harwell came up I closed it."

"Was it more than ten minutes?"

"Yes."

"More than twenty?"

"Perhaps." How pale her face was, and how she trembled!

"Miss Leavenworth, according to evidence, your uncle came to his death not very long after Mr. Harwell left him. If your door was open, you ought to have heard if any one went to his room, or any pistol shot was fired. Now, did you hear anything?"

"I heard no confusion; no, sir."

"Did you hear anything?"

"Nor any pistol shot."

"Miss Leavenworth, excuse my persistence, but did you hear anything?"

"I heard a door close."

"What door?"

"The library door."

"When?"

"I do not know." She clasped her hands hysterically. "I cannot say. Why do you ask me so many questions?"

I leaped to my feet; she was swaying, almost fainting. But before I could reach her, she had drawn herself up again, and resumed her former demeanor. "Excuse me," said she; "I am not myself this morning. I beg your pardon," and she turned steadily to the coroner. "What was it you asked?"

"I asked," and his voice grew thin and high,—evidently her manner was beginning to tell against her,—"when it was you heard the library door shut?"

"I cannot fix the precise time, but it was after Mr. Harwell came up, and before I closed my own."

"And you heard no pistol shot?"

"No, sir."

The coroner cast a quick look at the jury, who almost to a man glanced aside as he did so.

"Miss Leavenworth, we are told that Hannah, one of the servants, started for your room late last night after some medicine. Did she come there?"

"No, sir."

"When did you first learn of her remarkable disappearance from this house during the night?"

"This morning before breakfast. Molly met me in the hall, and asked how Hannah was. I thought the inquiry a strange one, and naturally questioned her. A

39

moment's talk made the conclusion plain that the girl was gone."

"What did you think when you became assured of this fact?"

"I did not know what to think."

"No suspicion of foul play crossed your mind?"

"No, sir."

"You did not connect the fact with that of your uncle's murder?"

"I did not know of this murder then."

"And afterwards?"

"Oh, some thought of the possibility of her knowing something about it may have crossed my mind; I cannot say."

"Can you tell us anything of this girl's past history?"

"I can tell you no more in regard to it than my cousin has done."

"Do you not know what made her sad at night?"

Her cheek flushed angrily; was it at his tone, or at the question itself? "No, sir! she never confided her secrets to my keeping."

"Then you cannot tell us where she would be likely to go upon leaving this house?"

"Certainly not."

"Miss Leavenworth, we are obliged to put another question to you. We are told it was by your order your uncle's body was removed from where it was found, into the next room."

She bowed her head.

"Didn't you know it to be improper for you or any one else to disturb the body of a person found dead, except in the presence and under the authority of the proper officer?"

"I did not consult my knowledge, sir, in regard to the subject: only my feelings."

"Then I suppose it was your feelings which prompted you to remain standing by the table at which he was murdered, instead of following the body in and seeing it properly deposited? Or perhaps," he went on, with relentless sarcasm, "you were too much interested, just then, in the piece of paper you took away, to think much of the proprieties of the occasion?"

"Paper?" lifting her head with determination. "Who says I took a piece of paper from the table?"

"One witness has sworn to seeing you bend over the table upon which several papers lay strewn; another, to meeting you a few minutes later in the hall just as you were putting a piece of paper into your pocket. The inference follows, Miss Leavenworth."

This was a home thrust, and we looked to see some show of agitation, but her haughty lip never quivered.

"You have drawn the inference, and you must prove the fact."

The answer was stateliness itself, and we were not surprised to see the coroner look a trifle baffled; but, recovering himself, he said:

"Miss Leavenworth, I must ask you again, whether you did or did not take anything from that table?"

She folded her arms. "I decline answering the question," she quietly said.

40

"Pardon me," he rejoined: "it is necessary that you should."

Her lip took a still more determined curve. "When any suspicious paper is found in my possession, it will be time enough then for me to explain how I came by it."

This defiance seemed to quite stagger the coroner.

"Do you realize to what this refusal is liable to subject you?"

She dropped her head. "I am afraid that I do; yes, sir."

Mr. Gryce lifted his hand, and softly twirled the tassel of the window curtain.

"And you still persist?"

She absolutely disdained to reply.

The coroner did not press it further.

It had now become evident to all, that Eleanore Leavenworth not only stood on her defence, but was perfectly aware of her position, and prepared to maintain it. Even her cousin, who until now had preserved some sort of composure, began to show signs of strong and uncontrollable agitation, as if she found it one thing to utter an accusation herself, and quite another to see it mirrored in the countenances of the men about her.

"Miss Leavenworth," the coroner continued, changing the line of attack, "you have always had free access to your uncle's apartments, have you not?"

"Yes, sir."

"Might even have entered his room late at night, crossed it and stood at his side, without disturbing him sufficiently to cause him to turn his head?"

"Yes," her hands pressing themselves painfully together.

"Miss Leavenworth, the key to the library door is missing."

She made no answer.

"It has been testified to, that previous to the actual discovery of the murder, you visited the door of the library alone. Will you tell us if the key was then in the lock?"

"It was not."

"Are you certain?"

"I am."

"Now, was there anything peculiar about this key, either in size or shape?"

She strove to repress the sudden terror which this question produced, glanced carelessly around at the group of servants stationed at her back, and trembled. "It was a little different from the others," she finally acknowledged.

"In what respect?"

"The handle was broken."

"Ah, gentlemen, the handle was broken!" emphasized the coroner, looking towards the jury.

Mr. Gryce seemed to take this information to himself, for he gave another of his quick nods.

"You would, then, recognize this key, Miss Leavenworth, if you should see it?"

She cast a startled look at him, as if she expected to behold it in his hand; but, seeming to gather courage at not finding it produced, replied quite easily:

"I think I should, sir."

The coroner seemed satisfied, and was about to dismiss the witness when Mr. Gryce quietly advanced and touched him on the arm. "One moment," said that gentleman, and stooping, he whispered a few words in the coroner's ear; then, recovering himself, stood with his right hand in his breast pocket and his eye upon the chandelier.

I scarcely dared to breathe. Had he repeated to the coroner the words he had inadvertently overheard in the hall above? But a glance at the latter's face satisfied me that nothing of such importance had transpired. He looked not only tired, but a trifle annoyed.

"Miss Leavenworth," said he, turning again in her direction; "you have declared that you did not visit your uncle's room last evening. Do you repeat the assertion?"

"I do."

He glanced at Mr. Gryce, who immediately drew from his breast a handkerchief curiously soiled. "It is strange, then, that your handkerchief should have been found this morning in that room."

The girl uttered a cry. Then, while Mary's face hardened into a sort of strong despair, Eleanore tightened her lips and coldly replied, "I do not see as it is so very strange. I was in that room early this morning."

"And you dropped it then?"

A distressed blush crossed her face; she did not reply.

"Soiled in this way?" he went on.

"I know nothing about the soil. What is it? let me see."

"In a moment. What we now wish, is to know how it came to be in your uncle's apartment."

"There are many ways. I might have left it there days ago. I have told you I was in the habit of visiting his room. But first, let me see if it is my handkerchief." And she held out her hand.

"I presume so, as I am told it has your initials embroidered in the corner," he remarked, as Mr. Gryce passed it to her.

But she with horrified voice interrupted him. "These dirty spots! What are they? They look like—"

"—what they are," said the coroner. "If you have ever cleaned a pistol, you must know what they are, Miss Leavenworth."

She let the handkerchief fall convulsively from her hand, and stood staring at it, lying before her on the floor. "I know nothing about it, gentlemen," she said. "It is my handkerchief, but—" for some cause she did not finish her sentence, but again repeated, "Indeed, gentlemen, I know nothing about it!"

This closed her testimony.

Kate, the cook, was now recalled, and asked to tell when she last washed the handkerchief?

"This, sir; this handkerchief? Oh, some time this week, sir," throwing a deprecatory glance at her mistress.

"What day?"

"Well, I wish I could forget, Miss Eleanore, but I can' t. It is the only one like it in the house. I washed it day before yesterday."

"When did you iron it?"

"Yesterday morning," half choking over the words.

"And when did you take it to her room?"

The cook threw her apron over her head. "Yesterday afternoon, with the rest of the clothes, just before dinner. Indade, I could not help it, Miss Eleanore!" she whispered; "it was the truth."

Eleanore Leavenworth frowned. This somewhat contradictory evidence had very sensibly affected her; and when, a moment later, the coroner, having dismissed the witness, turned towards her, and inquired if she had anything further to say in the way of explanation or otherwise, she threw her hands up almost spasmodically, slowly shook her head and, without word or warning, fainted quietly away in her chair.

A commotion, of course, followed, during which I noticed that Mary did not hasten to her cousin, but left it for Molly and Kate to do what they could toward her resuscitation. In a few moments this was in so far accomplished that they were enabled to lead her from the room. As they did so, I observed a tall man rise and follow her out.

A momentary silence ensued, soon broken, however, by an impatient stir as our little juryman rose and proposed that the jury should now adjourn for the day. This seeming to fall in with the coroner's views, he announced that the inquest would stand adjourned till three o'clock the next day, when he trusted all the jurors would be present.

A general rush followed, that in a few minutes emptied the room of all but Miss Leavenworth, Mr. Gryce, and myself.

IX. A DISCOVERY

"His rolling Eies did never rest in place,
But walkte each where for feare of hid mischance,
Holding a lattis still before his Pace,
Through which he still did peep as forward he did pace."

Faerie Queene.

MISS LEAVENWORTH, who appeared to have lingered from a vague terror of everything and everybody in the house not under her immediate observation, shrank from my side the moment she found herself left comparatively alone, and, retiring to a distant corner, gave herself up to grief. Turning my attention, therefore, in the direction of Mr. Gryce, I found that person busily engaged in counting his own fingers with a troubled expression upon his countenance, which may or may not have been the result of that arduous employment. But, at my approach, satisfied perhaps that he possessed no more than the requisite number, he dropped his hands and greeted me with a faint smile which was, considering all things, too suggestive to be pleasant.

43

"Well," said I, taking my stand before him, "I cannot blame you. You had a right to do as you thought best; but how had you the heart? Was she not sufficiently compromised without your bringing out that wretched handkerchief, which she may or may not have dropped in that room, but whose presence there, soiled though it was with pistol grease, is certainly no proof that she herself was connected with this murder?"

"Mr. Raymond," he returned, "I have been detailed as police officer and detective to look after this case, and I propose to do it."

"Of course," I hastened to reply. "I am the last man to wish you to shirk your duly; but you cannot have the temerity to declare that this young and tender creature can by any possibility be considered as at all likely to be implicated in a crime so monstrous and unnatural. The mere assertion of another woman's suspicions on the subject ought not——"

But here Mr. Gryce interrupted me. "You talk when your attention should be directed to more important matters. That other woman, as you are pleased to designate the fairest ornament of New York society, sits over there in tears; go and comfort her."

Looking at him in amazement, I hesitated to comply; but, seeing he was in earnest, crossed to Mary Leavenworth and sat down by her side. She was weeping, but in a slow, unconscious way, as if grief had been mastered by fear. The fear was too undisguised and the grief too natural for me to doubt the genuineness of either.

"Miss Leavenworth," said I, "any attempt at consolation on the part of a stranger must seem at a time like this the most bitter of mockeries; but do try and consider that circumstantial evidence is not always absolute proof."

Starting with surprise, she turned her eyes upon me with a slow, comprehensive gaze wonderful to see in orbs so tender and womanly.

"No," she repeated; "circumstantial evidence is not absolute proof, but Eleanore does not know this. She is so intense; she cannot see but one thing at a time. She has been running her head into a noose, and oh,—" Pausing, she clutched my arm with a passionate grasp: "Do you think there is any danger? Will they—" She could not go on.

"Miss Leavenworth," I protested, with a warning look toward the detective, "what do you mean?"

Like a flash, her glance followed mine, an instant change taking place in her bearing.

"Your cousin may be intense," I went on, as if nothing had occurred; "but I do not know to what you refer when you say she has been running her head into a noose."

"I mean this," she firmly returned: "that, wittingly or unwittingly, she has so parried and met the questions which have been put to her in this room that any one listening to her would give her the credit of knowing more than she ought to of this horrible affair. She acts"—Mary whispered, but not so low but that every word could be distinctly heard in all quarters of the room—"as if she were anxious to conceal something. But she is not; I am sure she is not. Eleanore and I

44

are not good friends; but all the world can never make me believe she has any more knowledge of this murder than I have. Won't somebody tell her, then—won't you—that her manner is a mistake; that it is calculated to arouse suspicion; that it has already done so? And oh, don't forget to add"—her voice sinking to a decided whisper now—"what you have just repeated to me: that circumstantial evidence is not always absolute proof."

I surveyed her with great astonishment. What an actress this woman was!

"You request me to tell her this," said I. "Wouldn't it be better for you to speak to her yourself?"

"Eleanore and I hold little or no confidential communication," she replied.

I could easily believe this, and yet I was puzzled. Indeed, there was something incomprehensible in her whole manner. Not knowing what else to say, I remarked, "That is unfortunate. She ought to be told that the straightforward course is the best by all means."

Mary Leavenworth only wept. "Oh, why has this awful trouble come to me, who have always been so happy before!"

"Perhaps for the very reason that you have always been so happy."

"It was not enough for dear uncle to die in this horrible manner; but she, my own cousin, had to——"

I touched her arm, and the action seemed to recall her to herself. Stopping short, she bit her lip.

"Miss Leavenworth," I whispered, "you should hope for the best. Besides, I honestly believe you to be disturbing yourself unnecessarily. If nothing fresh transpires, a mere prevarication or so of your cousin's will not suffice to injure her."

I said this to see if she had any reason to doubt the future. I was amply rewarded.

"Anything fresh? How could there be anything fresh, when she is perfectly innocent?"

Suddenly, a thought seemed to strike her. Wheeling round in her seat till her lovely, perfumed wrapper brushed my knee, she asked: "Why didn't they ask me more questions? I could have told them Eleanore never left her room last night."

"You could?" What was I to think of this woman?

"Yes; my room is nearer the head of the stairs than hers; if she had passed my door, I should have heard her, don't you see?"

Ah, that was all.

"That does not follow," I answered sadly. "Can you give no other reason?"

"I would say whatever was necessary," she whispered.

I started back. Yes, this woman would lie now to save her cousin; had lied during the inquest. But then I felt grateful, and now I was simply horrified.

"Miss Leavenworth," said I, "nothing can justify one in violating the dictates of his own conscience, not even the safety of one we do not altogether love."

"No?" she returned; and her lip took a tremulous curve, the lovely bosom heaved, and she softly looked away.

If Eleanore's beauty had made less of an impression on my fancy, or her

45

frightful situation awakened less anxiety in my breast, I should have been a lost man from that moment.

"I did not mean to do anything very wrong," Miss Leavenworth continued. "Do not think too badly of me."

"No, no," said I; and there is not a man living who would not have said the same in my place.

What more might have passed between us on this subject I cannot say, for just then the door opened and a man entered whom I recognized as the one who had followed Eleanore Leavenworth out, a short time before.

"Mr. Gryce," said he, pausing just inside the door; "a word if you please."

The detective nodded, but did not hasten towards him; instead of that, he walked deliberately away to the other end of the room, where he lifted the lid of an inkstand he saw there, muttered some unintelligible words into it, and speedily shut it again. Immediately the uncanny fancy seized me that if I should leap to that inkstand, open it and peer in, I should surprise and capture the bit of confidence he had intrusted to it. But I restrained my foolish impulse, and contented myself with noting the subdued look of respect with which the gaunt subordinate watched the approach of his superior.

"Well?" inquired the latter as he reached him: "what now?"

The man shrugged his shoulders, and drew his principal through the open door. Once in the hall their voices sank to a whisper, and as their backs only were visible, I turned to look at my companion. She was pale but composed.

"Has he come from Eleanore?"

"I do not know; I fear so. Miss Leavenworth," I proceeded, "can it be possible that your cousin has anything in her possession she desires to conceal?"

"Then you think she is trying to conceal something?"

"I do not say so. But there was considerable talk about a paper——"

"They will never find any paper or anything else suspicious in Eleanore's possession," Mary interrupted. "In the first place, there was no paper of importance enough"—I saw Mr. Gryce's form suddenly stiffen—"for any one to attempt its abstraction and concealment."

"Can you be sure of that? May not your cousin be acquainted with something ——"

"There was nothing to be acquainted with, Mr. Raymond. We lived the most methodical and domestic of lives. I cannot understand, for my part, why so much should be made out of this. My uncle undoubtedly came to his death by the hand of some intended burglar. That nothing was stolen from the house is no proof that a burglar never entered it. As for the doors and windows being locked, will you take the word of an Irish servant as infallible upon such an important point? I cannot. I believe the assassin to be one of a gang who make their living by breaking into houses, and if you cannot honestly agree with me, do try and consider such an explanation as possible; if not for the sake of the family credit, why then"—and she turned her face with all its fair beauty upon mine, eyes, cheeks, mouth all so exquisite and winsome—"why then, for mine."

Instantly Mr. Gryce turned towards us. "Mr. Raymond, will you be kind enough to step this way?"

Glad to escape from my present position, I hastily obeyed.

"What has happened?" I asked.

"We propose to take you into our confidence," was the easy response. "Mr. Raymond, Mr. Fobbs."

I bowed to the man I saw before me, and stood uneasily waiting. Anxious as I was to know what we really had to fear, I still intuitively shrank from any communication with one whom I looked upon as a spy.

"A matter of some importance," resumed the detective. "It is not necessary for me to remind you that it is in confidence, is it?"

"No."

"I thought not. Mr. Fobbs you may proceed."

Instantly the whole appearance of the man Fobbs changed. Assuming an expression of lofty importance, he laid his large hand outspread upon his heart and commenced.

"Detailed by Mr. Gryce to watch the movements of Miss Eleanore Leavenworth, I left this room upon her departure from it, and followed her and the two servants who conducted her up-stairs to her own apartment. Once there ——"

Mr. Gryce interrupted him. "Once there? where?"

"Her own room, sir."

"Where situated?"

"At the head of the stairs."

"That is not her room. Go on."

"Not her room? Then it *was* the fire she was after!" he cried, clapping himself on the knee.

"The fire?"

"Excuse me; I am ahead of my story. She did not appear to notice me much, though I was right behind her. It was not until she had reached the door of this room—which was not her room!" he interpolated dramatically, "and turned to dismiss her servants, that she seemed conscious of having been followed. Eying me then with an air of great dignity, quickly eclipsed, however, by an expression of patient endurance, she walked in, leaving the door open behind her in a courteous way I cannot sufficiently commend."

I could not help frowning. Honest as the man appeared, this was evidently anything but a sore subject with him. Observing me frown, he softened his manner.

"Not seeing any other way of keeping her under my eye, except by entering the room, I followed her in, and took a seat in a remote corner. She flashed one look at me as I did so, and commenced pacing the floor in a restless kind of way I'm not altogether unused to. At last she stopped abruptly, right in the middle of the room. 'Get me a glass of water!' she gasped; 'I'm faint again—quick! on the stand in the corner.' Now in order to get that glass of water it was necessary for me to pass behind a dressing mirror that reached almost to the ceiling; and I naturally hesitated. But she turned and looked at me, and—Well, gentlemen, I think either

47

of you would have hastened to do what she asked; or at least"—with a doubtful look at Mr. Gryce—"have given your two ears for the privilege, even if you didn't succumb to the temptation."

"Well, well!" exclaimed Mr. Gryce, impatiently.

"I am going on," said he. "I stepped out of sight, then, for a moment; but it seemed long enough for her purpose; for when I emerged, glass in hand, she was kneeling at the grate full five feet from the spot where she had been standing, and was fumbling with the waist of her dress in a way to convince me she had something concealed there which she was anxious to dispose of. I eyed her pretty closely as I handed her the glass of water, but she was gazing into the grate, and didn't appear to notice. Drinking barely a drop, she gave it back, and in another moment was holding out her hands over the fire. 'Oh, I am so cold!' she cried, 'so cold.' And I verily believe she was. At any rate, she shivered most naturally. But there were a few dying embers in the grate, and when I saw her thrust her hand again into the folds of her dress I became distrustful of her intentions and, drawing a step nearer, looked over her shoulder, when I distinctly saw her drop something into the grate that clinked as it fell. Suspecting what it was, I was about to interfere, when she sprang to her feet, seized the scuttle of coal that was upon the hearth, and with one move emptied the whole upon the dying embers. 'I want a fire,' she cried, 'a fire!' 'That is hardly the way to make one,' I returned, carefully taking the coal out with my hands, piece by piece, and putting it back into the scuttle, till—"

"Till what?" I asked, seeing him and Mr. Gryce exchange a hurried look.

"Till I found this!" opening his large hand, and showing me *a broken-handled key.*

X. MR. GRYCE RECEIVES NEW IMPETUS
"There's nothing ill
Can dwell in such a temple."

Tempest.

THIS astounding discovery made a most unhappy impression upon me. It was true, then. Eleanore the beautiful, the lovesome, was—I did not, could not finish the sentence, even in the silence of my own mind.

"You look surprised," said Mr. Gryce, glancing curiously towards the key. "Now, I ain't. A woman does not thrill, blush, equivocate, and faint for nothing; especially such a woman as Miss Leavenworth."

"A woman who could do such a deed would be the last to thrill, equivocate, and faint," I retorted. "Give me the key; let me see it."

He complacently put it in my hand. "It is the one we want. No getting out of that."

I returned it. "If she declares herself innocent, I will believe her."

He stared with great amazement. "You have strong faith in the women," he laughed. "I hope they will never disappoint you."

48

I had no reply for this, and a short silence ensued, first broken by Mr. Gryce. "There is but one thing left to do," said he. "Fobbs, you will have to request Miss Leavenworth to come down. Do not alarm her; only see that she comes. To the reception room," he added, as the man drew off.

No sooner were we left alone than I made a move to return to Mary, but he stopped me.

"Come and see it out," he whispered. "She will be down in a moment; see it out; you had best."

Glancing back, I hesitated; but the prospect of beholding Eleanore again drew me, in spite of myself. Telling him to wait, I returned to Mary's side to make my excuses.

"What is the matter—what has occurred?" she breathlessly asked.

"Nothing as yet to disturb you much. Do not be alarmed." But my face betrayed me.

"There is something!" said she.

"Your cousin is coming down."

"Down here?" and she shrank visibly.

"No, to the reception room."

"I do not understand. It is all dreadful; and no one tells me anything."

"I pray God there may be nothing to tell. Judging from your present faith in your cousin, there will not be. Take comfort, then, and be assured I will inform you if anything occurs which you ought to know."

Giving her a look of encouragement, I left her crushed against the crimson pillows of the sofa on which she sat, and rejoined Mr. Gryce. We had scarcely entered the reception room when Eleanore Leavenworth came in.

More languid than she was an hour before, but haughty still, she slowly advanced, and, meeting my eye, gently bent her head.

"I have been summoned here," said she, directing herself exclusively to Mr. Gryce, "by an individual whom I take to be in your employ. If so, may I request you to make your wishes known at once, as I am quite exhausted, and am in great need of rest."

"Miss Leavenworth," returned Mr. Gryce, rubbing his hands together and staring in quite a fatherly manner at the door-knob, "I am very sorry to trouble you, but the fact is I wish to ask you——"

But here she stopped him. "Anything in regard to the key which that man has doubtless told you he saw me drop into the ashes?"

"Yes, Miss."

"Then I must refuse to answer any questions concerning it. I have nothing to say on the subject, unless it is this:"—giving him a look full of suffering, but full of a certain sort of courage, too—"that he was right if he told you I had the key in hiding about my person, and that I attempted to conceal it in the ashes of the grate."

"Still, Miss——"

But she had already withdrawn to the door. "I pray you to excuse me," said she. "No argument you could advance would make any difference in my

49

determination; therefore it would be but a waste of energy on your part to attempt any." And, with a flitting glance in my direction, not without its appeal, she quietly left the room.

For a moment Mr. Gryce stood gazing after her with a look of great interest, then, bowing with almost exaggerated homage, he hastily followed her out.

I had scarcely recovered from the surprise occasioned by this unexpected movement when a quick step was heard in the hall, and Mary, flushed and anxious, appeared at my side.

"What is it?" she inquired. "What has Eleanore been saying?"

"Alas!" I answered, "she has not said anything. That is the trouble, Miss Leavenworth. Your cousin preserves a reticence upon certain points very painful to witness. She ought to understand that if she persists in doing this, that——"

"That what?" There was no mistaking the deep anxiety prompting this question.

"That she cannot avoid the trouble that will ensue."

For a moment she stood gazing at me, with great horror-stricken, incredulous eyes; then sinking back into a chair, flung her hands over her face with the cry:

"Oh, why were we ever born! Why were we allowed to live! Why did we not perish with those who gave us birth!"

In the face of anguish like this, I could not keep still.

"Dear Miss Leavenworth," I essayed, "there is no cause for such despair as this. The future looks dark, but not impenetrable. Your cousin will listen to reason, and in explaining——"

But she, deaf to my words, had again risen to her feet, and stood before me in an attitude almost appalling.

"Some women in my position would go mad! mad! mad!"

I surveyed her with growing wonder. I thought I knew what she meant. She was conscious of having given the cue which had led to this suspicion of her cousin, and that in this way the trouble which hung over their heads was of her own making. I endeavored to soothe her, but my efforts were all unavailing. Absorbed in her own anguish, she paid but little attention to me. Satisfied at last that I could do nothing more for her, I turned to go. The movement seemed to arouse her.

"I am sorry to leave," said I, "without having afforded you any comfort. Believe me; I am very anxious to assist you. Is there no one I can send to your side; no woman friend or relative? It is sad to leave you alone in this house at such a time."

"And do you expect me to remain here? Why, I should die! Here to-night?" and the long shudders shook her very frame.

"It is not at all necessary for you to do so, Miss Leavenworth," broke in a bland voice over our shoulders.

I turned with a start. Mr. Gryce was not only at our back, but had evidently been there for some moments. Seated near the door, one hand in his pocket, the other caressing the arm of his chair, he met our gaze with a sidelong smile that seemed at once to beg pardon for the intrusion, and to assure us it was made with no unworthy motive. "Everything will be properly looked after, Miss; you can leave with perfect safety."

I expected to see her resent this interference; but instead of that, she manifested a certain satisfaction in beholding him there.

Drawing me to one side, she whispered, "You think this Mr. Gryce very clever, do you not?"

"Well," I cautiously replied, "he ought to be to hold the position he does. The authorities evidently repose great confidence in him."

Stepping from my side as suddenly as she had approached it, she crossed the room and stood before Mr. Gryce.

"Sir," said she, gazing at him with a glance of entreaty: "I hear you have great talents; that you can ferret out the real criminal from a score of doubtful characters, and that nothing can escape the penetration of your eye. If this is so, have pity on two orphan girls, suddenly bereft of their guardian and protector, and use your acknowledged skill in finding out who has committed this crime. It would be folly in me to endeavor to hide from you that my cousin in her testimony has given cause for suspicion; but I here declare her to be as innocent of wrong as I am; and I am only endeavoring to turn the eye of justice from the guiltless to the guilty when I entreat you to look elsewhere for the culprit who committed this deed." Pausing, she held her two hands out before him. "It must have been some common burglar or desperado; can you not bring him, then, to justice?"

Her attitude was so touching, her whole appearance so earnest and appealing, that I saw Mr. Gryce's countenance brim with suppressed emotion, though his eye never left the coffee-urn upon which it had fixed itself at her first approach.

"You must find out—you can!" she went on. "Hannah—the girl who is gone—must know all about it. Search for her, ransack the city, do anything; my property is at your disposal. I will offer a large reward for the detection of the burglar who did this deed!"

Mr. Gryce slowly rose. "Miss Leavenworth," he began, and stopped; the man was actually agitated. "Miss Leavenworth, I did not need your very touching appeal to incite me to my utmost duty in this case. Personal and professional pride were in themselves sufficient. But, since you have honored me with this expression of your wishes, I will not conceal from you that I shall feel a certain increased interest in the affair from this hour. What mortal man can do, I will do, and if in one month from this day I do not come to you for my reward, Ebenezer Gryce is not the man I have always taken him to be."

"And Eleanore?"

"We will mention no names," said he, gently waving his hand to and fro.

A few minutes later, I left the house with Miss Leavenworth, she having expressed a wish to have me accompany her to the home of her friend, Mrs. Gilbert, with whom she had decided to take refuge. As we rolled down the street in the carriage Mr. Gryce had been kind enough to provide for us, I noticed my companion cast a look of regret behind her, as if she could not help feeling some compunctions at this desertion of her cousin.

But this expression was soon changed for the alert look of one who dreads to see a certain face start up from some unknown quarter. Glancing up and down the street, peering furtively into doorways as we passed, starting and trembling if a sudden figure appeared on the curbstone, she did not seem to breathe with perfect ease till we had left the avenue behind us and entered upon Thirty-seventh Street. Then, all at once her natural color returned and, leaning gently toward me, she asked if I had a pencil and piece of paper I could give her. I fortunately possessed both. Handing them to her, I watched her with some little curiosity while she wrote two or three lines, wondering she could choose such a time and place for the purpose.

"A little note I wish to send," she explained, glancing at the almost illegible scrawl with an expression of doubt. "Couldn't you stop the carriage a moment while I direct it?"

I did so, and in another instant the leaf which I had torn from my note-book was folded, directed, and sealed with a stamp which she had taken from her own pocket-book.

"That is a crazy-looking epistle," she muttered, as she laid it, direction downwards, in her lap.

"Why not wait, then, till you arrive at your destination, where you can seal it properly, and direct it at your leisure?"

"Because I am in haste. I wish to mail it now. Look, there is a box on the corner; please ask the driver to stop once more."

"Shall I not post it for you?" I asked, holding out my hand.

But she shook her head, and, without waiting for my assistance, opened the door on her own side of the carriage and leaped to the ground. Even then she paused to glance up and down the street, before venturing to drop her hastily written letter into the box. But when it had left her hand, she looked brighter and more hopeful than I had yet seen her. And when, a few moments later, she turned to bid me good-by in front of her friend's house, it was with almost a cheerful air she put out her hand and entreated me to call on her the next day, and inform her how the inquest progressed.

I shall not attempt to disguise from you the fact that I spent all that long evening in going over the testimony given at the inquest, endeavoring to reconcile what I had heard with any other theory than that of Eleanore's guilt. Taking a piece of paper, I jotted down the leading causes of suspicion as follows:

1. Her late disagreement with her uncle, and evident estrangement from him, as testified to by Mr. Harwell.

2. The mysterious disappearance of one of the servants of the house.

3. The forcible accusation made by her cousin,—overheard, however, only by Mr. Gryce and myself.

4. Her equivocation in regard to the handkerchief found stained with pistol smut on the scene of the tragedy.

5. Her refusal to speak in regard to the paper which she was supposed to have taken from Mr. Leavenworth's table immediately upon the removal of the body.

6. The finding of the library key in her possession.

"A dark record," I involuntarily decided, as I looked it over; but even in doing so began jotting down on the other side of the sheet the following explanatory notes:

1. Disagreements and even estrangements between relatives are common. Cases where such disagreements and estrangements have led to crime, rare.

2. The disappearance of Hannah points no more certainly in one direction than another.

3. If Mary's private accusation of her cousin was forcible and convincing, her public declaration that she neither knew nor suspected who might be the author of this crime, was equally so. To be sure, the former possessed the advantage of being uttered spontaneously; but it was likewise true that it was spoken under momentary excitement, without foresight of the consequences, and possibly without due consideration of the facts.

4, 5. An innocent man or woman, under the influence of terror, will often equivocate in regard to matters that seem to criminate them.

But the key! What could I say to that? Nothing. With that key in her possession, and unexplained, Eleanore Leavenworth stood in an attitude of suspicion which even I felt forced to recognize. Brought to this point, I thrust the paper into my pocket, and took up the evening *Express*. Instantly my eye fell upon these words:

SHOCKING MURDER

MR. LEAVENWORTH, THE WELL-KNOWN MILLIONAIRE, FOUND DEAD IN HIS ROOM

NO CLUE TO THE PERPETRATOR OF THE DEED

THE AWFUL CRIME COMMITTED WITH A PISTOL—
EXTRAORDINARY FEATURES OF
THE AFFAIR

Ah! here at least was one comfort; her name was not yet mentioned as that of a suspected party. But what might not the morrow bring? I thought of Mr. Gryce's expressive look as he handed me that key, and shuddered.

"She must be innocent; she cannot be otherwise," I reiterated to myself, and then pausing, asked what warranty I had of this? Only her beautiful face; only, only her beautiful face. Abashed, I dropped the newspaper, and went down-stairs just as a telegraph boy arrived with a message from Mr. Veeley. It was signed by the proprietor of the hotel at which Mr. Veeley was then stopping and ran thus:

"WASHINGTON, D. C.

"MR. Everett Raymond—

"Mr. Veeley is lying at my house ill. Have not shown him telegram, fearing results. Will do so as soon as advisable.

"Thomas Loworthy."

I went in musing. Why this sudden sensation of relief on my part? Could it be that I had unconsciously been guilty of cherishing a latent dread of my senior's return? Why, who else could know so well the secret springs which governed this

53

family? Who else could so effectually put me upon the right track? Was it possible that I, Everett Raymond, hesitated to know the truth in any case? No, that should never be said; and, sitting down again, I drew out the memoranda I had made and, looking them carefully over, wrote against No. 6 the word suspicious in good round characters. There! do one could say, after that, I had allowed myself to be blinded by a bewitching face from seeing what, in a woman with no claims to comeliness, would be considered at once an almost indubitable evidence of guilt.

And yet, after it was all done, I found myself repeating aloud as I gazed at it: "If she declares herself innocent, I will believe her." So completely are we the creatures of our own predilections.

XI. THE SUMMONS
"The pink of courtesy."
Romeo and Juliet.

THE morning papers contained a more detailed account of the murder than those of the evening before; but, to my great relief, in none of them was Eleanore's name mentioned in the connection I most dreaded.

The final paragraph in the *Times* ran thus: "The detectives are upon the track of the missing girl, Hannah." And in the *Herald* I read the following notice:

"*A Liberal Reward* will be given by the relatives of Horatio Leavenworth, Esq., deceased, for any news of the whereabouts of one Hannah Chester, disappeared from the house ———— Fifth Avenue since the evening of March 4. Said girl was of Irish extraction; in age about twenty-five, and may be known by the following characteristics. Form tall and slender; hair dark brown with a tinge of red; complexion fresh; features delicate and well made; hands small, but with the fingers much pricked by the use of the needle; feet large, and of a coarser type than the hands. She had on when last seen a checked gingham dress, brown and white, and was supposed to have wrapped herself in a red and green blanket shawl, very old. Beside the above distinctive marks, she had upon her right hand wrist the scar of a large burn; also a pit or two of smallpox upon the left temple."

This paragraph turned my thoughts in a new direction. Oddly enough, I had expended very little thought upon this girl; and yet how apparent it was that she was the one person upon whose testimony, if given, the whole case in reality hinged, I could not agree with those who considered her as personally implicated in the murder. An accomplice, conscious of what was before her, would have hid in her pockets whatever money she possessed. But the roll of bills found in Hannah's trunk proved her *to* have left too hurriedly for this precaution. On the other hand, if this girl had come unexpectedly upon the assassin at his work, how could she have been hustled from the house without creating a disturbance loud enough to have been heard by the ladies, one of whom had her door open? An innocent girl's first impulse upon such an occasion would have been to scream; and yet no scream was heard; she simply disappeared. What were we to think then? That the person seen by her was one both known and trusted? I would not

54

consider such a possibility; so laying down the paper, I endeavored to put away all further consideration of the affair till I had acquired more facts upon which to base the theory. But who can control his thoughts when over-excited upon any one theme? All the morning I found myself turning the case over in my mind, arriving ever at one of two conclusions. Hannah Chester must be found, or Eleanore Leavenworth must explain when and by what means the key of the library door came into her possession.

At two o'clock I started from my office to attend the inquest; but, being delayed on the way, missed arriving at the house until after the delivery of the verdict. This was a disappointment to me, especially as by these means I lost the opportunity of seeing Eleanore Leavenworth, she having retired to her room immediately upon the dismissal of the jury. But Mr. Harwell was visible, and from him I heard what the verdict had been.

"Death by means of a pistol shot from the hand of some person unknown."

The result of the inquest was a great relief to me. I had feared worse. Nor could I help seeing that, for all his studied self-command, the pale-faced secretary shared in my satisfaction.

What was less of a relief to me was the fact, soon communicated, that Mr. Gryce and his subordinates had left the premises immediately upon the delivery of the verdict. Mr. Gryce was not the man to forsake an affair like this while anything of importance connected with it remained unexplained. Could it be he meditated any decisive action? Somewhat alarmed, I was about to hurry from the house for the purpose of learning what his intentions were, when a sudden movement in the front lower window of the house on the opposite side of the way arrested my attention, and, looking closer, I detected the face of Mr. Fobbs peering out from behind the curtain. The sight assured me I was not wrong in my estimate of Mr. Gryce; and, struck with pity for the desolate girl left to meet the exigencies of a fate to which this watch upon her movements was but the evident precursor, I stepped back and sent her a note, in which, as Mr. Veeley's representative, I proffered my services in case of any sudden emergency, saying I was always to be found in my rooms between the hours of six and eight. This done, I proceeded to the house in Thirty-seventh Street where I had left Miss Mary Leavenworth the day before.

Ushered into the long and narrow drawing-room which of late years has been so fashionable in our uptown houses, I found myself almost immediately in the presence of Miss Leavenworth.

"Oh," she cried, with an eloquent gesture of welcome, "I had begun to think I was forsaken!" and advancing impulsively, she held out her hand. "What is the news from home?"

"A verdict of murder, Miss Leavenworth."

Her eyes did not lose their question.

"Perpetrated by party or parties unknown."

A look of relief broke softly across her features.

"And they are all gone?" she exclaimed.

"I found no one in the house who did not belong there."

"Oh! then we can breathe easily again."

I glanced hastily up and down the room.

"There is no one here," said she.

And still I hesitated. At length, in an awkward way enough, I turned towards her and said:

"I do not wish either to offend or alarm you, but I must say that I consider it your duty to return to your own home to-night."

"Why?" she stammered. "Is there any particular reason for my doing so? Have you not perceived the impossibility of my remaining in the same house with Eleanore?"

"Miss Leavenworth, I cannot recognize any so-called impossibility of this nature. Eleanore is your cousin; has been brought up to regard you as a sister; it is not worthy of you to desert her at the time of her necessity. You will see this as I do, if you will allow yourself a moment's dispassionate thought."

"Dispassionate thought is hardly possible under the circumstances," she returned, with a smile of bitter irony.

But before I could reply to this, she softened, and asked if I was very anxious to have her return; and when I replied, "More than I can say," she trembled and looked for a moment as if she were half inclined to yield; but suddenly broke into tears, crying it was impossible, and that I was cruel to ask it.

I drew back, baffled and sore. "Pardon me," said I, "I have indeed transgressed the bounds allotted to me. I will not do so again; you have doubtless many friends; let some of them advise you."

She turned upon me all fire. "The friends you speak of are flatterers. You alone have the courage to command me to do what is right."

"Excuse me, I do not command; I only entreat."

She made no reply, but began pacing the room, her eyes fixed, her hands working convulsively. "You little know what you ask," said she. "I feel as though the very atmosphere of that house would destroy me; but—why cannot Eleanore come here?" she impulsively inquired. "I know Mrs. Gilbert will be quite willing, and I could keep my room, and we need not meet."

"You forget that there is another call at home, besides the one I have already mentioned. To-morrow afternoon your uncle is to be buried."

"O yes; poor, poor uncle!"

"You are the head of the household," I now ventured, "and the proper one to attend to the final offices towards one who has done so much for you."

There was something strange in the look which she gave me. "It is true," she assented. Then, with a grand turn of her body, and a quick air of determination: "I am desirous of being worthy of your good opinion. I will go back to my cousin, Mr. Raymond."

I felt my spirits rise a little; I took her by the hand. "May that cousin have no need of the comfort which I am now sure you will be ready to give her."

Her hand dropped from mine. "I mean to do my duty," was her cold response.

As I descended the stoop, I met a certain thin and fashionably dressed young man, who gave me a very sharp look as he passed. As he wore his clothes a little too conspicuously for the perfect gentleman, and as I had some remembrance of having seen him at the inquest, I set him down for a man in Mr. Gryce's employ, and hasted on towards the avenue; when what was my surprise to find on the corner another person, who, while pretending to be on the look out for a car, cast upon me, as I approached, a furtive glance of intense inquiry. As this latter was, without question, a gentleman, I felt some annoyance, and, walking quietly up to him, asked if he found my countenance familiar, that he scrutinized it so closely.

"I find it a very agreeable one," was his unexpected reply, as he turned from me and walked down the avenue.

Nettled, and in no small degree mortified, at the disadvantage in which his courtesy had placed me, I stood watching him as he disappeared, asking myself who and what he was. For he was not only a gentleman, but a marked one; possessing features of unusual symmetry as well as a form of peculiar elegance. Not so very young—he might well be forty—there were yet evident on his face the impress of youth's strongest emotions, not a curve of his chin nor a glance of his eye betraying in any way the slightest leaning towards *ennui,* though face and figure were of that type which seems most to invite and cherish it.

"He can have no connection with the police force," thought I; "nor is it by any means certain that he knows me, or is interested in my affairs; but I shall not soon forget him, for all that."

The summons from Eleanore Leavenworth came about eight o'clock in the evening. It was brought by Thomas, and read as follows:

"Come, Oh, come! I—" there breaking off in a tremble, as if the pen had fallen from a nerveless hand.

It did not take me long to find my way to her home.

XII. ELEANORE.

"Constant you are—
... And for secrecy
No lady closer."

Henry IV.

"No, 't is slander,
Whose edge is sharper than the sword whose tongue
Outvenoms all the worms of Nile."

Cymbeline.

THE door was opened by Molly. "You will find Miss Eleanore in the drawing-room, sir," she said, ushering me in.

Fearing I knew not what, I hurried to the room thus indicated, feeling as never before the sumptuous-ness of the magnificent hall with its antique flooring, carved woods, and bronze ornamentations:—the mockery of *things* for the first time forcing itself upon me. Laying my hand on the drawing-room door, I listened. All was silent. Slowly pulling it open, I lifted the heavy satin curtains hanging before me to the floor, and looked within. What a picture met my eyes!

Sitting in the light of a solitary gas jet, whose faint glimmering just served to make visible the glancing satin and stainless marble of the gorgeous apartment, I beheld Eleanore Leavenworth. Pale as the sculptured image of the Psyche that towered above her from the mellow dusk of the bow-window near which she sat, beautiful as it, and almost as immobile, she crouched with rigid hands frozen in forgotten entreaty before her, apparently insensible to sound, movement, or touch; a silent figure of despair in presence of an implacable fate.

Impressed by the scene, I stood with my hand upon the curtain, hesitating if to advance or retreat, when suddenly a sharp tremble shook her impassive frame, the rigid hands unlocked, the stony eyes softened, and, springing to her feet, she uttered a cry of satisfaction, and advanced towards me.

"Miss Leavenworth!" I exclaimed, starting at the sound of my own voice.

She paused, and pressed her hands to her face, as if the world and all she had forgotten had rushed back upon her at this simple utterance of her name.

"What is it?" I asked.

Her hands fell heavily. "Do you not know? They—they are beginning to say that I—" she paused, and clutched her throat. "Read!" she gasped, pointing to a newspaper lying on the floor at her feet.

I stooped and lifted what showed itself at first glance to be the *Evening Telegram*. It needed but a single look to inform me to what she referred. There, in startling characters, I beheld:

THE LEAVENWORTH MURDER

LATEST DEVELOPMENTS IN THE MYSTERIOUS CASE

A MEMBER OF THE MURDERED MAN'S OWN FAMILY STRONGLY SUSPECTED OF THE CRIME

THE MOST BEAUTIFUL WOMAN IN NEW YORK UNDER A CLOUD

PAST HISTORY OF MISS ELEANORE LEAVENWORTH

I was prepared for it; had schooled myself for this very thing, you might say; and yet I could not help recoiling. Dropping the paper from my hand, I stood before her, longing and yet dreading to look into her face.

"What does it mean?" she panted; "what, what does it mean? Is the world mad?" and her eyes, fixed and glassy, stared into mine as if she found it impossible to grasp the sense of this outrage.

I shook my head. I could not reply.

"To accuse *me*" she murmured; "me, me!" striking her breast with her clenched hand, "who loved the very ground he trod upon; who would have cast my own body between him and the deadly bullet if I had only known his danger. Oh!" she cried, "it is not a slander they utter, but a dagger which they thrust into my heart!"

Overcome by her misery, but determined not to show my compassion until more thoroughly convinced of her complete innocence, I replied, after a pause:

"This seems to strike you with great surprise, Miss Leavenworth; were you not then able to foresee what must follow your determined reticence upon certain points? Did you know so little of human nature as to imagine that, situated as you are, you could keep silence in regard to any matter connected with this crime, without arousing the antagonism of the crowd, to say nothing of the suspicions of the police?"

"But—but——"

I hurriedly waved my hand. "When you defied the coroner to find any suspicious paper in your possession; when"—I forced myself to speak—"you refused to tell Mr. Gryce how you came in possession of the key—"

She drew hastily back, a heavy pall seeming to fall over her with my words.

"Don't," she whispered, looking in terror about her. "Don't! Sometimes I think the walls have ears, and that the very shadows listen."

"Ah," I returned; "then you hope to keep from the world what is known to the detectives?"

She did not answer.

"Miss Leavenworth," I went on, "I am afraid you do not comprehend your position. Try to look at the case for a moment in the light of an unprejudiced person; try to see for yourself the necessity of explaining——"

"But I cannot explain," she murmured huskily.

"Cannot!"

I do not know whether it was the tone of my voice or the word itself, but that simple expression seemed to affect her like a blow.

"Oh!" she cried, shrinking back: "you do not, cannot doubt me, too? I thought that you—" and stopped. "I did not dream that I—" and stopped again. Suddenly her whole form quivered. "Oh, I see! You have mistrusted me from the first; the appearances against me have been too strong"; and she sank inert, lost in the depths of her shame and humiliation. "Ah, but now I am forsaken!" she murmured.

The appeal went to my heart. Starting forward, I exclaimed: "Miss Leavenworth, I am but a man; I cannot see you so distressed. Say that you are innocent, and I will believe you, without regard to appearances."

Springing erect, she towered upon me. "Can any one look in my face and accuse me of guilt?" Then, as I sadly shook my head, she hurriedly gasped: "You want further proof!" and, quivering with an extraordinary emotion, she sprang to the door.

"Come, then," she cried, "come!" her eyes flashing full of resolve upon me.

Aroused, appalled, moved in spite of myself, I crossed the room to where she stood; but she was already in the hall. Hastening after her, filled with a fear I dared not express, I stood at the foot of the stairs; she was half-way to the top. Following her into the hall' above, I saw her form standing erect and noble at the door of her uncle's bedroom.

59

"Come!" she again cried, but this time in a calm and reverential tone; and flinging the door open before her, she passed in.

Subduing the wonder which I felt, I slowly followed her. There was no light in the room of death, but the flame of the gas-burner, at the far end of the hall, shone weirdly in, and by its glimmering I beheld her kneeling at the shrouded bed, her head bowed above that of the murdered man, her hand upon his breast.

"You have said that if I declared my innocence you would believe me," she exclaimed, lifting her head as I entered. "See here," and laying her cheek against the pallid brow of her dead benefactor, she kissed the clay-cold lips softly, wildly, agonizedly, then, leaping to her feet, cried, in a subdued but thrilling tone: "Could I do that if I were guilty? Would not the breath freeze on my lips, the blood congeal in my veins, and my heart faint at this contact? Son of a father loved and reverenced, can you believe me to be a woman stained with crime when I can do this?" and kneeling again she cast her arms over and about that inanimate form, looking in my face at the same time with an expression no mortal touch could paint, nor tongue describe.

"In olden times," she went on, "they used to say that a dead body would bleed if its murderer came in contact with it. What then would happen here if I, his daughter, his cherished child, loaded with benefits, enriched with his jewels, warm with his kisses, should be the thing they accuse me of? Would not the body of the outraged dead burst its very shroud and repel me?"

I could not answer; in the presence of some scenes the tongue forgets its functions.

"Oh!" she went on, "if there is a God in heaven who loves justice and hates a crime, let Him hear me now. If I, by thought or action, with or without intention, have been the means of bringing this dear head to this pass; if so much as the shadow of guilt, let alone the substance, lies upon my heart and across these feeble woman's hands, may His wrath speak in righteous retribution to the world, and here, upon the breast of the dead, let this guilty forehead fall, never to rise again!"

An awed silence followed this invocation; then a long, long sigh of utter relief rose tremulously from my breast, and all the feelings hitherto suppressed in my heart burst their bonds, and leaning towards her I took her hand in mine.

"You do not, cannot believe me tainted by crime now?" she whispered, the smile which does not stir the lips, but rather emanates from the countenance, like the flowering of an inner peace, breaking softly out on cheek and brow.

"Crime!" The word broke uncontrollably from my lips; "crime!"

"No," she said calmly, "the man does not live who could accuse me of crime, *here*."

For reply, I took her hand, which lay in mine, and placed it on the breast of the dead.

Softly, slowly, gratefully, she bowed her head.

"Now let the struggle come!" she whispered. "There is one who will believe in me, however dark appearances may be."

60

XIII. THE PROBLEM

"But who would force the soul, tilts with a straw
Against a champion cased in adamant."
Wordsworth.

WHEN we re-entered the parlor below, the first sight that met our eyes was Mary, standing wrapped in her long cloak in the centre of the room. She had arrived during our absence, and now awaited us with lifted head and countenance fixed in its proudest expression. Looking in her face, I realized what the embarrassment of this meeting must be to these women, and would have retreated, but something in the attitude of Mary Leavenworth seemed to forbid my doing so. At the same time, determined that the opportunity should not pass without some sort of reconcilement between them, I stepped forward, and, bowing to Mary, said:

"Your cousin has just succeeded in convincing me of her entire innocence, Miss Leavenworth. I am now ready to join Mr. Gryce, heart and soul, in finding out the true culprit."

"I should have thought one look into Eleanore Leavenworth's face would have been enough to satisfy you that she is incapable of crime," was her unexpected answer; and, lifting her head with a proud gesture, Mary Leavenworth fixed her eyes steadfastly on mine.

I felt the blood flash to my brow, but before I could speak, her voice rose again still more coldly than before.

"It is hard for a delicate girl, unused to aught but the most flattering expressions of regard, to be obliged to assure the world of her innocence in respect to the committal of a great crime. Eleanore has my sympathy." And sweeping her cloak from her shoulders with a quick gesture, she turned her gaze for the first time upon her cousin.

Instantly Eleanore advanced, as if to meet it; and I could not but feel that, for some reason, this moment possessed an importance for them which I was scarcely competent to measure. But if I found myself unable to realize its significance, I at least responded to its intensity. And indeed it was an occasion to remember. To behold two such women, either of whom might be considered the model of her time, face to face and drawn up in evident antagonism, was a sight to move the dullest sensibilities. But there was something more in this scene than that. It was the shock of all the most passionate emotions of the human soul; the meeting of waters of whose depth and force I could only guess by the effect. Eleanore was the first to recover. Drawing back with the cold haughtiness which, alas, I had almost forgotten in the display of later and softer emotions, she exclaimed:

"There is something better than sympathy, and that is justice"; and turned, as if to go. "I will confer with you in the reception room, Mr. Raymond."

But Mary, springing forward, caught her back with one powerful hand. "No," she cried, "you shall confer with *me!* I have something to say to you, Eleanore

61

Leavenworth." And, taking her stand in the centre of the room, she waited.

I glanced at Eleanore, saw this was no place for me, and hastily withdrew. For ten long minutes I paced the floor of the reception room, a prey to a thousand doubts and conjectures. What was the secret of this home? What had given rise to the deadly mistrust continually manifested between these cousins, fitted by nature for the completest companionship and the most cordial friendship? It was not a thing of to-day or yesterday. No sudden flame could awake such concentrated heat of emotion as that of which I had just been the unwilling witness. One must go farther back than this murder to find the root of a mistrust so great that the struggle it caused made itself felt even where I stood, though nothing but the faintest murmur came to my ears through the closed doors.

Presently the drawing-room curtain was raised, and Mary's voice was heard in distinct articulation.

"The same roof can never shelter us both after this. To-morrow, you or I find another home." And, blushing and panting, she stepped into the hall and advanced to where I stood. But at the first sight of my face, a change came over her; all her pride seemed to dissolve, and, flinging out her hands, as if to ward off scrutiny, she fled from my side, and rushed weeping up-stairs.

I was yet laboring under the oppression caused by this painful termination of the strange scene when the parlor curtain was again lifted, and Eleanore entered the room where I was. Pale but calm, showing no evidences of the struggle she had just been through, unless by a little extra weariness about the eyes, she sat down by my side, and, meeting my gaze with one unfathomable in its courage, said after a pause: "Tell me where I stand; let me know the worst at once; I fear that I have not indeed comprehended my own position."

Rejoiced to hear this acknowledgment from her lips, I hastened to comply. I began by placing before her the whole case as it appeared to an unprejudiced person; enlarged upon the causes of suspicion, and pointed out in what regard some things looked dark against her, which perhaps to her own mind were easily explainable and of small account; tried to make her see the importance of her decision, and finally wound up with an appeal. Would she not confide in me?

"But I thought you were satisfied?" she tremblingly remarked.

"And so I am; but I want the world to be so, too."

"Ah; now you ask too much! The finger of suspicion never forgets the way it has once pointed," she sadly answered. "My name is tainted forever."

"And you will submit to this, when a word——"

"I am thinking that any word of mine now would make very little difference," she murmured.

I looked away, the vision of Mr. Fobbs, in hiding behind the curtains of the opposite house, recurring painfully to my mind.

"If the affair looks as bad as you say it does," she pursued, "it is scarcely probable that Mr. Gryce will care much for any interpretation of mine in regard to the matter."

"Mr. Gryce would be glad to know where you procured that key, if only to assist him in turning his inquiries in the right direction."

She did not reply, and my spirits sank in renewed depression.

"It is worth your while to satisfy him," I pursued; "and though it may compromise some one you desire to shield——"

She rose impetuously. "I shall never divulge to any one how I came in possession of that key." And sitting again, she locked her hands in fixed resolve before her.

I rose in my turn and paced the floor, the fang of an unreasoning jealousy striking deep into my heart.

"Mr. Raymond, if the worst should come, and all who love me should plead on bended knees for me to tell, I will never do it."

"Then," said I, determined not to disclose my secret thought, but equally resolved to find out if possible her motive for this silence, "you desire to defeat the cause of justice."

She neither spoke nor moved.

"Miss Leavenworth," I now said, "this determined shielding of another at the expense of your own good name is no doubt generous of you; but your friends and the lovers of truth and justice cannot accept such a sacrifice."

She started haughtily. "Sir!" she said.

"If you will not assist us," I went on calmly, but determinedly, "we must do without your aid. After the scene I have just witnessed above; after the triumphant conviction which you have forced upon me, not only of your innocence, but your horror of the crime and its consequences, I should feel myself less than a man if I did not sacrifice even your own good opinion, in urging your cause, and clearing your character from this foul aspersion."

Again that heavy silence.

"What do you propose to do?" she asked, at last.

Crossing the room, I stood before her. "I propose to relieve you utterly and forever from suspicion, by finding out and revealing to the world the true culprit."

I expected to see her recoil, so positive had I become by this time as to who that culprit was. But instead of that, she merely folded her hands still more tightly and exclaimed:

"I doubt if you will be able to do that, Mr. Raymond."

"Doubt if I will be able to put my finger upon the guilty man, or doubt if I will be able to bring him to justice?"

"I doubt," she said with strong effort, "if any one ever knows who is the guilty person in this case."

"There is one who knows," I said with a desire to test her.

"One?"

"The girl Hannah is acquainted with the mystery of that night's evil doings, Miss Leavenworth. Find Hannah, and we find one who can point out to us the assassin of your uncle."

"That is mere supposition," she said; but I saw the blow had told.

"Your cousin has offered a large reward for the girl, and the whole country is on the lookout. Within a week we shall see her in our midst."

A change took place in her expression and bearing.

63

"The girl cannot help me," she said.

Baffled by her manner, I drew back. "Is there anything or anybody that can?"

She slowly looked away.

"Miss Leavenworth," I continued with renewed earnestness, "you have no brother to plead with you, you have no mother to guide you; let me then entreat, in default of nearer and dearer friends, that you will rely sufficiently upon me to tell me one thing."

"What is it?" she asked.

"Whether you took the paper imputed to you from the library table?"

She did not instantly respond, but sat looking earnestly before her with an intentness which seemed to argue that she was weighing the question as well as her reply. Finally, turning toward me, she said:

"In answering you, I speak in confidence. Mr. Raymond, I did."

Crushing back the sigh of despair that arose to my lips, I went on.

"I will not inquire what the paper was,"—she waved her hand deprecatingly, —"but this much more you will tell me. Is that paper still in existence?"

She looked me steadily in the face.

"It is not."

I could with difficulty forbear showing my disappointment. "Miss Leavenworth," I now said, "it may seem cruel for me to press you at this time; nothing less than my strong realization of the peril in which you stand would induce me to run the risk of incurring your displeasure by asking what under other circumstances would seem puerile and insulting questions. You have told me one thing which I strongly desired to know; will you also inform me what it was you heard that night while sitting in your room, between the time of Mr. Harwell's going up-stairs and the closing of the library door, of which you made mention at the inquest?"

I had pushed my inquiries too far, and I saw it immediately.

"Mr. Raymond," she returned, "influenced by my desire not to appear utterly ungrateful to you, I have been led to reply in confidence to one of your urgent appeals; but I can go no further. Do not ask me to."

Stricken to the heart by her look of reproach, I answered with some sadness that her wishes should be respected. "Not but what I intend to make every effort in my power to discover the true author of this crime. That is a sacred duty which I feel myself called upon to perform; but I will ask you no more questions, nor distress you with further appeals. What is done shall be done without your assistance, and with no other hope than that in the event of my success you will acknowledge my motives to have been pure and my action disinterested."

"I am ready to acknowledge that now," she began, but paused and looked with almost agonized entreaty in my face. "Mr. Raymond, cannot you leave things as they are? Won't you? I don't ask for assistance, nor do I want it; I would rather ———"

But I would not listen. "Guilt has no right to profit by the generosity of the guiltless. The hand that struck this blow shall not be accountable for the loss of a noble woman's honor and happiness as well.

"I shall do what I can, Miss Leavenworth."

As I walked down the avenue that night, feeling like an adventurous traveller that in a moment of desperation has set his foot upon a plank stretching in narrow perspective over a chasm of immeasurable depth, this problem evolved itself from the shadows before me: How, with no other clue than the persuasion that Eleanore Leavenworth was engaged in shielding another at the expense of her own good name, I was to combat the prejudices of Mr. Gryce, find out the real assassin of Mr. Leavenworth, and free an innocent woman from the suspicion that had, not without some show of reason, fallen upon her?

BOOK II. HENRY CLAVERING

XIV. MR. GRYCE AT HOME

"Nay, but hear me."

Measure for Measure.

THAT the guilty person for whom Eleanore Leavenworth stood ready to sacrifice herself was one for whom she had formerly cherished affection, I could no longer doubt; love, or the strong sense of duty growing out of love, being alone sufficient to account for such determined action. Obnoxious as it was to all my prejudices, one name alone, that of the commonplace secretary, with his sudden heats and changeful manners, his odd ways and studied self-possession, would recur to my mind whenever I asked myself who this person could be.

Not that, without the light which had been thrown upon the affair by Eleanore's strange behavior, I should have selected this man as one in any way open to suspicion; the peculiarity of his manner at the inquest not being marked enough to counteract the improbability of one in his relations to the deceased finding sufficient motive for a crime so manifestly without favorable results to himself. But if love had entered as a factor into the affair, what might not be expected? James Harwell, simple amanuensis to a retired tea-merchant, was one man; James Harwell, swayed by passion for a woman beautiful as Eleanore Leavenworth, was another; and in placing him upon the list of those parties open to suspicion I felt I was only doing what was warranted by a proper consideration of probabilities.

But, between casual suspicion and actual proof, what a gulf! To believe James Harwell capable of guilt, and to find evidence enough to accuse him of it, were two very different things. I felt myself instinctively shrink from the task, before I had fully made up my mind to attempt it; some relenting thought of his unhappy position, if innocent, forcing itself upon me, and making my very distrust of him seem personally ungenerous if not absolutely unjust. If I had liked the man better, I should not have been so ready to look upon him with doubt.

But Eleanore must be saved at all hazards. Once delivered up to the blight of suspicion, who could tell what the result might be? the arrest of her person perhaps,—a thing which, once accomplished, would cast a shadow over her young life that it would take more than time to dispel. The accusation of an impecunious secretary would be less horrible than this. I determined to make an early call upon Mr. Gryce.

Meanwhile the contrasted pictures of Eleanore standing with her hand upon the breast of the dead, her face upraised and mirroring a glory, I could not recall without emotion; and Mary, fleeing a short half-hour later indignantly from her presence, haunted me and kept me awake long after midnight. It was like a double vision of light and darkness that, while contrasting, neither assimilated nor harmonized. I could not flee from it. Do what I would, the two pictures followed me, filling my soul with alternate hope and distrust, till I knew not whether to place my hand with Eleanore on the breast of the dead, and swear implicit faith in her truth and purity, or to turn my face like Mary, and fly from what I could neither comprehend nor reconcile.

Expectant of difficulty, I started next morning upon my search for Mr. Gryce, with strong determination not to allow myself to become flurried by disappointment nor discouraged by premature failure. My business was to save Eleanore Leavenworth; and to do that, it was necessary for me to preserve, not only my equanimity, but my self-possession. The worst fear I anticipated was that matters would reach a crisis before I could acquire the right, or obtain the opportunity, to interfere. However, the fact of Mr. Leavenworth's funeral being announced for that day gave me some comfort in that direction; my knowledge of Mr. Gryce being sufficient, as I thought, to warrant me in believing he would wait till after that ceremony before proceeding to extreme measures.

I do not know that I had any vary definite ideas of what a detective's home should be; but when I stood before the neat three-story brick house to which I had been directed, I could not but acknowledge there was something in the aspect of its half-open shutters, over closely drawn curtains of spotless purity, highly suggestive of the character of its inmate.

A pale-looking youth, with vivid locks of red hair hanging straight down over either ear, answered my rather nervous ring. To my inquiry as to whether Mr. Gryce was in, he gave a kind of snort which might have meant no, but which I took to mean yes.

"My name is Raymond, and I wish to see him."

He gave me one glance that took in every detail of my person and apparel, and pointed to a door at the head of the stairs. Not waiting for further directions, I hastened up, knocked at the door he had designated, and went in. The broad back of Mr. Gryce, stooping above a desk that might have come over in the *Mayflower*, confronted me.

"Well!" he exclaimed; "this is an honor." And rising, he opened with a squeak and shut with a bang the door of an enormous stove that occupied the centre of the room. "Rather chilly day, eh?"

"Yes," I returned, eyeing him closely to see if he was in a communicative mood. "But I have had but little time to consider the state of the weather. My anxiety in regard to this murder——"

66

"To be sure," he interrupted, fixing his eyes upon the poker, though not with any hostile intention, I am sure. "A puzzling piece of business enough. But perhaps it is an open book to you. I see you have something to communicate."

"I have, though I doubt if it is of the nature you expect. Mr. Gryce, since I saw you last, my convictions upon a certain point have been strengthened into an absolute belief. The object of your suspicions is an innocent woman."

If I had expected him to betray any surprise at this, I was destined to be disappointed. "That is a very pleasing belief," he observed. "I honor you for entertaining it, Mr. Raymond."

I suppressed a movement of anger. "So thoroughly is it mine," I went on, in the determination to arouse him in some way, "that I have come here to-day to ask you in the name of justice and common humanity to suspend action in that direction till we can convince ourselves there is no truer scent to go upon."

But there was no more show of curiosity than before. "Indeed!" he cried; "that is a singular request to come from a man like you."

I was not to be discomposed, "Mr. Gryce," I went on, "a woman's name, once tarnished, remains so forever. Eleanore Leavenworth has too many noble traits to be thoughtlessly dealt with in so momentous a crisis. If you will give me your attention, I promise you shall not regret it."

He smiled, and allowed his eyes to roam from the poker to the arm of my chair. "Very well," he remarked; "I hear you; say on."

I drew my notes from my pocketbook, and laid them on the table.

"What! memoranda?" he exclaimed. "Unsafe, very; never put your plans on paper."

Taking no heed of the interruption, I went on.

"Mr. Gryce, I have had fuller opportunities than yourself for studying this woman. I have seen her in a position which no guilty person could occupy, and I am assured, beyond all doubt, that not only her hands, but her heart, are pure from this crime. She may have some knowledge of its secrets; that I do not presume to deny. The key seen in her possession would refute me if I did. But what if she has? You can never wish to see so lovely a being brought to shame for withholding information which she evidently considers it her duty to keep back, when by a little patient finesse we may succeed in our purposes without it."

"But," interposed the detective, "say this is so; how are we to arrive at the knowledge we want without following out the only clue which has yet been given us?"

"You will never reach it by following out any clue given you by Eleanore Leavenworth."

His eyebrows lifted expressively, but he said nothing.

"Miss Eleanore Leavenworth has been used by some one acquainted with her firmness, generosity, and perhaps love. Let us discover who possesses sufficient power over her to control her to this extent, and we find the man we seek."

"Humph!" came from Mr. Gryce's compressed lips, and no more.

Determined that he should speak, I waited.

"You have, then, some one in your mind"; he remarked at last, almost flippantly.

"I mention no names," I returned. "All I want is further time."

"You are, then, intending to make a personal business of this matter?"

"I am."

He gave a long, low whistle. "May I ask," he inquired at length, "whether you expect to work entirely by yourself; or whether, if a suitable coadjutor were provided, you would disdain his assistance and slight his advice?"

"I desire nothing more than to have you for my colleague."

The smile upon his face deepened ironically. "You must feel very sure of yourself!" said he.

"I am very sure of Miss Leavenworth."

The reply seemed to please him. "Let us hear what you propose doing."

I did not immediately answer. The truth was, I had formed no plans.

"It seems to me," he continued, "that you have undertaken a rather difficult task for an amateur. Better leave it to me, Mr. Raymond; better leave it to me."

"I am sure," I returned, "that nothing would please me better———"

"Not," he interrupted, "but that a word from you now and then would be welcome. I am not an egotist. I am open to suggestions: as, for instance, now, if you could conveniently inform me of all you have yourself seen and heard in regard to this matter, I should be most happy to listen."

Relieved to find him so amenable, I asked myself what I really had to tell; not so much that he would consider vital. However, it would not do to hesitate now.

"Mr. Gryce," said I, "I have but few facts to add to those already known to you. Indeed, I am more moved by convictions than facts. That Eleanore Leavenworth never committed this crime, I am assured. That, on the other hand, the real perpetrator is known to her, I am equally certain; and that for some reason she considers it a sacred duty to shield the assassin, even at the risk of her own safety, follows as a matter of course from the facts. Now, with such data, it cannot be a very difficult task for you or me to work out satisfactorily, to our own minds at least, who this person can be. A little more knowledge of the family—"

"You know nothing of its secret history, then?"

"Nothing."

"Do not even know whether either of these girls is engaged to be married?"

"I do not," I returned, wincing at this direct expression of my own thoughts.

He remained a moment silent. "Mr. Raymond," he cried at last, "have you any idea of the disadvantages under which a detective labors? For instance, now, you imagine I can insinuate myself into all sorts of society, perhaps; but you are mistaken. Strange as it may appear, I have never by any possibility of means succeeded with one class of persons at all. I cannot pass myself off for a gentleman. Tailors and barbers are no good; I am always found out."

He looked so dejected I could scarcely forbear smiling, notwithstanding my secret care and anxiety.

"I have even employed a French valet, who understood dancing and whiskers; but it was all of no avail. The first gentleman I approached stared at me,—real gentleman, I mean, none of your American dandies,—and I had no stare to return; I had forgotten that emergency in my confabs with Pierre Catnille Marie

Make-face."

Amused, but a little discomposed by this sudden turn in the conversation, I looked at Mr. Gryce inquiringly.

"Now you, I dare say, have no trouble? Was born one, perhaps. Can even ask a lady to dance without blushing, eh?"

"Well,—" I commenced.

"Just so," he replied; "now, I can't. I can enter a house, bow to the mistress of it, let her be as elegant as she will, so long as I have a writ of arrest in my hand, or some such professional matter upon my mind; but when it comes to visiting in kid gloves, raising a glass of champagne in response to a toast—and such like, I am absolutely good for nothing." And he plunged his two hands into his hair, and looked dolefully at the head of the cane I carried in my hand. "But it is much the same with the whole of us. When we are in want of a gentleman to work for us, we have to go outside of our profession."

I began to see what he was driving at; but held my peace, vaguely conscious I was likely to prove a necessity to him, after all.

"Mr. Raymond," he now said, almost abruptly; "do you know a gentleman by the name of Clavering residing at present at the Hoffman House?"

"Not that I am aware of."

"He is very polished in his manners; would you mind making his acquaintance?"

I followed Mr. Gryce's example, and stared at the chimney-piece. "I cannot answer till I understand matters a little better," I returned at length.

"There is not much to understand. Mr. Henry Clavering, a gentleman and a man of the world, resides at the Hoffman House. He is a stranger in town, without being strange; drives, walks, smokes, but never visits; looks at the ladies, but is never seen to bow to one. In short, a person whom it is desirable to know; but whom, being a proud man, with something of the old-world prejudice against Yankee freedom and forwardness, I could no more approach in the way of acquaintance than I could the Emperor of Austria."

"And you wish——"

"He would make a very agreeable companion for a rising young lawyer of good family and undoubted respectability. I have no doubt, if you undertook to cultivate him, you would find him well worth the trouble."

"But——"

"Might even desire to take him into familiar relations; to confide in him, and ——"

"Mr. Gryce," I hastily interrupted; "I can never consent to plot for any man's friendship for the sake of betraying him to the police."

"It is essential to your plans to make the acquaintance of Mr. Clavering," he dryly replied.

"Oh!" I returned, a light breaking in upon me; "he has some connection with this case, then?"

Mr. Gryce smoothed his coat-sleeve thoughtfully. "I don't know as it will be necessary for you to betray him. You wouldn't object to being introduced to him?"

69

"No."

"Nor, if you found him pleasant, to converse with him?"

"No."

"Not even if, in the course of conversation, you should come across something that might serve as a clue in your efforts to save Eleanore Leavenworth?"

The no I uttered this time was less assured; the part of a spy was the very last one I desired to play in the coming drama.

"Well, then," he went on, ignoring the doubtful tone in which my assent had been given, "I advise you to immediately take up your quarters at the Hoffman House."

"I doubt if that would do," I said. "If I am not mistaken, I have already seen this gentleman, and spoken to him."

"Where?"

"Describe him first."

"Well, he is tall, finely formed, of very upright carriage, with a handsome dark face, brown hair streaked with gray, a piercing eye, and a smooth address. A very imposing personage, I assure you."

"I have reason to think I have seen him," I returned; and in a few words told him when and where.

"Humph!" said he at the conclusion; "he is evidently as much interested in you as we are in him.

"How 's that? I think I see," he added, after a moment's thought. "Pity you spoke to him; may have created an unfavorable impression; and everything depends upon your meeting without any distrust."

He rose and paced the floor.

"Well, we must move slowly, that is all. Give him a chance to see you in other and better lights. Drop into the Hoffman House reading-room. Talk with the best men you meet while there; but not too much, or too indiscriminately. Mr. Clavering is fastidious, and will not feel honored by the attentions of one who is hail-fellow-well-met with everybody. Show yourself for what you are, and leave all advances to him; he 'll make them."

"Supposing we are under a mistake, and the man I met on the corner of Thirty-seventh Street was not Mr. Clavering?"

"I should be greatly surprised, that's all."

Not knowing what further objection to make, I remained silent.

"And this head of mine would have to put on its thinking-cap," he pursued jovially.

"Mr. Gryce," I now said, anxious to show that all this talk about an unknown party had not served to put my own plans from my mind, "there is one person of whom we have not spoken."

"No?" he exclaimed softly, wheeling around until his broad back confronted me. "And who may that be?"

"Why, who but Mr.—" I could get no further. What right had I to mention any man's name in this connection, without possessing sufficient evidence against him to make such mention justifiable? "I beg your pardon," said I; "but I think I will hold to my first impulse, and speak no names."

"Harwell?" he ejaculated easily.

The quick blush rising to my face gave an involuntary assent.

"I see no reason why we shouldn't speak of him," he went on; "that is, if there is anything to be gained by it."

"His testimony at the inquest was honest, you think?"

"It has not been disproved."

"He is a peculiar man."

"And so am I."

I felt myself slightly nonplussed; and, conscious of appearing at a disadvantage, lifted my hat from the table and prepared to take my leave; but, suddenly thinking of Hannah, turned and asked if there was any news of her.

He seemed to debate with himself, hesitating so long that I began to doubt if this man intended to confide in me, after all, when suddenly he brought his two hands down before him and exclaimed vehemently:

"The evil one himself is in this business! If the earth had opened and swallowed up this girl, she couldn't have more effectually disappeared."

I experienced a sinking of the heart. Eleanore had said: "Hannah can do nothing for me." Could it be that the girl was indeed gone, and forever?

"I have innumerable agents at work, to say nothing of the general public; and yet not so much as a whisper has come to me in regard to her whereabouts or situation. I am only afraid we shall find her floating in the river some fine morning, without a confession in her pocket."

"Everything hangs upon that girl's testimony," I remarked.

He gave a short grunt. "What does Miss Leavenworth say about it?"

"That the girl cannot help her."

I thought he looked a trifle surprised at this, but he covered it with a nod and an exclamation. "She must be found for all that," said he, "and shall, if I have to send out Q."

"Q?"

"An agent of mine who is a living interrogation point; so we call him _Q_, which is short for query." Then, as I turned again to go: "When the contents of the will are made known, come to me."

The will! I had forgotten the will.

XV. WAYS OPENING

"It is not and it cannot come to good."

Hamlet.

I ATTENDED the funeral of Mr. Leavenworth, but did not see the ladies before or after the ceremony. I, however, had a few moments' conversation with Mr. Harwell; which, without eliciting anything new, provided me with food for abundant conjecture. For he had asked, almost at first greeting, if I had seen the _Telegram_ of the night before; and when I responded in the affirmative, turned such

71

a look of mingled distress and appeal upon me, I was tempted to ask how such a frightful insinuation against a young lady of reputation and breeding could ever have got into the papers. It was his reply that struck me.

"That the guilty party might be driven by remorse to own himself the true culprit."

A curious remark to come from a person who had no knowledge or suspicion of the criminal and his character; and I would have pushed the conversation further, but the secretary, who was a man of few words, drew off at this, and could be induced to say no more. Evidently it was my business to cultivate Mr. Clavering, or any one else who could throw any light upon the secret history of these girls.

That evening I received notice that Mr. Veeley had arrived home, but was in no condition to consult with me upon so painful a subject as the murder of Mr. Leavenworth. Also a line from Eleanore, giving me her address, but requesting me at the same time not to call unless I had something of importance to communicate, as she was too ill to receive visitors. The little note affected me. Ill, alone, and in a strange home,—'twas pitiful!

The next day, pursuant to the wishes of Mr. Gryce, in I stepped into the Hoffman House, and took a seat in the reading room. I had been there but a few moments when a gentleman entered whom I immediately recognized as the same I had spoken to on the corner of Thirty-seventh Street and Sixth Avenue. He must have remembered me also, for he seemed to be slightly embarrassed at seeing me; but, recovering himself, took up a paper and soon became to all appearance lost in its contents, though I could feel his handsome black eye upon me, studying my features, figure, apparel, and movements with a degree of interest which equally astonished and disconcerted me. I felt that it would be injudicious on my part to return his scrutiny, anxious as I was to meet his eye and learn what emotion had so fired his curiosity in regard to a perfect stranger; so I rose, and, crossing to an old friend of mine who sat at a table opposite, commenced a desultory conversation, in the course of which I took occasion to ask if he knew who the handsome stranger was. Dick Furbish was a society man, and knew everybody.

"His name is Clavering, and he comes from London. I don't know anything more about him, though he is to be seen everywhere except in private houses. He has not been received into society yet; waiting for letters of introduction, perhaps."

"A gentleman?"

"Undoubtedly."

"One you speak to?"

"Oh, yes; I talk to him, but the conversation is very one-sided."

I could not help smiling at the grimace with which Dick accompanied this remark. "Which same goes to prove," he went on, "that he is the real thing."

Laughing outright this time, I left him, and in a few minutes sauntered from the room.

As I mingled again with the crowd on Broadway, I found myself wondering immensely over this slight experience. That this unknown gentleman from London, who went everywhere except into private houses, could be in any way connected with the affair I had so at heart, seemed not only improbable but absurd; and for the first time I felt tempted to doubt the sagacity of Mr. Gryce in recommending him to my attention.

The next day I repeated the experiment, but with no greater success than before. Mr. Clavering came into the room, but, seeing me, did not remain. I began to realize it was no easy matter to make his acquaintance. To atone for my disappointment, I called on Mary Leavenworth in the evening. She received me with almost a sister-like familiarity.

"Ah," she cried, after introducing me to an elderly lady at her side,—some connection of the family, I believe, who had come to remain with her for a while, —"you are here to tell me Hannah is found; is it not so?"

I shook my head, sorry to disappoint her. "No," said I; "not yet."

"But Mr. Gryce was here to-day, and he told me he hoped she would be heard from within twenty-four hours."

"Mr. Gryce here!"

"Yes; came to report how matters were progressing,—not that they seemed to have advanced very far."

"You could hardly have expected that yet. You must not be so easily discouraged."

"But I cannot help it; every day, every hour that passes in this uncertainty, is like a mountain weight here"; and she laid one trembling hand upon her bosom. "I would have the whole world at work. I would leave no stone unturned; I——"

"What would you do?"

"Oh, I don't know," she cried, her whole manner suddenly changing; "nothing, perhaps." Then, before I could reply to this: "Have you seen Eleanore to-day?"

I answered in the negative.

She did not seem satisfied, but waited till her friend left the room before saying more. Then, with an earnest look, inquired if I knew whether Eleanore was well.

"I fear she is not," I returned.

"It is a great trial to me, Eleanore being away. Not," she resumed, noting, perhaps, my incredulous look, "that I would have you think I wish to disclaim my share in bringing about the present unhappy state of things. I am willing to acknowledge I was the first to propose a separation. But it is none the easier to bear on that account."

"It is not as hard for you as for her," said I.

"Not as hard? Why? because she is left comparatively poor, while I am rich—is that what you would say? Ah," she went on, without waiting for my answer, "would I could persuade Eleanore to share my riches with me! Willingly would I bestow upon her the half I have received; but I fear she could never be induced to accept so much as a dollar from me."

"Under the circumstances it would be better for her not to."

"Just what I thought; yet it would ease me of a great weight if she would. This fortune, suddenly thrown into my lap, sits like an incubus upon me, Mr. Raymond.

When the will was read to-day which makes me possessor of so much wealth, I could not but feel that a heavy, blinding pall had settled upon me, spotted with blood and woven of horrors. Ah, how different from the feelings with which I have been accustomed to anticipate this day! For, Mr. Raymond," she went on, with a hurried gasp, "dreadful as it seems now, I have been reared to look forward to this hour with pride, if not with actual longing. Money has been made so much of in my small world. Not that I wish in this evil time of retribution to lay blame upon any one; least of all upon my uncle; but from the day, twelve years ago, when for the first time he took us in his arms, and looking down upon our childish faces, exclaimed: 'The light-haired one pleases me best; she shall be my heiress,' I have been petted, cajoled, and spoiled; called little princess, and uncle's darling, till it is only strange I retain in this prejudiced breast any of the impulses of generous womanhood; yes, though I was aware from the first that whim alone had raised this distinction between myself and cousin; a distinction which superior beauty, worth, or accomplishments could never have drawn; Eleanore being more than my equal in all these things." Pausing, she choked back the sudden sob that rose in her throat, with an effort at self-control which was at once touching and admirable. Then, while my eyes stole to her face, murmured in a low, appealing voice: "If I have faults, you see there is some slight excuse for them; arrogance, vanity, and selfishness being considered in the gay young heiress as no more than so many assertions of a laudable dignity. Ah! ah," she bitterly exclaimed "money alone has been the ruin of us all!" Then, with a falling of her voice: "And now it has come to me with its heritage of evil, and I—I would give it all for—But this is weakness! I have no right to afflict you with my griefs. Pray forget all I have said, Mr. Raymond, or regard my complaints as the utterances of an unhappy girl loaded down with sorrows and oppressed by the weight of many perplexities and terrors."

"But I do not wish to forget," I replied. "You have spoken some good words, manifested much noble emotion. Your possessions cannot but prove a blessing to you if you enter upon them with such feelings as these."

But, with a quick gesture, she ejaculated: "Impossible! they cannot prove a blessing." Then, as if startled at her own words, bit her lip and hastily added: "Very great wealth is never a blessing.

"And now," said she, with a total change of manner, "I wish to address you on a subject which may strike you as ill-timed, but which, nevertheless, I must mention, if the purpose I have at heart is ever to be accomplished. My uncle, as you know, was engaged at the time of his death in writing a book on Chinese customs and prejudices. It was a work which he was anxious to see published, and naturally I desire to carry out his wishes; but, in order to do so, I find it necessary not only to interest myself in the matter now,—Mr. Harwell's services being required, and it being my wish to dismiss that gentleman as soon as possible—but to find some one competent to supervise its completion. Now I have heard,—I have been told, —that you were the one of all others to do this; and though it is difficult if not improper for me to ask so great a favor of one who but a week ago was a perfect stranger to me, it would afford me the keenest pleasure if you would consent to look over this manuscript and tell me what remains to be done."

The timidity with which these words were uttered proved her to be in earnest, and I could not but wonder at the strange coincidence of this request with my secret wishes; it having been a question with me for some time how I was to gain free access to this house without in any way compromising either its inmates or myself. I did not know then that Mr. Gryce had been the one to recommend me to her favor in this respect. But, whatever satisfaction I may have experienced, I felt myself in duty bound to plead my incompetence for a task so entirely out of the line of my profession, and to suggest the employment of some one better acquainted with such matters than myself. But she would not listen to me.

"Mr. Harwell has notes and memoranda in plenty," she exclaimed, "and can give you all the information necessary. You will have no difficulty; indeed, you will not."

"But cannot Mr. Harwell himself do all that is requisite? He seems to be a clever and diligent young man."

But she shook her head. "He thinks he can; but I know uncle never trusted him with the composition of a single sentence."

"But perhaps he will not be pleased,—Mr. Harwell, I mean—with the intrusion of a stranger into his work."

She opened her eyes with astonishment. "That makes no difference," she cried. "Mr. Harwell is in my pay, and has nothing to say about it. But he will not object. I have already consulted him, and he expresses himself as satisfied with the arrangement."

"Very well," said I; "then I will promise to consider the subject. I can at any rate look over the manuscript and give you my opinion of its condition."

"Oh, thank you," said she, with the prettiest gesture of satisfaction. "How kind you are, and what can I ever do to repay you? But would you like to see Mr. Harwell himself?" and she moved towards the door; but suddenly paused, whispering, with a short shudder of remembrance: "He is in the library; do you mind?"

Crushing down the sick qualm that arose at the mention of that spot, I replied in the negative.

"The papers are all there, and he says he can work better in his old place than anywhere else; but if you wish, I can call him down."

But I would not listen to this, and myself led the way to the foot of the stairs.

"I have sometimes thought I would lock up that room," she hurriedly observed; "but something restrains me. I can no more do so than I can leave this house; a power beyond myself forces me to confront all its horrors. And yet I suffer continually from terror. Sometimes, in the darkness of the night—But I will not distress you. I have already said too much; come," and with a sudden lift of the head she mounted the stairs.

Mr. Harwell was seated, when we entered that fatal room, in the one chair of all others I expected to see unoccupied; and as I beheld his meagre figure bending where such a little while before his eyes had encountered the outstretched form of his murdered employer, I could not but marvel over the unimaginativeness of the man who, in the face of such memories, could not only appropriate that very spot for his own use, but pursue his avocations there with so much calmness and evident precision. But in another moment I discovered that the disposition of the light in the room made that one seat the only desirable one for his purpose; and instantly my wonder changed to admiration at this quiet surrender of personal feeling to the requirements of the occasion.

He looked up mechanically as we came in, but did not rise, his countenance wearing the absorbed expression which bespeaks the preoccupied mind.

"He is utterly oblivious," Mary whispered; "that is a way of his. I doubt if he knows who or what it is that has disturbed him." And, advancing into the room, she passed across his line of vision, as if to call attention to herself, and said: "I have brought Mr. Raymond up-stairs to see you, Mr. Harwell. He has been so kind as to accede to my wishes in regard to the completion of the manuscript now before you."

Slowly Mr. Harwell rose, wiped his pen, and put it away; manifesting, however, a reluctance in doing so that proved this interference to be in reality anything but agreeable to him. Observing this, I did not wait for him to speak, but took up the pile of manuscript, arranged in one mass on the table, saying:

"This seems to be very clearly written; if you will excuse me, I will glance over it and thus learn something of its general character."

He bowed, uttered a word or so of acquiescence, then, as Mary left the room, awkwardly reseated himself, and took up his pen.

Instantly the manuscript and all connected with it vanished from my thoughts; and Eleanore, her situation, and the mystery surrounding this family, returned upon me with renewed force. Looking the secretary steadily in the face, I remarked:

"I am very glad of this opportunity of seeing you a moment alone, Mr. Harwell, if only for the purpose of saying——"

"Anything in regard to the murder?"

"Yes," I began.

"Then you must pardon me," he respectfully but firmly replied. "It is a disagreeable subject which I cannot bear to think of, much less discuss."

Disconcerted and, what was more, convinced of the impossibility of obtaining any information from this man, I abandoned the attempt; and, taking up the manuscript once more, endeavored to master in some small degree the nature of its contents. Succeeding beyond my hopes, I opened a short conversation with him in regard to it, and finally, coming to the conclusion I could accomplish what Miss Leavenworth desired, left him and descended again to the reception room.

When, an hour or so later, I withdrew from the house, it was with the feeling that one obstacle had been removed from my path. If I failed in what I had undertaken, it would not be from lack of opportunity of studying the inmates of this dwelling.

XVI. THE WILL OF A MILLIONAIRE

"Our remedies oft in ourselves do lie,
Which we ascribe to Heaven."
All's Well that Ends Well.

THE next morning's *Tribune* contained a synopsis of Mr. Leavenworth's will. Its provisions were a surprise to me; for, while the bulk of his immense estate was, according to the general understanding, bequeathed to his niece, Mary, it appeared by a codicil, attached to his will some five years before, that Eleanore was not entirely forgotten, she having been made the recipient of a legacy which, if not large, was at least sufficient to support her in comfort. After listening to the various comments of my associates on the subject, I proceeded to the house of Mr. Gryce, in obedience to his request to call upon him as soon as possible after the publication of the will.

"Good-morning," he remarked as I entered, but whether addressing me or the frowning top of the desk before which he was sitting it would be difficult to say. "Won't you sit?" nodding with a curious back movement of his head towards a chair in his rear.

I drew up the chair to his side. "I am curious to know," I remarked, "what you have to say about this will, and its probable effect upon the matters we have in hand."

"What is your own idea in regard to it?"

"Well, I think upon the whole it will make but little difference in public opinion. Those who thought Eleanore guilty before will feel that they possess now greater cause than ever to doubt her innocence; while those who have hitherto hesitated to suspect her will not consider that the comparatively small amount bequeathed her would constitute an adequate motive for so great a crime."

"You have heard men talk; what seems to be the general opinion among those you converse with?"

"That the motive of the tragedy will be found in the partiality shown in so singular a will, though how, they do not profess to know."

Mr. Gryce suddenly became interested in one of the small drawers before him.

"And all this has not set you thinking?" said he.

"Thinking," returned I. "I don't know what you mean. I am sure I have done nothing but think for the last three days. I——"

"Of course—of course," he cried. "I didn't mean to say anything disagreeable. And so you have seen Mr. Clavering?"

"Just seen him; no more."

"And are you going to assist Mr. Harwell in finishing Mr. Leavenworth's book?"

"How did you learn that?"

He only smiled.

"Yes," said I; "Miss Leavenworth has requested me to do her that little favor."

"She is a queenly creature!" he exclaimed in a burst of enthusiasm. Then, with an instant return to his business-like tone: "You are going to have opportunities, Mr. Raymond. Now there are two things I want you to find out; first, what is the connection between these ladies and Mr. Clavering——"

77

"There is a connection, then?"

"Undoubtedly. And secondly, what is the cause of the unfriendly feeling which evidently exists between the cousins."

I drew back and pondered the position offered me. A spy in a fair woman's house! How could I reconcile it with my natural instincts as a gentleman?

"Cannot you find some one better adapted to learn these secrets for you?" I asked at length. "The part of a spy is anything but agreeable to my feelings, I assure you."

Mr. Gryce's brows fell.

"I will assist Mr. Harwell in his efforts to arrange Mr. Leavenworth's manuscript for the press," I said; "I will give Mr. Clavering an opportunity to form my acquaintance; and I will listen, if Miss Leavenworth chooses to make me her confidant in any way. But any hearkening at doors, surprises, unworthy feints or ungentlemanly subterfuges, I herewith disclaim as outside of my province; my task being to find out what I can in an open way, and yours to search into the nooks and corners of this wretched business."

"In other words, you are to play the hound, and I the mole; just so, I know what belongs to a gentleman."

"And now," said I, "what news of Hannah?" He shook both hands high in the air. "None."

I cannot say I was greatly surprised, that evening, when, upon descending from an hour's labor with Mr. Harwell, I encountered Miss Leavenworth standing at the foot of the stairs. There had been something in her bearing, the night before, which prepared me for another interview this evening, though her manner of commencing it was a surprise. "Mr. Raymond," said she, with an air of marked embarrassment, "I want to ask you a question. I believe you to be a good man, and I know you will answer me conscientiously. As a brother would," she added, lifting her eyes for a moment to my face. "I know it will sound strange; but remember, I have no adviser but you, and I must ask some one. Mr. Raymond, do you think a person could do something that was very wrong, and yet grow to be thoroughly good afterwards?"

"Certainly," I replied; "if he were truly sorry for his fault."

"But say it was more than a fault; say it was an actual harm; would not the memory of that one evil hour cast a lasting shadow over one's life?"

"That depends upon the nature of the harm and its effect upon others. If one had irreparably injured a fellow-being, it would be hard for a person of sensitive nature to live a happy life afterwards; though the fact of not living a happy life ought to be no reason why one should not live a good life."

"But to live a good life would it be necessary to reveal the evil you had done? Cannot one go on and do right without confessing to the world a past wrong?"

"Yes, unless by its confession he can in some way make reparation."

My answer seemed to trouble her. Drawing back, she stood for one moment in a thoughtful attitude before me, her beauty shining with almost a statuesque splendor in the glow of the porcelain-shaded lamp at her side. Nor, though she presently roused herself, leading the way into the drawing-room with a gesture that was allurement itself, did she recur to this topic again; but rather seemed to strive, in the conversation that followed, to make me forget what had already passed between us. That she did not succeed, was owing to my intense and unfailing interest in her cousin.

As I descended the stoop, I saw Thomas, the butler, leaning over the area gate. Immediately I was seized with an impulse to interrogate him in regard to a matter which had more or less interested me ever since the inquest; and that was, who was the Mr. Robbins who had called upon Eleanore the night of the murder? But Thomas was decidedly uncommunicative. He remembered such a person called, but could not describe his looks any further than to say that he was not a small man.

I did not press the matter.

XVII. THE BEGINNING OF GREAT SURPRISES

"Vous regardez une etoile pour deux motifs, parce qu'elle est
lumineuse et parce qu'elle est impenetrable. Vous avez aupres
de vous un plus doux rayonnement et un pas grand mystere, la femme."
    Les Miserables.

AND now followed days in which I seemed to make little or no progress. Mr. Clavering, disturbed perhaps by my presence, forsook his usual haunts, thus depriving me of all opportunity of making his acquaintance in any natural manner, while the evenings spent at Miss Leavenworth's were productive of little else than constant suspense and uneasiness.

The manuscript required less revision than I supposed. But, in the course of making such few changes as were necessary, I had ample opportunity of studying the character of Mr. Harwell. I found him to be neither more nor less than an excellent amanuensis. Stiff, unbending, and sombre, but true to his duty and reliable in its performance, I learned to respect him, and even to like him; and this, too, though I saw the liking was not reciprocated, whatever the respect may have been. He never spoke of Eleanore Leavenworth or, indeed, mentioned the family or its trouble in any way; till I began to feel that all this reticence had a cause deeper than the nature of the man, and that if he did speak, it would be to some purpose. This suspicion, of course, kept me restlessly eager in his presence. I could not forbear giving him sly glances now and then, to see how he acted when he believed himself unobserved; but he was ever the same, a passive, diligent, unexcitable worker.

This continual beating against a stone wall, for thus I regarded it, became at last almost unendurable. Clavering shy, and the secretary unapproachable—how was I to gain anything? The short interviews I had with Mary did not help matters. Haughty, constrained, feverish, pettish, grateful, appealing, everything at once, and never twice the same, I learned to dread, even while I coveted, an interview. She appeared to be passing through some crisis which occasioned her the keenest suffering. I have seen her, when she thought herself alone, throw up her hands with the gesture which we use to ward off a coming evil or shut out some hideous vision. I have likewise beheld her standing with her proud head abased, her nervous hands drooping, her whole form sinking and inert, as if the pressure of a weight she could neither upbear nor cast aside had robbed her even of the show of resistance. But this was only once. Ordinarily she was at least stately in her trouble. Even when the softest appeal came into her eyes she stood erect, and retained her expression of conscious power. Even the night she met me in the hall, with feverish cheeks and lips trembling with eagerness, only to turn and fly again without giving utterance to what she had to say, she comported herself with a fiery dignity that was well nigh imposing.

That all this meant something, I was sure; and so I kept my patience alive with the hope that some day she would make a revelation. Those quivering lips would not always remain closed; the secret involving Eleanore's honor and happiness would be divulged by this restless being, if by no one else. Nor was the memory of that extraordinary, if not cruel, accusation I had heard her make enough to destroy this hope—for hope it had grown to be—so that I found myself insensibly shortening my time with Mr. Harwell in the library, and extending my *tete-a-tete* visits with Mary in the reception room, till the imperturbable secretary was forced to complain that he was often left for hours without work.

But, as I say, days passed, and a second Monday evening came round without seeing me any further advanced upon the problem I had set myself to solve than when I first started upon it two weeks before. The subject of the murder had not even been broached; nor was Hannah spoken of, though I observed the papers were not allowed to languish an instant upon the stoop; mistress and servants betraying equal interest in their contents. All this was strange to me. It was as if you saw a group of human beings eating, drinking, and sleeping upon the sides of a volcano hot with a late eruption and trembling with the birth of a new one. I longed to break this silence as we shiver glass: by shouting the name of Eleanore through those gilded rooms and satin-draped vestibules. But this Monday evening I was in a calmer mood. I was determined to expect nothing from my visits to Mary Leavenworth's house; and entered it upon the eve in question with an equanimity such as I had not experienced since the first day I passed under its unhappy portals.

But when, upon nearing the reception room, I saw Mary pacing the floor with the air of one who is restlessly awaiting something or somebody, I took a sudden resolution, and, advancing towards her, said: "Do I see you alone, Miss Leavenworth?"

She paused in her hurried action, blushed and bowed, but, contrary to her usual custom, did not bid me enter.

"Will it be too great an intrusion on my part, if I venture to come in?" I asked.

Her glance flashed uneasily to the clock, and she seemed about to excuse herself, but suddenly yielded, and, drawing up a chair before the fire, motioned me towards it. Though she endeavored to appear calm, I vaguely felt I had chanced upon her in one of her most agitated moods, and that I had only to broach the subject I had in mind to behold her haughtiness disappear before me like melting snow. I also felt that I had but few moments in which to do it. I accordingly plunged immediately into the subject.

"Miss Leavenworth," said I, "in obtruding upon you to-night, I have a purpose other than that of giving myself a pleasure. I have come to make an appeal."

Instantly I saw that in some way I had started wrong. "An appeal to make to me?" she asked, breathing coldness from every feature of her face.

"Yes," I went on, with passionate recklessness. "Balked in every other endeavor to learn the truth, I have come to you, whom I believe to be noble at the core, for that help which seems likely to fail us in every other direction: for the word which, if it does not absolutely save your cousin, will at least put us upon the track of what will."

"I do not understand what you mean," she protested, slightly shrinking.

"Miss Leavenworth," I pursued, "it is needless for me to tell you in what position your cousin stands. You, who remember both the form and drift of the questions put to her at the inquest, comprehend it all without any explanation from me. But what you may not know is this, that unless she is speedily relieved from the suspicion which, justly or not, has attached itself to her name, the consequences which such suspicion entails must fall upon her, and——"

"Good God!" she cried; "you do not mean she will be——"

"Subject to arrest? Yes."

It was a blow. Shame, horror, and anguish were in every line of her white face. "And all because of that key!" she murmured.

"Key? How did you know anything about a key?"

"Why," she cried, flushing painfully; "I cannot say; didn't you tell me?"

"No," I returned.

"The papers, then?"

"The papers have never mentioned it."

She grew more and more agitated. "I thought every one knew. No, I did not, either," she avowed, in a sudden burst of shame and penitence. "I knew it was a secret; but—oh, Mr. Raymond, it was Eleanore herself who told me."

"Eleanore?"

"Yes, that last evening she was here; we were together in the drawing-room."

"What did she tell?"

"That the key to the library had been seen in her possession."

I could scarcely conceal my incredulity. Eleanore, conscious of the suspicion with which her cousin regarded her, inform that cousin of a fact calculated to add weight to that suspicion? I could not believe this.

"But you knew it?" Mary went on. "I have revealed nothing I ought to have kept secret?"

"No," said I; "and, Miss Leavenworth, it is this thing which makes your cousin's position absolutely dangerous. It is a fact that, left unexplained, must ever link her name with infamy; a bit of circumstantial evidence no sophistry can smother, and no denial obliterate. Only her hitherto spotless reputation, and the efforts of one who, notwithstanding appearances, believes in her innocence, keeps her so long from the clutch of the officers of justice. That key, and the silence preserved by

81

her in regard to it, is sinking her slowly into a pit from which the utmost endeavors of her best friends will soon be inadequate to extricate her."

"And you tell me this———"

"That you may have pity on the poor girl, who will not have pity on herself, and by the explanation of a few circumstances, which cannot be mysteries to you, assist in bringing her from under the dreadful shadow that threatens to overwhelm her."

"And would you insinuate, sir," she cried, turning upon me with a look of great anger, "that I know any more than you do of this matter? that I possess any knowledge which I have not already made public concerning the dreadful tragedy which has transformed our home into a desert, our existence into a lasting horror? Has the blight of suspicion fallen upon me, too; and have you come to accuse me in my own house———"

"Miss Leavenworth," I entreated; "calm yourself. I accuse you of nothing. I only desire you to enlighten me as to your cousin's probable motive for this criminating silence. You cannot be ignorant of it. You are her cousin, almost her sister, have been at all events her daily companion for years, and must know for whom or for what she seals her lips, and conceals facts which, if known, would direct suspicion to the real criminal—that is, if you really believe what you have hitherto stated, that your cousin is an innocent woman."

She not making any answer to this, I rose and confronted her. "Miss Leavenworth, do you believe your cousin guiltless of this crime, or not?"

"Guiltless? Eleanore? Oh! my God; if all the world were only as innocent as she!"

"Then," said I, "you must likewise believe that if she refrains from speaking in regard to matters which to ordinary observers ought to be explained, she does it only from motives of kindness towards one less guiltless than herself."

"What? No, no; I do not say that. What made you think of any such explanation?"

"The action itself. With one of Eleanore's character, such conduct as hers admits of no other construction. Either she is mad, or she is shielding another at the expense of herself."

Mary's lip, which had trembled, slowly steadied itself. "And whom have you settled upon, as the person for whom Eleanore thus sacrifices herself?"

"Ah," said I, "there is where I seek assistance from you. With your knowledge of her history———"

But Mary Leavenworth, sinking haughtily back into her chair, stopped me with a quiet gesture. "I beg your pardon," said she; "but you make a mistake. I know little or nothing of Eleanore's personal feelings. The mystery must be solved by some one besides me."

I changed my tactics.

"When Eleanore confessed to you that the missing key had been seen in her possession, did she likewise inform you where she obtained it, and for what reason she was hiding it?"

"No."

82

"Merely told you the fact, without any explanation?"

"Yes."

"Was not that a strange piece of gratuitous information for her to give one who, but a few hours before, had accused her to the face of committing a deadly crime?"

"What do you mean?'" she asked, her voice suddenly sinking.

"You will not deny that you were once, not only ready to believe her guilty, but that you actually charged her with having perpetrated this crime."

"Explain yourself!" she cried.

"Miss Leavenworth, do you not remember what you said in that room upstairs, when you were alone with your cousin on the morning of the inquest, just before Mr. Gryce and myself entered your presence?"

Her eyes did not fall, but they filled with sudden terror.

"You heard?" she whispered.

"I could not help it. I was just outside the door, and——"

"What did you hear?"

I told her.

"And Mr. Gryce?"

"He was at my side."

It seemed as if her eyes would devour my face. "Yet nothing was said when you came in?"

"No."

"You, however, have never forgotten it?"

"How could we, Miss Leavenworth?"

Her head fell forward in her hands, and for one wild moment she seemed lost in despair. Then she roused, and desperately exclaimed:

"And that is why you come here to-night. With that sentence written upon your heart, you invade my presence, torture me with questions——"

"Pardon me," I broke in; "are my questions such as you, with reasonable regard for the honor of one with whom you are accustomed to associate, should hesitate to answer? Do I derogate from my manhood in asking you how and why you came to make an accusation of so grave a nature, at a time when all the circumstances of the case were freshly before you, only to insist fully as strongly upon your cousin's innocence when you found there was even more cause for your imputation than you had supposed?"

She did not seem to hear me. "Oh, my cruel fate!" she murmured. "Oh, my cruel fate!"

"Miss Leavenworth," said I, rising, and taking my stand before her; "although there is a temporary estrangement between you and your cousin, you cannot wish to seem her enemy. Speak, then; let me at least know the name of him for whom she thus immolates herself. A hint from you——"

But rising, with a strange look, to her feet, she interrupted me with a stern remark: "If you do not know, I cannot inform you; do not ask me, Mr. Raymond." And she glanced at the clock for the second time.

I took another turn.

83

"Miss Leavenworth, you once asked me if a person who had committed a wrong ought necessarily to confess it; and I replied no, unless by the confession reparation could be made. Do you remember?"

Her lips moved, but no words issued from them.

"I begin to think," I solemnly proceeded, following the lead of her emotion, "that confession is the only way out of this difficulty: that only by the words you can utter Eleanore can be saved from the doom that awaits her. Will you not then show yourself a true woman by responding to my earnest entreaties?"

I seemed to have touched the right chord; for she trembled, and a look of wistfulness filled her eyes. "Oh, if I could!" she murmured.

"And why can you not? You will never be happy till you do. Eleanore persists in silence; but that is no reason why you should emulate her example. You only make her position more doubtful by it."

"I know it; but I cannot help myself. Fate has too strong a hold upon me; I cannot break away."

"That is not true. Any one can escape from bonds imaginary as yours."

"No, no," she protested; "you do not understand."

"I understand this: that the path of rectitude is a straight one, and that he who steps into devious byways is going astray."

A nicker of light, pathetic beyond description, flashed for a moment across her face; her throat rose as with one wild sob; her lips opened; she seemed yielding, when—A sharp ring at the front door-bell!

"Oh," she cried, sharply turning, "tell him I cannot see him; tell him——"

"Miss Leavenworth," said I, taking her by both hands, "never mind the door; never mind anything but this. I have asked you a question which involves the mystery of this whole affair; answer me, then, for your soul's sake; tell me, what the unhappy circumstances were which could induce you—"

But she tore her hands from mine. "The door!" she cried; "it will open, and—"

Stepping into the hall, I met Thomas coming up the basement stairs. "Go back," said I; "I will call you when you are wanted."

With a bow he disappeared.

"You expect me to answer," she exclaimed, when I re-entered, "now, in a moment? I cannot."

"But——"

"Impossible!" fastening her gaze upon the front door.

"Miss Leavenworth!"

She shuddered.

"I fear the time will never come, if you do not speak now."

"Impossible," she reiterated.

Another twang at the bell.

"You hear!" said she.

I went into the hall and called Thomas. "You may open the door now," said I, and moved to return to her side.

But, with a gesture of command, she pointed up-stairs. "Leave me!" and her glance passed on to Thomas, who stopped where he was.

"I will see you again before I go," said I, and hastened up-stairs.

Thomas opened the door. "Is Miss Leavenworth in?" I heard a rich, tremulous voice inquire.

"Yes, sir," came in the butler's most respectful and measured accents, and, leaning over the banisters I beheld, to my amazement, the form of Mr. Clavering enter the front hall and move towards the reception room.

XVIII. ON THE STAIRS

"You cannot *say* I did it."

　　Macbeth.

EXCITED, tremulous, filled with wonder at this unlooked-for event, I paused for a moment to collect my scattered senses, when the sound of a low, monotonous voice breaking upon my ear from the direction of the library, I approached and found Mr. Harwell reading aloud from his late employer's manuscript. It would be difficult for me to describe the effect which this simple discovery made upon me at this time. There, in that room of late death, withdrawn from the turmoil of the world, a hermit in his skeleton-lined cell, this man employed himself in reading and rereading, with passive interest, the words of the dead, while above and below, human beings agonized in doubt and shame. Listening, I heard these words:

"By these means their native rulers will not only lose their jealous terror of our institutions, but acquire an actual curiosity in regard to them."

Opening the door I went in.

"Ah! you are late, sir," was the greeting with which he rose and brought forward a chair.

My reply was probably inaudible, for he added, as he passed to his own seat:

"I am afraid you are not well."

I roused myself.

"I am not ill." And, pulling the papers towards me, I began looking them over. But the words danced before my eyes, and I was obliged to give up all attempt at work for that night.

"*I* fear I am unable to assist you this evening, Mr. Harwell. The fact is, I find it difficult to give proper attention to this business while the man who by a dastardly assassination has made it necessary goes unpunished."

The secretary in his turn pushed the papers aside, as if moved by a sudden distaste of them, but gave me no answer.

"You told me, when you first came to me with news of this fearful tragedy, that it was a mystery; but it is one which must be solved, Mr. Harwell; it is wearing out the lives of too many whom we love and respect."

The secretary gave me a look. "Miss Eleanore?" he murmured.

"And Miss Mary," I went on; "myself, you, and many others."

"You have manifested much interest in the matter from the beginning,"—he said, methodically dipping his pen into the ink.

85

I stared at him in amazement.

"And you," said I; "do you take no interest in that which involves not only the safety, but the happiness and honor, of the family in which you have dwelt so long?"

He looked at me with increased coldness. "I have no wish to discuss this subject. I believe I have before prayed you to spare me its introduction." And he arose.

"But I cannot consider your wishes in this regard," I persisted. "If you know any facts, connected with this affair, which have not yet been made public, it is manifestly your duty to state them. The position which Miss Eleanore occupies at this time is one which should arouse the sense of justice in every true breast; and if you——"

"If I knew anything which would serve to release her from her unhappy position, Mr. Raymond, I should have spoken long ago."

I bit my lip, weary of these continual bafflings, and rose also.

"If you have nothing more to say," he went on, "and feel utterly disinclined to work, why, I should be glad to excuse myself, as I have an engagement out."

"Do not let me keep you," I said, bitterly. "I can take care of myself."

He turned upon me with a short stare, as if this display of feeling was well nigh incomprehensible to him; and then, with a quiet, almost compassionate bow left the room. I heard him go up-stairs, felt the jar when his room door closed, and sat down to enjoy my solitude. But solitude in that room was unbearable. By the time Mr. Harwell again descended, I felt I could remain no longer, and, stepping into the hall, told him that if he had no objection I would accompany him for a short stroll.

He bowed a stiff assent, and hastened before me down the stairs. By the time I had closed the library door, he was half-way to the foot, and I was just remarking to myself upon the unpliability of his figure and the awkwardness of his carriage, as seen from my present standpoint, when suddenly I saw him stop, clutch the banister at his side, and hang there with a startled, deathly expression upon his half-turned countenance, which fixed me for an instant where I was in breathless astonishment, and then caused me to rush down to his side, catch him by the arm, and cry:

"What is it? what is the matter?"

But, thrusting out his hand, he pushed me upwards. "Go back!" he whispered, in a voice shaking with in-tensest emotion, "go back." And catching me by the arm, he literally pulled me up the stairs. Arrived at the top, he loosened his grasp, and leaning, quivering from head to foot, over the banisters, glared below.

"Who is that?" he cried. "Who is that man? What is his name?"

Startled in my turn, I bent beside him, and saw Henry Clavering come out of the reception room and cross the hall.

"That is Mr. Clavering," I whispered, with all the self-possession I could muster; "do you know him?"

Mr. Harwell fell back against the opposite wall. "Clavering, Clavering," he murmured with quaking lips; then, suddenly bounding forward, clutched the railing before him, and fixing me with his eyes, from which all the stoic calmness had gone down forever in flame and frenzy, gurgled into my ear: "You want to know who the assassin of Mr. Leavenworth is, do you? Look there, then: that is the man, Clavering!" And with a leap, he bounded from my side, and, swaying like a drunken man, disappeared from my gaze in the hall above.

My first impulse was to follow him. Rushing upstairs, I knocked at the door of his room, but no response came to my summons. I then called his name in the hall, but without avail; he was determined not to show himself. Resolved that he should not thus escape me, I returned to the library, and wrote him a short note, in which I asked for an explanation of his tremendous accusation, saying I would be in my rooms the next evening at six, when I should expect to see him. This done I descended to rejoin Mary.

But the evening was destined to be full of disappointments. She had retired to her room while I was in the library, and I lost the interview from which I expected so much. "The woman is slippery as an eel," I inwardly commented, pacing the hall in my chagrin. "Wrapped in mystery, she expects me to feel for her the respect due to one of frank and open nature."

I was about to leave the house, when I saw Thomas descending the stairs with a letter in his hand.

"Miss Leavenworth's compliments, sir, and she is too fatigued to remain below this evening."

I moved aside to read the note he handed me, feeling a little conscience-stricken as I traced the hurried, trembling handwriting through the following words:

"You ask more than I can give. Matters must be received as they are
without explanation from me. It is the grief of my life to deny you;
but I have no choice. God forgive us all and keep us from despair.

"M."

And below:
"As we cannot meet now without embarrassment, it is better we should
bear our burdens in silence and apart. Mr. Harwell will visit you.
Farewell!"

As I was crossing Thirty-second Street, I heard a quick footstep behind me, and turning, saw Thomas at my side. "Excuse me, sir," said he, "but I have something a little particular to say to you. When you asked me the other night what sort of a person the gentleman was who called on Miss Eleanore the evening of the murder, I didn't answer you as I should. The fact is, the detectives had been talking to me about that very thing, and I felt shy; but, sir, I know you are a friend of the family, and I want to tell you now that that same gentleman, whoever he was,—Mr. Robbins, he called himself then,—was at the house again tonight, sir, and the name he gave me this time to carry to Miss Leavenworth was Clavering. Yes, sir," he went on, seeing me start; "and, as I told Molly, he acts queer for a stranger. When he came the other night, he hesitated a long time before asking for Miss Eleanore, and when I wanted his name, took out a card and wrote on it the one I told you of, sir, with a look on his face a little peculiar for a caller; besides

_____"

"Well?"

"Mr. Raymond," the butler went on, in a low, excited voice, edging up very closely to me in the darkness. "There is something I have never told any living being but Molly, sir, which may be of use to those as wishes to find out who committed this murder."

"A fact or a suspicion?" I inquired.

"A fact, sir; which I beg your pardon for troubling you with at this time; but Molly will give me no rest unless I speak of it to you or Mr. Gryce; her feelings being so worked up on Hannah's account, whom we all know is innocent, though folks do dare to say as how she must be guilty just because she is not to be found the minute they want her."

"But this fact?" I urged.

"Well, the fact is this. You see—I would tell Mr. Gryce," he resumed, unconscious of my anxiety, "but I have my fears of detectives, sir; they catch you up so quick at times, and seem to think you know so much more than you really do."

"But this fact," I again broke in.

"O yes, sir; the fact is, that that night, the one of the murder you know, I saw Mr. Clavering, Robbins, or whatever his name is, enter the house, but neither I nor any one else saw him go out of it; nor do I know that he _did._"

"What do you mean?"

"Well, sir, what I mean is this. When I came down from Miss Eleanore and told Mr. Robbins, as he called himself at that time, that my mistress was ill and unable to see him (the word she gave me, sir, to deliver) Mr. Robbins, instead of bowing and leaving the house like a gentleman, stepped into the reception room and sat down. He may have felt sick, he looked pale enough; at any rate, he asked me for a glass of water. Not knowing any reason then for suspicionat-ing any one's actions, I immediately went down to the kitchen for it, leaving him there in the reception room alone. But before I could get it, I heard the front door close. 'What's that?' said Molly, who was helping me, sir. 'I don't know,' said I, 'unless it's the gentleman has got tired of waiting and gone.' 'If he's gone, he won't want the water,' she said. So down I set the pitcher, and up-stairs I come; and sure enough he was gone, or so I thought then. But who knows, sir, if he was not in that room or the drawing-room, which was dark that night, all the time I was a-shutting up of the house?"

I made no reply to this; I was more startled than I cared to reveal.

"You see, sir, I wouldn't speak of such a thing about any person that comes to see the young ladies; but we all know some one who was in the house that night murdered my master, and as it was not Hannah——"

"You say that Miss Eleanore refused to see him," I interrupted, in the hope that the simple suggestion would be enough to elicitate further details of his interview with Eleanore.

"Yes, sir. When she first looked at the card, she showed a little hesitation; but in a moment she grew very flushed in the face, and bade me say what I told you. I should never have thought of it again if I had not seen him come blazoning and bold into the house this evening, with a new name on his tongue. Indeed, and I do not like to think any evil of him now; but Molly would have it I should speak to you, sir, and ease my mind,—and that is all, sir."

When I arrived home that night, I entered into my memorandum-book a new list of suspicious circumstances, but this time they were under the caption "C" instead of "E."

XIX. IN MY OFFICE
"Something between an hindrance and a help."
Wordsworth.

THE next day as, with nerves unstrung and an exhausted brain, I entered my office, I was greeted by the announcement:

"A gentleman, sir, in your private room—been waiting some time, very impatient."

Weary, in no mood to hold consultation with clients new or old, I advanced with anything but an eager step towards my room, when, upon opening the door, I saw —Mr. Clavering.

Too much astounded for the moment to speak, I bowed to him silently, whereupon he approached me with the air and dignity of a highly bred gentleman, and presented his card, on which I saw written, in free and handsome characters, his whole name, Henry Ritchie Clavering. After this introduction of himself, he apologized for making so unceremonious a call, saying, in excuse, that he was a stranger in town; that his business was one of great urgency; that he had casually heard honorable mention of me as a lawyer and a gentleman, and so had ventured to seek this interview on behalf of a friend who was so unfortunately situated as to require the opinion and advice of a lawyer upon a question which not only involved an extraordinary state of facts, but was of a nature peculiarly embarrassing to him, owing to his ignorance of American laws, and the legal bearing of these facts upon the same.

Having thus secured my attention, and awakened my curiosity, he asked me if I would permit him to relate his story. Recovering in a measure from my astonishment, and subduing the extreme repulsion, almost horror, I felt for the man, I signified my assent; at which he drew from his pocket a memorandum-book from which he read in substance as follows:

"An Englishman travelling in this country meets, at a fashionable watering-place, an American girl, with whom he falls deeply in love, and whom, after a few days, he desires to marry. Knowing his position to be good, his fortune ample, and his intentions highly honorable, he offers her his hand, and is accepted. But a decided opposition arising in the family to the match, he is compelled to disguise his sentiments, though the engagement remained unbroken. While matters were in this uncertain condition, he received advices from England demanding his instant return, and, alarmed at the prospect of a protracted absence from the object of

89

his affections, he writes to the lady, informing her of the circumstances, and proposing a secret marriage. She consents with stipulations; the first of which is, that he should leave her instantly upon the conclusion of the ceremony, and the second, that he should intrust the public declaration of the marriage to her. It was not precisely what he wished, but anything which served to make her his own was acceptable at such a crisis. He readily enters into the plans proposed. Meeting the lady at a parsonage, some twenty miles from the watering-place at which she was staying, he stands up with her before a Methodist preacher, and the ceremony of marriage is performed. There were two witnesses, a hired man of the minister, called in for the purpose, and a lady friend who came with the bride; but there was no license, and the bride had not completed her twenty-first year. Now, was that marriage legal? If the lady, wedded in good faith upon that day by my friend, chooses to deny that she is his lawful wife, can he hold her to a compact entered into in so informal a manner? In short, Mr. Raymond, is my friend the lawful husband of that girl or not?"

While listening to this story, I found myself yielding to feelings greatly in contrast to those with which I greeted the relator but a moment before. I became so interested in his "friend's" case as to quite forget, for the time being, that I had ever seen or heard of Henry Clavering; and after learning that the marriage ceremony took place in the State of New York, I replied to him, as near as I can remember, in the following words: "In this State, and I believe it to be American law, marriage is a civil contract, requiring neither license, priest, ceremony, nor certificate—and in some cases witnesses are not even necessary to give it validity. Of old, the modes of getting a wife were the same as those of acquiring any other species of property, and they are not materially changed at the present time. It is enough that the man and woman say to each other, 'From this time we are married,' or, 'You are now my wife,' or, 'my husband,' as the case may be. The mutual consent is all that is necessary. In fact, you may contract marriage as you contract to lend a sum of money, or to buy the merest trifle."

"Then your opinion is——"

"That upon your statement, your friend is the lawful husband of the lady in question; presuming, of course, that no legal disabilities of either party existed to prevent such a union. As to the young lady's age, I will merely say that any fourteen-year-old girl can be a party to a marriage contract."

Mr. Clavering bowed, his countenance assuming a look of great satisfaction. "I am very glad to hear this," said he; "my friend's happiness is entirely involved in the establishment, of his marriage."

He appeared so relieved, my curiosity was yet further aroused. I therefore said: "I have given you my opinion as to the legality of this marriage; but it may be quite another thing to prove it, should the same be contested."

He started, cast me an inquiring look, and murmured:

"True."

"Allow me to ask you a few questions. Was the lady married under her own name?"

"She was."

90

"The gentleman?"

"Yes, sir."

"Did the lady receive a certificate?"

"She did."

"Properly signed by the minister and witnesses?"

He bowed his head in assent.

"Did she keep this?"

"I cannot say; but I presume she did."

"The witnesses were——"

"A hired man of the minister——"

"Who can be found?"

"Who cannot be found."

"Dead or disappeared?"

"The minister is dead, the man has disappeared."

"The minister dead!"

"Three months since."

"And the marriage took place when?"

"Last July."

"The other witness, the lady friend, where is she?"

"She can be found; but her action is not to be depended upon."

"Has the gentleman himself no proofs of this marriage?"

Mr. Clavering shook his head. "He cannot even prove he was in the town where it took place on that particular day."

"The marriage certificate was, however, filed with the clerk of the town?" said I.

"It was not, sir."

"How was that?"

"I cannot say. I only know that my friend has made inquiry, and that no such paper is to be found."

I leaned slowly back and looked at him. "I do not wonder your friend is concerned in regard to his position, if what you hint is true, and the lady seems disposed to deny that any such ceremony ever took place. Still, if he wishes to go to law, the Court may decide in his favor, though I doubt it. His sworn word is all he would have to go upon, and if she contradicts his testimony under oath, why the sympathy of a jury is, as a rule, with the woman."

Mr. Clavering rose, looked at me with some earnestness, and finally asked, in a tone which, though somewhat changed, lacked nothing of its former suavity, if I would be kind enough to give him in writing that portion of my opinion which directly bore upon the legality of the marriage; that such a paper would go far towards satisfying his friend that his case had been properly presented; as he was aware that no respectable lawyer would put his name to a legal opinion without first having carefully arrived at his conclusions by a thorough examination of the law bearing upon the facts submitted.

This request seeming so reasonable, I unhesitatingly complied with it, and handed him the opinion. He took it, and, after reading it carefully over, deliberately copied it into his memorandum-book. This done, he turned towards me, a strong, though hitherto subdued, emotion showing itself in his countenance.

"Now, sir," said he, rising upon me to the full height of his majestic figure, "I have but one more request to make; and that is, that you will receive back this opinion into your own possession, and in the day you think to lead a beautiful woman to the altar, pause and ask yourself: 'Am I sure that the hand I clasp with such impassioned fervor is free? Have I any certainty for knowing that it has not already been given away, like that of the lady whom, in this opinion of mine, I have declared to be a wedded wife according to the laws of my country? '"

"Mr. Clavering!"

But he, with an urbane bow, laid his hand upon the knob of the door. "I thank you for your courtesy, Mr. Raymond, and I bid you good-day. I hope you will have no need of consulting that paper before I see you again." And with another bow, he passed out.

It was the most vital shock I had yet experienced; and for a moment I stood paralyzed. Me! me! Why should he mix me up with the affair unless—but I would not contemplate that possibility. Eleanore married, and to this man? No, no; anything but that! And yet I found myself continually turning the supposition over in my mind until, to escape the torment of my own conjectures, I seized my hat, and rushed into the street in the hope of finding him again and extorting from him an explanation of his mysterious conduct. But by the time I reached the sidewalk, he was nowhere to be seen. A thousand busy men, with their various cares and purposes, had pushed themselves between us, and I was obliged to return to my office with my doubts unsolved.

I think I never experienced a longer day; but it passed, and at five o'clock I had the satisfaction of inquiring for Mr. Clavering at the Hoffman House. Judge of my surprise when I learned that his visit to my office was his last action before taking passage upon the steamer leaving that day for Liverpool; that he was now on the high seas, and all chance of another interview with him was at an end. I could scarcely believe the fact at first; but after a talk with the cabman who had driven him off to my office and thence to the steamer, I became convinced. My first feeling was one of shame. I had been brought face to face with the accused man, had received an intimation from him that he was not expecting to see me again for some time, and had weakly gone on attending to my own affairs and allowed him to escape, like the simple tyro that I was. My next, the necessity of notifying Mr. Gryce of this man's departure. But it was now six o'clock, the hour set apart for my interview with Mr. Harwell. I could not afford to miss that, so merely stopping to despatch a line to Mr. Gryce, in which I promised to visit him that evening, I turned my steps towards home. I found Mr. Harwell there before me.

XX. "TRUEMAN! TRUEMAN! TRUEMAN!"

"Often do the spirits
Of great events stride on before the events,
And in to-day already walks to-morrow."
  Coleridge.

INSTANTLY a great dread seized me. What revelations might not this man be going to make! But I subdued the feeling; and, greeting him with what cordiality I could, settled myself to listen to his explanations.

But Trueman Harwell had no explanations to give, or so it seemed; on the contrary, he had come to apologize for the very violent words he had used the evening before; words which, whatever their effect upon me, he now felt bound to declare had been used without sufficient basis in fact to make their utterance of the least importance.

"But you must have thought you had grounds for so tremendous an accusation, or your act was that of a madman."

His brow wrinkled heavily, and his eyes assumed a very gloomy expression. "It does not follow," he returned. "Under the pressure of surprise, I have known men utter convictions no better founded than mine without running the risk of being called mad."

"Surprise? Mr. Clavering's face or form must; then, have been known to you. The mere fact of seeing a strange gentleman in the hall would have been insufficient to cause you astonishment, Mr. Harwell."

He uneasily fingered the back of the chair before which he stood, but made no reply.

"Sit down," I again urged, this time with a touch of command in my voice. "This is a serious matter, and I intend to deal with it as it deserves. You once said that if you knew anything which might serve to exonerate Eleanore Leavenworth from the suspicion under which she stands, you would be ready to impart it."

"Pardon me. I said that if I had ever known anything calculated to release her from her unhappy position, I would have spoken," he coldly corrected.

"Do not quibble. You know, and I know, that you are keeping something back; and I ask you, in her behalf, and in the cause of justice, to tell me what it is."

"You are mistaken," was his dogged reply. "I have reasons, perhaps, for certain conclusions I may have drawn; but my conscience will not allow me in cold blood to give utterance to suspicions which may not only damage the reputation of an honest man, but place me in the unpleasant position of an accuser without substantial foundation for my accusations."

"You occupy that position already," I retorted, with equal coldness. "Nothing can make me forget that in my presence you have denounced Henry Clavering as the murderer of Mr. Leavenworth. You had better explain yourself, Mr. Harwell."

He gave me a short look, but moved around and took the chair. "You have me at a disadvantage," he said, in a lighter tone. "If you choose to profit by your position, and press me to disclose the little I know, I can only regret the necessity under which I lie, and speak."

93

"Then you are deterred by conscientious scruples alone?"

"Yes, and by the meagreness of the facts at my command."

"I will judge of the facts when I have heard them."

He raised his eyes to mine, and I was astonished to observe a strange eagerness in their depths; evidently his convictions were stronger than his scruples. "Mr. Raymond," he began, "you are a lawyer, and undoubtedly a practical man; but you may know what it is to scent danger before you see it, to feel influences working in the air over and about you, and yet be in ignorance of what it is that affects you so powerfully, till chance reveals that an enemy has been at your side, or a friend passed your window, or the shadow of death crossed your book as you read, or mingled with your breath as you slept?"

I shook my head, fascinated by the intensity of his gaze into some sort of response.

"Then you cannot understand me, or what I have suffered these last three weeks." And he drew back with an icy reserve that seemed to promise but little to my now thoroughly awakened curiosity.

"I beg your pardon," I hastened to say; "but the fact of my never having experienced such sensations does not hinder me from comprehending the emotions of others more affected by spiritual influences than myself."

He drew himself slowly forward. "Then you will not ridicule me if I say that upon the eve of Mr. Leavenworth's murder I experienced in a dream all that afterwards occurred; saw him murdered, saw"—and he clasped his hands before him, in an attitude inexpressibly convincing, while his voice sank to a horrified whisper, "saw the face of his murderer!"

I started, looked at him in amazement, a thrill as at a ghostly presence running through me.

"And was that——" I began.

"My reason for denouncing the man I beheld before me in the hall of Miss Leavenworth's house last night? It was." And, taking out his handkerchief, he wiped his forehead, on which the perspiration was standing in large drops.

"You would then intimate that the face you saw in your dream and the face you saw in the hall last night were the same?"

He gravely nodded his head.

I drew my chair nearer to his. "Tell me your dream," said I.

"It was the night before Mr. Leavenworth's murder. I had gone to bed feeling especially contented with myself and the world at large; for, though my life is anything but a happy one," and he heaved a short sigh, "some pleasant words had been said to me that day, and I was revelling in the happiness they conferred, when suddenly a chill struck my heart, and the darkness which a moment before had appeared to me as the abode of peace thrilled to the sound of a supernatural cry, and I heard my name, 'Trueman, Trueman, True-man,' repeated three times in a voice I did not recognize, and starting from my pillow beheld at my bedside a woman. Her face was strange to me," he solemnly proceeded, "but I can give you each and every detail of it, as, bending above me, she stared into my eyes with a growing terror that seemed to implore help, though her lips were quiet, and only the memory of that cry echoed in my ears."

"Describe the face," I interposed.

"It was a round, fair, lady's face. Very lovely in contour, but devoid of coloring; not beautiful, but winning from its childlike look of trust. The hair, banded upon the low, broad forehead, was brown; the eyes, which were very far apart, gray; the mouth, which was its most charming feature, delicate of make and very expressive. There was a dimple in the chin, but none in the cheeks. It was a face to be remembered."

"Go on," said I.

"Meeting the gaze of those imploring eyes, I started up. Instantly the face and all vanished, and I became conscious, as we sometimes do in dreams, of a certain movement in the hall below, and the next instant the gliding figure of a man of imposing size entered the library. I remember experiencing a certain thrill at this, half terror, half curiosity, though I seemed to know, as if by intuition, what he was going to do. Strange to say, I now seemed to change my personality, and to be no longer a third party watching these proceedings, but Mr. Leavenworth himself, sitting at his library table and feeling his doom crawling upon him without capacity for speech or power of movement to avert it. Though my back was towards the man, I could feel his stealthy form traverse the passage, enter the room beyond, pass to that stand where the pistol was, try the drawer, find it locked, turn the key, procure the pistol, weigh it in an accustomed hand, and advance again. I could feel each footstep he took as though his feet were in truth upon my heart, and I remember staring at the table before me as if I expected every moment to see it run with my own blood. I can see now how the letters I had been writing danced upon the paper before me, appearing to my eyes to take the phantom shapes of persons and things long ago forgotten; crowding my last moments with regrets and dead shames, wild longings, and unspeakable agonies, through all of which that face, the face of my former dream, mingled, pale, sweet, and searching, while closer and closer behind me crept that noiseless foot till I could feel the glaring of the assassin's eyes across the narrow threshold separating me from death and hear the click of his teeth as he set his lips for the final act. Ah!" and the secretary's livid face showed the touch of awful horror, "what words can describe such an experience as that? In one moment, all the agonies of hell in the heart and brain, the next a blank through which I seemed to see afar, and as if suddenly removed from all this, a crouching figure looking at its work with starting eyes and pallid back-drawn lips; and seeing, recognize no face that I had ever known, but one so handsome, so remarkable, so unique in its formation and character, that it would be as easy for me to mistake the countenance of my father as the look and figure of the man revealed to me in my dream."

"And this face?" said I, in a voice I failed to recognize as my own.

"Was that of him whom we saw leave Mary Leavenworth's presence last night and go down the hall to the front door."

95

XXI. A PREJUDICE

"True, I talk of dreams,
'Which are the children of an idle brain
Begot of nothing but vain phantasy."
—Romeo and Juliet.

FOR one moment I sat a prey to superstitious horror; then, my natural incredulity asserting itself, I looked up and remarked:

"You say that all this took place the night previous to the actual occurrence?"

He bowed his head. "For a warning," he declared.

"But you did not seem to take it as such?"

"No; I am subject to horrible dreams. I thought but little of it in a superstitious way till I looked next day upon Mr. Leavenworth's dead body."

"I do not wonder you behaved strangely at the inquest."

"Ah, sir," he returned, with a slow, sad smile; "no one knows what I suffered in my endeavors not to tell more than I actually knew, irrespective of my dream, of this murder and the manner of its accomplishment."

"You believe, then, that your dream foreshadowed the manner of the murder as well as the fact?"

"I do."

"It is a pity it did not go a little further, then, and tell us how the assassin escaped from, if not how he entered, a house so securely fastened."

His face flushed. "That would have been convenient," he repeated. "Also, if I had been informed where Hannah was, and why a stranger and a gentleman should have stooped to the committal of such a crime."

Seeing that he was nettled, I dropped my bantering vein. "Why do you say a stranger?" I asked; "are you so well acquainted with all who visit that house as to be able to say who are and who are not strangers to the family?

"I am well acquainted with the faces of their friends, and Henry Clavering is not amongst the number; but——"

"Were you ever with Mr. Leavenworth," I interrupted, "when he has been away from home; in the country, for instance, or upon his travels?"

"No." But the negative came with some constraint.

"Yet I suppose he was in the habit of absenting himself from home?"

"Certainly."

"Can you tell me where he was last July, he and the ladies?"

"Yes, sir; they went to R——. The famous watering-place, you know. Ah," he cried, seeing a change in my face, "do you think he could have met them there?"

I looked at him for a moment, then, rising in my turn, stood level with him, and exclaimed:

"You are keeping something back, Mr. Harwell; you have more knowledge of this man than you have hitherto given me to understand. What is it?"

He seemed astonished at my penetration, but replied: "I know no more of the man than I have already informed you; but"—and a burning flush crossed his face, "if you are determined to pursue this matter——" and he paused, with an inquiring look.

96

"I am resolved to find out all I can about Henry Clavering," was my decided answer.

"Then," said he, "I can tell you this much. Henry Clavering wrote a letter to Mr. Leavenworth a few days before the murder, which I have some reason to believe produced a marked effect upon the household." And, folding his arms, the secretary stood quietly awaiting my next question.

"How do you know?" I asked.

"I opened it by mistake. I was in the habit of reading Mr. Leavenworth's business letters, and this, being from one unaccustomed to write to him, lacked the mark which usually distinguished those of a private nature."

"And you saw the name of Clavering?"

"I did; Henry Ritchie Clavering."

"Did you read the letter?" I was trembling now.

The secretary did not reply.

"Mr. Harwell," I reiterated, "this is no time for false delicacy. Did you read that letter?"

"I did; but hastily, and with an agitated conscience."

"You can, however, recall its general drift?"

"It was some complaint in regard to the treatment received by him at the hand of one of Mr. Leavenworth's nieces. I remember nothing more."

"Which niece?"

"There were no names mentioned."

"But you inferred——"

"No, sir; that is just what I did not do. I forced myself to forget the whole thing."

"And yet you say it produced an effect upon the family?"

"I can see now that it did. None of them have ever appeared quite the same as before."

"Mr. Harwell," I gravely continued; "when you were questioned as to the receipt of any letter by Mr. Leavenworth, which might seem in any manner to be connected with this tragedy, you denied having seen any such; how was that?"

"Mr. Raymond, you are a gentleman; have a chivalrous regard for the ladies; do you think you could have brought yourself (even if in your secret heart you considered some such result possible, which I am not ready to say I did) to mention, at such a time as that, the receipt of a letter complaining of the treatment received from one of Mr. Leavenworth's nieces, as a suspicious circumstance worthy to be taken into account by a coroner's jury?"

I shook my head. I could not but acknowledge the impossibility.

"What reason had I for thinking that letter was one of importance? I knew of no Henry Ritchie Clavering."

"And yet you seemed to think it was. I remember you hesitated before replying."

"It is true; but not as I should hesitate now, if the question were put to me again."

Silence followed these words, during which I took two or three turns up and down the room.

"This is all very fanciful," I remarked, laughing in the vain endeavor to throw off the superstitious horror his words had awakened.

He bent his head in assent. "I know it," said he. "I am practical myself in broad daylight, and recognize the nimsiness of an accusation based upon a poor, hardworking secretary's dream, as plainly as you do. This is the reason I desired to keep from speaking at all; but, Mr. Raymond," and his long, thin hand fell upon my arm with a nervous intensity which gave me almost the sensation of an electrical shock, "if the murderer of Mr. Leavenworth is ever brought to confess his deed, mark my words, he will prove to be the man of my dream."

I drew a long breath. For a moment his belief was mine; and a mingled sensation of relief and exquisite pain swept over me as I thought of the possibility of Eleanore being exonerated from crime only to be plunged into fresh humiliation and deeper abysses of suffering.

"He stalks the streets in freedom now," the secretary went on, as if to himself; "even dares to enter the house he has so wofully desecrated; but justice is justice and, sooner or later, something will transpire which will prove to you that a premonition so wonderful as that I received had its significance; that the voice calling 'Trueman, Trueman,' was something more than the empty utterances of an excited brain; that it was Justice itself, calling attention to the guilty."

I looked at him in wonder. Did he know that the officers of justice were already upon the track of this same Clavering? I judged not from his look, but felt an inclination to make an effort and see.

"You speak with strange conviction," I said; "but in all probability you are doomed to be disappointed. So far as we know, Mr. Clavering is a respectable man."

He lifted his hat from the table. "I do not propose to denounce him; I do not even propose to speak his name again. I am not a fool, Mr. Raymond. I have spoken thus plainly to you only in explanation of last night's most unfortunate betrayal; and while I trust you will regard what I have told you as confidential, I also hope you will give me credit for behaving, on the whole, as well as could be expected under the circumstances." And he held out his hand.

"Certainly," I replied as I took it. Then, with a sudden impulse to test the accuracy of this story of his, inquired if he had any means of verifying his statement of having had this dream at the time spoken of: that is, before the murder and not afterwards.

"No, sir; I know myself that I had it the night previous to that of Mr. Leavenworth's death; but I cannot prove the fact."

"Did not speak of it next morning to any one?"

"O no, sir; I was scarcely in a position to do so."

"Yet it must have had a great effect upon you, unfitting you for work———"

"Nothing unfits me for work," was his bitter reply.

"I believe you," I returned, remembering his diligence for the last few days. "But you must at least have shown some traces of having passed an uncomfortable night. Have you no recollection of any one speaking to you in regard to your appearance the next morning?"

98

"Mr. Leavenworth may have done so; no one else would be likely to notice." There was sadness in the tone, and my own voice softened as I said:

"I shall not be at the house to-night, Mr. Harwell; nor do I know when I shall return there. Personal considerations keep me from Miss Leavenworth's presence for a time, and I look to you to carry on the work we have undertaken without my assistance, unless you can bring it here——"

"I can do that."

"I shall expect you, then, to-morrow evening."

"Very well, sir"; and he was going, when a sudden thought seemed to strike him. "Sir," he said, "as we do not wish to return to this subject again, and as I have a natural curiosity in regard to this man, would you object to telling me what you know of him? You believe him to be a respectable man; are you acquainted with him, Mr. Raymond?"

"I know his name, and where he resides."

"And where is that?"

"In London; he is an Englishman."

"Ah!" he murmured, with a strange intonation.

"Why do you say that?"

He bit his lip, looked down, then up, finally fixed his eyes on mine, and returned, with marked emphasis: "I used an exclamation, sir, because I was startled."

"Startled?"

"Yes; you say he is an Englishman. Mr. Leavenworth had the most bitter antagonism to the English. It was one of his marked peculiarities. He would never be introduced to one if he could help it."

It was my turn to look thoughtful.

"You know," continued the secretary, "that Mr. Leavenworth was a man who carried his prejudices to the extreme. He had a hatred for the English race amounting to mania. If he had known the letter I have mentioned was from an Englishman, I doubt if he would have read it. He used to say he would sooner see a daughter of his dead before him than married to an Englishman."

I turned hastily aside to hide the effect which this announcement made upon me.

"You think I am exaggerating," he said. "Ask Mr. Veeley."

"No," I replied. "I have no reason for thinking so."

"He had doubtless some cause for hating the English with which we are unacquainted," pursued the secretary. "He spent some time in Liverpool when young, and had, of course, many opportunities for studying their manners and character." And the secretary made another movement, as if to leave.

But it was my turn to detain him now. "Mr. Harwell, you must excuse me. You have been on familiar terms with Mr. Leavenworth for so long. Do you think that, in the case of one of his nieces, say, desiring to marry a gentleman of that nationality, his prejudice was sufficient to cause him to absolutely forbid the match?"

"I do."

99

I moved back. I had learned what I wished, and saw no further reason for prolonging the interview.

XXII. PATCH-WORK

"Come, give us a taste of your quality."
Hamlet.

STARTING with the assumption that Mr. Clavering in his conversation of the morning had been giving me, with more or less accuracy, a detailed account of his own experience and position regarding Eleanore Leavenworth, I asked myself what particular facts it would be necessary for me to establish in order to prove the truth of this assumption, and found them to be:

I. That Mr. Clavering had not only been in this country at the time designated, but that he had been located for some little time at a watering-place in New York State.

II. That this watering-place should correspond to the one in which Miss Eleanore Leavenworth was staying at the same time.

III. That they had been seen while there to hold more or less communication.

IV. That they had both been absent from town, at Lorne one time, long enough to have gone through the ceremony of marriage at a point twenty miles or so away.

V. That a Methodist clergyman, who has since died, lived at that time within a radius of twenty miles of said watering-place.

I next asked myself how I was to establish these acts. Mr. Clavering's life was as yet too little known to me to offer me any assistance; so, leaving it for the present, I took up the thread of Eleanore's history, and found that at the time given me she had been in R——, a fashionable watering-place in this State. Now, if his was true, and my theory correct, he must have been there also. To prove this fact, became, consequently, my first business. I resolved to go to R—— on the morrow.

But before proceeding in an undertaking of such importance, I considered it expedient to make such inquiries and collect such facts as the few hours I had left to work in rendered possible. I went first to the house of Mr. Gryce.

I found him lying upon a hard sofa, in the bare sitting-room I have before mentioned, suffering from a severe attack of rheumatism. His hands were done up in bandages, and his feet incased in multiplied folds of a dingy red shawl which looked as if it had been through the wars. Greeting me with a short nod that was both a welcome and an apology, he devoted a few words to an explanation of his unwonted position; and then, without further preliminaries, rushed into the subject which was uppermost in both our minds by inquiring, in a slightly sarcastic way, if I was very much surprised to find my bird flown when I returned to the Hoffman House that afternoon.

"I was astonished to find you allowed him to fly at this time," I replied. "From the manner in which you requested me to make his acquaintance, I supposed you considered him an important character in the tragedy which has just been enacted."

"And what makes you think I don't? Oh, the fact that I let him go off so easily? That's no proof. I never fiddle with the brakes till the car starts down-hill. But let that pass for the present; Mr. Clavering, then, did not explain himself before going?"

"That is a question which I find it exceedingly difficult to answer. Hampered by circumstances, I cannot at present speak with the directness which is your due, but what I can say, I will. Know, then, that in my opinion Mr. Clavering did explain himself in an interview with me this morning. But it was done in so blind a way, it will be necessary for me to make a few investigations before I shall feel sufficiently sure of my ground to take you into my confidence. He has given me a possible clue——"

"Wait," said Mr. Gryce; "does he know this? Was it done intentionally and with sinister motive, or unconsciously and in plain good faith?"

"In good faith, I should say."

Mr. Gryce remained silent for a moment. "It is very unfortunate you cannot explain yourself a little more definitely," he said at last. "I am almost afraid to trust you to make investigations, as you call them, on your own hook. You are not used to the business, and will lose time, to say nothing of running upon false scents, and using up your strength on unprofitable details."

"You should have thought of that when you admitted me into partnership."

"And you absolutely insist upon working this mine alone?"

"Mr. Gryce, the matter stands just here. Mr. Clavering, for all I know, is a gentleman of untarnished reputation. I am not even aware for what purpose you set me upon his trail. I only know that in thus following it I have come upon certain facts that seem worthy of further investigation."

"Well, well; you know best. But the days are slipping by. Something must be done, and soon. The public are becoming clamorous."

"I know it, and for that reason I have come to you for such assistance as you can give me at this stage of the proceedings. You are in possession of certain facts relating to this man which it concerns me to know, or your conduct in reference to him has been purposeless. Now, frankly, will you make me master of those facts: in short, tell me all you know of Mr. Clavering, without requiring an immediate return of confidence on my part?"

"That is asking a great deal of a professional detective."

"I know it, and under other circumstances I should hesitate long before preferring such a request; but as things are, I don't see how I am to proceed in the matter without some such concession on your part. At all events——"

"Wait a moment! Is not Mr. Clavering the lover of one of the young ladies?"

Anxious as I was to preserve the secret of my interest in that gentleman, I could not prevent the blush from rising to my face at the suddenness of this question.

"I thought as much," he went on. "Being neither a relative nor acknowledged friend, I took it for granted he must occupy some such position as that in the family."

101

"I do not see why you should draw such an inference," said I, anxious to determine how much he knew about him. "Mr. Clavering is a stranger in town; has not even been in this country long; has indeed had no time to establish himself upon any such footing as you suggest."

"This is not the only time Mr. Clavering has been in New York. He was here a year ago to my certain knowledge."

"You know that?"

"Yes."

"How much more do you know? Can it be possible I am groping blindly about for facts which are already in your possession? I pray you listen to my entreaties, Mr. Gryce, and acquaint me at once with what I want to know. You will not regret it. I have no selfish motive in this matter. If I succeed, the glory shall be yours; it I fail, the shame of the defeat shall be mine."

"That is fair," he muttered. "And how about the reward?"

"My reward will be to free an innocent woman from the imputation of crime which hangs over her."

This assurance seemed to satisfy him. His voice and appearance changed; for a moment he looked quite confidential. "Well, well," said he; "and what is it you want to know?"

"I should first like to know how your suspicions came to light on him at all. What reason had you for thinking a gentleman of his bearing and position was in any way connected with this affair?"

"That is a question you ought not to be obliged to put," he returned.

"How so?"

"Simply because the opportunity of answering it was in your hands before ever it came into mine."

"What do you mean?"

"Don't you remember the letter mailed in your presence by Miss Mary Leavenworth during your drive from her home to that of her friend in Thirty-seventh Street?"

"On the afternoon of the inquest?"

"Yes."

"Certainly, but——"

"You never thought to look at its superscription before it was dropped into the box."

"I had neither opportunity nor right to do so."

"Was it not written in your presence?"

"It was."

"And you never regarded the affair as worth your attention?"

"However I may have regarded it, I did not see how I could prevent Miss Leavenworth from dropping a letter into a box if she chose to do so."

"That is because you are a *gentleman*. Well, it has its disadvantages," he muttered broodingly.

"But you," said I; "how came you to know anything about this letter? Ah, I see," remembering that the carriage in which we were riding at the time had been procured for us by him. "The man on the box was in your pay, and informed, as you call it."

Mr. Gryce winked at his muffled toes mysteriously. "That is not the point," he said. "Enough that I heard that a letter, which might reasonably prove to be of some interest to me, had been dropped at such an hour into the box on the corner of a certain street. That, coinciding in the opinion of my informant, I telegraphed to the station connected with that box to take note of the address of a suspicious-looking letter about to pass through their hands on the way to the General Post Office, and following up the telegram in person, found that a curious epistle addressed in lead pencil and sealed with a stamp, had just arrived, the address of which I was allowed to see———"

"And which was?"

"Henry R. Clavering, Hoffman House, New York."

I drew a deep breath. "And so that is how your attention first came to be directed to this man?"

"Yes."

"Strange. But go on—what next?"

"Why, next I followed up the clue by going to the Hoffman House and instituting inquiries. I learned that Mr. Clavering was a regular guest of the hotel. That he had come there, direct from the Liverpool steamer, about three months since, and, registering his name as Henry R. Clavering, Esq., London, had engaged a first-class room which he had kept ever since. That, although nothing definite was known concerning him, he had been seen with various highly respectable people, both of his own nation and ours, by all of whom he was treated with respect. And lastly, that while not liberal, he had given many evidences of being a man of means. So much done, I entered the office, and waited for him to come in, in the hope of having an opportunity to observe his manner when the clerk handed him that strange-looking letter from Mary Leavenworth."

"And did you succeed?"

"No; an awkward gawk of a fellow stepped between us just at the critical moment, and shut off my view. But I heard enough that evening from the clerk and servants, of the agitation he had shown on receiving it, to convince me I was upon a trail worth following. I accordingly put on my men, and for two days Mr. Clavering was subjected to the most rigid watch a man ever walked under. But nothing was gained by it; his interest in the murder, if interest at all, was a secret one; and though he walked the streets, studied the papers, and haunted the vicinity of the house in Fifth Avenue, he not only refrained from actually approaching it, but made no attempt to communicate with any of the family. Meanwhile, you crossed my path, and with your determination incited me to renewed effort. Convinced from Mr. Clavering's bearing, and the gossip I had by this time gathered in regard to him, that no one short of a gentleman and a friend could succeed in getting at the clue of his connection with this family, I handed him over to you, and———"

"Found me rather an unmanageable colleague."

Mr. Gryce smiled very much as if a sour plum had been put in his mouth, but made no reply; and a momentary pause ensued.

"Did you think to inquire," I asked at last, "if any one knew where Mr. Clavering had spent the evening of the murder?"

"Yes; but with no good result. It was agreed he went out during the evening; also that he was in his bed in the morning when the servant came in to make his fire; but further than this no one seemed posted."

"So that, in fact, you gleaned nothing that would in any way connect this man with the murder except his marked and agitated interest in it, and the fact that a niece of the murdered man had written a letter to him?"

"That is all."

"Another question; did you hear in what manner and at what time he procured a newspaper that evening?"

"No; I only learned that he was observed, by more than one, to hasten out of the dining-room with the *Post* in his hand, and go immediately to his room without touching his dinner."

"Humph! that does not look——"

"If Mr. Clavering had had a guilty knowledge of the crime, he would either have ordered dinner before opening the paper, or, having ordered it, he would have eaten it."

"Then you do not believe, from what you have learned, that Mr. Clavering is the guilty party?"

Mr. Gryce shifted uneasily, glanced at the papers protruding from my coat pocket and exclaimed: "I am ready to be convinced by you that he is."

That sentence recalled me to the business in hand. Without appearing to notice his look, I recurred to my questions.

"How came you to know that Mr. Clavering was in this city last summer? Did you learn that, too, at the Hoffman House?"

"No; I ascertained that in quite another way. In short, I have had a communication from London in regard to the matter.

"From London?"

"Yes; I've a friend there in my own line of business, who sometimes assists me with a bit of information, when requested."

"But how? You have not had time to write to London, and receive an answer since the murder."

"It is not necessary to write. It is enough for me to telegraph him the name of a person, for him to understand that I want to know everything he can gather in a reasonable length of time about that person."

"And you sent the name of Mr. Clavering to him?"

"Yes, in cipher."

"And have received a reply?"

"This morning."

I looked towards his desk.

"It is not there," he said; "if you will be kind enough to feel in my breast pocket you will find a letter——"

It was in my hand before he finished his sentence. "Excuse my eagerness," I

104

said. "This kind of business is new to me, you know."

He smiled indulgently at a very old and faded picture hanging on the wall before him. "Eagerness is not a fault; only the betrayal of it. But read out what you have there. Let us hear what my friend Brown has to tell us of Mr. Henry Ritchie Clavering, of Portland Place, London."

I took the paper to the light and read as follows:

"Henry Ritchie Clavering, Gentleman, aged 43. Born in

———, Hertfordshire, England. His father was Chas. Clavering, for short time in the army. Mother was Helen Ritchie, of Dumfriesshire, Scotland; she is still living. Home with H. R. C., in Portland Place, London. H. R. C. is a bachelor, 6 ft. high, squarely built, weight about 12 stone. Dark complexion, regular features. Eyes dark brown; nose straight. Called a handsome man; walks erect and rapidly. In society is considered a good fellow; rather a favorite, especially with ladies. Is liberal, not extravagant; reported to be worth about 5000 pounds per year, and appearances give color to this statement. Property consists of a small estate in Hertfordshire, and some funds, amount not known. Since writing this much, a correspondent sends the following in regard to his history. In '46 went from uncle's house to Eton. From Eton went to Oxford, graduating in '56. Scholarship good. In 1855 his uncle died, and his father succeeded to the estates. Father died in '57 by a fall from his horse or a similar accident. Within a very short time H. R. C. took his mother to London, to the residence named, where they have lived to the present time.

"Travelled considerably in 1860; part of the time was with ———, of Munich; also in party of Vandervorts from New York; went as far east as Cairo. Went to America in 1875 alone, but at end of three months returned on account of mother's illness. Nothing is known of his movements while in America.

"From servants learn that he was always a favorite from a boy. More recently has become somewhat taciturn. Toward last of his stay watched the post carefully, especially foreign ones. Posted scarcely anything but newspapers. Has written to Munich. Have seen, from waste-paper basket, torn envelope directed to Amy Belden, no address. American correspondents mostly in Boston; two in New York. Names not known, but supposed to be bankers. Brought home considerable luggage, and fitted up part of house, as for a lady. This was closed soon afterwards. Left for America two months since. Has been, I understand, travelling in the south. Has telegraphed twice to Portland Place. His friends hear from him but rarely. Letters rec'd recently, posted in New York. One by last steamer posted in F———, k. Y.

105

"Business here conducted by ———. In the country, ——— of ——— has charge of the property.

"BROWN."

The document fell from my hands.

F———, N. Y., was a small town near R———.

"Your friend is a trump," I declared. "He tells me just what I wanted most to know." And, taking out my book, I made memoranda of the facts which had most forcibly struck me during my perusal of the communication before me. "With the aid of what he tells me, I shall ferret out the mystery of Henry Clavering in a week; see if I do not."

"And how soon," inquired Mr. Gryce, "may I expect to be allowed to take a hand in the game?"

"As soon as I am reasonably assured I am upon the right tack."

"And what will it take to assure you of that?"

"Not much; a certain point settled, and———"

"Hold on; who knows but what I can do that for you?" And, looking towards the desk which stood in the corner, Mr. Gryce asked me if I would be kind enough to open the top drawer and bring him the bits of partly-burned paper I would find there.

Hastily complying, I brought three or four strips of ragged paper, and laid them on the table at his side.

"Another result of Fobbs' researches under the coal on the first day of the inquest," Mr. Gryce abruptly explained. "You thought the key was all he found. Well, it wasn't. A second turning over of the coal brought these to light, and very interesting they are, too."

I immediately bent over the torn and discolored scraps with great anxiety. They were four in number, and appeared at first glance to be the mere remnants of a sheet of common writing-paper, torn lengthwise into strips, and twisted up into lighters; but, upon closer inspection, they showed traces of writing upon one side, and, what was more important still, the presence of one or more drops of spattered blood. This latter discovery was horrible to me, and so overcame me for the moment that I put the scraps down, and, turning towards Mr. Gryce, inquired:

"What do you make of them?"

"That is just the question I was going to put to you."

Swallowing my disgust, I took them up again. "They look like the remnants of some old letter," said I.

"They have that appearance," Mr. Gryce grimly assented.

"A letter which, from the drop of blood observable on the written side, must have been lying face up on Mr. Leavenworth's table at the time of the murder—"

"Just so."

"And from the uniformity in width of each of these pieces, as well as their tendency to curl up when left alone, must first have been torn into even strips, and then severally rolled up, before being tossed into the grate where they were afterwards found."

106

"That is all good," said Mr. Gryce; "go on."

"The writing, so far as discernible, is that of a cultivated gentleman. It is not that of Mr. Leavenworth; for I have studied his chirography too much lately not to know it at a glance; but it may be—Hold!" I suddenly exclaimed, "have you any mucilage handy? I think, if I could paste these strips down upon a piece of paper, so that they would remain flat, I should be able to tell you what I think of them much more easily."

"There is mucilage on the desk," signified Mr. Gryce.

Procuring it, I proceeded to consult the scraps once more for evidence to guide me in their arrangement. These were more marked than I expected; the longer and best preserved strip, with its "Mr. Hor" at the top, showing itself at first blush to be the left-hand margin of the letter, while the machine-cut edge of the next in length presented tokens fully as conclusive of its being the right-hand margin of the same. Selecting these, then, I pasted them down on a piece of paper at just the distance they would occupy if the sheet from which they were torn was of the ordinary commercial note size. Immediately it became apparent: first, that it would take two other strips of the same width to fill up the space left between them; and secondly, that the writing did not terminate at the foot of the sheet, but was carried on to another page.

Taking up the third strip, I looked at its edge; it was machine-cut at the top, and showed by the arrangement of its words that it was the margin strip of a second leaf. Pasting that down by itself, I scrutinized the fourth, and finding it also machine-cut at the top but not on the side, endeavored to fit it to the piece already pasted down, but the words would not match. Moving it along to the position it would hold if it were the third strip, I fastened it down; the whole presenting, when completed, the appearance seen on the opposite page.

"Well!" exclaimed Mr. Gryce, "that's business." Then, as I held it up before his eyes: "But don't show it to me. Study it yourself, and tell me what you think of it."

"Well," said I, "this much is certain: that it is a letter directed to Mr. Leavenworth from some House, and dated—let's see; that is an *h*, isn't it?" And I pointed to the one letter just discernible on the line under the word House.

"I should think so; but don't ask me."

"It must be an *h*. The year is 1875, and this is not the termination of either January or February. Dated, then, March 1st, 1876, and signed——"

Mr. Gryce rolled his eyes in anticipatory ecstasy towards the ceiling.

"By Henry Clavering," I announced without hesitation.

Mr. Gryce's eyes returned to his swathed finger-ends. "Humph! how do you know that?"

"Wait a moment, and I'll show you"; and, taking out of my pocket the card which Mr. Clavering had handed me as an introduction at our late interview, I laid it underneath the last line of writing on the second page. One glance was sufficient. Henry Ritchie Clavering on the card; H——chie—in the same handwriting on the letter.

"Clavering it is," said he, "without a doubt." But I saw he was not surprised.

"And now," I continued, "for its general tenor and meaning." And, commencing

107

at the beginning, I read aloud the words as they came, with pauses at the breaks, something as follows: "Mr. Hor—Dear—a niece whom yo—one too who see— the love and trus—any other man ca—autiful, so char——s she in face fo—— conversation, ery rose has its——rose is no exception——ely as she is, char ——tender as she is, s——pable of tramplin——one who trusted—— heart——————. ——————— him to——he owes a——honor ——ance.

"If——t believe —— her to——cruel——face,—— what is——ble serv ——yours

"H——tchie"

"It reads like a complaint against one of Mr. Leavenworth's nieces," I said, and started at my own words.

"What is it?" cried Mr. Gryce; "what is the matter?"

"Why," said I, "the fact is I have heard this very letter spoken of. It *is* a complaint against one of Mr. Leavenworth's nieces, and was written by Mr. Clavering." And I told him of Mr. Harwell's communication in regard to the matter.

"Ah! then Mr. Harwell has been talking, has he? I thought he had forsworn gossip."

"Mr. Harwell and I have seen each other almost daily for the last two weeks," I replied. "It would be strange if he had nothing to tell me."

"And he says he has read a letter written to Mr. Leavenworth by Mr. Clavering?"

"Yes; but the particular words of which he has now forgotten."

"These few here may assist him in recalling the rest."

"I would rather not admit him to a knowledge of the existence of this piece of evidence. I don't believe in letting any one into our confidence whom we can conscientiously keep out."

"I see you don't," dryly responded Mr. Gryce.

Not appearing to notice the fling conveyed by these words, I took up the letter once more, and began pointing out such half-formed words in it as I thought we might venture to complete, as the Hor—, yo—, see—utiful——, har——, for ——, tramplin——, pable——, serv——.

This done, I next proposed the introduction of such others as seemed necessary to the sense, as *Leavenworth* after *Horatio; Sir* after *Dear; have* with a possible *you* before *a niece; thorn* after *Us* in the phrase *rose has its; on after trampling; whom* after *to; debt after a; you* after *If; me ask* after *believe; beautiful* after *cruel.*

Between the columns of words thus furnished I interposed a phrase or two, here and there, the whole reading upon its completion as follows:

"——————— House." March 1st, 1876.

"*Mr. Horatio Leavenworth; Dear Sir:*

"(You) have a niece whom you one too who seems worthy the love and trust of any other man ca so beautiful, so charming is she in face form and conversation. But every rose has its thorn and (this) rose is no exception lovely as she is, charming (as she is,) tender as she is, she is capable of trampling on one who trusted her heart a

108

him to whom she owes a debt of honor a ance

"If you don't believe me ask her to her cruel beautiful face what is (her) humble servant yours:

"Henry Ritchie Clavering."

"I think that will do," said Mr. Gryce. "Its general tenor is evident, and that is all we want at this time."

"The whole tone of it is anything but complimentary to the lady it mentions," I remarked. "He must have had, or imagined he had, some desperate grievance, to provoke him to the use of such plain language in regard to one he can still characterize as tender, charming, beautiful."

"Grievances are apt to lie back of mysterious crimes."

"I think I know what this one was," I said; "but"—seeing him look up—"must decline to communicate my suspicion to you for the present. My theory stands unshaken, and in some degree confirmed; and that is all I can say."

"Then this letter does not supply the link you wanted?"

"No: it is a valuable bit of evidence; but it is not the link I am in search of just now."

"Yet it must be an important clue, or Eleanore Leavenworth would not have been to such pains, first to take it in the way she did from her uncle's table, and secondly——"

"Wait! what makes you think this is the paper she took, or was believed to have taken, from Mr. Leavenworth's table on that fatal morning?"

"Why, the fact that it was found together with the key, which we know she dropped into the grate, and that there are drops of blood on it."

I shook my head.

"Why do you shake your head?" asked Mr. Gryce.

"Because I am not satisfied with your reason for believing this to be the paper taken by her from Mr. Leavenworth's table."

"And why?"

"Well, first, because Fobbs does not speak of seeing any paper in her hand, when she bent over the fire; leaving us to conclude that these pieces were in the scuttle of coal she threw upon it; which surely you must acknowledge to be a strange place for her to have put a paper she took such pains to gain possession of; and, secondly, for the reason that these scraps were twisted as if they had been used for curl papers, or something of that kind; a fact hard to explain by your hypothesis."

The detective's eye stole in the direction of my necktie, which was as near as he ever came to a face. "You are a bright one," said he; "a very bright one. I quite admire you, Mr. Raymond."

A little surprised, and not altogether pleased with this unexpected compliment, I regarded him doubtfully for a moment and then asked:

"What is your opinion upon the matter?"

"Oh, you know I have no opinion. I gave up everything of that kind when I put

109

the affair into your hands."

"Still——"

"That the letter of which these scraps are the remnant was on Mr. Leavenworth's table at the time of the murder is believed. That upon the body being removed, a paper was taken from the table by Miss Eleanore Leavenworth, is also believed. That, when she found her action had been noticed, and attention called to this paper and the key, she resorted to subterfuge in order to escape the vigilance of the watch that had been set over her, and, partially succeeding in her endeavor, flung the key into the fire from which these same scraps were afterwards recovered, is also known. The conclusion I leave to your judgment."

"Very well, then," said I, rising; "we will let conclusions go for the present. My mind must be satisfied in regard to the truth or falsity of a certain theory of mine, for my judgment to be worth much on this or any other matter connected with the affair."

And, only waiting to get the address of his subordinate P., in case I should need assistance in my investigations, I left Mr. Gryce, and proceeded immediately to the house of Mr. Veeley.

XXIII. THE STORY OF A CHARMING WOMAN

"Fe, fi, fo, fum, I smell the blood of an Englishman."
—Old Song.

"I hold you as a thing enskied and sainted."
—Measure for Measure.

"YOU have never heard, then, the particulars of Mr. Leavenworth's marriage?"

It was my partner who spoke. I had been asking him to explain to me Mr. Leavenworth's well-known antipathy to the English race.

"No."

"If you had, you would not need to come to me for this explanation. But it is not strange you are ignorant of the matter. I doubt if there are half a dozen persons in existence who could tell you where Horatio Leavenworth found the lovely woman who afterwards became his wife, much less give you any details of the circumstances which led to his marriage."

"I am very fortunate, then, in being in the confidence of one who can. What were those circumstances, Mr. Veeley?"

"It will aid you but little to hear. Horatio Leavenworth, when a young man, was very ambitious; so much so, that at one time he aspired to marry a wealthy lady of Providence. But, chancing to go to England, he there met a young woman whose grace and charm had such an effect upon him that he relinquished all thought of the Providence lady, though it was some time before he could face the prospect of marrying the one who had so greatly interested him; as she was not only in humble circumstances, but was encumbered with a child concerning whose parentage the neighbors professed ignorance, and she had nothing to say. But, as

110

is very apt to be the case in an affair like this, love and admiration soon got the better of worldly wisdom. Taking his future in his hands, he offered himself as her husband, when she immediately proved herself worthy of his regard by entering at once into those explanations he was too much of a gentleman to demand. The story she told was pitiful. She proved to be an American by birth, her father having been a well-known merchant of Chicago. While he lived, her home was one of luxury, but just as she was emerging into womanhood he died. It was at his funeral she met the man destined to be her ruin. How he came there she never knew; he was not a friend of her father's. It is enough he was there, and saw her, and that in three weeks—don't shudder, she was such a child—they were married. In twenty-four hours she knew what that word meant for her; it meant blows. Everett, I am telling no fanciful story. In twenty-four hours after that girl was married, her husband, coming drunk into the house, found her in his way, and knocked her down. It was but the beginning. Her father's estate, on being settled up, proving to be less than expected, he carried her off to England, where he did not wait to be drunk in order to maltreat her. She was not free from his cruelty night or day. Before she was sixteen, she had run the whole gamut of human suffering; and that, not at the hands of a coarse, common ruffian, but from an elegant, handsome, luxury-loving gentleman, whose taste in dress was so nice he would sooner fling a garment of hers into the fire than see her go into company clad in a manner he did not consider becoming. She bore it till her child was born, then she fled. Two days after the little one saw the light, she rose from her bed and, taking her baby in her arms, ran out of the house. The few jewels she had put into her pocket supported her till she could set up a little shop. As for her husband, she neither saw him, nor heard from him, from the day she left him till about two weeks before Horatio Leavenworth first met her, when she learned from the papers that he was dead. She was, therefore, free; but though she loved Horatio Leavenworth with all her heart, she would not marry him. She felt herself forever stained and soiled by the one awful year of abuse and contamination. Nor could he persuade her. Not till the death of her child, a month or so after his proposal, did she consent to give him her hand and what remained of her unhappy life. He brought her to New York, surrounded her with luxury and every tender care, but the arrow had gone too deep; two years from the day her child breathed its last, she too died. It was the blow of his life to Horatio Leavenworth; he was never the same man again. Though Mary and Eleanore shortly after entered his home, he never recovered his old light-heartedness. Money became his idol, and the ambition to make and leave a great fortune behind him modified all his views of life. But one proof remained that he never forgot the wife of his youth, and that was, he could not bear to have the word 'Englishman' uttered in his hearing."

Mr. Veeley paused, and I rose to go. "Do you remember how Mrs. Leavenworth looked?" I asked. "Could you describe her to me?"

He seemed a little astonished at my request, but immediately replied: "She was a very pale woman; not strictly beautiful, but of a contour and expression of great charm. Her hair was brown, her eyes gray—"

"And very wide apart?"

He nodded, looking still more astonished. "How came you to know? Have you seen her picture?"

I did not answer that question.

On my way downstairs, I bethought me of a letter which I had in my pocket for Mr. Veeley's son Fred, and, knowing of no surer way of getting it to him that night than by leaving it on the library table, I stepped to the door of that room, which in this house was at the rear of the parlors, and receiving no reply to my knock, opened it and looked in.

The room was unlighted, but a cheerful fire was burning in the grate, and by its glow I espied a lady crouching on the hearth, whom at first glance I took for Mrs. Veeley. But, upon advancing and addressing her by that name, I saw my mistake; for the person before me not only refrained from replying, but, rising at the sound of my voice, revealed a form of such noble proportions that all possibility of its being that of the dainty little wife of my partner fled.

"I see I have made a mistake," said I. "I beg your pardon"; and would have left the room, but something in the general attitude of the lady before me restrained me, and, believing it to be Mary Leavenworth, I inquired:

"Can it be this is Miss Leavenworth?"

The noble figure appeared to droop, the gently lifted head to fall, and for a moment I doubted if I had been correct in my supposition. Then form and head slowly erected themselves, a soft voice spoke, and I heard a low "yes," and hurriedly advancing, confronted—not Mary, with her glancing, feverish gaze, and scarlet, trembling lips—but Eleanore, the woman whose faintest look had moved me from the first, the woman whose husband I believed myself to be even then pursuing to his doom!

The surprise was too great; I could neither sustain nor conceal it. Stumbling slowly back, I murmured something about having believed it to be her cousin; and then, conscious only of the one wish to fly a presence I dared not encounter in my present mood, turned, when her rich, heart-full voice rose once more and I heard:

"You will not leave me without a word, Mr. Raymond, now that chance has thrown us together?" Then, as I came slowly forward: "Were you so very much astonished to find me here?"

"I do not know—I did not expect—" was my incoherent reply. "I had heard you were ill; that you went nowhere; that you had no wish to see your friends."

"I have been ill," she said; "but I am better now, and have come to spend the night with Mrs. Veeley, because I could not endure the stare of the four walls of my room any longer."

This was said without any effort at plaintiveness, but rather as if she thought it necessary to excuse herself for being where she was.

"I am glad you did so," said I. "You ought to be here all the while. That dreary, lonesome boarding-house is no place for you, Miss Leavenworth. It distresses us all to feel that you are exiling yourself at this time."

"I do not wish anybody to be distressed," she returned. "It is best for me to be

112

where I am. Nor am I altogether alone. There is a child there whose innocent eyes see nothing but innocence in mine. She will keep me from despair. Do not let my friends be anxious; I can bear it." Then, in a lower tone: "There is but one thing which really unnerves me; and that is my ignorance of what is going on at home. Sorrow I can bear, but suspense is killing me. Will you not tell me something of Mary and home? I cannot ask Mrs. Veeley; she is kind, but has no real knowledge of Mary or me, nor does she know anything of our estrangement. She thinks me obstinate, and blames me for leaving my cousin in her trouble. But you know I could not help it. You know,—" her voice wavered off into a tremble, and she did not conclude.

"I cannot tell you much," I hastened to reply; "but whatever knowledge is at my command is certainly yours. Is there anything in particular you wish to know?"

"Yes, how Mary is; whether she is well, and—and composed."

"Your cousin's health is good," I returned; "but I fear I cannot say she is composed. She is greatly troubled about you."

"You see her often, then?"

"I am assisting Mr. Harwell in preparing your uncle's book for the press, and necessarily am there much of the time."

"My uncle's book!" The words came in a tone of low horror.

"Yes, Miss Leavenworth. It has been thought best to bring it before the world, and——"

"And Mary has set you at the task?"

"Yes."

It seemed as if she could not escape from the horror which this caused. "How could she? Oh, how could she!"

"She considers herself as fulfilling her uncle's wishes. He was very anxious, as you know, to have the book out by July."

"Do not speak of it!" she broke in, "I cannot bear it." Then, as if she feared she had hurt my feelings by her abruptness, lowered her voice and said: "I do not, however, know of any one I should be better pleased to have charged with the task than yourself. With you it will be a work of respect and reverence; but a stranger—Oh, I could not have endured a stranger touching it."

She was fast falling into her old horror; but rousing herself, murmured: "I wanted to ask you something; ah, I know"—and she moved so as to face me. "I wish to inquire if everything is as before in the house; the servants the same and —and other things?"

"There is a Mrs. Darrell there; I do not know of any other change."

"Mary does not talk of going away?"

"I think not."

"But she has visitors? Some one besides Mrs. Darrell to help her bear her loneliness?"

I knew what was coming, and strove to preserve my composure.

"Yes," I replied; "a few."

"Would you mind naming them?" How low her tones were, but how distinct!

"Certainly not. Mrs. Veeley, Mrs. Gilbert, Miss Martin, and a—a——"

"Go on," she whispered.

"A gentleman by the name of Clavering."

"You speak that name with evident embarrassment," she said, after a moment of intense anxiety on my part. "May I inquire why?"

Astounded, I raised my eyes to her face. It was very pale, and wore the old look of self-repressed calm I remembered so well. I immediately dropped my gaze.

"Why? because there are some circumstances surrounding him which have struck me as peculiar."

"How so?" she asked.

"He appears under two names. To-day it is Clavering; a short time ago it was _____"

"Go on."

"Robbins."

Her dress rustled on the hearth; there was a sound of desolation in it; but her voice when she spoke was expressionless as that of an automaton.

"How many times has this person, of whose name you do not appear to be certain, been to see Mary?"

"Once."

"When was it?"

"Last night."

"Did he stay long?"

"About twenty minutes, I should say."

"And do you think he will come again?"

"No."

"Why?"

"He has left the country."

A short silence followed this, I felt her eyes searching my face, but doubt whether, if I had known she held a loaded pistol, I could have looked up at that moment.

"Mr. Raymond," she at length observed, in a changed tone, "the last time I saw you, you told me you were going to make some endeavor to restore me to my former position before the world. I did not wish you to do so then; nor do I wish you to do so now. Can you not make me comparatively happy, then, by assuring me you have abandoned or will abandon a project so hopeless?"

"It is impossible," I replied with emphasis. "I cannot abandon it. Much as I grieve to be a source of sorrow to you, it is best you should know that I can never give up the hope of righting you while I live."

She put out her hand in a sort of hopeless appeal inexpressibly touching to behold in the fast waning firelight. But I was relentless.

"I should never be able to face the world or my own conscience if, through any weakness of my own, I should miss the blessed privilege of setting the wrong right, and saving a noble woman from unmerited disgrace." And then, seeing she was not likely to reply to this, drew a step nearer and said: "Is there not some little kindness I can show you, Miss Leavenworth? Is there no message you would like taken, or act it would give you pleasure to see performed?"

114

She stopped to think. "No," said she; "I have only one request to make, and that you refuse to grant."

"For the most unselfish of reasons," I urged.

She slowly shook her head. "You think so"; then, before I could reply, "I could desire one little favor shown me, however."

"What is that?"

"That if anything should transpire; if Hannah should be found, or—or my presence required in any way,—you will not keep me in ignorance. That you will let me know the worst when it comes, without fail."

"I will."

"And now, good-night. Mrs. Veeley is coming back, and you would scarcely wish to be found here by her."

"No," said I.

And yet I did not go, but stood watching the firelight flicker on her black dress till the thought of Clavering and the duty I had for the morrow struck coldly to my heart, and I turned away towards the door. But at the threshold I paused again, and looked back. Oh, the flickering, dying fire flame! Oh, the crowding, clustering shadows! Oh, that drooping figure in their midst, with its clasped hands and its hidden face! I see it all again; I see it as in a dream; then darkness falls, and in the glare of gas-lighted streets, I am hastening along, solitary and sad, to my lonely home.

XXIV. A REPORT FOLLOWED BY SMOKE

"Oft expectation fails, and most oft there
Where most it promises; and oft it hits
Where Hope is coldest, and Despair most sits."
—All's Well that Ends Well.

WHEN I told Mr. Gryce I only waited for the determination of one fact, to feel justified in throwing the case unreservedly into his hands, I alluded to the proving or disproving of the supposition that Henry Clavering had been a guest at the same watering-place with Eleanore Leavenworth the summer before.

When, therefore, I found myself the next morning with the Visitor Book of the Hotel Union at R—— in my hands, it was only by the strongest effort of will I could restrain my impatience. The suspense, however, was short. Almost immediately I encountered his name, written not half a page below those of Mr. Leavenworth and his nieces, and, whatever may have been my emotion at finding my suspicions thus confirmed, I recognized the fact that I was in the possession of a clue which would yet lead to the solving of the fearful problem which had been imposed upon me.

Hastening to the telegraph office, I sent a message for the man promised me by Mr. Gryce, and receiving for an answer that he could not be with me before three o'clock, started for the house of Mr. Monell, a client of ours, living in R——. I found him at home and, during our interview of two hours, suffered the ordeal

115

of appearing at ease and interested in what he had to say, while my heart was heavy with its first disappointment and my brain on fire with the excitement of the work then on my hands.

I arrived at the depot just as the train came in.

There was but one passenger for R———, a brisk young man, whose whole appearance differed so from the description which had been given me of Q that I at once made up my mind he could not be the man I was looking for, and was turning away disappointed, when he approached, and handed me a card on which was inscribed the single character "?" Even then I could not bring myself to believe that the slyest and most successful agent in Mr. Gryce's employ was before me, till, catching his eye, I saw such a keen, enjoyable twinkle sparkling in its depths that all doubt fled, and, returning his bow with a show of satisfaction, I remarked:

"You are very punctual. I like that."

He gave another short, quick nod. "Glad, sir, to please you. Punctuality is too cheap a virtue not to be practised by a man on the lookout for a rise. But what orders, sir? Down train due in ten minutes; no time to spare."

"Down train? What have we to do with that?"

"I thought you might wish to take it, sir. Mr. Brown"—winking expressively at the name, "always checks his carpet-bag for home when he sees me coming. But that is your affair; I am not particular."

"I wish to do what is wisest under the circumstances."

"Go home, then, as speedily as possible." And he gave a third sharp nod exceedingly business-like and determined.

"If I leave you, it is with the understanding that you bring your information first to me; that you are in my employ, and in that of no one else for the time being; and that *mum* is the word till I give you liberty to speak."

"Yes, sir. When I work for Brown & Co. I do not work for Smith & Jones. That you can count on."

"Very well then, here are your instructions."

He looked at the paper I handed him with a certain degree of care, then stepped into the waiting-room and threw it into the stove, saying in a low tone: "So much in case I should meet with some accident: have an apoplectic fit, or anything of that sort."

"But———"

"Oh, don't worry; I sha'n't forget. I've a memory, sir. No need of anybody using pen and paper with me."

And laughing in the short, quick way one would expect from a person of his appearance and conversation, he added: "You will probably hear from me in a day or so," and bowing, took his brisk, free way down the street just as the train came rushing in from the West.

My instructions to Q were as follows:

1. To find out on what day, and in whose company, the Misses Leavenworth arrived at R——— the year before. What their movements had been while there, and in whose society they were oftenest to be seen. Also the date of their

116

departure, and such facts as could be gathered in regard to their habits, etc.

2. Ditto in respect to a Mr. Henry Clavering, fellow-guest and probable friend of said ladies.

3. Name of individual fulfilling the following requirements: Clergyman, Methodist, deceased since last December or thereabouts, who in July of Seventy-five was located in some town not over twenty miles from R——.

4. Also name and present whereabouts of a man at that time in service of the above.

To say that the interval of time necessary to a proper inquiry into these matters was passed by me in any reasonable frame of mind, would be to give myself credit for an equanimity of temper which I unfortunately do not possess. Never have days seemed so long as the two which interposed between my return from R—— and the receipt of the following letter:

"Sir:

"Individuals mentioned arrived in R—— July 3, 1875. Party consisted of four; the two ladies, their uncle, and the girl named Hannah. Uncle remained three days, and then left for a short tour through Massachusetts. Gone two weeks, during which ladies were seen more or less with the gentleman named between us, but not to an extent sufficient to excite gossip or occasion remark, when said gentleman left R—— abruptly, two days after uncle's return. Date July 19. As to habits of ladies, more or less social. They were always to be seen at picnics, rides, etc., and in the ballroom. M—— liked best. E——considered grave, and, towards the last of her stay, moody. It is remembered now that her manner was always peculiar, and that she was more or less shunned by her cousin.

However, in the opinion of one girl still to be found at the hotel, she was the sweetest lady that ever breathed. No particular reason for this opinion. Uncle, ladies, and servants left R—— for New York, August 7, 1875.

"2. H. C. arrived at the hotel in R——July 6, 1875, in-company with Mr. and Mrs. Vandervort, friends of the above. Left July 19, two weeks from day of arrival. Little to be learned in regard to him. Remembered as the handsome gentleman who was in the party with the L, girls, and that is all.

"3. F——, a small town, some sixteen or seventeen miles from R——, had for its Methodist minister, in July of last year, a man who has since died, Samuel Stebbins by name. Date of decease, Jan. 7 of this year.

"4. Name of man in employ of S. S. at that time is Timothy Cook. He has been absent, but returned to P—— two days ago. Can be seen if required."

"Ah, ha!" I cried aloud at this point, in my sudden surprise and satisfaction; "now we have something to work upon!" And sitting down I penned the following reply:

"T. C. wanted by all means. Also any evidence going to prove that H. C. and E. L. were married at the house of Mr. S. on any day of July or August last."

Next morning came the following telegram:

"T. C. on the road. Remembers a marriage. Will be with you by 2 p.m."

At three o'clock of that same day, I stood before Mr. Gryce. "I am here to make my report," I announced.

117

The nicker of a smile passed over his face, and he gazed for the first time at his bound-up finger-ends with a softening aspect which must have done them good. "I'm ready," said he.

"Mr. Gryce," I began, "do you remember the conclusion we came to at our first interview in this house?"

"I remember the *one you* came to."

"Well, well," I acknowledged a little peevishly, "the one I came to, then. It was this: that if we could find to whom Eleanore Leavenworth felt she owed her best duty and love, we should discover the man who murdered her uncle."

"And do you imagine you have done this?"

"I do."

His eyes stole a little nearer my face. "Well! that is good; go on."

"When I undertook this business of clearing Eleanore Leavenworth from suspicion," I resumed, "it was with the premonition that this person would prove to be her lover; but I had no idea he would prove to be her husband."

Mr. Gryce's gaze flashed like lightning to the ceiling.

"What!" he ejaculated with a frown.

"The lover of Eleanore Leavenworth is likewise her husband," I repeated. "Mr. Clavering holds no lesser connection to her than that."

"How have you found that out?" demanded Mr. Gryce, in a harsh tone that argued disappointment or displeasure.

"That I will not take time to state. The question is not how I became acquainted with a certain thing, but is what I assert in regard to it true. If you will cast your eye over this summary of events gleaned by me from the lives of these two persons, I think you will agree with me that it is." And I held up before his eyes the following:

"During the two weeks commencing July 6, of the year 1875, and ending July 19, of the same year, Henry R. Clavering, of London, and Eleanore Leavenworth, of New York, were guests of the same hotel. *Fact proved by Visitor Book of the Hotel Union at R———, New York.*

"They were not only guests of the same hotel, but are known to have held more or less communication with each other. *Fact proved by such servants now employed in R——— as were in the hotel at that time.*

"July 19. Mr. Clavering left R——— abruptly, a circumstance that would not be considered remarkable if Mr. Leavenworth, whose violent antipathy to Englishmen as husbands is publicly known, had not just returned from a journey.

"July 30. Mr. Clavering was seen in the parlor of Mr. Stebbins, the Methodist minister at F———, a town about sixteen miles from R———, where he was married to a lady of great beauty. *Proved by Timothy Cook, a man in the employ of Mr. Stebbins, who was called in from the garden to witness the ceremony and sign a paper supposed to be a certificate.*

"July 31. Mr. Clavering takes steamer for Liverpool. *Proved by newspapers of that date.*

"September. Eleanore Leavenworth in her uncle's house in New York, conducting herself as usual, but pale of face and preoccupied in manner. *Proved by*

118

servants then in her service. Mr. Clavering in London; watches the United States mails with eagerness, but receives no letters. Fits up room elegantly, as for a lady. *Proved by secret communication from London.*

"November. Miss Leavenworth still in uncle's house. No publication of her marriage ever made. Mr. Clavering in London; shows signs of uneasiness; the room prepared for lady closed. *Proved as above.*

"January 17, 1876. Mr. Clavering, having returned to America, engages room at Hoffman House, New York.

"March 1 or 2. Mr. Leavenworth receives a letter signed by Henry Clavering, in which he complains of having been ill-used by one of that gentleman's nieces. A manifest shade falls over the family at this time.

"March 4. Mr. Clavering under a false name inquires at the door of Mr. Leavenworth's house for Miss Eleanore Leavenworth. *Proved by Thomas.'"*

"March 4th?" exclaimed Mr. Gryce at this point. "That was the night of the murder.-"

"Yes; the Mr. Le Roy Robbins said to have called that evening was none other than Mr. Clavering."

"March 19. Miss Mary Leavenworth, in a conversation with me, acknowledges that there is a secret in the family, and is just upon the point of revealing its nature, when Mr. Clavering enters the house. Upon his departure she declares her unwillingness ever to mention the subject again."

Mr. Gryce slowly waved the paper aside. "And from these facts you draw the inference that Eleanore Leavenworth is the wife of Mr. Clavering?"

"I do."

"And that, being his wife——"

"It would be natural for her to conceal anything she knew likely to criminate him."

"Always supposing Clavering himself had done anything criminal!"

"Of course."

"Which latter supposition you now propose to justify!"

"Which latter supposition it is left for *us* to justify."

A peculiar gleam shot over Mr. Gryce's somewhat abstracted countenance. "Then you have no new evidence against Mr. Clavering?"

"I should think the fact just given, of his standing in the relation of unacknowledged husband to the suspected party was something."

"No positive evidence as to his being the assassin of Mr. Leavenworth, I mean?"

I was obliged to admit I had none which he would consider positive. "But I can show the existence of motive; and I can likewise show it was not only possible, but probable, he was in the house at the time of the murder."

"Ah, you can!" cried Mr. Gryce, rousing a little from his abstraction.

"The motive was the usual one of self-interest. Mr. Leavenworth stood in the way of Eleanore's acknowledging him as a husband, and he must therefore be put out of the way."

"Weak!"

119

"Motives for murders are sometimes weak."

"The motive for this was not. Too much calculation was shown for the arm to have been nerved by anything short of the most deliberate intention, founded upon the deadliest necessity of passion or avarice."

"Avarice?"

"One should never deliberate upon the causes which have led to the destruction of a rich man without taking into account that most common passion of the human race."

"But——"

"Let us hear what you have to say of Mr. Clavering's presence in the house at the time of the murder."

I related what Thomas the butler had told me in regard to Mr. Clavering's call upon Miss Leavenworth that night, and the lack of proof which existed as to his having left the house when supposed to do so.

"That is worth remembering," said Mr. Gryce at the conclusion. "Valueless as direct evidence, it might prove of great value as corroborative." Then, in a graver tone, he went on to say: "Mr. Raymond, are you aware that in all this you have been strengthening the case against Eleanore Leavenworth instead of weakening it?"

I could only ejaculate, in my sudden wonder and dismay.

"You have shown her to be secret, sly, and unprincipled; capable of wronging those to whom she was most bound, her uncle and her husband."

"You put it very strongly," said I, conscious of a shocking discrepancy between this description of Eleanore's character and all that I had preconceived in regard to it.

"No more so than your own conclusions from this story warrant me in doing." Then, as I sat silent, murmured low, and as if to himself: "If the case was dark against her before, it is doubly so with this supposition established of her being the woman secretly married to Mr. Clavering."

"And yet," I protested, unable to give up my hope without a struggle; "you do not, cannot, believe the noble-looking Eleanore guilty of this horrible crime?"

"No," he slowly said; "you might as well know right here what I think about that. I believe Eleanore Leavenworth to be an innocent woman."

"You do? Then what," I cried, swaying between joy at this admission and doubt as to the meaning of his former expressions, "remains to be done?"

Mr. Gryce quietly responded: "Why, nothing but to prove your supposition a false one."

XXV. TIMOTHY COOK

"Look here upon this picture and on this."
—Hamlet.

I STARED at him in amazement. "I doubt if it will be so very difficult," said he. Then, in a sudden burst, "Where is the man Cook?"

"He is below with Q."

"That was a wise move; let us see the boys; have them up."

Stepping to the door I called them.

"I expected, of course, you would want to question them," said I, coming back.

In another moment the spruce Q and the shock-headed Cook entered the room.

"Ah," said Mr. Gryce, directing his attention at the latter in his own whimsical, non-committal way; "this is the deceased Mr. Stebbins' hired man, is it? Well, you look as though you could tell the truth."

"I usually calculate to do that thing, sir; at all events, I was never called a liar as I can remember."

"Of course not, of course not," returned the affable detective. Then, without any further introduction: "What was the first name of the lady you saw married in your master's house last summer?"

"Bless me if I know! I don't think I heard, sir."

"But you recollect how she looked?"

"As well as if she was my own mother. No disrespect to the lady, sir, if you know her," he made haste to add, glancing hurriedly at me. "What I mean is, she was so handsome, I could never forget the look of her sweet face if I lived a hundred years."

"Can you describe her?"

"I don't know, sirs; she was tall and grand-looking, had the brightest eyes and the whitest hand, and smiled in a way to make even a common man like me wish he had never seen her."

"Would you know her in a crowd?"

"I would know her anywhere."

"Very well; now tell us all you can about that marriage."

"Well, sirs, it was something like this. I had been in Mr. Stebbins' employ about a year, when one morning as I was hoeing in the garden I saw a gentleman walk rapidly up the road to our gate and come in. I noticed him particularly, because he was so fine-looking; unlike anybody in F——, and, indeed, unlike anybody I had ever seen, for that matter; but I shouldn't have thought much about that if there hadn't come along, not five minutes after, a buggy with two ladies in it, which stopped at our gate, too. I saw they wanted to get out, so I went and held their horse for them, and they got down and went into the house."

"Did you see their faces?"

"No, sir; not then. They had veils on."

"Very well, go on."

"I hadn't been to work long, before I heard some one calling my name, and looking up, saw Mr. Stebbins standing in the doorway beckoning. I went to him, and he said, 'I want you, Tim; wash your hands and come into the parlor.' I had never been asked to do that before, and it struck me all of a heap; but I did what he asked, and was so taken aback at the looks of the lady I saw standing up on the floor with the handsome gentleman, that I stumbled over a stool and made a great racket, and didn't know much where I was or what was going on, till I heard Mr.

121

Stebbins say 'man and wife'; and then it came over me in a hot kind of way that it was a marriage I was seeing."

Timothy Cook stopped to wipe his forehead, as if overcome with the very recollection, and Mr. Gryce took the opportunity to remark:

"You say there were two ladies; now where was the other one at this time?"

"She was there, sir; but I didn't mind much about her, I was so taken up with the handsome one and the way she had of smiling when any one looked at her. I never saw the beat."

I felt a quick thrill go through me.

"Can you remember the color of her hair or eyes?"

"No, sir; I had a feeling as if she wasn't dark, and that is all I know."

"But you remember her face?"

"Yes, sir!"

Mr. Gryce here whispered me to procure two pictures which I would find in a certain drawer in his desk, and set them up in different parts of the room unbeknown to the man.

"You have before said," pursued Mr. Gryce, "that you have no remembrance of her name. Now, how was that? Weren't you called upon to sign the certificate?"

"Yes, sir; but I am most ashamed to say it; I was in a sort of maze, and didn't hear much, and only remember it was a Mr. Clavering she was married to, and that some one called some one else Elner, or something like that. I wish I hadn't been so stupid, sir, if it would have done you any good."

"Tell us about the signing of the certificate," said Mr. Gryce.

"Well, sir, there isn't much to tell. Mr. Stebbins asked me to put my name down in a certain place on a piece of paper he pushed towards me, and I put it down there; that is all."

"Was there no other name there when you wrote yours?"

"No, sir. Afterwards Mr. Stebbins turned towards the other lady, who now came forward, and asked her if she wouldn't please sign it, too; and she said,' yes,' and came very quickly and did so."

"And didn't you see her face then?"

"No, sir; her back was to me when she threw by her veil, and I only saw Mr. Stebbins staring at her as she stooped, with a kind of wonder on his face, which made me think she might have been something worth looking at too; but I didn't see her myself."

"Well, what happened then?"

"I don't know, sir. I went stumbling out of the room, and didn't see anything more."

"Where were you when the ladies went away?"

"In the garden, sir. I had gone back to my work."

"You saw them, then. Was the gentleman with them?"

"No, sir; that was the queer part of it all. They went back as they came, and so did he; and in a few minutes Mr. Stebbins came out where I was, and told me I was to say nothing about what I had seen, for it was a secret."

"Were you the only one in the house who knew anything about it? Weren't there

122

any women around?"

"No, sir; Miss Stebbins had gone to the sewing circle."

I had by this time some faint impression of what Mr. Gryce's suspicions were, and in arranging the pictures had placed one, that of Eleanore, on the mantelpiece, and the other, which was an uncommonly fine photograph of Mary, in plain view on the desk. But Mr. Cook's back was as yet towards that part of the room, and, taking advantage of the moment, I returned and asked him if that was all he had to tell us about this matter.

"Yes, sir."

"Then," said Mr. Gryce, with a glance at Q, "isn't there something you can give Mr. Cook in payment for his story? Look around, will you?"

Q nodded, and moved towards a cupboard in the wall at the side of the mantelpiece; Mr. Cook following him with his eyes, as was natural, when, with a sudden start, he crossed the room and, pausing before the mantelpiece, looked at the picture of Eleanore which I had put there, gave a low grunt of satisfaction or pleasure, looked at it again, and walked away. I felt my heart leap into my throat, and, moved by what impulse of dread or hope I cannot say, turned my back, when suddenly I heard him give vent to a startled exclamation, followed by the words: "Why! here she is; this is her, sirs," and turning around saw him hurrying towards us with Mary's picture in his hands.

I do not know as I was greatly surprised. I was powerfully excited, as well as conscious of a certain whirl of thought, and an unsettling of old conclusions that was very confusing; but surprised? No. Mr. Gryce's manner had too well prepared me.

"This the lady who was married to Mr. Clavering, my good man? I guess you are mistaken," cried the detective, in a very incredulous tone.

"Mistaken? Didn't I say I would know her anywhere? This is the lady, if she is the president's wife herself." And Mr. Cook leaned over it with a devouring look that was not without its element of homage.

"I am very much astonished," Mr. Gryce went on, winking at me in a slow, diabolical way which in another mood would have aroused my fiercest anger. "Now, if you had said the other lady was the one"—pointing to the picture on the mantelpiece," I shouldn't have wondered."

"She? I never saw that lady before; but this one—would you mind telling me her name, sirs?"

"If what you say is true, her name is Mrs. Clavering."

"Clavering? Yes, that was his name."

"And a very lovely lady," said Mr. Gryce. "Morris, haven't you found anything yet?"

Q, for answer, brought forward glasses and a bottle.

But Mr. Cook was in no mood for liquor. I think he was struck with remorse; for, looking from the picture to Q, and from Q to the picture, he said:

"If I have done this lady wrong by my talk, I'll never forgive myself. You told me I would help her to get her rights; if you have deceived me ——"

"Oh, I haven't deceived you," broke in Q, in his short, sharp way. "Ask that

123

gentleman there if we are not all interested in Mrs. Clavering getting her due."

He had designated me; but I was in no mood to reply. I longed to have the man dismissed, that I might inquire the reason of the great complacency which I now saw overspreading Mr. Gryce's frame, to his very finger-ends.

"Mr. Cook needn't be concerned," remarked Mr. Gryce. "If he will take a glass of warm drink to fortify him for his walk, I think he may go to the lodgings Mr. Morris has provided for him without fear. Give the gent a glass, and let him mix for himself."

But it was full ten minutes before we were delivered of the man and his vain regrets. Mary's image had called up every latent feeling in his heart, and I could but wonder over a loveliness capable of swaying the low as well as the high. But at last he yielded to the seductions of the now wily Q, and departed.

Left alone with Mr. Gryce, I must have allowed some of the confused emotions which filled my breast to become apparent on my countenance; for after a few minutes of ominous silence, he exclaimed very grimly, and yet with a latent touch of that complacency I had before noticed:

"This discovery rather upsets you, doesn't it? Well, it don't me," shutting his mouth like a trap. "I expected it."

"Your conclusions must differ very materially from mine," I returned; "or you would see that this discovery alters the complexion of the whole affair."

"It does not alter the truth."

"What is the truth?"

Mr. Gryce's very legs grew thoughtful; his voice sank to its deepest tone. "Do you very much want to know?"

"Want to know the truth? What else are we after?"

"Then," said he, "to my notion, the complexion of things has altered, but very much for the better. As long as Eleanore was believed to be the wife, her action in this matter was accounted for; but the tragedy itself was not. Why should Eleanore or Eleanore's husband wish the death of a man whose bounty they believed would end with his life? But with Mary, the heiress, proved the wife!—I tell you, Mr. Raymond, it all hangs together now. You must never, in reckoning up an affair of murder like this, forget who it is that most profits by the deceased man's death."

"But Eleanore's silence? her concealment of certain proofs and evidences in her own breast—how will you account for that? I can imagine a woman devoting herself to the shielding of a husband from the consequences of crime; but a cousin's husband, never."

Mr. Gryce put his feet very close together, and softly grunted. "Then you still think Mr. Clavering the assassin of Mr. Leavenworth?"

I could only stare at him in my sudden doubt and dread. "Still think?" I repeated.

"Mr. Clavering the murderer of Mr. Leavenworth?"

"Why, what else is there to think? You don't—you can't—suspect Eleanore of having deliberately undertaken to help her cousin out of a difficulty by taking the life of their mutual benefactor?"

124

"No," said Mr. Gryce; "no, I do not think Eleanore Leavenworth had any hand in the business."

"Then who—" I began, and stopped, lost in the dark vista that was opening before me.

"Who? Why, who but the one whose past deceit and present necessity demanded his death as a relief? Who but the beautiful, money-loving, man-deceiving goddess——"

I leaped to my feet in my sudden horror and repugnance. "Do not mention the name! You are wrong; but do not speak the name."

"Excuse me," said he; "but it will have to be spoken many times, and we may as well begin here and now—who then but Mary Leavenworth; or, if you like it better, Mrs. Henry Clavering? Are you so much surprised? It has been my thought from the beginning."

XXVI. MR. GRYCE EXPLAINS HIMSELF

"Sits the wind in that corner?"
　　—Much Ado about Nothing.

I DO not propose to enter into a description of the mingled feelings aroused in me by this announcement. As a drowning man is said to live over in one terrible instant the events of a lifetime, so each word uttered in my hearing by Mary, from her first introduction to me in her own room, on the morning of the inquest, to our final conversation on the night of Mr. Clavering's call, swept in one wild phantasmagoria through my brain, leaving me aghast at the signification which her whole conduct seemed to acquire from the lurid light which now fell upon it.

"I perceive that I have pulled down an avalanche of doubts about your ears," exclaimed my companion from the height of his calm superiority. "You never thought of this possibility, then, yourself?"

"Do not ask me what I have thought. I only know I will never believe your suspicions true. That, however much Mary may have been benefited by her uncle's death, she never had a hand in it; actual hand, I mean."

"And what makes you so sure of this?"

"And what makes you so sure of the contrary? It is for you to prove, not for me to prove her innocence."

"Ah," said Mr. Gryce, in his slow, sarcastic way, "you recollect that principle of law, do you? If I remember rightly, you have not always been so punctilious in regarding it, or wishing to have it regarded, when the question was whether Mr. Clavering was the assassin or not."

"But he is a man. It does not seem so dreadful to accuse a man of a crime. But a woman! and such a woman! I cannot listen to it; it is horrible. Nothing short of absolute confession on her part will ever make me believe Mary Leavenworth, or any other woman, committed this deed. It was too cruel, too deliberate, too——"

"Read the criminal records," broke in Mr. Gryce.

But I was obstinate. "I do not care for the criminal records. All the criminal

125

records in the world would never make me believe Eleanore perpetrated this crime, nor will I be less generous towards her cousin Mary Leavenworth is a faulty woman, but not a guilty one."

"You are more lenient in your judgment of her than her cousin was, it appears."

"I do not understand you," I muttered, feeling a new and yet more fearful light breaking upon me.

"What! have you forgotten, in the hurry of these late events, the sentence of accusation which we overheard uttered between these ladies on the morning of the inquest?"

"No, but———"

"You believed it to have been spoken by Mary to Eleanore?"

"Of course; didn't you?"

Oh, the smile which crossed Mr. Gryce's face! "Scarcely. I left that baby-play for you. I thought one was enough to follow on that tack."

The light, the light that was breaking upon me! "And do you mean to say it was Eleanore who was speaking at that time? That I have been laboring all these weeks under a terrible mistake, and that you could have righted me with a word, and did not?"

"Well, as to that, I had a purpose in letting you follow your own lead for a while. In the first place, I was not sure myself which spoke; though I had but little doubt about the matter. The voices are, as you must have noticed, very much alike, while the attitudes in which we found them upon entering were such as to be explainable equally by the supposition that Mary was in the act of launching a denunciation, or in that of repelling one. So that, while I did not hesitate myself as to the true explanation of the scene before me, I was pleased to find you accept a contrary one; as in this way both theories had a chance of being tested; as was right in a case of so much mystery. You accordingly took up the affair with one idea for your starting-point, and I with another. You saw every fact as it developed through the medium of Mary's belief in Eleanore's guilt, and I through the opposite. And what has been the result? With you, doubt, contradiction, constant unsettlement, and unwarranted resorts to strange sources for reconcilement between appearances and your own convictions; with me, growing assurance, and a belief which each and every development so far has but served to strengthen and make more probable."

Again that wild panorama of events, looks, and words swept before me. Mary's reiterated assertions of her cousin's innocence, Eleanore's attitude of lofty silence in regard to certain matters which might be considered by her as pointing towards the murderer.

"Your theory must be the correct one," I finally admitted; "it was undoubtedly Eleanore who spoke. She believes in Mary's guilt, and I have been blind, indeed, not to have seen it from the first."

"If Eleanore Leavenworth believes in her cousin's criminality, she must have some good reasons for doing so."

I was obliged to admit that too. "She did not conceal in her bosom that telltale key,—found who knows where?—and destroy, or seek to destroy, it and the letter

126

which introduced her cousin to the public as the unprincipled destroyer of a trusting man's peace, for nothing."

"No, no."

"And yet you, a stranger, a young man who have never seen Mary Leavenworth in any other light than that in which her coquettish nature sought to display itself, presume to say she is innocent, in the face of the attitude maintained from the first by her cousin!"

"But," said I, in my great unwillingness to accept his conclusions, "Eleanore Leavenworth is but mortal. She may have been mistaken in her inferences. She has never stated what her suspicion was founded upon; nor can we know what basis she has for maintaining the attitude you speak of. Clavering is as likely as Mary to be the assassin, for all we know, and possibly for all she knows."

"You seem to be almost superstitious in your belief in Clavering's guilt."

I recoiled. Was I? Could it be that Mr. Harwell's fanciful conviction in regard to this man had in any way influenced me to the detriment of my better judgment?

"And you may be right," Mr. Gryce went on. "I do not pretend to be set in my notions. Future investigation may succeed in fixing something upon him; though I hardly think it likely. His behavior as the secret husband of a woman possessing motives for the commission of a crime has been too consistent throughout."

"All except his leaving her."

"No exception at all; for he hasn't left her."

"What do you mean?"

"I mean that, instead of leaving the country, Mr. Clavering has only made pretence of doing so. That, in place of dragging himself off to Europe at her command, he has only changed his lodgings, and can now be found, not only in a house opposite to hers, but in the window of that house, where he sits day after day watching who goes in and out of her front door."

I remembered his parting injunction to me, in that memorable interview we had in my office, and saw myself compelled to put a new construction upon it.

"But I was assured at the Hoffman House that he had sailed for Europe, and myself saw the man who professes to have driven him to the steamer."

"Just so."

"And Mr. Clavering returned to the city after that?"

"In another carriage, and to another house."

"And you tell me that man is all right?"

"No; I only say there isn't the shadow of evidence against him as the person who shot Mr. Leavenworth."

Rising, I paced the floor, and for a few minutes silence fell between us. But the clock, striking, recalled me to the necessity of the hour, and, turning, I asked Mr. Gryce what he proposed to do now.

"There is but one thing I can do," said he.

"And that is?"

"To go upon such lights as I have, and cause the arrest of Miss Leavenworth."

I had by this time schooled myself to endurance, and was able to hear this without uttering an exclamation. But I could not let it pass without making one

127

effort to combat his determination.

"But," said I, "I do not see what evidence you have, positive enough in its character, to warrant extreme measures. You have yourself intimated that the existence of motive is not enough, even though taken with the fact of the suspected party being in the house at the time of the murder; and what more have you to urge against Miss Leavenworth?"

"Pardon me. I said 'Miss Leavenworth'; I should have said 'Eleanore Leavenworth.'"

"Eleanore? What! when you and all unite in thinking that she alone of all these parties to the crime is utterly guiltless of wrong?"

"And yet who is the only one against whom positive testimony of any kind can be brought."

I could but acknowledge that.

"Mr. Raymond," he remarked very gravely; "the public is becoming clamorous; something must be done to satisfy it, if only for the moment. Eleanore has laid herself open to the suspicion of the police, and must take the consequences of her action. I am sorry; she is a noble creature; I admire her; but justice is justice, and though I think her innocent, I shall be forced to put her under arrest unless———"

"But I cannot be reconciled to it. It is doing an irretrievable injury to one whose only fault is an undue and mistaken devotion to an unworthy cousin. If Mary is the———."

"Unless something occurs between now and tomorrow morning," Mr. Gryce went on, as if I had not spoken.

"To-morrow morning?"

"Yes."

I tried to realize it; tried to face the fact that all my efforts had been for nothing, and failed.

"Will you not grant me one more day?" I asked in my desperation.

"What to do?"

Alas, I did not know. "To confront Mr. Clavering, and force from him the truth."

"To make a mess of the whole affair!" he growled. "No, sir; the die is cast. Eleanore Leavenworth knows the one point which fixes this crime upon her cousin, and she must tell us that point or suffer the consequences of her refusal."

I made one more effort.

"But why to-morrow? Having exhausted so much time already in our inquiries, why not take a little more; especially as the trail is constantly growing warmer? A little more moleing———"

"A little more folderol!" exclaimed Mr. Gryce, losing his temper. "No, sir; the hour for moleing has passed; something decisive has got to be done now; though, to be sure, if I could find the one missing link I want———"

"Missing link? What is that?"

"The immediate motive of the tragedy; a bit of proof that Mr. Leavenworth threatened his niece with his displeasure, or Mr. Clavering with his revenge, would

128

place me on the vantage-point at once; no arresting of Eleanore then! No, my lady! I would walk right into your own gilded parlors, and when you asked me if I had found the murderer yet, say 'yes,' and show you a bit of paper which would surprise you! But missing links are not so easily found. This has been moled for, and moled for, as you are pleased to call our system of investigation, and totally without result. Nothing but the confession of some one of these several parties to the crime will give us what we want. I will tell you what I will do," he suddenly cried. "Miss Leavenworth has desired me to report to her; she is very anxious for the detection of the murderer, you know, and offers an immense reward. Well, I will gratify this desire of hers. The suspicions I have, together with my reasons for them, will make an interesting disclosure. I should not greatly wonder if they produced an equally interesting confession."

I could only jump to my feet in my horror.

"At all events, I propose to try it. Eleanore is worth that much risk any way."

"It will do no good," said I. "If Mary is guilty, she will never confess it. If not ____"

"She will tell us who is."

"Not if it is Clavering, her husband."

"Yes; even if it is Clavering, her husband. She has not the devotion of Eleanore."

That I could but acknowledge. She would hide no keys for the sake of shielding another: no, if Mary were accused, she would speak. The future opening before us looked sombre enough. And yet when, in a short time from that, I found myself alone in a busy street, the thought that Eleanore was free rose above all others, filling and moving me till my walk home in the rain that day has become a marked memory of my life. It was only with nightfall that I began to realize the truly critical position in which Mary stood if Mr. Gryce's theory was correct. But, once seized with this thought, nothing could drive it from my mind. Shrink as I would, it was ever before me, haunting me with the direst forebodings. Nor, though I retired early, could I succeed in getting either sleep or rest. All night I tossed on my pillow, saying over to myself with dreary iteration: "Something must happen, something will happen, to prevent Mr. Gryce doing this dreadful thing." Then I would start up and ask what could happen; and my mind would run over various contingencies, such as,—Mr. Clavering might confess; Hannah might come back; Mary herself wake up to her position and speak the word I had more than once seen trembling on her lips. But further thought showed me how unlikely any of these things were to happen, and it was with a brain utterly exhausted that I fell asleep in the early dawn, to dream I saw Mary standing above Mr. Gryce with a pistol in her hand. I was awakened from this pleasing vision by a heavy knock at the door. Hastily rising, I asked who was there. The answer came in the shape of an envelope thrust under the door. Raising it, I found it to be a note. It was from Mr. Gryce, and ran thus:

"Come at once; Hannah Chester is found."

"Hannah found?"

"So we have reason to think."

129

"When? where? by whom?"

"Sit down, and I will tell you."

Drawing up a chair in a flurry of hope and fear, I sat down by Mr. Gryce's side.

"She is not in the cupboard," that person dryly assured me, noting without doubt how my eyes went travelling about the room in my anxiety and impatience. "We are not absolutely sure that she is anywhere. But word has come to us that a girl's face believed to be Hannah's has been seen at the upper window of a certain house in—don't start—R——, where a year ago she was in the habit of visiting while at the hotel with the Misses Leavenworth. Now, as it has already been determined that she left New York the night of the murder, by the —— —— Railroad, though for what point we have been unable to ascertain, we consider the matter worth inquiring into."

"But—"

"If she is there," resumed Mr. Gryce, "she is secreted; kept very close. No one except the informant has ever seen her, nor is there any suspicion among the neighbors of her being in town."

"Hannah secreted at a certain house in R——? Whose house?"

Mr. Gryce honored me with one of his grimmest smiles. "The name of the lady she's with is given in the communication as Belden; Mrs. Amy Belden."

"Amy Belden! the name found written on a torn envelope by Mr. Clavering's servant girl in London?"

"Yes."

I made no attempt to conceal my satisfaction. "Then we are upon the verge of some discovery; Providence has interfered, and Eleanore will be saved! But when did you get this word?"

"Last night, or rather this morning; Q brought it."

"It was a message, then, to Q?"

"Yes, the result of his moleings while in R——, I suppose."

"Whom was it signed by?"

"A respectable tinsmith who lives next door to Mrs. B."

"And is this the first you knew of an Amy Belden living in R——?"

"Yes."

"Widow or wife?"

"Don't know; don't know anything about her but her name."

"But you have already sent Q to make inquiries?"

"No; the affair is a little too serious for him to manage alone. He is not equal to great occasions, and might fail just for the lack of a keen mind to direct him."

"In short——"

"I wish you to go. Since I cannot be there myself, I know of no one else sufficiently up in the affair to conduct it to a successful issue. You see, it is not enough to find and identify the girl. The present condition of things demands that the arrest of so important a witness should be kept secret. Now, for a man to walk into a strange house in a distant village, find a girl who is secreted there, frighten her, cajole her, force her, as the case may be, from her hiding-place to a detective's office in New York, and all without the knowledge of the next-door

130

neighbor, if possible, requires judgment, brains, genius. Then the woman who conceals her! She must have her reasons for doing so; and they must be known. Altogether, the affair is a delicate one. Do you think you can manage it?"

"I should at least like to try."

Mr. Gryce settled himself on the sofa. "To think what pleasure I am losing on your account!" he grumbled, gazing reproachfully at his helpless limbs. "But to business. How soon can you start?"

"Immediately."

"Good! a train leaves the depot at 12.15. Take that. Once in R——, it will be for you to decide upon the means of making Mrs. Belden's acquaintance without arousing her suspicions. Q, who will follow you, will hold himself in readiness to render you any assistance you may require. Only this thing is to be understood: as he will doubtless go in disguise, you are not to recognize him, much less interfere with him and his plans, till he gives you leave to do so, by some preconcerted signal. You are to work in your way, and he in his, till circumstances seem to call for mutual support and countenance. I cannot even say whether you will see him or not; he may find it necessary to keep out of the way; but you may be sure of one thing, that he will know where you are, and that the display of, well, let us say a red silk handkerchief—have you such a thing?"

"I will get one."

"Will be regarded by him as a sign that you desire his presence or assistance, whether it be shown about your person or at the window of your room."

"And these are all the instructions you can give me?" I said, as he paused.

"Yes, I don't know of anything else. You must depend largely upon your own discretion, and the exigencies of the moment. I cannot tell you now what to do. Your own wit will be the best guide. Only, if possible, let me either hear from you or see you by to-morrow at this time."

And he handed me a cipher in case I should wish to telegraph.

BOOK III. HANNAH

XXVII. AMY BELDEN

"A merrier man
Within the limits of becoming mirth,
I never spent an hour's talk withal."
—Love's Labour's Last.

I HAD a client in R—— by the name of Monell; and it was from him I had planned to learn the best way of approaching Mrs. Belden. When, therefore, I was so fortunate as to meet him, almost on my arrival, driving on the long road behind his famous trotter Alfred, I regarded the encounter as a most auspicious beginning of a very doubtful enterprise.

131

"Well, and how goes the day?" was his exclamation as, the first greetings passed, we drove rapidly into town.

"Your part in it goes pretty smoothly," I returned; and thinking I could never hope to win his attention to my own affairs till I had satisfied him in regard to his, I told him all I could concerning the law-suit then pending; a subject so prolific of question and answer, that we had driven twice round the town before he remembered he had a letter to post. As it was an important one, admitting of no delay, we hasted at once to the post-office, where he went in, leaving me outside to watch the rather meagre stream of goers and comers who at that time of day make the post-office of a country town their place of rendezvous. Among these, for some reason, I especially noted one middle-aged woman; why, I cannot say; her appearance was anything but remarkable. And yet when she came out, with two letters in her hand, one in a large and one in a small envelope, and meeting my eye hastily drew them under her shawl, I found myself wondering what was in her letters and who she could be, that the casual glance of a stranger should unconsciously move her to an action so suspicious. But Mr. Monell's reappearance at the same moment, diverted my attention, and in the interest of the conversation that followed, I soon forgot both the woman and her letters. For determined that he should have no opportunity to revert to that endless topic, a law case, I exclaimed with the first crack of the whip,--"There, I knew there was something I wanted to ask you. It is this: Are you acquainted with any one is this town by the name of Belden?" "There is a widow Belden in town; I don't know of any other." "Is her first name Amy?" "Yes, Mrs. Amy Belden." "That is the one," said I. "Who is she, what is she, and what is the extent of your acquaintance with her?" "Well," said he, " I cannot conceive why you should be interested in such an antiquated piece of commonplace goodness as she is, but seeing you ask, I have no objection to telling you that she is the very respectable relict of a deceased cabinetmaker of this town; that she lives in a little house down the street there, and that if you have any forlorn old tramp to be lodged over night, or any destitute family of little ones to be looked after, she is the one to go to. As to knowing her, I know her as I do a dozen other members of our church there up over the hill. When I see her I speak to her, and that is all." "A respectable widow, you say. Any family?" "No; lives alone, has a little income, I believe; must have, to put the money on the plate she always does; but spends her time in plain sewing and such deeds of charity, as one with small means but willing heart can find the opportunity of doing in a town like this. But why in the name of wonders do you ask?" "Business," said I, "business. Mrs. Belden--don't mention it by the way--has got mixed up in a case of mine, and I felt it due to my curiosity if not to my purse, to find out something about her. And I am not satisfied yet. The fact is I would give something, Monell, for the opportunity of studying this woman's character. Now couldn't you manage to get me introduced into her house in some way that would make it possible and proper for me to converse with her at my leisure? Business would thank you if you could." "Well, I don't know; I suppose it could be done. She used to take lodgers in the summer when the hotel was full, and might be induced to give a bed to a friend of mine who is very anxious to be near the post-office on account of a business telegram he is expecting, and which when it comes will demand his immediate attention." And Mr. Monell gave me a sly wink of his eye, little imagining how near the mark he had struck.

"You need not say that. Tell her I have a peculiar dislike to sleeping in a public house, and that you know of no one better fitted to accommodate me, for the short time I desire to be in town, than herself."

"And what will be said of my hospitality in allowing you under these circumstances to remain in any other house than my own?"

"I don't know; very hard things, no doubt; but I guess your hospitality can stand it."

"Well, if you persist, we will see what can be done." And driving up to a neat white cottage of homely, but sufficiently attractive appearance, he stopped.

"This is her house," said he, jumping to the ground; "let's go in and see what we can do."

Glancing up at the windows, which were all closed save the two on the veranda overlooking the street, I thought to myself, "If she has anybody in hiding here, whose presence in the house she desires to keep secret, it is folly to hope she will take me in, however well recommended I may come." But, yielding to the example of my friend, I alighted in my turn and followed him up the short, grass-bordered walk to the front door.

"As she has no servant, she will come to the door herself, so be ready," he remarked as he knocked.

I had barely time to observe that the curtains to the window at my left suddenly dropped, when a hasty step made itself heard within, and a quick hand drew open the door; and I saw before me the woman whom I had observed at the post-office, and whose action with the letters had struck me as peculiar. I recognized her at first glance, though she was differently dressed, and had evidently passed through some worry or excitement that had altered the expression of her countenance, and made her manner what it was not at that time, strained and a trifle uncertain. But I saw no reason for thinking she remembered me. On the contrary, the look she directed towards me had nothing but inquiry in it, and when Mr. Monell pushed me forward with the remark, "A friend of mine; in fact my lawyer from New York," she dropped a hurried old-fashioned curtsey whose only expression was a manifest desire to appear sensible of the honor conferred upon her, through the mist of a certain trouble that confused everything about her.

"We have come to ask a favor, Mrs. Belden; but may we not come in? "said my client in a round, hearty voice well calculated to recall a person's thoughts into their proper channel. "I have heard many times of your cosy home, and am glad of this opportunity of seeing it." And with a blind disregard to the look of surprised resistance with which she met his advance, he stepped gallantly into the little room whose cheery red carpet and bright picture-hung walls showed invitingly through the half-open door at our left.

Finding her premises thus invaded by a sort of French *coup d'etat,* Mrs. Belden made the best of the situation, and pressing me to enter also, devoted herself to hospitality. As for Mr. Monell, he quite blossomed out in his endeavors to make himself agreeable; so much so, that I shortly found myself laughing at his sallies, though my heart was full of anxiety lest, after all, our efforts should fail of the success they certainly merited. Meanwhile, Mrs. Belden softened more and more, joining in the conversation with an ease hardly to be expected from one in her humble circumstances. Indeed, I soon saw she was no common woman. There was a refinement in her speech and manner, which, combined with her motherly presence and gentle air, was very pleasing. The last woman in the world to suspect of any underhanded proceeding, if she had not shown a peculiar hesitation when Mr. Monell broached the subject of my entertainment there.

"I don't know, sir; I would be glad, but," and she turned a very scrutinizing look upon me, "the fact is, I have not taken lodgers of late, and I have got out of the way of the whole thing, and am afraid I cannot make him comfortable. In short, you will have to excuse me."

"But we can't," returned Mr. Monell. "What, entice a fellow into a room like this"——and he cast a hearty admiring glance round the apartment which, for all its simplicity, both its warm coloring and general air of cosiness amply merited, "and then turn a cold shoulder upon him when he humbly entreats the honor of staying a single night in the enjoyment of its attractions? No, no, Mrs. Belden; I know you too well for that. Lazarus himself couldn't come to your door and be turned away; much less a good-hearted, clever-headed young gentleman like my friend here."

"You are very good," she began, an almost weak love of praise showing itself for a moment in her eyes; "but I have no room prepared. I have been house-cleaning, and everything is topsy-turvy Mrs. Wright, now, over the way——"

"My young friend is going to stop here," Mr. Mouell broke in, with frank positiveness. "If I cannot have him at my own house,——and for certain reasons it is not advisable,——I shall at least have the satisfaction of knowing he is in the charge of the best housekeeper in R——."

"Yes," I put in, but without too great a show of interest; "I should be sorry, once introduced here, to be obliged to go elsewhere."

The troubled eye wavered away from us to the door.

"I was never called inhospitable," she commenced; "but everything in such disorder. What time would you like to come?"

"I was in hopes I might remain now," I replied; "I have some letters to write, and ask nothing better than for leave to sit here and write them."

At the word letters I saw her hand go to her pocket in a movement which must have been involuntary, for her countenance did not change, and she made the quick reply:

"Well, you may. If you can put up with such poor accommodations as I can offer, it shall not be said I refused you what Mr. Monell is pleased to call a favor."

And, complete in her reception as she had been in her resistance, she gave us a pleasant smile, and, ignoring my thanks, bustled out with Mr. Monell to the buggy, where she received my bag and what was, doubtless, more to her taste, the compliments he was now more than ever ready to bestow upon her.

134

"I will see that a room is got ready for you in a very short space of time," she said, upon re-entering. "Meanwhile, make yourself at home here; and if you wish to write, why I think you will find everything for the purpose in these drawers." And wheeling up a table to the easy chair in which I sat, she pointed to the small compartments beneath, with an air of such manifest desire to have me make use of anything and everything she had, that I found myself wondering over my position with a sort of startled embarrassment that was not remote from shame.

"Thank you; I have materials of my own," said I, and hastened to open my bag and bring out the writing-case, which I always carried with me.

"Then I will leave you," said she; and with a quick bend and a short, hurried look out of the window, she hastily quitted the room.

I could hear her steps cross the hall, go up two or three stairs, pause, go up the rest of the flight, pause again, and then pass on. I was left on the first floor alone.

XXVIII. A WEIRD EXPERIENCE

"Flat burglary as ever was committed."
—Much Ado about Nothing.

THE first thing I did was to inspect with greater care the room in which I sat.

It was a pleasant apartment, as I have already said; square, sunny, and well furnished. On the floor was a crimson carpet, on the walls several pictures, at the windows, cheerful curtains of white, tastefully ornamented with ferns and autumn leaves; in one corner an old melodeon, and in the centre of the room a table draped with a bright cloth, on which were various little knick-knacks which, without being rich or expensive, were both pretty and, to a certain extent, ornamental. But it was not these things, which I had seen repeated in many other country homes, that especially attracted my attention, or drew me forward in the slow march which I now undertook around the room. It was the something underlying all these, the evidences which I found, or sought to find, not only in the general aspect of the room, but in each trivial object I encountered, of the character, disposition, and history of the woman with whom I now had to deal. It was for this reason I studied the daguerreotypes on the mantel-piece, the books on the shelf, and the music on the rack; for this and the still further purpose of noting if any indications were to be found of there being in the house any such person as Hannah.

First then, for the little library, which I was pleased to see occupied one corner of the room. Composed of a few well-chosen books, poetical, historical, and narrative, it was of itself sufficient to account for the evidences of latent culture observable in Mrs. Belden's conversation. Taking out a well-worn copy of *Byron*, I opened it. There were many passages marked, and replacing the book with a mental comment upon her evident impressibility to the softer emotions, I turned towards the melodeon fronting me from the opposite wall. It was closed, but on its neatly-covered top lay one or two hymn-books, a basket of russet apples, and a piece of half-completed knitting work.

135

I took up the latter, but was forced to lay it down again without a notion for what it was intended. Proceeding, I next stopped before a window opening upon the small yard that ran about the house, and separated it from the one adjoining. The scene without failed to attract me, but the window itself drew my attention, for, written with a diamond point on one of the panes, I perceived a row of letters which, as nearly as I could make out, were meant for some word or words, but which utterly failed in sense or apparent connection. Passing it by as the work of some school-girl, I glanced down at the work-basket standing on a table at my side. It was full of various kinds of work, among which I spied a pair of stockings, which were much too small, as well as in too great a state of disrepair, to belong to Mrs. Belden; and drawing them carefully out, I examined them for any name on them. Do not start when I say I saw the letter H plainly marked upon them. Thrusting them back, I drew a deep breath of relief, gazing, as I did so, out of the window, when those letters again attracted my attention.

What could they mean? Idly I began to read them backward, when—But try for yourself, reader, and judge of my surprise! Elate at the discovery thus made, I sat down to write my letters. I had barely finished them, when Mrs. Belden came in with the announcement that supper was ready. "As for your room," said she, "I have prepared my own room for your use, thinking you would like to remain on the first floor." And, throwing open a door at my side, she displayed a small, but comfortable room, in which I could dimly see a bed, an immense bureau, and a shadowy looking-glass in a dark, old-fashioned frame.

"I live in very primitive fashion," she resumed, leading the way into the dining-room; "but I mean to be comfortable and make others so."

"I should say you amply succeeded," I rejoined, with an appreciative glance at her well-spread board.

She smiled, and I felt I had paved the way to her good graces in a way that would yet redound to my advantage.

Shall I ever forget that supper! its dainties, its pleasant freedom, its mysterious, pervading atmosphere of unreality: and the constant sense which every bountiful dish she pressed upon me brought of the shame of eating this woman's food with such feelings of suspicion in my heart! Shall I ever forget the emotion I experienced when I first perceived she had something on her mind, which she longed, yet hesitated, to give utterance to! Or how she started when a cat jumped from the sloping roof of the kitchen on to the grass-plot at the back of the house; or how my heart throbbed when I heard, or thought I heard, a board creak overhead! We were in a long and narrow room which seemed, curiously enough, to run crosswise of the house, opening on one side into the parlor, and on the other into the small bedroom, which had been allotted to my use.

"You live in this house alone, without fear?" I asked, as Mrs. Belden, contrary to my desire, put another bit of cold chicken on my plate. "Have you no marauders in this town: no tramps, of whom a solitary woman like you might reasonably be afraid?"

"No one will hurt me," said she; "and no one ever came here for food or shelter but got it."

136

"I should think, then, that living as you do, upon a railroad, you would be constantly overrun with worthless beings whose only trade is to take all they can get without giving a return."

"I cannot turn them away. It is the only luxury I have: to feed the poor."

"But the idle, restless ones, who neither will work, nor let others work——"

"Are still the poor."

Mentally remarking, here is the woman to shield an unfortunate who has somehow become entangled in the meshes of a great crime, I drew back from the table. As I did so, the thought crossed me that, in case there was any such person in the house as Hannah, she would take the opportunity of going up-stairs with something for her to eat; and that she might not feel hampered by my presence, I stepped out on the veranda with my cigar.

While smoking it, I looked about for Q. I felt that the least token of his presence in town would be very encouraging at this time. But it seemed I was not to be afforded even that small satisfaction. If Q was anywhere near, he was lying very low.

Once again seated with Mrs. Belden (who I know came down-stairs with an empty plate, for going into the kitchen for a drink, I caught her in the act of setting it down on the table), I made up my mind to wait a reasonable length of time for what she had to say; and then, if she did not speak, make an endeavor on my own part to surprise her secret.

But her avowal was nearer and of a different nature from what I expected, and brought its own train of consequences with it.

"You are a lawyer, I believe," she began, taking down her knitting work, with a forced display of industry.

"Yes," I said; "that is my profession."

She remained for a moment silent, creating great havoc in her work I am sure, from the glance of surprise and vexation she afterwards threw it. Then, in a hesitating voice, remarked:

"Perhaps you may be willing, then, to give me some advice. The truth is, I am in a very curious predicament; one from which I don't know how to escape, and yet which demands immediate action. I should like to tell you about it; may I?"

"You may; I shall be only too happy to give you any advice in my power."

She drew in her breath with a sort of vague relief, though her forehead did not lose its frown.

"It can all be said in a few words. I have in my possession a package of papers which were intrusted to me by two ladies, with the understanding that I should neither return nor destroy them without the full cognizance and expressed desire of both parties, given in person or writing. That they were to remain in my hands till then, and that nothing or nobody should extort them from me."

"That is easily understood," said I; for she stopped.

"But, now comes word from one of the ladies, the one, too, most interested in the matter, that, for certain reasons, the immediate destruction of those papers is necessary to her peace and safety."

"And do you want to know what your duty is in this case?"

137

"Yes," she tremulously replied.

I rose. I could not help it: a flood of conjectures rushing in tumult over me.

"It is to hold on to the papers like grim death till released from your guardianship by the combined wish of both parties."

"Is that your opinion as a lawyer?"

"Yes, and as a man. Once pledged in that way, you have no choice. It would be a betrayal of trust to yield to the solicitations of one party what you have undertaken to return to both. The fact that grief or loss might follow your retention of these papers does not release you from your bond. You have nothing to do with that; besides, you are by no means sure that the representations of the so-called interested party are true. You might be doing a greater wrong, by destroying in this way, what is manifestly considered of value to them both, than by preserving the papers intact, according to compact."

"But the circumstances? Circumstances alter cases; and in short, it seems to me that the wishes of the one most interested ought to be regarded, especially as there is an estrangement between these ladies which may hinder the other's consent from ever being obtained."

"No," said I; "two wrongs never make a right; nor are we at liberty to do an act of justice at the expense of an injustice. The papers must be preserved, Mrs. Belden."

Her head sank very despondingly; evidently it had been her wish to please the interested party. "Law is very hard," she said; "very hard."

"This is not only law, but plain duty," I remarked. "Suppose a case different; suppose the honor and happiness of the other party depended upon the preservation of the papers; where would your duty be then?"

"But——"

"A contract is a contract," said I, "and cannot be tampered with. Having accepted the trust and given your word, you are obliged to fulfil, to the letter, all its conditions. It would be a breach of trust for you to return or destroy the papers without the mutual consent necessary."

An expression of great gloom settled slowly over her features. "I suppose you are right," said she, and became silent.

Watching her, I thought to myself, "If I were Mr. Gryce, or even Q, I would never leave this seat till I had probed this matter to the bottom, learned the names of the parties concerned, and where those precious papers are hidden, which she declares to be of so much importance." But being neither, I could only keep her talking upon the subject until she should let fall some word that might serve as a guide to my further enlightenment; I therefore turned, with the intention of asking her some question, when my attention was attracted by the figure of a woman coming out of the back-door of the neighboring house, who, for general dilapidation and uncouthness of bearing, was a perfect type of the style of tramp of whom we had been talking at the supper table. Gnawing a crust which she threw away as she reached the street, she trudged down the path, her scanty dress, piteous in its rags and soil, flapping in the keen spring wind, and revealing ragged shoes red with the mud of the highway.

138

"There is a customer that may interest you," said I.

Mrs. Belden seemed to awake from a trance. Rising slowly, she looked out, and with a rapidly softening gaze surveyed the forlorn creature before her.

"Poor thing!" she muttered; "but I cannot do much for her to-night. A good supper is all I can give her."

And, going to the front door, she bade her step round the house to the kitchen, where, in another moment, I heard the rough creature's voice rise in one long "Bless you!" that could only have been produced by the setting before her of the good things with which Mrs. Belden's larder seemed teeming.

But supper was not all she wanted. After a decent length of time, employed as I should judge in mastication, I heard her voice rise once more in a plea for shelter.

"The barn, ma'am, or the wood-house. Any place where I can lie out of the wind." And she commenced a long tale of want and disease, so piteous to hear that I was not at all surprised when Mrs. Belden told me, upon re-entering, that she had consented, notwithstanding her previous determination, to allow the woman to lie before the kitchen fire for the night.

"She has such an honest eye," said she; "and charity is my only luxury."

The interruption of this incident effectually broke up our conversation. Mrs. Belden went up-stairs, and for some time I was left alone to ponder over what I had heard, and determine upon my future course of action. I had just reached the conclusion that she would be fully as liable to be carried away by her feelings to the destruction of the papers in her charge, as to be governed by the rules of equity I had laid down to her, when I heard her stealthily descend the stairs and go out by the front door. Distrustful of her intentions, I took up my hat and hastily followed her. She was on her way down the main street, and my first thought was, that she was bound for some neighbor's house or perhaps for the hotel itself; but the settled swing into which she soon altered her restless pace satisfied me that she had some distant goal in prospect; and before long I found myself passing the hotel with its appurtenances, even the little schoolhouse, that was the last building at this end of the village, and stepping out into the country beyond. What could it mean?

But still her fluttering figure hasted on, the outlines of her form, with its close shawl and neat bonnet, growing fainter and fainter in the now settled darkness of an April night; and still I followed, walking on the turf at the side of the road lest she should hear my footsteps and look round. At last we reached a bridge. Over this I could hear her pass, and then every sound ceased. She had paused, and was evidently listening. It would not do for me to pause too, so gathering myself into as awkward a shape as possible, I sauntered by her down the road, but arrived at a certain point, stopped, and began retracing my steps with a sharp lookout for her advancing figure, till I had arrived once more at the bridge. She was not there.

Convinced now that she had discovered my motive for being in her house and, by leading me from it, had undertaken to supply Hannah with an opportunity for escape, I was about to hasten back to the charge I had so incautiously left, when a strange sound heard at my left arrested me. It came from the banks of the puny stream which ran under the bridge, and was like the creaking of an old door on worn-out hinges.

Leaping the fence, I made my way as best I could down the sloping field in the direction from which the sound came. It was quite dark, and my progress was slow; so much so, that I began to fear I had ventured upon a wild-goose chase, when an unexpected streak of lightning shot across the sky, and by its glare I saw before me what seemed, in the momentary glimpse I had of it, an old barn. From the rush of waters near at hand, I judged it to be somewhere on the edge of the stream, and consequently hesitated to advance, when I heard the sound of heavy breathing near me, followed by a stir as of some one feeling his way over a pile of loose boards; and presently, while I stood there, a faint blue light flashed up from the interior of the barn, and I saw, through the tumbled-down door that faced me, the form of Mrs. Belden standing with a lighted match in her hand, gazing round on the four walls that encompassed her. Hardly daring to breathe, lest I should alarm her, I watched her while she turned and peered at the roof above her, which was so old as to be more than half open to the sky, at the flooring beneath, which was in a state of equal dilapidation, and finally at a small tin box which she drew from under her shawl and laid on the ground at her feet. The sight of that box at once satisfied me as to the nature of her errand. She was going to hide what she dared not destroy; and, relieved upon this point, I was about to take a step forward when the match went out in her hand. While she was engaged in lighting another, I considered that perhaps it would be better for me not to arouse her apprehensions by accosting her at this time, and thus endanger the success of my main scheme; but to wait till she was gone, before I endeavored to secure the box. Accordingly I edged my way up to the side of the barn and waited till she should leave it, knowing that if I attempted to peer in at the door, I ran great risk of being seen, owing to the frequent streaks of lightning which now flashed about us on every side. Minute after minute went by, with its weird alternations of heavy darkness and sudden glare; and still she did not come. At last, just as I was about to start impatiently from my hiding-place, she reappeared, and began to withdraw with faltering steps toward the bridge. When I thought her quite out of hearing, I stole from my retreat and entered the barn. It was of course as dark as Erebus, but thanks to being a smoker I was as well provided with matches as she had been, and having struck one, I held it up; but the light it gave was very feeble, and as I did not know just where to look, it went out before I had obtained more than a cursory glimpse of the spot where I was. I thereupon lit another; but though I confined my attention to one place, namely, the floor at my feet, it too went out before I could conjecture by means of any sign seen there where she had hidden the box. I now for the first time realized the difficulty before me. She had probably made up her mind, before she left home, in just what portion of this old barn she would conceal her treasure; but I had nothing to guide me: I could only waste matches. And I did waste them. A dozen had been lit and extinguished before I was so much as sure the box was not under a pile of debris that lay in one corner, and I had taken the last in my hand before I became aware that one of the broken boards of the floor was pushed a little out of its proper position. One match! and that board was to be raised, the space beneath examined, and the box, if there, lifted safely out. I concluded not to waste my resources, so kneeling down in the darkness, I groped for the board, tried it, and found it to be loose. Wrenching at it with all my strength, I tore it free and cast it aside; then lighting my match looked into the hole thus made. Something, I could not tell what, stone or box, met my eye, but while I reached for it, the match flew out of my hand. Deploring my carelessness, but determined at all hazards to secure what I had seen, I dived down deep into the hole, and in another moment had the object of my curiosity in my hands. It was the box!

Satisfied at this result of my efforts, I turned to depart, my one wish now being to arrive home before Mrs. Belden. Was this possible? She had several minutes the start of me; I would have to pass her on the road, and in so doing might be recognized. Was the end worth the risk? I decided that it was.

Regaining the highway, I started at a brisk pace. For some little distance I kept it up, neither overtaking nor meeting any one. But suddenly, at a turn in the road, I came unexpectedly upon Mrs. Belden, standing in the middle of the path, looking back. Somewhat disconcerted, I hastened swiftly by her, expecting her to make some effort to stop me. But she let me pass without a word. Indeed, I doubt now if she even saw or heard me. Astonished at this treatment, and still more surprised that she made no attempt to follow me, I looked back, when I saw what enchained her to the spot, and made her so unmindful of my presence. The barn behind us was on fire!

Instantly I realized it was the work of my hands; I had dropped a half-extinguished match, and it had fallen upon some inflammable substance.

Aghast at the sight, I paused in my turn, and stood staring. Higher and higher the red flames mounted, brighter and brighter glowed the clouds above, the stream beneath; and in the fascination of watching it all, I forgot Mrs. Belden. But a short, agitated gasp in my vicinity soon recalled her presence to my mind, and drawing nearer, I heard her exclaim like a person speaking in a dream, "Well, I didn't mean to do it"; then lower, and with a certain satisfaction in her tone, "But it's all right, any way; the thing is lost now for good, and Mary will be satisfied without any one being to blame."

I did not linger to hear more; if this was the conclusion she had come to, she would not wait there long, especially as the sound of distant shouts and running feet announced that a crowd of village boys was on its way to the scene of the conflagration.

The first thing I did, upon my arrival at the house, was to assure myself that no evil effects had followed my inconsiderate desertion of it to the mercies of the tramp she had taken in; the next to retire to my room, and take a peep at the box. I found it to be a neat tin coffer, fastened with a lock. Satisfied from its weight that it contained nothing heavier than the papers of which Mrs. Belden had spoken, I hid it under the bed and returned to the sitting-room. I had barely taken a seat and lifted a book when Mrs. Belden came in.

"Well!" cried she, taking off her bonnet and revealing a face much flushed with exercise, but greatly relieved in expression; "this *is* a night! It lightens, and there is a fire somewhere down street, and altogether it is perfectly dreadful out. I hope

141

you have not been lonesome," she continued, with a keen searching of my face which I bore in the best way I could. "I had an errand to attend to, but didn't expect to stay so long."

I returned some nonchalant reply, and she hastened from the room to fasten up the house.

I waited, but she did not come back; fearful, perhaps, of betraying herself, she had retired to her own apartment, leaving me to take care of myself as best I might. I own that I was rather relieved at this. The fact is, I did not feel equal to any more excitement that night, and was glad to put off further action until the next day. As soon, then, as the storm was over, I myself went to bed, and, after several ineffectual efforts, succeeded in getting asleep.

XXIX. THE MISSING WITNESS

"I fled and cried out death."

—Milton.

"MR. RAYMOND!"

The voice was low and searching; it reached me in my dreams, waked me, and caused me to look up. Morning had begun to break, and by its light I saw, standing in the open door leading into the dining-room, the forlorn figure of the tramp who had been admitted into the house the night before. Angry and perplexed, I was about to bid her be gone, when, to my great surprise, she pulled out a red handkerchief from her pocket, and I recognized Q.

"Read that," said he, hastily advancing and putting a slip of paper into my hand. And, without another word or look, left the room, closing the door behind him.

Rising in considerable agitation, I took it to the window, and by the rapidly increasing light, succeeded in making out the rudely scrawled lines as follows:

"She is here; I have seen her; in the room marked with a cross in the accompanying plan. Wait till eight o'clock, then go up. I will contrive some means of getting Mrs. B—— out of the house."

Sketched below this was the following plan of the upper floor:

Hannah, then, was in the small back room over the dining-room, and I had not been deceived in thinking I had heard steps overhead, the evening before. Greatly relieved, and yet at the same time much moved at the near prospect of being brought face to face with one who we had every reason to believe was acquainted with the dreadful secret involved in the Leavenworth murder, I lay down once more, and endeavored to catch another hour's rest. But I soon gave up the effort in despair, and contented myself with listening to the sounds of awakening life which now began to make themselves heard in the house and neighborhood.

As Q had closed the door after him, I could only faintly hear Mrs. Belden when she came down-stairs. But the short, surprised exclamation which she uttered upon reaching the kitchen and finding the tramp gone and the back-door wide open, came plainly enough to my ears, and for a moment I was not sure but that Q had made a mistake in thus leaving so unceremoniously. But he had not studied

142

Mrs. Belden's character in vain. As she came, in the course of her preparations for breakfast, into the room adjoining mine, I could hear her murmur to herself:

"Poor thing! She has lived so long in the fields and at the roadside, she finds it unnatural to be cooped up in the house all night."

The trial of that breakfast! The effort to eat and appear unconcerned, to chat and make no mistake,—may I never be called upon to go through such another! But at last it was over, and I was left free to await in my own room the time for the dreaded though much-to-be-desired interview. Slowly the minutes passed; eight o'clock struck, when, just as the last vibration ceased, there came a loud knock at the backdoor, and a little boy burst into the kitchen, crying at the top of his voice: "Papa's got a fit! Oh, Mrs. Belden! papa's got a fit; do come!"

Rising, as was natural, I hastened towards the kitchen, meeting Mrs. Belden's anxious face in the doorway.

"A poor wood-chopper down the street has fallen in a fit," she said. "Will you please watch over the house while I see what I can do for him? I won't be absent any longer than I can help."

And almost without waiting for my reply, she caught up a shawl, threw it over her head, and followed the urchin, who was in a state of great excitement, out into the street.

Instantly the silence of death seemed to fill the house, and a dread the greatest I had ever experienced settled upon me. To leave the kitchen, go up those stairs, and confront that girl seemed for the moment beyond my power; but, once on the stair, I found myself relieved from the especial dread which had overwhelmed me, and possessed, instead, of a sort of combative curiosity that led me to throw open the door which I saw at the top with a certain fierceness new to my nature, and not altogether suitable, perhaps, to the occasion.

I found myself in a large bedroom, evidently the one occupied by Mrs. Belden the night before. Barely stopping to note certain evidences of her having passed a restless night, I passed on to the door leading into the room marked with a cross in the plan drawn for me by Q. It was a rough affair, made of pine boards rudely painted. Pausing before it, I listened. All was still. Raising the latch, I endeavored to enter. The door was locked. Pausing again, I bent my ear to the keyhole. Not a sound came from within; the grave itself could not have been stiller. Awe-struck and irresolute, I looked about me and questioned what I had best do. Suddenly I remembered that, in the plan Q had given me, I had seen intimation of another door leading into this same room from the one on the opposite side of the hall. Going hastily around to it, I tried it with my hand. But it was as fast as the other. Convinced at last that nothing was left me but force, I spoke for the first time, and, calling the girl by name, commanded her to open the door. Receiving no response, I said aloud with an accent of severity:

"Hannah Chester, you are discovered; if you do not open the door, we shall be obliged to break it down; save us the trouble, then, and open immediately."

Still no reply.

Going back a step, I threw my whole weight against the door. It creaked ominously, but still resisted.

143

Stopping only long enough to be sure no movement had taken place within, I pressed against it once more, this time with all my strength, when it flew from its hinges, and I fell forward into a room so stifling, chill, and dark that I paused for a moment to collect my scattered senses before venturing to look around me. It was well I did so. In another moment, the pallor and fixity of the pretty Irish face staring upon me from amidst the tumbled clothes of a bed, drawn up against the wall at my side, struck me with so deathlike a chill that, had it not been for that one instant of preparation, I should have been seriously dismayed. As it was, I could not prevent a feeling of sickly apprehension from seizing me as I turned towards the silent figure stretched so near, and observed with what marble-like repose it lay beneath the patchwork quilt drawn across it, asking myself if sleep could be indeed so like death in its appearance. For that it was a sleeping woman I beheld, I did not seriously doubt. There were too many evidences of careless life in the room for any other inference. The clothes, left just as she had stepped from them in a circle on the floor; the liberal plate of food placed in waiting for her on the chair by the door, —food amongst which I recognized, even in this casual glance, the same dish which we had had for breakfast —all and everything in the room spoke of robust life and reckless belief in the morrow.

And yet so white was the brow turned up to the bare beams of the unfinished wall above her, so glassy the look of the half-opened eyes, so motionless the arm lying half under, half over, the edge of the coverlid that it was impossible not to shrink from contact with a creature so sunk in unconsciousness. But contact seemed to be necessary; any cry which I could raise at that moment would be ineffectual enough to pierce those dull ears. Nerving myself, therefore, I stooped and lifted the hand which lay with its telltale scar mockingly uppermost, intending to speak, call, do something, anything, to arouse her. But at the first touch of her hand on mine an unspeakable horror thrilled me. It was not only icy cold, but stiff. Dropping it in my agitation, I started back and again surveyed the face. Great God! when did life ever look like that? What sleep ever wore such pallid hues, such accusing fixedness? Bending once more I listened at the lips. Not a breath, nor a stir. Shocked to the core of my being, I made one final effort. Tearing down the clothes, I laid my hand upon her heart. It was pulseless as stone.

XXX. BURNED PAPER

"I could have better spared a better man."
—Henry IV.

I DO not think I called immediately for help. The awful shock of this discovery, coming as it did at the very moment life and hope were strongest within me; the sudden downfall which it brought of all the plans based upon this woman's expected testimony; and, worst of all, the dread coincidence between this sudden death and the exigency in which the guilty party, whoever it was, was supposed to be at that hour were much too appalling for instant action. I could only stand and stare at the quiet face before me, smiling in its peaceful rest as if death were

144

pleasanter than we think, and marvel over the providence which had brought us renewed fear instead of relief, complication instead of enlightenment, disappointment instead of realization. For eloquent as is death, even on the faces of those unknown and unloved by us, the causes and consequences of this one were much too important to allow the mind to dwell upon the pathos of the scene itself. Hannah, the girl, was lost in Hannah the witness.

But gradually, as I gazed, the look of expectation which I perceived hovering about the wistful mouth and half-open lids attracted me, and I bent above her with a more personal interest, asking myself if she were quite dead, and whether or not immediate medical assistance would be of any avail. But the more closely I looked, the more certain I became that she had been dead for some hours; and the dismay occasioned by this thought, taken with the regrets which I must ever feel, that I had not adopted the bold course the evening before, and, by forcing my way to the hiding-place of this poor creature, interrupted, if not prevented the consummation of her fate, startled me into a realization of my present situation; and, leaving her side, I went into the next room, threw up the window, and fastened to the blind the red handkerchief which I had taken the precaution to bring with me.

Instantly a young man, whom I was fain to believe Q, though he bore not the least resemblance, either in dress or facial expression to any renderings of that youth which I had yet seen, emerged from the tinsmith's house, and approached the one I was in.

Observing him cast a hurried glance in my direction, I crossed the floor, and stood awaiting him at the head of the stairs.

"Well?" he whispered, upon entering the house and meeting my glance from below; "have you seen her?"

"Yes," I returned bitterly, "I have seen her!"

He hurriedly mounted to my side. "And she has confessed?"

"No; I have had no talk with her." Then, as I perceived him growing alarmed at my voice and manner, I drew him into Mrs. Belden's room and hastily inquired: "What did you mean this morning when you informed me you had seen this girl? that she was in a certain room where I might find her?"

"What I said."

"You have, then, been to her room?"

"No; I have only been on the outside of it. Seeing a light, I crawled up on to the ledge of the slanting roof last night while both you and Mrs. Belden were out, and, looking through the window, saw her moving round the room." He must have observed my countenance change, for he stopped. "What is to pay?" he cried.

I could restrain myself no longer. "Come," I said, "and see for yourself!" And, leading him to the little room I had just left, I pointed to the silent form lying within. "You told me I should find Hannah here; but you did not tell me I should find her in this condition."

"Great heaven!" he cried with a start: "not dead?"

"Yes," I said, "dead."

145

It seemed as if he could not realize it. "But it is impossible!" he returned. "She is in a heavy sleep, has taken a narcotic——"

"It is not sleep," I said, "or if it is, she will never wake. Look!" And, taking the hand once more in mine, I let it fall in its stone weight upon the bed.

The sight seemed to convince him. Calming down, he stood gazing at her with a very strange expression upon his face. Suddenly he moved and began quietly turning over the clothes that were lying on the floor.

"What are you doing?" I asked. "What are you looking for?"

"I am looking for the bit of paper from which I saw her take what I supposed to be a dose of medicine last night. Oh, here it is!" he cried, lifting a morsel of paper that, lying on the floor under the edge of the bed, had hitherto escaped his notice.

"Let me see!" I anxiously exclaimed.

He handed me the paper, on the inner surface of which I could dimly discern the traces of an impalpable white powder.

"This is important," I declared, carefully folding the paper together. "If there is enough of this powder remaining to show that the contents of this paper were poisonous, the manner and means of the girl's death are accounted for, and a case of deliberate suicide made evident."

"I am not so sure of that," he retorted. "If I am any judge of countenances, and I rather flatter myself I am, this girl had no more idea she was taking poison than I had. She looked not only bright but gay; and when she tipped up the paper, a smile of almost silly triumph crossed her face. If Mrs. Belden gave her that dose to take, telling her it was medicine——"

"That is something which yet remains to be learned; also whether the dose, as you call it, was poisonous or not. It may be she died of heart disease."

He simply shrugged his shoulders, and pointed first at the plate of breakfast left on the chair, and secondly at the broken-down door.

"Yes," I said, answering his look, "Mrs. Belden has been in here this morning, and Mrs. Belden locked the door when she went out; but that proves nothing beyond her belief in the girl's hearty condition."

"A belief which that white face on its tumbled pillow did not seem to shake?"

"Perhaps in her haste she may not have looked at the girl, but have set the dishes down without more than a casual glance in her direction?"

"I don't want to suspect anything wrong, but it is such a coincidence!"

This was touching me on a sore point, and I stepped back. "Well," said I, "there is no use in our standing here busying ourselves with conjectures. There is too much to be done. Come!" and I moved hurriedly towards the door.

"What are you going to do?" he asked. "Have you forgotten this is but an episode in the one great mystery we are sent here to unravel? If this girl has come to her death by some foul play, it is our business to find it out."

"That must be left for the coroner. It has now passed out of our hands."

"I know; but we can at least take full note of the room and everything in it before throwing the affair into the hands of strangers. Mr. Gryce will expect that much of us, I am sure."

146

"I have looked at the room. The whole is photographed on my mind. I am only afraid I can never forget it."

"And the body? Have you noticed its position? the lay of the bed-clothes around it? the lack there is of all signs of struggle or fear? the repose of the countenance? the easy fall of the hands?"

"Yes, yes; don't make me look at it any more."

"Then the clothes hanging on the wall?"—rapidly pointing out each object as he spoke. "Do you see? a calico dress, a shawl,—not the one in which she was believed to have run away, but an old black one, probably belonging to Mrs. Belden. Then this chest,"—opening it,—"containing a few underclothes marked, —let us see, ah, with the name of the lady of the house, but smaller than any she ever wore; made for Hannah, you observe, and marked with her own name to prevent suspicion. And then these other clothes lying on the floor, all new, all marked in the same way. Then this—Halloo! look here!" he suddenly cried.

Going over to where he stood I stooped down, when a wash-bowl half full of burned paper met my eye.

"I saw her bending over something in this corner, and could not think what it was. Can it be she is a suicide after all? She has evidently destroyed something here which she didn't wish any one to see."

"I do not know," I said. "I could almost hope so."

"Not a scrap, not a morsel left to show what it was; how unfortunate!"

"Mrs. Belden must solve this riddle," I cried.

"Mrs. Belden must solve the whole riddle," he replied; "the secret of the Leavenworth murder hangs upon it." Then, with a lingering look towards the mass of burned paper, "Who knows but what that was a confession?"

The conjecture seemed only too probable.

"Whatever it was," said I, "it is now ashes, and we have got to accept the fact and make the best of it."

"Yes," said he with a deep sigh; "that's so; but Mr. Gryce will never forgive me for it, never. He will say I ought to have known it was a suspicious circumstance for her to take a dose of medicine at the very moment detection stood at her back."

"But she did not know that; she did not see you."

"We don't know what she saw, nor what Mrs. Belden saw. Women are a mystery; and though I flatter myself that ordinarily I am a match for the keenest bit of female flesh that ever walked, I must say that in this case I feel myself thoroughly and shamefully worsted."

"Well, well," I said, "the end has not come yet; who knows what a talk with Mrs. Belden will bring out? And, by the way, she will be coming back soon, and I must be ready to meet her. Everything depends upon finding out, if I can, whether she is aware of this tragedy or not. It is just possible she knows nothing about it."

And, hurrying him from the room, I pulled the door to behind me, and led the way down-stairs.

"Now," said I, "there is one thing you must attend to at once. A telegram must be sent Mr. Gryce acquainting him with this unlooked-for occurrence."

147

"All right, sir," and Q started for the door.

"Wait one moment," said I. "I may not have another opportunity to mention it. Mrs. Belden received two letters from the postmaster yesterday; one in a large and one in a small envelope; if you could find out where they were postmarked———"

Q put his hand in his pocket. "I think I will not have to go far to find out where one of them came from. Good George, I have lost it!" And before I knew it, he had returned up-stairs.

That moment I heard the gate click.

XXXI. "THEREBY HANGS A TALE."
—Taming of the Shrew.

"IT was all a hoax; nobody was ill; I have been imposed upon, meanly imposed upon!" And Mrs. Belden, flushed and panting, entered the room where I was, and proceeded to take off her bonnet; but whilst doing so paused, and suddenly exclaimed: "What is the matter? How you look at me! Has anything happened?"

"Something very serious has occurred," I replied; "you have been gone but a little while, but in that time a discovery has been made—" I purposely paused here that the suspense might elicit from her some betrayal; but, though she turned pale, she manifested less emotion than I expected, and I went on—"which is likely to produce very important consequences."

To my surprise she burst violently into tears. "I knew it, I knew it!" she murmured. "I always said it would be impossible to keep it secret if I let anybody into the house; she is so restless. But I forget," she suddenly said, with a frightened look; "you haven't told me what the discovery was. Perhaps it isn't what I thought; perhaps———"

I did not hesitate to interrupt her. "Mrs. Belden," I said, "I shall not try to mitigate the blow. A woman who, in the face of the most urgent call from law and justice, can receive into her house and harbor there a witness of such importance as Hannah, cannot stand in need of any great preparation for hearing that her efforts, have been too successful, that she has accomplished her design of suppressing valuable testimony, that law and justice are outraged, and that the innocent woman whom this girl's evidence might have saved stands for ever compromised in the eyes of the world, if not in those of the officers of the law."

Her eyes, which had never left me during this address, flashed wide with dismay.

"What do you mean?" she cried. "I have intended no wrong; I have only tried to save people. I—I—But who are you? What have you got to do with all this? What is it to you what I do or don't do? You said you were a lawyer. Can it be you are come from Mary Leavenworth to see how I am fulfilling her commands, and ———"

"Mrs. Belden," I said, "it is of small importance now as to who I am, or for what purpose I am here. But that my words may have the more effect, I will say, that whereas I have not deceived you, either as to my name or position, it is true that I am the friend of the Misses Leavenworth, and that anything which is likely to affect them, is of interest to me. When, therefore, I say that Eleanore Leavenworth is irretrievably injured by this girl's death——"

"Death? What do you mean? Death!"

The burst was too natural, the tone too horror-stricken for me to doubt for another moment as to this woman's ignorance of the true state of affairs.

"Yes," I repeated, "the girl you have been hiding so long and so well is now beyond your control. Only her dead body remains, Mrs. Belden."

I shall never lose from my ears the shriek which she uttered, nor the wild, "I don't believe it! I don't believe it!" with which she dashed from the room and rushed up-stairs.

Nor that after-scene when, in the presence of the dead, she stood wringing her hands and protesting, amid sobs of the sincerest grief and terror, that she knew nothing of it; that she had left the girl in the best of spirits the night before; that it was true she had locked her in, but this she always did when any one was in the house; and that if she died of any sudden attack, it must have been quietly, for she had heard no stir all night, though she had listened more than once, being naturally anxious lest the girl should make some disturbance that would arouse me.

"But you were in here this morning?" said I.

"Yes; but I didn't notice. I was in a hurry, and thought she was asleep; so I set the things down where she could get them and came right away, locking the door as usual."

"It is strange she should have died this night of all others. Was she ill yesterday?"

"No, sir; she was even brighter than common; more lively. I never thought of her being sick then or ever. If I had——"

"You never thought of her being sick?" a voice here interrupted. "Why, then, did you take such pains to give her a dose of medicine last night?" And Q entered from the room beyond.

"I didn't!" she protested, evidently under the supposition it was I who had spoken. "Did I, Hannah, did I, poor girl?" stroking the hand that lay in hers with what appeared to be genuine sorrow and regret.

"How came she by it, then? Where she did she get it if you didn't give it to her?"

This time she seemed to be aware that some one besides myself was talking to her, for, hurriedly rising, she looked at the man with a wondering stare, before replying.

"I don't know who you are, sir; but I can tell you this, the girl had no medicine, —took no dose; she wasn't sick last night that I know of."

"Yet I saw her swallow a powder."

"Saw her!—the world is crazy, or I am—saw her swallow a powder! How could you see her do that or anything else? Hasn't she been shut up in this room for twenty-four hours?"

"Yes; but with a window like that in the roof, it isn't so very difficult to see into the room, madam."

"Oh," she cried, shrinking, "I have a spy in the house, have I? But I deserve it; I kept her imprisoned in four close walls, and never came to look at her once all night. I don't complain; but what was it you say you saw her take? medicine? poison?"

"I didn't say poison."

"But you meant it. You think she has poisoned herself, and that I had a hand in it!"

"No," I hastened to remark, "he does not think you had a hand in it. He says he saw the girl herself swallow something which he believes to have been the occasion of her death, and only asks you now where she obtained it."

"How can I tell? I never gave her anything; didn't know she had anything."

Somehow, I believed her, and so felt unwilling to prolong the present interview, especially as each moment delayed the action which I felt it incumbent upon us to take. So, motioning Q to depart upon his errand, I took Mrs. Belden by the hand and endeavored to lead her from the room. But she resisted, sitting down by the side of the bed with the expression, "I will not leave her again; do not ask it; here is my place, and here I will stay," while Q, obdurate for the first time, stood staring severely upon us both, and would not move, though I urged him again to make haste, saying that the morning was slipping away, and that the telegram to Mr. Gryce ought to be sent.

"Till that woman leaves the room, I don't; and unless you promise to take my place in watching her, I don't quit the house."

Astonished, I left her side and crossed to him.

"You carry your suspicions too far," I whispered, "and I think you are too rude. We have seen nothing, I am sure, to warrant us in any such action; besides, she can do no harm here; though, as for watching her, I promise to do that much if it will relieve your mind."

"I don't want her watched here; take her below. I cannot leave while she remains."

"Are you not assuming a trifle the master?"

"Perhaps; I don't know. If I am, it is because I have something in my possession which excuses my conduct."

"What is that? the letter?"

"Yes."

Agitated now in my turn, I held out my hand. "Let me see," I said.

"Not while that woman remains in the room."

Seeing him implacable, I returned to Mrs. Belden.

"I must entreat you to come with me," said I. "This is not a common death; we shall be obliged to have the coroner here and others. You had better leave the room and go below."

"I don't mind the coroner; he is a neighbor of mine; his coming won't prevent my watching over the poor girl until he arrives."

"Mrs. Belden," I said, "your position as the only one conscious of the presence of this girl in your house makes it wiser for you not to invite suspicion by lingering any longer than is necessary in the room where her dead body lies."

"As if my neglect of her now were the best surety of my good intentions

150

towards her in time past!"

"It will not be neglect for you to go below with me at my earnest request. You can do no good here by staying; will, in fact, be doing harm. So listen to me or I shall be obliged to leave you in charge of this man and go myself to inform the authorities."

This last argument seemed to affect her, for with one look of shuddering abhorrence at Q she rose, saying, "You have me in your power," and then, without another word, threw her handkerchief over the girl's face and left the room. In two minutes more I had the letter of which Q had spoken in my hands.

"It is the only one I could find, sir. It was in the pocket of the dress Mrs. Belden had on last night. The other must be lying around somewhere, but I haven't had time to find it. This will do, though, I think. You will not ask for the other."

Scarcely noticing at the time with what deep significance he spoke, I opened the letter. It was the smaller of the two I had seen her draw under her shawl the day before at the post-office, and read as follows:

"DEAR, DEAR FRIEND:

"I am in awful trouble. You who love me must know it. I cannot
explain, I can only make one prayer. Destroy what you have,
to-day, instantly, without question or hesitation. The consent
of any one else has nothing to do with it. You must obey. I am
lost if you refuse. Do then what I ask, and save

"ONE WHO LOVES YOU."

It was addressed to Mrs. Belden; there was no signature or date, only the postmark New York; but I knew the handwriting. It was Mary Leavenworth's.

"A damning letter!" came in the dry tones which Q seemed to think fit to adopt on this occasion. "And a damning bit of evidence against the one who wrote it, and the woman who received it!"

"A terrible piece of evidence, indeed," said I, "if I did not happen to know that this letter refers to the destruction of something radically different from what you suspect. It alludes to some papers in Mrs. Belden's charge; nothing else."

"Are you sure, sir?"

"Quite; but we will talk of this hereafter. It is time you sent your telegram, and went for the coroner."

"Very well, sir." And with this we parted; he to perform his role and I mine.

I found Mrs. Belden walking the floor below, bewailing her situation, and uttering wild sentences as to what the neighbors would say of her; what the minister would think; what Clara, whoever that was, would do, and how she wished she had died before ever she had meddled with the affair.

Succeeding in calming her after a while, I induced her to sit down and listen to what I had to say. "You will only injure yourself by this display of feeling," I remarked, "besides unfitting yourself for what you will presently be called upon to go through." And, laying myself out to comfort the unhappy woman, I first explained the necessities of the case, and next inquired if she had no friend upon

151

whom she could call in this emergency.

To my great surprise she replied no; that while she had kind neighbors and good friends, there was no one upon whom she could call in a case like this, either for assistance or sympathy, and that, unless I would take pity on her, she would have to meet it alone—"As I have met everything," she said, "from Mr. Belden's death to the loss of most of my little savings in a town fire last year."

I was touched by this,—that she who, in spite of her weakness and inconsistencies of character, possessed at least the one virtue of sympathy with her kind, should feel any lack of friends. Unhesitatingly, I offered to do what I could for her, providing she would treat me with the perfect frankness which the case demanded. To my great relief, she expressed not only her willingness, but her strong desire, to tell all she knew. "I have had enough secrecy for my whole life," she said. And indeed I do believe she was so thoroughly frightened, that if a police-officer had come into the house and asked her to reveal secrets compromising the good name of her own son, she would have done so without cavil or question. "I feel as if I wanted to take my stand out on the common, and, in the face of the whole world, declare what I have done for Mary Leavenworth. But first," she whispered, "tell me, for God's sake, how those girls are situated. I have not dared to ask or write. The papers say a good deal about Eleanore, but nothing about Mary; and yet Mary writes of her own peril only, and of the danger she would be in if certain facts were known. What is the truth? I don't want to injure them, only to take care of myself."

"Mrs. Belden," I said, "Eleanore Leavenworth has got into her present difficulty by not telling all that was required of her. Mary Leavenworth—but I cannot speak of her till I know what you have to divulge. Her position, as well as that of her cousin, is too anomalous for either you or me to discuss. What we want to learn from you is, how you became connected with this affair, and what it was that Hannah knew which caused her to leave New York and take refuge here."

But Mrs. Belden, clasping and unclasping her hands, met my gaze with one full of the most apprehensive doubt. "You will never believe me," she cried; "but I don't know what Hannah knew. I am in utter ignorance of what she saw or heard on that fatal night; she never told, and I never asked. She merely said that Miss Leavenworth wished me to secrete her for a short time; and I, because I loved Mary Leavenworth and admired her beyond any one I ever saw, weakly consented, and——"

"Do you mean to say," I interrupted, "that after you knew of the murder, you, at the mere expression of Miss Leavenworth's wishes, continued to keep this girl concealed without asking her any questions or demanding any explanations?"

"Yes, sir; you will never believe me, but it is so. I thought that, since Mary had sent her here, she must have her reasons; and—and—I cannot explain it now; it all looks so differently; but I did do as I have said."

"But that was very strange conduct. You must have had strong reason for obeying Mary Leavenworth so blindly."

"Oh, sir," she gasped, "I thought I understood it all; that Mary, the bright young creature, who had stooped from her lofty position to make use of me and to love

152

me, was in some way linked to the criminal, and that it would be better for me to remain in ignorance, do as I was bid, and trust all would come right. I did not reason about it; I only followed my impulse. I couldn't do otherwise; it isn't my nature. When I am requested to do anything for a person I love, I cannot refuse."

"And you love Mary Leavenworth; a woman whom you yourself seem to consider capable of a great crime?"

"Oh, I didn't say that; I don't know as I thought that. She might be in some way connected with it, without being the actual perpetrator. She could never be that; she is too dainty."

"Mrs. Belden," I said, "what do you know of Mary Leavenworth which makes even that supposition possible?"

The white face of the woman before me flushed. "I scarcely know what to reply," she cried. "It is a long story, and——"

"Never mind the long story," I interrupted. "Let me hear the one vital reason."

"Well," said she, "it is this; that Mary was in an emergency from which nothing but her uncle's death could release her."

"Ah, how's that?"

But here we were interrupted by the sound of steps on the porch, and, looking out, I saw Q entering the house alone. Leaving Mrs. Belden where she was, I stepped into the hall.

"Well," said I, "what is the matter? Haven't you found the coroner? Isn't he at home?"

"No, gone away; off in a buggy to look after a man that was found some ten miles from here, lying in a ditch beside a yoke of oxen." Then, as he saw my look of relief, for I was glad of this temporary delay, said, with an expressive wink: "It would take a fellow a long time to go to him—if he wasn't in a hurry—hours, I think."

"Indeed!" I returned, amused at his manner. "Rough road?"

"Very; no horse I could get could travel it faster than a walk."

"Well," said I, "so much the better for us. Mrs. Belden has a long story to tell, and——"

"Doesn't wish to be interrupted. I understand."

I nodded and he turned towards the door.

"Have you telegraphed Mr. Gryce?" I asked.

"Yes, sir."

"Do you think he will come?"

"Yes, sir; if he has to hobble on two sticks."

"At what time do you look for him?"

"*You* will look for him as early as three o'clock. I shall be among the mountains, ruefully eying my broken-down team." And leisurely donning his hat he strolled away down the street like one who has the whole day on his hands and does not know what to do with it.

An opportunity being thus given for Mrs. Belden's story, she at once composed herself to the task, with the following result.

153

XXXII. MRS. BELDEN'S NARRATIVE

"Cursed, destructive Avarice,
Thou everlasting foe to Love and Honor."
—Trap's Atram.

"Mischief never thrives
Without the help of Woman."
—The Same.

IT will be a year next July since I first saw Mary Leavenworth. I was living at that time a most monotonous existence. Loving what was beautiful, hating what was sordid, drawn by nature towards all that was romantic and uncommon, but doomed by my straitened position and the loneliness of my widowhood to spend my days in the weary round of plain sewing, I had begun to think that the shadow of a humdrum old age was settling down upon me, when one morning, in the full tide of my dissatisfaction, Mary Leavenworth stepped across the threshold of my door and, with one smile, changed the whole tenor of my life.

This may seem exaggeration to you, especially when I say that her errand was simply one of business, she having heard I was handy with my needle; but if you could have seen her as she appeared that day, marked the look with which she approached me, and the smile with which she left, you would pardon the folly of a romantic old woman, who beheld a fairy queen in this lovely young lady. The fact is, I was dazzled by her beauty and her charms. And when, a few days after, she came again, and crouching down on the stool at my feet, said she was so tired of the gossip and tumult down at the hotel, that it was a relief to run away and hide with some one who would let her act like the child she was, I experienced for the moment, I believe, the truest happiness of my life. Meeting her advances with all the warmth her manner invited, I found her ere long listening eagerly while I told her, almost without my own volition, the story of my past life, in the form of an amusing allegory.

The next day saw her in the same place; and the next; always with the eager, laughing eyes, and the fluttering, uneasy hands, that grasped everything they touched, and broke everything they grasped.

But the fourth day she was not there, nor the fifth, nor the sixth, and I was beginning to feel the old shadow settling back upon me, when one night, just as the dusk of twilight was merging into evening gloom, she came stealing in at the front door, and, creeping up to my side, put her hands over my eyes with such a low, ringing laugh, that I started.

"You don't know what to make of me!" she cried, throwing aside her cloak, and revealing herself in the full splendor of evening attire. "I don't know what to make of myself. Though it seems folly, I felt that I must run away and tell some one that a certain pair of eyes have been looking into mine, and that for the first time in my life I feel myself a woman as well as a queen." And with a glance in which coyness struggled with pride, she gathered up her cloak around her, and

154

laughingly cried:

"Have you had a visit from a flying sprite? Has one little ray of moonlight found its way into your prison for a wee moment, with Mary's laugh and Mary's snowy silk and flashing diamonds? Say!" and she patted my cheek, and smiled so bewilderingly, that even now, with all the dull horror of these after-events crowding upon me, I cannot but feel something like tears spring to my eyes at the thought of it.

"And so the Prince has come for you?" I whispered, alluding to a story I had told her the last time she had visited me; a story in which a girl, who had waited all her life in rags and degradation for the lordly knight who was to raise her from a hovel to a throne, died just as her one lover, an honest peasant-lad whom she had discarded in her pride, arrived at her door with the fortune he had spent all his days in amassing for her sake.

But at this she flushed, and drew back towards the door. "I don't know; I am afraid not. I—I don't think anything about that. Princes are not so easily won," she murmured.

"What! are you going?" I said, "and alone? Let me accompany you."

But she only shook her fairy head, and replied: "No, no; that would be spoiling the romance, indeed. I have come upon you like a sprite, and like a sprite I will go." And, flashing like the moonbeam she was, she glided out into the night, and floated away down the street.

When she next came, I observed a feverish excitement in her manner, which assured me, even plainer than the coy sweetness displayed in our last interview, that her heart had been touched by her lover's attentions. Indeed, she hinted as much before she left, saying in a melancholy tone, when I had ended my story in the usual happy way, with kisses and marriage, "I shall never marry!" finishing the exclamation with a long-drawn sigh, that somehow emboldened me to say, perhaps because I knew she had no mother:

"And why? What reason can there be for such rosy lips saying their possessor will never marry?"

She gave me one quick look, and then dropped her eyes. I feared I had offended her, and was feeling very humble, when she suddenly replied, in an even but low tone, "I said I should never marry, because the one man who pleases me can never be my husband."

All the hidden romance in my nature started at once into life. "Why not? What do you mean? Tell me."

"There is nothing to tell," said she; "only I have been so weak as to"—she would not say, fall in love, she was a proud woman—"admire a man whom my uncle will never allow me to marry."

And she rose as if to go; but I drew her back. "Whom your uncle will not allow you to marry!" I repeated. "Why? because he is poor?"

"No; uncle loves money, but not to such an extent as that. Besides, Mr. Clavering is not poor. He is the owner of a beautiful place in his own country ——"

"Own country?" I interrupted. "Is he not an American?"

155

"No," she returned; "he is an Englishman."

I did not see why she need say that in just the way she did, but, supposing she was aggravated by some secret memory, went on to inquire: "Then what difficulty can there be? Isn't he——" I was going to say steady, but refrained.

"He is an Englishman," she emphasized in the same bitter tone as before. "In saying that, I say it all. Uncle will never let me marry an Englishman."

I looked at her in amazement. Such a puerile reason as this had never entered my mind.

"He has an absolute mania on the subject," resumed she. "I might as well ask him to allow me to drown myself as to marry an Englishman."

A woman of truer judgment than myself would have said: "Then, if that is so, why not discard from your breast all thought of him? Why dance with him, and talk to him, and let your admiration develop into love?" But I was all romance then, and, angry at a prejudice I could neither understand nor appreciate, I said:

"But that is mere tyranny! Why should he hate the English so? And why, if he does, should you feel yourself obliged to gratify him in a whim so unreasonable?"

"Why? Shall I tell you, auntie?" she said, flushing and looking away.

"Yes," I returned; "tell me everything."

"Well, then, if you want to know the worst of me, as you already know the best, I hate to incur my uncle's displeasure, because—because—I have always been brought up to regard myself as his heiress, and I know that if I were to marry contrary to his wishes, he would instantly change his mind, and leave me penniless."

"But," I cried, my romance a little dampened by this admission, "you tell me Mr. Clavering has enough to live upon, so you would not want; and if you love—"

Her violet eyes fairly flashed in her amazement.

"You don't understand," she said; "Mr. Clavering is not poor; but uncle is rich. I shall be a queen—" There she paused, trembling, and falling on my breast. "Oh, it sounds mercenary, I know, but it is the fault of my bringing up. I have been taught to worship money. I would be utterly lost without it. And yet"—her whole face softening with the light of another emotion, "I cannot say to Henry Clavering, 'Go! my prospects are dearer to me than you!' I cannot, oh, I cannot!"

"You love him, then?" said I, determined to get at the truth of the matter if possible.

She rose restlessly. "Isn't that a proof of love? If you knew me, you would say it was." And, turning, she took her stand before a picture that hung on the wall of my sitting-room.

"That looks like me," she said.

It was one of a pair of good photographs I possessed.

"Yes," I remarked, "that is why I prize it."

She did not seem to hear me; she was absorbed in gazing at the exquisite face before her. "That is a winning face," I heard her say. "Sweeter than mine. I wonder if she would ever hesitate between love and money. I do not believe she would," her own countenance growing gloomy and sad as she said so; "she would think only of the happiness she would confer; she is not hard like me. Eleanore herself

156

would love this girl."

I think she had forgotten my presence, for at the mention of her cousin's name she turned quickly round with a half suspicious look, saying lightly:

"My dear old Mamma Hubbard looks horrified. She did not know she had such a very unromantic little wretch for a listener, when she was telling all those wonderful stories of Love slaying dragons, and living in caves, and walking over burning ploughshares as if they were tufts of spring grass?"

"No," I said, taking her with an irresistible impulse of admiring affection into my arms; "but if I had, it would have made no difference. I should still have talked about love, and of all it can do to make this weary workaday world sweet and delightful."

"Would you? Then you do not think me such a wretch?"

What could I say? I thought her the winsomest being in the world, and frankly told her so. Instantly she brightened into her very gayest self. Not that I thought then, much less do I think now, she partially cared for my good opinion; but her nature demanded admiration, and unconsciously blossomed under it, as a flower under the sunshine.

"And you will still let me come and tell you how bad I am,—that is, if I go on being bad, as I doubtless shall to the end of the chapter? You will not turn me off?"

"I will never turn you off."

"Not if I should do a dreadful thing? Not if I should run away with my lover some fine night, and leave uncle to discover how his affectionate partiality had been requited?"

It was lightly said, and lightly meant, for she did not even wait for my reply. But its seed sank deep into our two hearts for all that. And for the next few days I spent my time in planning how I should manage, if it should ever fall to my lot to conduct to a successful issue so enthralling a piece of business as an elopement. You may imagine, then, how delighted I was, when one evening Hannah, this unhappy girl who is now lying dead under my roof, and who was occupying the position of lady's maid to Miss Mary Leavenworth at that time, came to my door with a note from her mistress, running thus:

"Have the loveliest story of the season ready for me tomorrow; and
let the prince be as handsome as—as some one you have heard of,
and the princess as foolish as your little yielding pet,

"MARY."

Which short note could only mean that she was engaged. But the next day did not bring me my Mary, nor the next, nor the next; and beyond hearing that Mr. Leavenworth had returned from his trip I received neither word nor token. Two more days dragged by, when, just as twilight set in, she came. It had been a week since I had seen her, but it might have been a year from the change I observed in her countenance and expression. I could scarcely greet her with any show of pleasure, she was so unlike her former self.

"You are disappointed, are you not?" said she, looking at me. "You expected revelations, whispered hopes, and all manner of sweet confidences; and you see, instead, a cold, bitter woman, who for the first time in your presence feels inclined to be reserved and uncommunicative."

"That is because you have had more to trouble than encourage you in your love," I returned, though not without a certain shrinking, caused more by her manner than words.

She did not reply to this, but rose and paced the floor, coldly at first, but afterwards with a certain degree of excitement that proved to be the prelude to a change in her manner; for, suddenly pausing, she turned to me and said: "Mr. Clavering has left R——, Mrs. Belden."

"Left!"

"Yes, my uncle commanded me to dismiss him, and I obeyed."

The work dropped from my hands, in my heartfelt disappointment. "Ah! then he knows of your engagement to Mr. Clavering?"

"Yes; he had not been in the house five minutes before Eleanore told him."

"Then *she* knew?"

"Yes," with a half sigh. "She could hardly help it. I was foolish enough to give her the cue in my first moment of joy and weakness. I did not think of the consequences; but I might have known. She is so conscientious."

"I do not call it conscientiousness to tell another's secrets," I returned.

"That is because you are not Eleanore."

Not having a reply for this, I said, "And so your uncle did not regard your engagement with favor?"

"Favor! Did I not tell you he would never allow me to marry an Englishman? He said he would sooner see me buried."

"And you yielded? Made no struggle? Let the hard, cruel man have his way?"

She was walking off to look again at that picture which had attracted her attention the time before, but at this word gave me one little sidelong look that was inexpressibly suggestive.

"I obeyed him when he commanded, if that is what you mean."

"And dismissed Mr. Clavering after having given him your word of honor to be his wife?"

"Why not, when I found I could not keep my word."

"Then you have decided not to marry him?"

She did not reply at once, but lifted her face mechanically to the picture.

"My uncle would tell you that I had decided to be governed wholly by his wishes!" she responded at last with what I felt was self-scornful bitterness.

Greatly disappointed, I burst into tears. "Oh, Mary!" I cried, "Oh, Mary!" and instantly blushed, startled that I had called her by her first name.

But she did not appear to notice.

"Have you any complaint to make?" she asked. "Is it not my manifest duty to be governed by my uncle's wishes? Has he not brought me up from childhood? lavished every luxury upon me? made me all I am, even to the love of riches which he has instilled into my soul with every gift he has thrown into my lap, every word he has dropped into my ear, since I was old enough to know what

158

riches meant? Is it for me now to turn my back upon fostering care so wise, beneficent, and free, just because a man whom I have known some two weeks chances to offer me in exchange what he pleases to call his love?"

"But," I feebly essayed, convinced perhaps by the tone of sarcasm in which this was uttered that she was not far from my way of thinking after all, "if in two weeks you have learned to love this man more than everything else, even the riches which make your uncle's favor a thing of such moment—"

"Well," said she, "what then?"

"Why, then I would say, secure your happiness with the man of your choice, if you have to marry him in secret, trusting to your influence over your uncle to win the forgiveness he never can persistently deny."

You should have seen the arch expression which stole across her face at that. "Would it not be better," she asked, creeping to my arms, and laying her head on my shoulder, "would it not be better for me to make sure of that uncle's favor first, before undertaking the hazardous experiment of running away with a too ardent lover?"

Struck by her manner, I lifted her face and looked at it. It was one amused smile.

"Oh, my darling," said I, "you have not, then dismissed Mr. Clavering?"

"I have sent him away," she whispered demurely.

"But not without hope?"

She burst into a ringing laugh.

"Oh, you dear old Mamma Hubbard; what a matchmaker you are, to be sure! You appear as much interested as if you were the lover yourself."

"But tell me," I urged.

In a moment her serious mood returned. "He will wait for me," said she.

The next day I submitted to her the plan I had formed for her clandestine intercourse with Mr. Clavering. It was for them both to assume names, she taking mine, as one less liable to provoke conjecture than a strange name, and he that of LeRoy Robbins. The plan pleased her, and with the slight modification of a secret sign being used on the envelope, to distinguish her letters from mine, was at once adopted.

And so it was I took the fatal step that has involved me in all this trouble. With the gift of my name to this young girl to use as she would and sign what she would, I seemed to part with what was left me of judgment and discretion. Henceforth, I was only her scheming, planning, devoted slave; now copying the letters which she brought me, and enclosing them to the false name we had agreed upon, and now busying myself in devising ways to forward to her those which I received from him, without risk of discovery. Hannah was the medium we employed, as Mary felt it would not be wise for her to come too often to my house. To this girl's charge, then, I gave such notes as I could not forward in any other way, secure in the reticence of her nature, as well as in her inability to read, that these letters addressed to Mrs. Amy Belden would arrive at their proper destination without mishap. And I believe they always did. At all events, no difficulty that I ever heard of arose out of the use of this girl as a go-between.

But a change was at hand. Mr. Clavering, who had left an invalid mother in

England, was suddenly summoned home. He prepared to go, but, flushed with love, distracted by doubts, smitten with the fear that, once withdrawn from the neighborhood of a woman so universally courted as Mary, he would stand small chance of retaining his position in her regard, he wrote to her, telling his fears and asking her to marry him before he went.

"Make me your husband, and I will follow your wishes in all things," he wrote. "The certainty that you are mine will make parting possible; without it, I cannot go; no, not if my mother should die without the comfort of saying good-bye to her only child."

By some chance she was in my house when I brought this letter from the post-office, and I shall never forget how she started when she read it. But, from looking as if she had received an insult, she speedily settled down into a calm consideration of the subject, writing and delivering into my charge for copying a few lines in which she promised to accede to his request, if he would agree to leave the public declaration of the marriage to her discretion, and consent to bid her farewell at the door of the church or wherever the ceremony of marriage should take place, never to come into her presence again till such declaration had been made. Of course this brought in a couple of days the sure response: "Anything, so you will be mine."

And Amy Belden's wits and powers of planning were all summoned into requisition for the second time, to devise how this matter could be arranged without subjecting the parties to the chance of detection. I found the thing very difficult. In the first place, it was essential that the marriage should come off within three days, Mr. Clavering having, upon the receipt of her letter, secured his passage upon a steamer that sailed on the following Saturday; and, next, both he and Miss Leavenworth were too conspicuous in their personal appearance to make it at all possible for them to be secretly married anywhere within gossiping distance of this place. And yet it was desirable that the scene of the ceremony should not be too far away, or the time occupied in effecting the journey to and from the place would necessitate an absence from the hotel on the part of Miss Leavenworth long enough to arouse the suspicions of Eleanore; something which Mary felt it wiser to avoid. Her uncle, I have forgotten to say, was not here— having gone away again shortly after the apparent dismissal of Mr. Clavering. F——, then, was the only town I could think of which combined the two advantages of distance and accessibility. Although upon the railroad, it was an insignificant place, and had, what was better yet, a very obscure man for its clergyman, living, which was best of all, not ten rods from the depot. If they could meet there? Making inquiries, I found that it could be done, and, all alive to the romance of the occasion, proceeded to plan the details.

And now I am coming to what might have caused the overthrow of the whole scheme: I allude to the detection on the part of Eleanore of the correspondence between Mary and Mr. Clavering. It happened thus. Hannah, who, in her frequent visits to my house, had grown very fond of my society, had come in to sit with me for a while one evening. She had not been in the house, however, more than ten minutes, before there came a knock at the front door; and going to it I saw Mary,

160

as I supposed, from the long cloak she wore, standing before me. Thinking she had come with a letter for Mr. Clavering, I grasped her arm and drew her into the hall, saying, "Have you got it? I must post it to-night, or he will not receive it in time."

There I paused, for, the panting creature I had by the arm turning upon me, I saw myself confronted by a stranger.

"You have made a mistake," she cried. "I am Eleanore Leavenworth, and I have come for my girl Hannah. Is she here?"

I could only raise my hand in apprehension, and point to the girl sitting in the corner of the room before her. Miss Leavenworth immediately turned back.

"Hannah, I want you," said she, and would have left the house without another word, but I caught her by the arm.

"Oh, miss—" I began, but she gave me such a look, I dropped her arm.

"I have nothing to say to you!" she cried in a low, thrilling voice. "Do not detain me." And, with a glance to see if Hannah were following her, she went out.

For an hour I sat crouched on the stair just where she had left me. Then I went to bed, but I did not sleep a wink that night. You can imagine, then, my wonder when, with the first glow of the early morning light, Mary, looking more beautiful than ever, came running up the steps and into the room where I was, with the letter for Mr. Clavering trembling in her hand.

"Oh!" I cried in my joy and relief, "didn't she understand me, then?"

The gay look on Mary's face turned to one of reckless scorn. "If you mean Eleanore, yes. She is duly initiated, Mamma Hubbard. Knows that I love Mr. Clavering and write to him. I couldn't keep it secret after the mistake you made last evening; so I did the next best thing, told her the truth."

"Not that you were about to be married?"

"Certainly not. I don't believe in unnecessary communications."

"And you did not find her as angry as you expected?"

"I will not say that; she was angry enough. And yet," continued Mary, with a burst of self-scornful penitence, "I will not call Eleanore's lofty indignation anger. She was grieved, Mamma Hubbard, grieved." And with a laugh which I believe was rather the result of her own relief than of any wish to reflect on her cousin, she threw her head on one side and eyed me with a look which seemed to say, "Do I plague you so very much, you dear old Mamma Hubbard?"

She did plague me, and I could not conceal it. "And will she not tell her uncle?" I gasped.

The naive expression on Mary's face quickly changed. "No," said she.

I felt a heavy hand, hot with fever, lifted from my heart. "And we can still go on?"

She held out the letter for reply.

The plan agreed upon between us for the carrying out of our intentions was this. At the time appointed, Mary was to excuse herself to her cousin upon the plea that she had promised to take me to see a friend in the next town. She was then to enter a buggy previously ordered, and drive here, where I was to join her. We were then to proceed immediately to the minister's house in F——, where we had reason to believe we should find everything prepared for us. But in this plan, simple as it was, one thing was forgotten, and that was the character of Eleanore's love for her cousin. That her suspicions would be aroused we did not doubt; but that she would actually follow Mary up and demand an explanation of her conduct, was what neither she, who knew her so well, nor I, who knew her so little, ever imagined possible. And yet that was just what occurred. But let me explain. Mary, who had followed out the programme to the point of leaving a little note of excuse on Eleanore's dressing-table, had come to my house, and was just taking off her long cloak to show me her dress, when there came a commanding knock at the front door. Hastily pulling her cloak about her I ran to open it, intending, you may be sure, to dismiss my visitor with short ceremony, when I heard a voice behind me say, "Good heavens, it is Eleanore!" and, glancing back, saw Mary looking through the window-blind upon the porch without.

"What shall we do?" I cried, in very natural dismay.

"Do? why, open the door and let her in; I am not afraid of Eleanore."

I immediately did so, and Eleanore Leavenworth, very pale, but with a resolute countenance, walked into the house and into this room, confronting Mary in very nearly the same spot where you are now sitting. "I have come," said she, lifting a face whose expression of mingled sweetness and power I could not but admire, even in that moment of apprehension, "to ask you without any excuse for my request, if you will allow me to accompany you upon your drive this morning?"

Mary, who had drawn herself up to meet some word of accusation or appeal, turned carelessly away to the glass. "I am very sorry," she said, "but the buggy holds only two, and I shall be obliged to refuse."

"I will order a carriage."

"But I do not wish your company, Eleanore. We are off on a pleasure trip, and desire to have our fun by ourselves."

"And you will not allow me to accompany you?"

"I cannot prevent your going in another carriage."

Eleanore's face grew yet more earnest in its expression. "Mary," said she, "we have been brought up together. I am your sister in affection if not in blood, and I cannot see you start upon this adventure with no other companion than this woman. Then tell me, shall I go with you, as a sister, or on the road behind you as the enforced guardian of your honor against your will?"

"My honor?"

"You are going to meet Mr. Clavering."

"Well?"

"Twenty miles from home."

"Well?"

"Now is it discreet or honorable in you to do this?"

Mary's haughty lip took an ominous curve. "The same hand that raised you has raised me," she cried bitterly.

"This is no time to speak of that," returned Eleanore.

Mary's countenance flushed. All the antagonism of her nature was aroused. She looked absolutely Juno-like in her wrath and reckless menace. "Eleanore," she

162

cried, "I am going to F—— to marry Mr. Clavering! *Now* do you wish to accompany me?"

"I do."

Mary's whole manner changed. Leaping forward, she grasped her cousin's arm and shook it. "For what reason?" she cried. "What do you intend to do?"

"To witness the marriage, if it be a true one; to step between you and shame if any element of falsehood should come in to affect its legality."

Mary's hand fell from her cousin's arm. "I do not understand you," said she. "I thought you never gave countenance to what you considered wrong."

"Nor do I. Any one who knows me will understand that I do not give my approval to this marriage just because I attend its ceremonial in the capacity of an unwilling witness."

"Then why go?"

"Because I value your honor above my own peace. Because I love our common benefactor, and know that he would never pardon me if I let his darling be married, however contrary her union might be to his wishes, without lending the support of my presence to make the transaction at least a respectable one."

"But in so doing you will be involved in a world of deception—which you hate."

"Any more so than now?"

"Mr. Clavering does not return with me, Eleanore."

"No, I supposed not."

"I leave him immediately after the ceremony."

Eleanore bowed her head.

"He goes to Europe." A pause.

"And I return home."

"There to wait for what, Mary?"

Mary's face crimsoned, and she turned slowly away.

"What every other girl does under such circumstances, I suppose. The development of more reasonable feelings in an obdurate parent's heart."

Eleanore sighed, and a short silence ensued, broken by Eleanore's suddenly falling upon her knees, and clasping her cousin's hand. "Oh, Mary," she sobbed, her haughtiness all disappearing in a gush of wild entreaty, "consider what you are doing! Think, before it is too late, of the consequences which must follow such an act as this. Marriage founded upon deception can never lead to happiness. Love— but it is not that. Love would have led you either to have dismissed Mr. Clavering at once, or to have openly accepted the fate which a union with him would bring. Only passion stoops to subterfuge like this. And you," she continued, rising and turning toward me in a sort of forlorn hope very touching to see, "can you see this young motherless girl, driven by caprice, and acknowledging no moral restraint, enter upon the dark and crooked path she is planning for herself, without uttering one word of warning and appeal? Tell me, mother of children dead and buried, what excuse you will have for your own part in this day's work, when she, with her face marred by the sorrows which must follow this deception, comes to you——"

163

"The same excuse, probably," Mary's voice broke in, chill and strained, "which you will have when uncle inquires how you came to allow such an act of disobedience to be perpetrated in his absence: that she could not help herself, that Mary would gang her ain gait, and every one around must accommodate themselves to it."

It was like a draught of icy air suddenly poured into a room heated up to fever point. Eleanore stiffened immediately, and drawing back, pale and composed, turned upon her cousin with the remark:

"Then nothing can move you?"

The curling of Mary's lips was her only reply.

Mr. Raymond, I do not wish to weary you with my feelings, but the first great distrust I ever felt of my wisdom in pushing this matter so far came with that curl of Mary's lip. More plainly than Eleanore's words it showed me the temper with which she was entering upon this undertaking; and, struck with momentary dismay, I advanced to speak when Mary stopped me.

"There, now, Mamma Hubbard, don't you go and acknowledge that you are frightened, for I won't hear it. I have promised to marry Henry Clavering to-day, and I am going to keep my word—if I don't love him," she added with bitter emphasis. Then, smiling upon me in a way which caused me to forget everything save the fact that she was going to her bridal, she handed me her veil to fasten. As I was doing this, with very trembling fingers, she said, looking straight at Eleanore:

"You have shown yourself more interested in my fate than I had any reason to expect. Will you continue to display this concern all the way to F——, or may I hope for a few moments of peace in which to dream upon the step which, according to you, is about to hurl upon me such dreadful consequences?"

"If I go with you to F——," Eleanore returned, "it is as a witness, no more. My sisterly duty is done."

"Very well, then," Mary said, dimpling with sudden gayety; "I suppose I shall have to accept the situation. Mamma Hubbard, I am so sorry to disappoint you, but the buggy *won't* hold three. If you are good you shall be the first to congratulate me when I come home to-night." And, almost before I knew it, the two had taken their seats in the buggy that was waiting at the door. "Good-by," cried Mary, waving her hand from the back; "wish me much joy—of my ride."

I tried to do so, but the words wouldn't come. I could only wave my hand in response, and rush sobbing into the house.

Of that day, and its long hours of alternate remorse and anxiety, I cannot trust myself to speak. Let me come at once to the time when, seated alone in my lamp-lighted room, I waited and watched for the token of their return which Mary had promised me. It came in the shape of Mary herself, who, wrapped in her long cloak, and with her beautiful face aglow with blushes, came stealing into the house just as I was beginning to despair.

A strain of wild music from the hotel porch, where they were having a dance, entered with her, producing such a weird effect upon my fancy that I was not at all surprised when, in flinging off her cloak, she displayed garments of bridal white and a head crowned with snowy roses.

"Oh, Mary!" I cried, bursting into tears; "you are then——"

"Mrs. Henry Clavering, at your service. I'm a bride, Auntie."

"Without a bridal," I murmured, taking her passionately into my embrace.

She was not insensible to my emotion. Nestling close to me, she gave herself up for one wild moment to a genuine burst of tears, saying between her sobs all manner of tender things; telling me how she loved me, and how I was the only one in all the world to whom she dared come on this, her wedding night, for comfort or congratulation, and of how frightened she felt now it was all over, as if with her name she had parted with something of inestimable value.

"And does not the thought of having made some one the proudest of men solace you?" I asked, more than dismayed at this failure of mine to make these lovers happy.

"I don't know," she sobbed. "What satisfaction can it be for him to feel himself tied for life to a girl who, sooner than lose a prospective fortune, subjected him to such a parting?"

"Tell me about it," said I.

But she was not in the mood at that moment. The excitement of the day had been too much for her. A thousand fears seemed to beset her mind. Crouching down on the stool at my feet, she sat with her hands folded and a glare on her face that lent an aspect of strange unreality to her brilliant attire. "How shall I keep it secret! The thought haunts me every moment; how can I keep it secret!"

"Why, is there any danger of its being known?" I inquired. "Were you seen or followed?"

"No," she murmured. "It all went off well, but——"

"Where is the danger, then?"

"I cannot say; but some deeds are like ghosts. They will not be laid; they reappear; they gibber; they make themselves known whether we will or not. I did not think of this before. I was mad, reckless, what you will. But ever since the night has come, I have felt it crushing upon me like a pall that smothers life and youth and love out of my heart. While the sunlight remained I could endure it; but now—oh, Auntie, I have done something that will keep me in constant fear. I have allied myself to a living apprehension. I have destroyed my happiness."

I was too aghast to speak.

"For two hours I have played at being gay. Dressed in my bridal white, and crowned with roses, I have greeted my friends as if they were wedding-guests, and made believe to myself that all the compliments bestowed upon me—and they are only too numerous—were just so many congratulations upon my marriage. But it was no use; Eleanore knew it was no use. She has gone to her room to pray, while I—I have come here for the first time, perhaps for the last, to fall at some one's feet and cry,—' God have mercy upon me!'"

I looked at her in uncontrollable emotion. "Oh, Mary, have I only succeeded, then, in making you miserable?"

She did not answer; she was engaged in picking up the crown of roses which had fallen from her hair to the floor.

"If I had not been taught to love money so!" she said at length. "If, like Eleanore, I could look upon the splendor which has been ours from childhood as a mere accessory of life, easy to be dropped at the call of duty or affection! If prestige, adulation, and elegant belongings were not so much to me; or love, friendship, and domestic happiness more! If only I could walk a step without dragging the chain of a thousand luxurious longings after me. Eleanore can. Imperious as she often is in her beautiful womanhood, haughty as she can be when the delicate quick of her personality is touched too rudely, I have known her to sit by the hour in a low, chilly, ill-lighted and ill-smelling garret, cradling a dirty child on her knee, and feeding with her own hand an impatient old woman whom no one else would consent to touch. Oh, oh! they talk about repentance and a change of heart! If some one or something would only change mine! But there is no hope of that! no hope of my ever being anything else than what I am: a selfish, wilful, mercenary girl."

Nor was this mood a mere transitory one. That same night she made a discovery which increased her apprehension almost to terror. This was nothing less than the fact that Eleanore had been keeping a diary of the last few weeks. "Oh," she cried in relating this to me the next day, "what security shall I ever feel as long as this diary of hers remains to confront me every time I go into her room? And she will not consent to destroy it, though I have done my best to show her that it is a betrayal of the trust I reposed in her. She says it is all she has to show in the way of defence, if uncle should ever accuse her of treachery to him and his happiness. She promises to keep it locked up; but what good will that do! A thousand accidents might happen, any of them sufficient to throw it into uncle's hands. I shall never feel safe for a moment while it exists."

I endeavored to calm her by saying that if Eleanore was without malice, such fears were groundless. But she would not be comforted, and seeing her so wrought up, I suggested that Eleanore should be asked to trust it into my keeping till such time as she should feel the necessity of using it. The idea struck Mary favorably. "O yes," she cried; "and I will put my certificate with it, and so get rid of all my care at once." And before the afternoon was over, she had seen Eleanore and made her request.

It was acceded to with this proviso, that I was neither to destroy nor give up all or any of the papers except upon their united demand. A small tin box was accordingly procured, into which were put all the proofs of Mary's marriage then existing, viz.: the certificate, Mr. Clavering's letters, and such leaves from Eleanore's diary as referred to this matter. It was then handed over to me with the stipulation I have already mentioned, and I stowed it away in a certain closet upstairs, where it has lain undisturbed till last night.

Here Mrs. Belden paused, and, blushing painfully, raised her eyes to mine with a look in which anxiety and entreaty were curiously blended.

"I don't know what you will say," she began, "but, led away by my fears, I took that box out of its hiding-place last evening and, notwithstanding your advice, carried it from the house, and it is now———"

"In my possession," I quietly finished.

166

I don't think I ever saw her look more astounded, not even when I told her of Hannah's death. "Impossible!" she exclaimed. "I left it last night in the old barn that was burned down. I merely meant to hide it for the present, and could think of no better place in my hurry; for the barn is said to be haunted—a man hung himself there once—and no one ever goes there. I—I—you cannot have it!" she cried, "unless——"

"Unless I found and brought it away before the barn was destroyed," I suggested.

Her face flushed deeper. "Then you followed me?"

"Yes," said I. Then, as I felt my own countenance redden, hastened to add: "We have been playing strange and unaccustomed parts, you and I. Some time, when all these dreadful events shall be a mere dream of the past, we will ask each other's pardon. But never mind all this now. The box is safe, and I am anxious to hear the rest of your story."

This seemed to compose her, and after a minute she continued:

Mary seemed more like herself after this. And though, on account of Mr. Leavenworth's return and their subsequent preparations for departure, I saw but little more of her, what I did see was enough to make me fear that, with the locking up of the proofs of her marriage, she was indulging the idea that the marriage itself had become void. But I may have wronged her in this.

The story of those few weeks is almost finished. On the eve of the day before she left, Mary came to my house to bid me good-by. She had a present in her hand the value of which I will not state, as I did not take it, though she coaxed me with all her prettiest wiles. But she said something that night that I have never been able to forget. It was this. I had been speaking of my hope that before two months had elapsed she would find herself in a position to send for Mr. Clavering, and that when that day came I should wish to be advised of it; when she suddenly interrupted me by saying:

"Uncle will never be won upon, as you call it, while he lives. If I was convinced of it before, I am sure of it now. Nothing but his death will ever make it possible for me to send for Mr. Clavering." Then, seeing me look aghast at the long period of separation which this seemed to betoken, blushed a little and whispered: "The prospect looks somewhat dubious, doesn't it? But if Mr. Clavering loves me, he can wait."

"But," said I, "your uncle is only little past the prime of life and appears to be in robust health; it will be years of waiting, Mary."

"I don't know," she muttered, "I think not. Uncle is not as strong as he looks and—" She did not say any more, horrified perhaps at the turn the conversation was taking. But there was an expression on her countenance that set me thinking at the time, and has kept me thinking ever since.

Not that any actual dread of such an occurrence as has since happened came to oppress my solitude during the long months which now intervened. I was as yet too much under the spell of her charm to allow anything calculated to throw a shadow over her image to remain long in my thoughts. But when, some time in the fall, a letter came to me personally from Mr. Clavering, filled with a vivid

167

appeal to tell him something of the woman who, in spite of her vows, doomed him to a suspense so cruel, and when, on the evening of the same day, a friend of mine who had just returned from New York spoke of meeting Mary Leavenworth at some gathering, surrounded by manifest admirers, I began to realize the alarming features of the affair, and, sitting down, I wrote her a letter. Not in the strain in which I had been accustomed to talk to her,—I had not her pleading eyes and trembling, caressing hands ever before me to beguile my judgment from its proper exercise,—but honestly and earnestly, telling her how Mr. Clavering felt, and what a risk she ran in keeping so ardent a lover from his rights. The reply she sent rather startled me.

"I have put Mr. Robbins out of my calculations for the present, and advise you to do the same. As for the gentleman himself, I have told him that when I could receive him I would be careful to notify him. That day has not yet come.

"But do not let him be discouraged," she added in a postscript. "When he does receive his happiness, it will be a satisfying one."

When, I thought. Ah, it is that *when* which is likely to ruin all! But, intent only upon fulfilling her will, I sat down and wrote a letter to Mr. Clavering, in which I stated what she had said, and begged him to have patience, adding that I would surely let him know if any change took place in Mary or her circumstances. And, having despatched it to his address in London, awaited the development of events.

They were not slow in transpiring. In two weeks I heard of the sudden death of Mr. Stebbins, the minister who had married them; and while yet laboring under the agitation produced by this shock, was further startled by seeing in a New York paper the name of Mr. Clavering among the list of arrivals at the Hoffman House; showing that my letter to him had failed in its intended effect, and that the patience Mary had calculated upon so blindly was verging to its end. I was consequently far from being surprised when, in a couple of weeks or so afterwards, a letter came from him to my address, which, owing to the careless omission of the private mark upon the envelope, I opened, and read enough to learn that, driven to desperation by the constant failures which he had experienced in all his endeavors to gain access to her in public or private, a failure which he was not backward in ascribing to her indisposition to see him, he had made up his mind to risk everything, even her displeasure; and, by making an appeal to her uncle, end the suspense under which he was laboring, definitely and at once. "I want you," he wrote; "dowered or dowerless, it makes little difference to me. If you will not come of yourself, then I must follow the example of the brave knights, my ancestors; storm the castle that holds you, and carry you off by force of arms."

Neither can I say I was much surprised, knowing Mary as I did, when, in a few days from this, she forwarded to me for copying, this reply: "If Mr. Robbins ever expects to be happy with Amy Belden, let him reconsider the determination of which he speaks. Not only would he by such an action succeed in destroying the happiness of her he professes to love, but run the greater risk of effectually annulling the affection which makes the tie between them endurable."

168

To this there was neither date nor signature. It was the cry of warning which a spirited, self-contained creature gives when brought to bay. It made even me recoil, though I had known from the first that her pretty wilfulness was but the tossing foam floating above the soundless depths of cold resolve and most deliberate purpose.

What its real effect was upon him and her fate I can only conjecture. All I know is that in two weeks thereafter Mr. Leavenworth was found murdered in his room, and Hannah Chester, coming direct to my door from the scene of violence, begged me to take her in and secrete her from public inquiry, as I loved and desired to serve Mary Leavenworth.

XXXIII. UNEXPECTED TESTIMONY

Pol. What do you read, my lord?
Ham. Words, words, words.
   —Hamlet.

MRS. BELDEN paused, lost in the sombre shadow which these words were calculated to evoke, and a short silence fell upon the room. It was broken by my asking for some account of the occurrence she had just mentioned, it being considered a mystery how Hannah could have found entrance into her house without the knowledge of the neighbors.

"Well," said she, "it was a chilly night, and I had gone to bed early (I was sleeping then in the room off this) when, at about a quarter to one—the last train goes through R—— at 12.50—there came a low knock on the window-pane at the head of my bed. Thinking that some of the neighbors were sick, I hurriedly rose on my elbow and asked who was there. The answer came in low, muffled tones, 'Hannah, Miss Leavenworth's girl! Please let me in at the kitchen door.' Startled at hearing the well-known voice, and fearing I knew not what, I caught up a lamp and hurried round to the door. 'Is any one with you?' I asked. 'No,' she replied. 'Then come in.' But no sooner had she done so than my strength failed me, and I had to sit down, for I saw she looked very pale and strange, was without baggage, and altogether had the appearance of some wandering spirit. 'Hannah!' I gasped, 'what is it? what has happened? what brings you here in this condition and at this time of night?' 'Miss Leavenworth has sent me,' she replied, in the low, monotonous tone of one repeating a lesson by rote. 'She told me to come here; said you would keep me. I am not to go out of the house, and no one is to know I am here.' 'But why?' I asked, trembling with a thousand undefined fears; 'what has occurred?' 'I dare not say,' she whispered; 'I am forbid; I am just to stay here, and keep quiet.' 'But,' I began, helping her to take off her shawl,—the dingy blanket advertised for in the papers—'you must tell me. She surely did not forbid you to tell *me?*' 'Yes she did; every one,' the girl replied, growing white in her persistence, 'and I never break my word; fire couldn't draw it out of me.' She looked so determined, so utterly unlike herself, as I remembered her in the meek, unobtrusive days of our old acquaintance, that I could do nothing but stare at her.

169

'You will keep me,' she said; 'you will not turn me away?' 'No,' I said, 'I will not turn you away.' 'And tell no one?' she went on. 'And tell no one,' I repeated.

"This seemed to relieve her. Thanking me, she quietly followed me up-stairs. I put her into the room in which you found her, because it was the most secret one in the house; and there she has remained ever since, satisfied and contented, as far as I could see, till this very same horrible day."

"And is that all?" I asked. "Did you have no explanation with her afterwards? Did she never give you any information in regard to the transactions which led to her flight?"

"No, sir. She kept a most persistent silence. Neither then nor when, upon the next day, I confronted her with the papers in my hand, and the awful question upon my lips as to whether her flight had been occasioned by the murder which had taken place in Mr. Leavenworth's household, did she do more than acknowledge she had run away on this account. Some one or something had sealed her lips, and, as she said, 'Fire and torture should never make her speak.'"

Another short pause followed this; then, with my mind still hovering about the one point of intensest interest to me, I said:

"This story, then, this account which you have just given me of Mary Leavenworth's secret marriage and the great strait it put her into—a strait from which nothing but her uncle's death could relieve her—together with this acknowledgment of Hannah's that she had left home and taken refuge here on the insistence of Mary Leavenworth, is the groundwork you have for the suspicions you have mentioned?"

"Yes, sir; that and the proof of her interest in the matter which is given by the letter I received from her yesterday, and which you say you have now in your possession."

Oh, that letter!

"I know," Mrs. Belden went on in a broken voice, "that it is wrong, in a serious case like this, to draw hasty conclusions; but, oh, sir, how can I help it, knowing what I do?"

I did not answer; I was revolving in my mind the old question: was it possible, in face of all these later developments, still to believe Mary Leavenworth's own hand guiltless of her uncle's blood?

"It is dreadful to come to such conclusions," proceeded Mrs. Belden, "and nothing but her own words written in her own hand would ever have driven me to them, but——"

"Pardon me," I interrupted; "but you said in the beginning of this interview that you did not believe Mary herself had any direct hand in her uncle's murder. Are you ready to repeat that assertion?"

"Yes, yes, indeed. Whatever I may think of her influence in inducing it, I never could imagine her as having anything to do with its actual performance. Oh, no! oh, no! whatever was done on that dreadful night, Mary Leavenworth never put hand to pistol or ball, or even stood by while they were used; that you may be sure of. Only the man who loved her, longed for her, and felt the impossibility of obtaining her by any other means, could have found nerve for an act so horrible."

170

"Then you think——"

"Mr. Clavering is the man? I do: and oh, sir, when you consider that he is her husband, is it not dreadful enough?"

"It is, indeed," said I, rising to conceal how much I was affected by this conclusion of hers.

Something in my tone or appearance seemed to startle her. "I hope and trust I have not been indiscreet," she cried, eying me with something like an incipient distrust. "With this dead girl lying in my house, I ought to be very careful, I know, but——"

"You have said nothing," was my earnest assurance as I edged towards the door in my anxiety to escape, if but for a moment, from an atmosphere that was stifling me. "No one can blame you for anything you have either said or done to-day. But"—and here I paused and walked hurriedly back,—"I wish to ask one question more. Have you any reason, beyond that of natural repugnance to believing a young and beautiful woman guilty of a great crime, for saying what you have of Henry Clavering, a gentleman who has hitherto been mentioned by you with respect?"

"No," she whispered, with a touch of her old agitation.

I felt the reason insufficient, and turned away with something of the same sense of suffocation with which I had heard that the missing key had been found in Eleanore Leavenworth's possession. "You must excuse me," I said; "I want to be a moment by myself, in order to ponder over the facts which I have just heard; I will soon return"; and without further ceremony, hurried from the room.

By some indefinable impulse, I went immediately up-stairs, and took my stand at the western window of the large room directly over Mrs. Belden. The blinds were closed; the room was shrouded in funereal gloom, but its sombreness and horror were for the moment unfelt; I was engaged in a fearful debate with myself. Was Mary Leavenworth the principal, or merely the accessory, in this crime? Did the determined prejudice of Mr. Gryce, the convictions of Eleanore, the circumstantial evidence even of such facts as had come to our knowledge, preclude the possibility that Mrs. Belden's conclusions were correct? That all the detectives interested in the affair would regard the question as settled, I did not doubt; but need it be? Was it utterly impossible to find evidence yet that Henry Clavering was, after all, the assassin of Mr. Leavenworth?

Filled with the thought, I looked across the room to the closet where lay the body of the girl who, according to all probability, had known the truth of the matter, and a great longing seized me. Oh, why could not the dead be made to speak? Why should she lie there so silent, so pulseless, so inert, when a word from her were enough to decide the awful question? Was there no power to compel those pallid lips to move?

Carried away by the fervor of the moment, I made my way to her side. Ah, God, how still! With what a mockery the closed lips and lids confronted my demanding gaze! A stone could not have been more unresponsive.

With a feeling that was almost like anger, I stood there, when—what was it I saw protruding from beneath her shoulders where they crushed against the bed?

171

An envelope? a letter? Yes.

Dizzy with the sudden surprise, overcome with the wild hopes this discovery awakened, I stooped in great agitation and drew the letter out. It was sealed but not directed. Breaking it hastily open, I took a glance at its contents. Good heavens! it was the work of the girl herself!—its very appearance was enough to make that evident! Feeling as if a miracle had happened, I hastened with it into the other room, and set myself to decipher the awkward scrawl.

This is what I saw, rudely printed in lead pencil on the inside of a sheet of common writing-paper:

"I am a wicked girl. I have knone things all the time which I had ought to have told but I didn't dare to he said he would kill me if I did I mene the tall splendud looking gentulman with the black mustash who I met coming out of Mister Levenworth's room with a key in his hand the night Mr. Levenworth was murdered. He was so scared he gave me money and made me go away and come here and keep every thing secret but I can't do so no longer. I seem to see Miss Elenor all the time crying and asking me if I want her sent to prisun. God knows I'd rathur die. And this is the truth and my last words and I pray every body's forgivness and hope nobody will blame me and that they wont bother Miss Elenor any more but go and look after the handsome gentulman with the black mushtash."

BOOK IV. THE PROBLEM SOLVED

XXXIV. MR. GRYCE RESUMES CONTROL
"It out-herods Herod."
—Hamlet.

"A thing devised by the enemy."
—Richard III

A HALF-HOUR had passed. The train upon which I had every reason to expect Mr. Gryce had arrived, and I stood in the doorway awaiting with indescribable agitation the slow and labored approach of the motley group of men and women whom I had observed leave the depot at the departure of the cars. Would he be among them? Was the telegram of a nature peremptory enough to make his presence here, sick as he was, an absolute certainty? The written confession of Hannah throbbing against my heart, a heart all elation now, as but a short half-hour before it had been all doubt and struggle, seemed to rustle distrust, and the prospect of a long afternoon spent in impatience was rising before me, when a portion of the advancing crowd turned off into a side street, and I saw the form of Mr. Gryce hobbling, not on two sticks, but very painfully on one, coming slowly down the street.

172

His face, as he approached, was a study.

"Well, well, well," he exclaimed, as we met at the gate; "this is a pretty how-dye-do, I must say. Hannah dead, eh? and everything turned topsy-turvy! Humph, and what do you think of Mary Leavenworth now?"

It would therefore seem natural, in the conversation which followed his introduction into the house and installment in Mrs. Belden's parlor, that I should begin my narration by showing him Hannah's confession; but it was not so. Whether it was that I felt anxious to have him go through the same alternations of hope and fear it had been my lot to experience since I came to R——; or whether, in the depravity of human nature, there lingered within me sufficient resentment for the persistent disregard he had always paid to my suspicions of Henry Clavering to make it a matter of moment to me to spring this knowledge upon him just at the instant his own convictions seemed to have reached the point of absolute certainty, I cannot say. Enough that it was not till I had given him a full account of every other matter connected with my stay in this house; not till I saw his eye beaming, and his lip quivering with the excitement incident upon the perusal of the letter from Mary, found in Mrs. Belden's pocket; not, indeed, until I became assured from such expressions as "Tremendous! The deepest game of the season! Nothing like it since the Lafarge affair!" that in another moment he would be uttering some theory or belief that once heard would forever stand like a barrier between us, did I allow myself to hand him the letter I had taken from under the dead body of Hannah.

I shall never forget his expression as he received it; "Good heavens!" cried he, "what's this?"

"A dying confession of the girl Hannah. I found it lying in her bed when I went up, a half-hour ago, to take a second look at her."

Opening it, he glanced over it with an incredulous air that speedily, however, turned to one of the utmost astonishment, as he hastily perused it, and then stood turning it over and over in his hand, examining it.

"A remarkable piece of evidence," I observed, not without a certain feeling of triumph; "quite changes the aspect of affairs!"

"Think so?" he sharply retorted; then, whilst I stood staring at him in amazement, his manner was so different from what I expected, looked up and said: "You tell me that you found this in her bed. Whereabouts in her bed?"

"Under the body of the girl herself," I returned. "I saw one corner of it protruding from beneath her shoulders, and drew it out."

He came and stood before me. "Was it folded or open, when you first looked at it?"

"Folded; fastened up in this envelope," showing it to him.

He took it, looked at it for a moment, and went on with his questions.

"This envelope has a very crumpled appearance, as well as the letter itself. Were they so when you found them?"

"Yes, not only so, but doubled up as you see."

"Doubled up? You are sure of that? Folded, sealed, and then doubled up as if her body had rolled across it while alive?"

"Yes."

"No trickery about it? No look as if the thing had been insinuated there since her death?"

"Not at all. I should rather say that to every appearance she held it in her hand when she lay down, but turning over, dropped it and then laid upon it."

Mr. Gryce's eyes, which had been very bright, ominously clouded; evidently he had been disappointed in my answers, paying the letter down, he stood musing, but suddenly lifted it again, scrutinized the edges of the paper on which it was written, and, darting me a quick look, vanished with it into the shade of the window curtain. His manner was so peculiar, I involuntarily rose to follow; but he waved me back, saying:

"Amuse yourself with that box on the table, which you had such an ado over; see if it contains all we have a right to expect to find in it. I want to be by myself for a moment."

Subduing my astonishment, I proceeded to comply with his request, but scarcely had I lifted the lid of the box before me when he came hurrying back, flung the letter down on the table with an air of the greatest excitement, and cried:

"Did I say there had never been anything like it since the Lafarge affair? I tell you there has never been anything like it in any affair. It is the rummest case on record! Mr. Raymond," and his eyes, in his excitement, actually met mine for the first time in my experience of him, "prepare yourself for a disappointment. This pretended confession of Hannah's is a fraud!"

"A fraud?"

"Yes; fraud, forgery, what you will; the girl never wrote it."

Amazed, outraged almost, I bounded from my chair. "How do you know that?" I cried.

Bending forward, he put the letter into my hand. "Look at it," said he; "examine it closely. Now tell me what is the first thing you notice in regard to it?"

"Why, the first thing that strikes me, is that the words are printed, instead of written; something which might be expected from this girl, according to all accounts."

"Well?"

"That they are printed on the inside of a sheet of ordinary paper——"

"Ordinary paper?"

"Yes."

"That is, a sheet of commercial note of the ordinary quality."

"Of course."

"But is it?"

"Why, yes; I should say so."

"Look at the lines."

"What of them? Oh, I see, they run up close to the top of the page; evidently the scissors have been used here."

"In short, it is a large sheet, trimmed down to the size of commercial note?"

"Yes."

"And is that all you see?"

174

"All but the words."

"Don't you perceive what has been lost by means of this trimming down?"

"No, unless you mean the manufacturer's stamp in the corner." Mr. Gryce's glance took meaning. "But I don't see why the loss of that should be deemed a matter of any importance."

"Don't you? Not when you consider that by it we seem to be deprived of all opportunity of tracing this sheet back to the quire of paper from which it was taken?"

"No."

"Humph! then you are more of an amateur than I thought you. Don't you see that, as Hannah could have had no motive for concealing where the paper came from on which she wrote her dying words, this sheet must have been prepared by some one else?"

"No," said I; "I cannot say that I see all that."

"Can't! Well then, answer me this. Why should Hannah, a girl about to commit suicide, care whether any clue was furnished, in her confession, to the actual desk, drawer, or quire of paper from which the sheet was taken, on which she wrote it?"

"She wouldn't."

"Yet especial pains have been taken to destroy that clue."

"But——"

"Then there is another thing. Read the confession itself, Mr. Raymond, and tell me what you gather from it."

"Why," said I, after complying, "that the girl, worn out with constant apprehension, has made up her mind to do away with herself, and that Henry Clavering——"

"Henry Clavering?"

The interrogation was put with so much meaning, I looked up. "Yes," said I.

"Ah, I didn't know that Mr. Clavering's name was mentioned there; excuse me."

"His name is not mentioned, but a description is given so strikingly in accordance——"

Here Mr. Gryce interrupted me. "Does it not seem a little surprising to you that a girl like Hannah should have stopped to describe a man she knew by name?"

I started; it was unnatural surely.

"You believe Mrs. Belden's story, don't you?"

"Yes."

"Consider her accurate in her relation of what took place here a year ago?"

"I do."

"Must believe, then, that Hannah, the go-between, was acquainted with Mr. Clavering and with his name?"

"Undoubtedly."

"Then why didn't she use it? If her intention was, as she here professes, to save Eleanore Leavenworth from the false imputation which had fallen upon her, she would naturally take the most direct method of doing it. This description of a man whose identity she could have at once put beyond a doubt by the mention of his name is the work, not of a poor, ignorant girl, but of some person who, in attempting to play the *role* of one, has signally failed. But that is not all. Mrs. Belden, according to you, maintains that Hannah told her, upon entering the house, that Mary Leavenworth sent her here. But in this document, she declares it to have been the work of Black Mustache."

"I know; but could they not have both been parties to the transaction?"

"Yes," said he; "yet it is always a suspicious circumstance, when there is a discrepancy between the written and spoken declaration of a person. But why do we stand here fooling, when a few words from this Mrs. Belden, you talk so much about, will probably settle the whole matter!"

"A few words from Mrs. Belden," I repeated. "I have had thousands from her to-day, and find the matter no nearer settled than in the beginning."

"*You* have had," said he, "but I have not. Fetch her in, Mr. Raymond."

I rose. "One thing," said I, "before I go. What if Hannah had found the sheet of paper, trimmed just as it is, and used it without any thought of the suspicions it would occasion!"

"Ah!" said he, "that is just what we are going to find out."

Mrs. Belden was in a flutter of impatience when I entered the sitting-room. When did I think the coroner would come? and what did I imagine this detective would do for us? It was dreadful waiting there alone for something, she knew not what.

I calmed her as well as I could, telling her the detective had not yet informed me what he could do, having some questions to ask her first. Would she come in to see him? She rose with alacrity. Anything was better than suspense.

Mr. Gryce, who in the short interim of my absence had altered his mood from the severe to the beneficent, received Mrs. Belden with just that show of respectful courtesy likely to impress a woman as dependent as she upon the good opinion of others.

"Ah! and this is the lady in whose house this very disagreeable event has occurred," he exclaimed, partly rising in his enthusiasm to greet her. "May I request you to sit," he asked; "if a stranger may be allowed to take the liberty of inviting a lady to sit in her own house."

"It does not seem like my own house any longer," said she, but in a sad, rather than an aggressive tone; so much had his genial way imposed upon her. "Little better than a prisoner here, go and come, keep silence or speak, just as I am bidden; and all because an unhappy creature, whom I took in for the most unselfish of motives, has chanced to die in my house!"

"Just so!" exclaimed Mr. Gryce; "it is very unjust. But perhaps we can right matters. I have every reason to believe we can. This sudden death ought to be easily explained. You say you had no poison in the house?"

"No, sir."

"And that the girl never went out?"

"Never, sir."

"And that no one has been here to see her?"

"No one, sir."

"So that she could not have procured any such thing if she had wished?"

176

"No, sir."

"Unless," he added suavely, "she had it with her when she came here?"

"That couldn't have been, sir. She brought no baggage; and as for her pocket, I know everything there was in it, for I looked."

"And what did you find there?"

"Some money in bills, more than you would have expected such a girl to have, some loose pennies, and a common handkerchief."

"Well, then, it is proved the girl didn't die of poison, there being none in the house."

He said this in so convinced a tone she was deceived.

"That is just what I have been telling Mr. Raymond," giving me a triumphant look.

"Must have been heart disease," he went on, "You say she was well yesterday?"

"Yes, sir; or seemed so."

"Though not cheerful?"

"I did not say that; she was, sir, very."

"What, ma'am, this girl?" giving me a look. "I don't understand that. I should think her anxiety about those she had left behind her in the city would have been enough to keep her from being very cheerful."

"So you would," returned Mrs. Belden; "but it wasn't so. On the contrary, she never seemed to worry about them at all."

"What! not about Miss Eleanore, who, according to the papers, stands in so cruel a position before the world? But perhaps she didn't know anything about that—Miss Leavenworth's position, I mean?"

"Yes, she did, for I told her. I was so astonished I could not keep it to myself. You see, I had always considered Eleanore as one above reproach, and it so shocked me to see her name mentioned in the newspaper in such a connection, that I went to Hannah and read the article aloud, and watched her face to see how she took it."

"And how did she?"

"I can't say. She looked as if she didn't understand; asked me why I read such things to her, and told me she didn't want to hear any more; that I had promised not to trouble her about this murder, and that if I continued to do so she wouldn't listen."

"Humph! and what else?"

"Nothing else. She put her hand over her ears and frowned in such a sullen way I left the room."

"That was when?"

"About three weeks ago."

"She has, however, mentioned the subject since?"

"No, sir; not once."

"What! not asked what they were going to do with her mistress?"

"No, sir."

"She has shown, however, that something was preying on her mind—fear, remorse, or anxiety?"

177

"No, sir; on the contrary, she has oftener appeared like one secretly elated."

"But," exclaimed Mr. Gryce, with another sidelong look at me, "that was very strange and unnatural. I cannot account for it."

"Nor I, sir. I used to try to explain it by thinking her sensibilities had been blunted, or that she was too ignorant to comprehend the seriousness of what had happened; but as I learned to know her better, I gradually changed my mind. There was too much method in her gayety for that. I could not help seeing she had some future before her for which she was preparing herself. As, for instance, she asked me one day if I thought she could learn to play on the piano. And I finally came to the conclusion she had been promised money if she kept the secret intrusted to her, and was so pleased with the prospect that she forgot the dreadful past, and all connected with it. At all events, that was the only explanation I could find for her general industry and desire to improve herself, or for the complacent smiles I detected now and then stealing over her face when she didn't know I was looking."

Not such a smile as crept over the countenance of Mr. Gryce at that moment, I warrant.

"It was all this," continued Mrs. Belden, "which made her death such a shock to me. I couldn't believe that so cheerful and healthy a creature could die like that, all in one night, without anybody knowing anything about it. But——"

"Wait one moment," Mr. Gryce here broke in. "You speak of her endeavors to improve herself. What do you mean by that?"

"Her desire to learn things she didn't know; as, for instance, to write and read writing. She could only clumsily print when she came here."

I thought Mr. Gryce would take a piece out of my arm, he griped it so.

"When she came here! Do you mean to say that since she has been with you she has learned to write?"

"Yes, sir; I used to set her copies and——"

"Where are these copies?" broke in Mr. Gryce, subduing his voice to its most professional tone. "And where are her attempts at writing? I'd like to see some of them. Can't you get them for us?"

"I don't know, sir. I always made it a point to destroy them as soon as they had answered their purpose. I didn't like to have such things lying around. But I will go see."

"Do," said he; "and I will go with you. I want to take a look at things upstairs, any way." And, heedless of his rheumatic feet, he rose and prepared to accompany her.

"This is getting very intense," I whispered, as he passed me.

The smile he gave me in reply would have made the fortune of a Thespian Mephistopheles.

Of the ten minutes of suspense which I endured in their absence, I say nothing. At the end of that time they returned with their hands full of paper boxes, which they flung down on the table.

"The writing-paper of the household," observed Mr. Gryce; "every scrap and half-sheet which could be found. But, before you examine it, look at this." And he

178

held out a sheet of bluish foolscap, on which were written some dozen imitations of that time-worn copy, "BE GOOD AND YOU WILL BE HAPPY"; with an occasional "*Beauty soon fades,*" and "*Evil communications corrupt good manners.*"

"What do you think of that?"

"Very neat and very legible."

"That is Hannah's latest. The only specimens of her writing to be found. Not much like some scrawls we have seen, eh?"

"No."

"Mrs. Belden says this girl has known how to write as good as this for more than a week. Took great pride in it, and was continually talking about how smart she was." Leaning over, he whispered in my ear, "This thing you have in your hand must have been scrawled some time ago, if she did it." Then aloud: "But let us look at the paper she used to write on."

Dashing open the covers of the boxes on the table, he took out the loose sheets lying inside, and scattered them out before me. One glance showed they were all of an utterly different quality from that used in the confession. "This is all the paper in the house," said he.

"Are you sure of that?" I asked, looking at Mrs. Belden, who stood in a sort of maze before us. "Wasn't there one stray sheet lying around somewhere, foolscap or something like that, which she might have got hold of and used without your knowing it?"

"No, sir; I don't think so. I had only these kinds; besides, Hannah had a whole pile of paper like this in her room, and wouldn't have been apt to go hunting round after any stray sheets."

"But you don't know what a girl like that might do. Look at this one," said I, showing her the blank side of the confession. "Couldn't a sheet like this have come from somewhere about the house? Examine it well; the matter is important."

"I have, and I say, no, I never had a sheet of paper like that in my house."

Mr. Gryce advanced and took the confession from my hand. As he did so, he whispered: "What do you think now? Many chances that Hannah got up this precious document?"

I shook my head, convinced at last; but in another moment turned to him and whispered back: "But, if Hannah didn't write it, who did? And how came it to be found where it was?"

"That," said he, "is just what is left for us to learn." And, beginning again, he put question after question concerning the girl's life in the house, receiving answers which only tended to show that she could not have brought the confession with her, much less received it from a secret messenger. Unless we doubted Mrs. Belden's word, the mystery seemed impenetrable, and I was beginning to despair of success, when Mr. Gryce, with an askance look at me, leaned towards Mrs. Belden and said:

"You received a letter from Miss Mary Leavenworth yesterday, I hear."

"Yes, sir."

"*This* letter?" he continued, showing it to her.

179

"Yes, sir."

"Now I want to ask you a question. Was the letter, as you see it, the only contents of the envelope in which it came? Wasn't there one for Hannah enclosed with it?"

"No, sir. There was nothing in my letter for her; but she had a letter herself yesterday. It came in the same mail with mine."

"Hannah had a letter!" we both exclaimed; "and in the mail?"

"Yes; but it was not directed to her. It was"—casting me a look full of despair, "directed to me. It was only by a certain mark in the corner of the envelope that I knew——"

"Good heaven!" I interrupted; "where is this letter? Why didn't you speak of it before? What do you mean by allowing us to flounder about here in the dark, when a glimpse at this letter might have set us right at once?"

"I didn't think anything about it till this minute. I didn't know it was of importance. I——"

But I couldn't restrain myself. "Mrs. Belden, where is this letter?" I demanded. "Have you got it?"

"No," said she; "I gave it to the girl yesterday; I haven't seen it since."

"It must be upstairs, then. Let us take another look." and I hastened towards the door.

"You won't find it," said Mr. Gryce at my elbow. "I have looked. There is nothing but a pile of burned paper in the corner. By the way, what could that have been?" he asked of Mrs. Belden.

"I don't know, sir. She hadn't anything to burn unless it was the letter."

"We will see about that," I muttered, hurrying upstairs and bringing down the wash-bowl with its contents. "If the letter was the one I saw in your hand at the post-office, it was in a yellow envelope."

"Yes, sir."

"Yellow envelopes burn differently from white paper. I ought to be able to tell the tinder made by a yellow envelope when I see it. Ah, the letter has been destroyed; here is a piece of the envelope," and I drew out of the heap of charred scraps a small bit less burnt than the rest, and held it up.

"Then there is no use looking here for what the letter contained," said Mr. Gryce, putting the wash-bowl aside. "We will have to ask you, Mrs. Belden."

"But I don't know. It was directed to me, to be sure; but Hannah told me, when she first requested me to teach her how to write, that she expected such a letter, so I didn't open it when it came, but gave it to her just as it was."

"You, however, stayed by to see her read it?"

"No, sir; I was in too much of a flurry. Mr. Raymond had just come and I had no time to think of her. My own letter, too, was troubling me."

"But you surely asked her some questions about it before the day was out?"

"Yes, sir, when I went up with her tea things; but she had nothing to say. Hannah could be as reticent as any one I ever knew, when she pleased. She didn't even admit it was from her mistress."

"Ah! then you thought it was from Miss Leavenworth?"

180

"Why, yes, sir; what else was I to think, seeing that mark in the corner? Though, to be sure, it might have been put there by Mr. Clavering," she thoughtfully added.

"You say she was cheerful yesterday; was she so after receiving this letter?"

"Yes, sir; as far as I could see. I wasn't with her long; the necessity I felt of doing something with the box in my charge—but perhaps Mr. Raymond has told you?"

Mr. Gryce nodded.

"It was an exhausting evening, and quite put Hannah out of my head, but——"

"Wait!" cried Mr. Gryce, and beckoning me into a corner, he whispered, "Now comes in that experience of Q's. While you are gone from the house, and before Mrs. Belden sees Hannah again, he has a glimpse of the girl bending over something in the corner of her room which may very fairly be the wash-bowl we found there. After which, he sees her swallow, in the most lively way, a dose of something from a bit of paper. Was there anything more?"

"No," said I.

"Very well, then," he cried, going back to Mrs. Belden. "But——"

"But when I went upstairs to bed, I thought of the girl, and going to her door opened it. The light was extinguished, and she seemed asleep, so I closed it again and came out."

"Without speaking?"

"Yes, sir."

"Did you notice how she was lying?"

"Not particularly. I think on her back."

"In something of the same position in which she was found this morning?"

"Yes, sir."

"And that is all you can tell us, either of her letter or her mysterious death?"

"All, sir."

Mr. Gryce straightened himself up.

"Mrs. Belden," said he, "you know Mr. Clavering's handwriting when *you* see it?"

"I do."

"And Miss Leavenworth's?"

"Yes, sir."

"Now, which of the two was upon the envelope of the letter you gave Hannah?"

"I couldn't say. It was a disguised handwriting and might have been that of either; but I think——"

"Well?"

"That it was more like hers than his, though it wasn't like hers either."

With a smile, Mr. Gryce enclosed the confession in his hand in the envelope in which it had been found. "You remember how large the letter was which you gave her?"

"Oh, it was large, very large; one of the largest sort."

"And thick?"

"O yes; thick enough for two letters."

"Large enough and thick enough to contain this?" laying the confession, folded and enveloped as it was, before her.

"Yes, sir," giving it a look of startled amazement, "large enough and thick enough to contain that."

Mr. Gryce's eyes, bright as diamonds, flashed around the room, and finally settled upon a fly traversing my coat-sleeve. "Do you need to ask now," he whispered, in a low voice, "where, and from whom, this so-called confession comes?"

He allowed himself one moment of silent triumph, then rising, began folding the papers on the table and putting them in his pocket.

"What are you going to do?" I asked, hurriedly approaching.

He took me by the arm and led me across the hall into toe sitting-room. "I am going back to New York, I am going to pursue this matter. I am going to find out from whom came the poison which killed this girl, and by whose hand this vile forgery of a confession was written."

"But," said I, rather thrown off my balance by all this, "Q and the coroner will be here presently, won't you wait to see them?"

"No; clues such as are given here must be followed while the trail is hot; I can't afford to wait."

"If I am not mistaken, they have already come," I remarked, as a tramping of feet without announced that some one stood at the door.

"That is so," he assented, hastening to let them in.

Judging from common experience, we had every reason to fear that an immediate stop would be put to all proceedings on our part, as soon as the coroner was introduced upon the scene. But happily for us and the interest at stake, Dr. Fink, of R ———, proved to be a very sensible man. He had only to hear a true story of the affair to recognize at once its importance and the necessity of the most cautious action in the matter. Further, by a sort of sympathy with Mr. Gryce, all the more remarkable that he had never seen him before, he expressed himself as willing to enter into our plans, offering not only to allow us the temporary use of such papers as we desired, but even undertaking to conduct the necessary formalities of calling a jury and instituting an inquest in such a way as to give us time for the investigations we proposed to make.

The delay was therefore short. Mr. Gryce was enabled to take the 6:30 train for New York, and I to follow on the 10 p.m.,—the calling of a jury, ordering of an autopsy, and final adjournment of the inquiry till the following Tuesday, having all taken place in the interim.

XXXV. FINE WORK

"No hinge nor loop
   To hang a doubt on!"
"But yet the pity of it, Iago!
   Oh, Iago, the pity of it, Iago."
      —Othello.

One sentence dropped by Mr. Gryce before leaving R—— prepared me for his next move.

"The clue to this murder is supplied by the paper on which the confession is written. Find from whose desk or portfolio this especial sheet was taken, and you find the double murderer," he had said.

Consequently, I was not surprised when, upon visiting his house, early the next morning, I beheld him seated before a table on which lay a lady's writing-desk and a pile of paper, till told the desk was Eleanore's. Then I did show astonishment. "What," said I, "are you not satisfied yet of her innocence?"

"O yes; but one must be thorough. No conclusion is valuable which is not preceded by a full and complete investigation. Why," he cried, casting his eyes complacently towards the fire-tongs, "I have even been rummaging through Mr. Clavering's effects, though the confession bears the proof upon its face that it could not have been written by him. It is not enough to look for evidence where you expect to find it. You must sometimes search for it where you don't. Now," said he, drawing the desk before him, "I don't anticipate finding anything here of a criminating character; but it is among the possibilities that I may; and that is enough for a detective."

"Did you see Miss Leavenworth this morning?" I asked, as he proceeded to fulfil his intention by emptying the contents of the desk upon the table.

"Yes; I was unable to procure what I desired without it. And she behaved very handsomely, gave me the desk with her own hands, and never raised an objection. To be sure, she had little idea what I was looking for; thought, perhaps, I wanted to make sure it did not contain the letter about which so much has been said. But it would have made but little difference if she had known the truth. This desk contains nothing *we* want."

"Was she well; and had she heard of Hannah's sudden death?" I asked, in my irrepressible anxiety.

"Yes, and feels it, as you might expect her to. But let us see what we have here," said he, pushing aside the desk, and drawing towards him the stack of paper I have already referred to. "I found this pile, just as you see it, in a drawer of the library table at Miss Mary Leavenworth's house in Fifth Avenue. If I am not mistaken, it will supply us with the clue we want."

"But——"

"But this paper is square, while that of the confession is of the size and shape of commercial note? I know; but you remember the sheet used in the confession was trimmed down. Let us compare the quality."

Taking the confession from his pocket and the sheet from the pile before him, he carefully compared them, then held them out for my inspection. A glance showed them to be alike in color.

"Hold them up to the light," said he.

I did so; the appearance presented by both was precisely alike.

"Now let us compare the ruling." And, laying them both down on the table, he placed the edges of the two sheets together. The lines on the one accommodated themselves to the lines on the other; and that question was decided.

His triumph was assured. "I was convinced of it," said he. "From the moment I pulled open that drawer and saw this mass of paper, I knew the end was come."

"But," I objected, in my old spirit of combativeness, "isn't there any room for doubt? This paper is of the commonest kind. Every family on the block might easily have specimens of it in their library."

"That isn't so," he said. "It is letter size, and that has gone out. Mr. Leavenworth used it for his manuscript, or I doubt if it would have been found in his library. But, if you are still incredulous, let us see what can be done," and jumping up, he carried the confession to the window, looked at it this way and that, and, finally discovering what he wanted, came back and, laying it before me, pointed out one of the lines of ruling which was markedly heavier than the rest, and another which was so faint as to be almost undistinguishable. "Defects like these often run through a number of consecutive sheets," said he. "If we could find the identical half-quire from which this was taken, I might show you proof that would dispel every doubt," and taking up the one that lay on top, he rapidly counted the sheets. There were but eight. "It might have been taken from this one," said he; but, upon looking closely at the ruling, he found it to be uniformly distinct. "Humph! that won't do!" came from his lips.

The remainder of the paper, some dozen or so half-quires, looked undisturbed. Mr. Gryce tapped his fingers on the table and a frown crossed his face. "Such a pretty thing, if it could have been done!" he longingly exclaimed. Suddenly he took up the next half-quire. "Count the sheets," said he, thrusting it towards me, and himself lifting another.

I did as I was bid. "Twelve."

He counted his and laid it down. "Go on with the rest," he cried.

I counted the sheets in the next; twelve. He counted those in the one following, and paused. "Eleven!"

"Count again," I suggested.

He counted again, and quietly put them aside. "I made a mistake," said he.

But he was not to be discouraged. Taking another half-quire, he went through with the same operation;—in vain. With a sigh of impatience he flung it down on the table and looked up. "Halloo!" he cried, "what is the matter?"

"There are but eleven sheets in this package," I said, placing it in his hand.

The excitement he immediately evinced was contagious. Oppressed as I was, I could not resist his eagerness. "Oh, beautiful!" he exclaimed. "Oh, beautiful! See! the light on the inside, the heavy one on the outside, and both in positions precisely corresponding to those on this sheet of Hannah's. What do you think now? Is any further proof necessary?"

184

"The veriest doubter must succumb before this," returned I.

With something like a considerate regard for my emotion, he turned away. "I am obliged to congratulate myself, notwithstanding the gravity of the discovery that has been made," said he. "It is so neat, so very neat, and so conclusive. I declare I am myself astonished at the perfection of the thing. But what a woman that is!" he suddenly cried, in a tone of the greatest admiration. "What an intellect she has! what shrewdness! what skill! I declare it is almost a pity to entrap a woman who has done as well as this—taken a sheet from the very bottom of the pile, trimmed it into another shape, and then, remembering the girl couldn't write, put what she had to say into coarse, awkward printing, Hannah-like. *Splendid*! or would have been, if any other man than myself had had this thing in charge." And, all animated and glowing with his enthusiasm, he eyed the chandelier above him as if it were the embodiment of his own sagacity.

Sunk in despair, I let him go on.

"Could she have done any better?" he now asked. "Watched, circumscribed as she was, could she have done any better? I hardly think so; the fact of Hannah's having learned to write after she left here was fatal. No, she could not have provided against that contingency."

"Mr. Gryce," I here interposed, unable to endure this any longer; "did you have an interview with Miss Mary Leavenworth this morning?"

"No," said he; "it was not in the line of my present purpose to do so. I doubt, indeed, if she knew I was in her house. A servant maid who has a grievance is a very valuable assistant to a detective. With Molly at my side, I didn't need to pay my respects to the mistress."

"Mr. Gryce," I asked, after another moment of silent self-congratulation on his part, and of desperate self-control on mine, "what do you propose to do now? You have followed your clue to the end and are satisfied. Such knowledge as this is the precursor of action."

"Humph! we will see," he returned, going to his private desk and bringing out the box of papers which we had no opportunity of looking at while in R——. "First let us examine these documents, and see if they do not contain some hint which may be of service to us." And taking out the dozen or so loose sheets which had been torn from Eleanore's Diary, he began turning them over.

While he was doing this, I took occasion to examine the contents of the box. I found them to be precisely what Mrs. Belden had led me to expect,—a certificate of marriage between Mary and Mr. Clavering and a half-dozen or more letters. While glancing over the former, a short exclamation from Mr. Gryce startled me into looking up.

"What is it?" I cried.

He thrust into my hand the leaves of Eleanore's Diary. "Read," said he. "Most of it is a repetition of what you have already heard from Mrs. Belden, though given from a different standpoint; but there is one passage in it which, if I am not mistaken, opens up the way to an explanation of this murder such as we have not had yet. Begin at the beginning; you won't find it dull."

Dull! Eleanore's feelings and thoughts during that anxious time, dull!

185

Mustering up my self-possession, I spread out the leaves in their order and commenced:

"R——, July 6,-"

"Two days after they got there, you perceive," Mr. Gryce explained.

"—A gentleman was introduced to us to-day upon the *piazza* whom I cannot forbear mentioning; first, because he is the most perfect specimen of manly beauty I ever beheld, and secondly, because Mary, who is usually so voluble where gentlemen are concerned, had nothing to say when, in the privacy of our own apartment, I questioned her as to the effect his appearance and conversation had made upon her. The fact that he is an Englishman may have something to do with this; Uncle's antipathy to every one of that nation being as well known to her as to me. But somehow I cannot feel satisfied of this. Her experience with Charlie Somerville has made me suspicious. What if the story of last summer were to be repeated here, with an Englishman for the hero! But I will not allow myself to contemplate such a possibility. Uncle will return in a few days, and then all communication with one who, however prepossessing, is of a family and race with whom it is impossible for us to unite ourselves, must of necessity cease. I doubt if I should have thought twice of all this if Mr. Clavering had not betrayed, upon his introduction to Mary, such intense and unrestrained admiration.

"July 8. The old story is to be repeated. Mary not only submits to the attentions of Mr. Clavering, but encourages them. To-day she sat two hours at the piano singing over to him her favorite songs, and to-night—But I will not put down every trivial circumstance that comes under my observation; it is unworthy of me. And yet, how can I shut my eyes when the happiness of so many I love is at stake!

"July 11. If Mr. Clavering is not absolutely in love with Mary, he is on the verge of it. He is a very fine-looking man, and too honorable to be trifled with in this reckless fashion.

"July 13. Mary's beauty blossoms like the rose. She was absolutely wonderful to-night in scarlet and silver. I think her smile the sweetest I ever beheld, and in this I am sure Mr. Clavering passionately agrees with me; he never looked away from her to-night. But it is not so easy to read *her* heart. To be sure, she appears anything but indifferent to his fine appearance, strong sense, and devoted affection. But did she not deceive us into believing she loved Charlie Somerville? In her case, blush and smile go for little, I fear. Would it not be wiser under the circumstances to say, I hope?

"July 17. Oh, my heart! Mary came into my room this evening, and absolutely startled me by falling at my side and burying her face in my lap. 'Oh, Eleanore, Eleanore!' she murmured, quivering with what seemed to me very happy sobs. But when I strove to lift her head to my breast, she slid from my arms, and drawing herself up into her old attitude of reserved pride, raised her hand as if to impose silence, and haughtily left the room. There is but one interpretation to put upon this. Mr. Clavering has expressed his sentiments, and she is filled with that reckless delight which in its first flush makes one insensible to the existence of barriers which have hitherto been deemed impassable. When will Uncle come?

"July 18. Little did I think when I wrote the above that Uncle was already in the

186

house. He arrived unexpectedly on the last train, and came into my room just as I was putting away my diary. Looking a little care-worn, he took me in his arms and then asked for Mary. I dropped my head, and could not help stammering as I replied that she was in her own room. Instantly his love took alarm, and leaving me, he hastened to her apartment, where I afterwards learned he came upon her sitting abstractedly before her dressing-table with Mr. Clavering's family ring on her finger. I do not know what followed. An unhappy scene, I fear, for Mary is ill this morning, and Uncle exceedingly melancholy and stern.

"Afternoon. We are an unhappy family! Uncle not only refuses to consider for a moment the question of Mary's alliance with Mr. Clavering, but even goes so far as to demand his instant and unconditional dismissal. The knowledge of this came to me in the most distressing way. Recognizing the state of affairs, but secretly rebelling against a prejudice which seemed destined to separate two persons otherwise fitted for each other, I sought Uncle's presence this morning after breakfast, and attempted to plead their cause. But he almost instantly stopped me with the remark, 'You are the last one, Eleanore, who should seek to promote this marriage.' Trembling with apprehension, I asked him why. 'For the reason that by so doing you work entirely for your own interest.' More and more troubled, I begged him to explain himself. 'I mean,' said he, 'that if Mary disobeys me by marrying this Englishman, I shall disinherit her, and substitute your name for hers in my will as well as in my affection.'

"For a moment everything swam before my eyes. 'You will never make me so wretched!' I entreated. 'I will make you my heiress, if Mary persists in her present determination,' he declared, and without further word sternly left the room. What could I do but fall on my knees and pray! Of all in this miserable house, I am the most wretched. To supplant her! But I shall not be called upon to do it; Mary will give up Mr. Clavering."

"There!" exclaimed Mr. Gryce. "What do you think of that? Isn't it becoming plain enough what was Mary's motive for this murder? But go on; let us hear what followed."

With sinking heart, I continued. The next entry is dated July 19, and runs thus:

"I was right. After a long struggle with Uncle's invincible will, Mary has consented to dismiss Mr. Clavering. I was in the room when she made known her decision, and I shall never forget our Uncle's look of gratified pride as he clasped her in his arms and called her his own True Heart. He has evidently been very much exercised over this matter, and I cannot but feel greatly relieved that affairs have terminated so satisfactorily. But Mary? What is there in her manner that vaguely disappoints me? I cannot say. I only know that I felt a powerful shrinking overwhelm me when she turned her face to me and asked if I were satisfied now. But I conquered my feelings and held out my hand. She did not take it.

"July 26. How long the days are! The shadow of our late trial is upon me yet; I cannot shake it off. I seem to see Mr. Clavering's despairing face wherever I go. How is it that Mary preserves her cheerfulness? If she does not love him, I should think the respect which she must feel for his disappointment would keep her from levity at least.

187

"Uncle has gone away again. Nothing I could say sufficed to keep him.

"July 28. It has all come out. Mary has only nominally separated from Mr. Clavering; she still cherishes the idea of one day uniting herself to him in marriage. The fact was revealed to me in a strange way not necessary to mention here; and has since been confirmed by Mary herself. 'I admire the man,' she declares, 'and have no intention of giving him up.' 'Then why not tell Uncle so?' I asked. Her only answer was a bitter smile and a short,—'I leave that for you to do.'

"July 30. Midnight. Worn completely out, but before my blood cools let me write. Mary is a wife. I have just returned from seeing her give her hand to Henry Clavering. Strange that I can write it without quivering when my whole soul is one flush of indignation and revolt. But let me state the facts. Having left my room for a few minutes this morning, I returned to find on my dressing-table a note from Mary in which she informed me that she was going to take Mrs. Belden for a drive and would not be back for some hours. Convinced, as I had every reason to be, that she was on her way to meet Mr. Clavering, I only stopped to put on my hat—"

There the Diary ceased.

"She was probably interrupted by Mary at this point," explained Mr. Gryce. "But we have come upon the one thing we wanted to know. Mr. Leavenworth threatened to supplant Mary with Eleanore if she persisted in marrying contrary to his wishes. She did so marry, and to avoid the consequences of her act she ____"

"Say no more," I returned, convinced at last. "It is only too clear."

Mr. Gryce rose.

"But the writer of these words is saved," I went on, trying to grasp the one comfort left me. "No one who reads this Diary will ever dare to insinuate she is capable of committing a crime."

"Assuredly not; the Diary settles that matter effectually."

I tried to be man enough to think of that and nothing else. To rejoice in her deliverance, and let every other consideration go; but in this I did not succeed. "But Mary, her cousin, almost her sister, is lost," I muttered.

Mr. Gryce thrust his hands into his pockets and, for the first time, showed some evidence of secret disturbance. "Yes, I am afraid she is; I really am afraid she is." Then after a pause, during which I felt a certain thrill of vague hope: "Such an entrancing creature too! It is a pity, it positively is a pity! I declare, now that the thing is worked up, I begin to feel almost sorry we have succeeded so well. Strange, but true. If there was the least loophole out of it," he muttered. "But there isn't. The thing is clear as A, B, C." Suddenly he rose, and began pacing the floor very thoughtfully, casting his glances here, there, and everywhere, except at me, though I believe now, as then, my face was all he saw.

"Would it be a very great grief to you, Mr. Raymond, if Miss Mary Leavenworth should be arrested on this charge of murder?" he asked, pausing before a sort of tank in which two or three disconsolate-looking fishes were slowly swimming about.

188

"Yes," said I, "it would; a very great grief." "Yet it must be done," said he, though with a strange lack of his usual decision. "As an honest official, trusted to bring the murderer of Mr. Leavenworth to the notice of the proper authorities, I have got to do it."

Again that strange thrill of hope at my heart induced by his peculiar manner.

"Then my reputation as a detective! I ought surely to consider that. I am not so rich or so famous that I can afford to forget all that a success like this may bring me. No, lovely as she is, I have got to push it through." But even as he said this, he became still more thoughtful, gazing down into the murky depths of the wretched tank before him with such an intent-ness I half expected the fascinated fishes to rise from the water and return his gaze. What was in his mind?

After a little while he turned, his indecision utterly gone. "Mr. Raymond, come here again at three. I shall then have my report ready for the Superintendent. I should like to show it to you first, so don't fail me."

There was something so repressed in his expression, I could not prevent myself from venturing one question. "Is your mind made up?" I asked.

"Yes," he returned, but in a peculiar tone, and with a peculiar gesture.

"And you are going to make the arrest you speak of?"

"Come at three!"

XXXVI. GATHERED THREADS

"This is the short and the long of it."

—Merry Wives of Windsor.

PROMPTLY at the hour named, I made my appearance at Mr. Gryce's door. I found him awaiting me on the threshold.

"I have met you," said he gravely, "for the purpose of requesting you not to speak during the coming interview. I am to do the talking; you the listening. Neither are you to be surprised at anything I may do or say. I am in a facetious mood"—he did not look so—"and may take it into my head to address you by another name than your own. If I do, don't mind it. Above all, don't talk: remember that." And without waiting to meet my look of doubtful astonishment, he led me softly up-stairs.

The room in which I had been accustomed to meet him was at the top of the first flight, but he took me past that into what appeared to be the garret story, where, after many cautionary signs, he ushered me into a room of singularly strange and unpromising appearance. In the first place, it was darkly gloomy, being lighted simply by a very dim and dirty skylight. Next, it was hideously empty; a pine table and two hard-backed chairs, set face to face at each end of it, being the only articles in the room. Lastly, it was surrounded by several closed doors with blurred and ghostly ventilators over their tops which, being round, looked like the blank eyes of a row of staring mummies. Altogether it was a lugubrious spot, and in the present state of my mind made me feel as if something unearthly and threatening lay crouched in the very atmosphere. Nor,

189

sitting there cold and desolate, could I imagine that the sunshine glowed without, or that life, beauty, and pleasure paraded the streets below.

Mr. Gryce's expression, as he took a seat and beckoned me to do the same, may have had something to do with this strange sensation, it was so mysteriously and sombrely expectant.

"You'll not mind the room," said he, in so muffled a tone I scarcely heard him. "It's an awful lonesome spot, I know; but folks with such matters before them mustn't be too particular as to the places in which they hold their consultations, if they don't want all the world to know as much as they do. Smith," and he gave me an admonitory shake of his finger, while his voice took a more distinct tone, "I have done the business; the reward is mine; the assassin of Mr. Leavenworth is found, and in two hours will be in custody. Do you want to know who it is?" leaning forward with every appearance of eagerness in tone and expression.

I stared at him in great amazement. Had anything new come to light? any great change taken place in his conclusions? All this preparation could not be for the purpose of acquainting me with what I already knew, yet—

He cut short my conjectures with a low, expressive chuckle. "It was a long chase, I tell you," raising his voice still more; "a tight go; a woman in the business too; but all the women in the world can't pull the wool over the eyes of Ebenezer Gryce when he is on a trail; and the assassin of Mr. Leavenworth and"—here his voice became actually shrill in his excitement—"and of Hannah Chester is found.

"Hush!" he went on, though I had neither spoken nor made any move; "you didn't know Hannah Chester was murdered. Well, she wasn't in one sense of the word, but in another she was, and by the same hand that killed the old gentleman. How do I know this? look here! This scrap of paper was found on the floor of her room; it had a few particles of white powder sticking to it; those particles were tested last night and found to be poison. But you say the girl took it herself, that she was a suicide. You are right, she did take it herself, and it was a suicide; but who terrified her into this act of self-destruction? Why, the one who had the most reason to fear her testimony, of course. But the proof, you say. Well, sir, this girl left a confession behind her, throwing the onus of the whole crime on a certain party believed to be innocent; this confession was a forged one, known from three facts; first, that the paper upon which it was written was unobtainable by the girl in the place where she was; secondly, that the words used therein were printed in coarse, awkward characters, whereas Hannah, thanks to the teaching of the woman under whose care she has been since the murder, had learned to write very well; thirdly, that the story told in the confession does not agree with the one related by the girl herself. Now the fact of a forged confession throwing the guilt upon an innocent party having been found in the keeping of this ignorant girl, killed by a dose of poison, taken with the fact here stated, that on the morning of the day on which she killed herself the girl received from some one manifestly acquainted with the customs of the Leavenworth family a letter large enough and thick enough to contain the confession folded, as it was when found, makes it almost certain to my mind that the murderer of Mr. Leavenworth sent this powder and this so-called confession to the girl, meaning her to use them

190

precisely as she did: for the purpose of throwing off suspicion from the right track and of destroying herself at the same time; for, as you know, dead men tell no tales."

He paused and looked at the dingy skylight above us. Why did the air seem to grow heavier and heavier? Why did I shudder in vague apprehension? I knew all this before; why did it strike me, then, as something new?

"But who was this? you ask. Ah, that is the secret; that is the bit of knowledge which is to bring me fame and fortune. But, secret or not, I don't mind telling you"; lowering his voice and rapidly raising it again. "The fact is, *I* can't keep it to myself; it burns like a new dollar in my pocket. Smith, my boy, the murderer of Mr. Leavenworth—but stay, who does the world say it is? Whom do the papers point at and shake their heads over? A woman! a young, beautiful, bewitching woman! Ha, ha, ha! The papers are right; it is a woman; young, beautiful, and bewitching too. But what one? Ah, that's the question. There is more than one woman in this affair. Since Hannah's death I have heard it openly advanced that she was the guilty party in the crime: bah! Others cry it is the niece who was so unequally dealt with by her uncle in his will: bah! again. But folks are not without some justification for this latter assertion. Eleanore Leavenworth did know more of this matter than appeared. Worse than that, Eleanore Leavenworth stands in a position of positive peril to-day. If you don't think so, let me show you what the detectives have against her.

"First, there is the fact that a handkerchief, with her name on it, was found stained with pistol grease upon the scene of murder; a place which she explicitly denies having entered for twenty-four hours previous to the discovery of the dead body.

"Secondly, the fact that she not only evinced terror when confronted with this bit of circumstantial evidence, but manifested a decided disposition, both at this time and others, to mislead inquiry, shirking a direct answer to some questions and refusing all answer to others.

"Thirdly, that an attempt was made by her to destroy a certain letter evidently relating to this crime.

"Fourthly, that the key to the library door was seen in her possession.

"All this, taken with the fact that the fragments of the letter which this same lady attempted to destroy within an hour after the inquest were afterwards put together, and were found to contain a bitter denunciation of one of Mr. Leavenworth's nieces, by a gentleman we will call X in other words, an unknown quantity—makes out a dark case against *you*, especially as after investigations revealed the fact that a secret underlay the history of the Leavenworth family. That, unknown to the world at large, and Mr. Leavenworth in particular, a marriage ceremony had been performed a year before in a little town called F —— between a Miss Leavenworth and this same X. That, in other words, the unknown gentleman who, in the letter partly destroyed by Miss Eleanore Leavenworth, complained to Mr. Leavenworth of the treatment received by him from one of his nieces, was in fact the secret husband of that niece. And that, moreover, this same gentle man, under an assumed name, called on the night of the murder at the house of Mr. Leavenworth and asked for Miss Eleanore's.

"Now you see, with all this against her, Eleanore Leavenworth is lost if it cannot be proved, first that the articles testifying against her, viz.: the handkerchief, letter, and key, passed after the murder through other hands, before reaching hers; and secondly, that some one else had even a stronger reason than she for desiring Mr. Leavenworth's death at this time.

"Smith, my boy, both of these hypotheses have been established by me. By dint of moleing into old secrets, and following unpromising clues, I have finally come to the conclusion that not Eleanore Leavenworth, dark as are the appearances against her, but another woman, beautiful as she, and fully as interesting, is the true criminal. In short, that her cousin, the exquisite Mary, is the murderer of Mr. Leavenworth, and by inference of Hannah Chester also."

He brought this out with such force, and with such a look of triumph and appearance of having led up to it, that I was for the moment dumbfounded, and started as if I had not known what he was going to say. The stir I made seemed to awake an echo. Something like a suppressed cry was in the air about me. All the room appeared to breathe horror and dismay. Yet when, in the excitement of this fancy, I half turned round to look, I found nothing but the blank eyes of those dull ventilators staring upon me.

"You are taken aback!" Mr. Gryce went on. "I don't wonder. Every one else is engaged in watching the movements of Eleanore Leavenworth; I only know where to put my hand upon the real culprit. You shake your head!" (Another fiction.) "You don't believe me! Think I am deceived. Ha, ha! Ebenezer Gryce deceived after a month of hard work! You are as bad as Miss Leavenworth herself, who has so little faith in my sagacity that she offered me, of all men, an enormous reward if I would find for her the assassin of her uncle! But that is neither here nor there; you have your doubts, and you are waiting for me to solve them. Well, nothing is easier. Know first that on the morning of the inquest I made one or two discoveries not to be found in the records, viz.: that the handkerchief picked up, as I have said, in Mr. Leavenworth's library, had notwithstanding its stains of pistol grease, a decided perfume lingering about it. Going to the dressing-table of the two ladies, I sought for that perfume, and found it in Mary's room, not Eleanore's. This led me to examine the pockets of the dresses respectively worn by them the evening before. In that of Eleanore I found a handkerchief, presumably the one she had carried at that time. But in Mary's there was none, nor did I see any lying about her room as if tossed down on her retiring. The conclusion I drew from this was, that she, and not Eleanore, had carried the handkerchief into her uncle's room, a conclusion emphasized by the fact privately communicated to me by one of the servants, that Mary was in Eleanore's room when the basket of clean clothes was brought up with this handkerchief lying on top.

"But knowing the liability we are to mistake in such matters as these, I made another search in the library, and came across a very curious thing. Lying on the table was a penknife, and scattered on the floor beneath, in close proximity to the chair, were two or three minute portions of wood freshly chipped off from the leg of the table; all of which looked as if some one of a nervous disposition had been sitting there, whose hand in a moment of self-forgetfulness had caught up the knife and unconsciously whittled the table, A little thing, you say; but when the question is, which of two ladies, one of a calm and self-possessed nature, the other restless in her ways and excitable in her disposition, was in a certain spot at a certain time, it is these little things that become almost deadly in their significance. No one who has been with these two women an hour can hesitate as to whose delicate hand made that cut in Mr. Leavenworth's library table.

"But we are not done. I distinctly overheard Eleanore accuse her cousin of this deed. Now such a woman as Eleanore Leavenworth has proved herself to be never would accuse a relative of crime without the strongest and most substantial reasons. First, she must have been sure her cousin stood in a position of such emergency that nothing but the death of her uncle could release her from it; secondly, that her cousin's character was of such a nature she would not hesitate to relieve herself from a desperate emergency by the most desperate of means; and lastly, been in possession of some circumstantial evidence against her cousin, seriously corroborative of her suspicions. Smith, all this was true of Eleanore Leavenworth. As to the character of her cousin, she has had ample proof of her ambition, love of money, caprice and deceit, it having been Mary Leavenworth, and not Eleanore, as was first supposed, who had contracted the secret marriage already spoken of. Of the critical position in which she stood, let the threat once made by Mr. Leavenworth to substitute her cousin's name for hers in his will in case she had married this x be remembered, as well as the tenacity with which Mary clung to her hopes of future fortune; while for the corroborative testimony of her guilt which Eleanore is supposed to have had, remember that previous to the key having been found in Eleanore's possession, she had spent some time in her cousin's room; and that it was at Mary's fireplace the half-burned fragments of that letter were found,—and you have the outline of a report which in an hour's time from this will lead to the arrest of Mary Leavenworth as the assassin of her uncle and benefactor."

A silence ensued which, like the darkness of Egypt, could be felt; then a great and terrible cry rang through the room, and a man's form, rushing from I knew not where, shot by me and fell at Mr. Gryce's feet shrieking out:

"It is a lie! a lie! Mary Leavenworth is innocent as a babe unborn. I am the murderer of Mr. Leavenworth. I! I! I!"

It was Trueman Harwell.

XXXVII. CULMINATION

"Saint seducing gold."
—Romeo and Juliet.

"When our actions do not,
Our fears do make us traitors."
--Macbeth.

I NEVER saw such a look of mortal triumph on the face of a man as that which crossed the countenance of the detective.

"Well," said he, "this is unexpected, but not wholly unwelcome. I am truly glad to learn that Miss Leavenworth is innocent; but I must hear some few more particulars before I shall be satisfied. Get up, Mr. Harwell, and explain yourself. If you are the murderer of Mr. Leavenworth, how comes it that things look so black against everybody but yourself?"

But in the hot, feverish eyes which sought him from the writhing form at his feet, there was mad anxiety and pain, but little explanation. Seeing him making unavailing efforts to speak, I drew near.

"Lean on me," said I, lifting him to his feet.

His face, relieved forever from its mask of repression, turned towards me with the look of a despairing spirit. "Save! save!" he gasped. "Save her—Mary—they are sending a report—stop it!"

"Yes," broke in another voice. "If there is a man here who believes in God and prizes woman's honor, let him stop the issue of that report." And Henry Clavering, dignified as ever, but in a state of extreme agitation, stepped into our midst through an open door at our right.

But at the sight of his face, the man in our arms quivered, shrieked, and gave one bound that would have overturned Mr. Clavering, herculean of frame as he was, had not Mr. Gryce interposed.

"Wait!" he cried; and holding back the secretary with one hand—where was his rheumatism now!—he put the other in his pocket and drew thence a document which he held up before Mr. Clavering. "It has not gone yet," said he; "be easy. And you," he went on, turning towards Trueman Harwell, "be quiet, or——"

His sentence was cut short by the man springing from his grasp. "Let me go!" he shrieked. "Let me have my revenge on him who, in face of all I have done for Mary Leavenworth, dares to call her his wife! Let me—" But at this point he paused, his quivering frame stiffening into stone, and his clutching hands, outstretched for his rival's throat, falling heavily back. "Hark!" said he, glaring over Mr. Clavering's shoulder: "it is she! I hear her! I feel her! She is on the stairs! she is at the door! she—" a low, shuddering sigh of longing and despair finished the sentence: the door opened, and Mary Leavenworth stood before us!

It was a moment to make young hairs turn gray. To see her face, so pale, so haggard, so wild in its fixed horror, turned towards Henry Clavering, to the utter ignoring of the real actor in this most horrible scene! Trueman Harwell could not

194

stand it.

"Ah, ah!" he cried; "look at her! cold, cold; not one glance for me, though I have just drawn the halter from her neck and fastened it about my own!"

And, breaking from the clasp of the man who in his jealous rage would now have withheld him, he fell on his knees before Mary, clutching her dress with frenzied hands. "You *shall* look at me," he cried; "you *shall* listen to me! I will not lose body and soul for nothing. Mary, they said you were in peril! I could not endure that thought, so I uttered the truth,—yes, though I knew what the consequence would be,—and all I want now is for you to say you believe me, when I swear that I only meant to secure to you the fortune you so much desired; that I never dreamed it would come to this; that it was because I loved you, and hoped to win your love in return that I——"

But she did not seem to see him, did not seem to hear him. Her eyes were fixed upon Henry Clavering with an awful inquiry in their depths, and none but he could move her.

"You do not hear me!" shrieked the poor wretch. "Ice that you are, you would not turn your head if I should call to you from the depths of hell!"

But even this cry fell unheeded. Pushing her hands down upon his shoulders as though she would sweep some impediment from her path, she endeavored to advance. "Why is that man here?" she cried, indicating her husband with one quivering hand. "What has he done that he should be brought here to confront me at this awful time?"

"'I told her to come here to meet her uncle's murderer," whispered Mr. Gryce into my ear.

But before I could reply to her, before Mr. Clavering himself could murmur a word, the guilty wretch before her had started to his feet.

"Don't you know? then I will tell you. It is because these gentlemen, chivalrous and honorable as they consider themselves, think that you, the beauty and the Sybarite, committed with your own white hand the deed of blood which has brought you freedom and fortune. Yes, yes, this man"—turning and pointing at me—"friend as he has made himself out to be, kindly and honorable as you have doubtless believed him, but who in every look he has bestowed upon you, every word he has uttered in your hearing during all these four horrible weeks, has been weaving a cord for your neck—thinks you the assassin of your uncle, unknowing that a man stood at your side ready to sweep half the world from your path if that same white hand rose in bidding. That I——"

"You?" Ah! now she could see him: now she could hear him!

"Yes," clutching her robe again as she hastily recoiled; "didn't you know it? When in that dreadful hour of your rejection by your uncle, you cried aloud for some one to help you, didn't you know——"

"Don't!" she shrieked, bursting from him with a look of unspeakable horror. "Don't say that! Oh!" she gasped, "is the mad cry of a stricken woman for aid and sympathy the call for a murderer?" And turning away in horror, she moaned: "Who that ever looks at me now will forget that a man—such a man!—dared to think that, because I was in mortal perplexity, I would accept the murder of my

195

best friend as a relief from it!" Her horror was unbounded. "Oh, what a chastisement for folly!" she murmured. "What a punishment for the love of money which has always been my curse!"

Henry Clavering could no longer restrain himself, leaping to her side, he bent over her. "Was it nothing but folly, Mary? Are you guiltless of any deeper wrong? Is there no link of complicity between you two? Have you nothing on your soul but an inordinate desire to preserve your place in your uncle's will, even at the risk of breaking my heart and wronging your noble cousin? Are you innocent in this matter? Tell me!" placing his hand on her head, he pressed it slowly back and gazed into her eyes; then, without a word, took her to his breast and looked calmly around him.

"She is innocent!" said he.

It was the uplifting of a stifling pall. No one in the room, unless it was the wretched criminal shivering before us, but felt a sudden influx of hope. Even Mary's own countenance caught a glow. "Oh!" she whispered, withdrawing from his arms to look better into his face, "and is this the man I have trifled with, injured, and tortured, till the very name of Mary Leavenworth might well make him shudder? Is this he whom I married in a fit of caprice, only to forsake and deny? Henry, do you declare me innocent in face of all you have seen and heard; in face of that moaning, chattering wretch before us, and my own quaking flesh and evident terror; with the remembrance on your heart and in your mind of the letter I wrote you the morning after the murder, in which I prayed you to keep away from me, as I was in such deadly danger the least hint given to the world that I had a secret to conceal would destroy me? Do you, can you, will you, declare me innocent before God and the world?"

"I do," said he.

A light such as had never visited her face before passed slowly over it. "Then God forgive me the wrong I have done this noble heart, for I can never forgive myself! Wait!" said she, as he opened his lips. "Before I accept any further tokens of your generous confidence, let me show you what I am. You shall know the worst of the woman you have taken to your heart. Mr. Raymond," she cried, turning towards me for the first time, "in those days when, with such an earnest desire for my welfare (you see I do not believe this man's insinuations), you sought to induce me to speak out and tell all I knew concerning this dreadful deed, I did not do it because of my selfish fears. I knew the case looked dark against me. Eleanore had told me so. Eleanore herself—and it was the keenest pang I had to endure—believed me guilty. She had her reasons. She knew first, from the directed envelope she had found lying underneath my uncle's dead body on the library table, that he had been engaged at the moment of death in summoning his lawyer to make that change in his will which would transfer my claims to her; secondly, that notwithstanding my denial of the same, I had been down to his room the night before, for she had heard my door open and my dress rustle as I passed out. But that was not all; the key that every one felt to be a positive proof of guilt wherever found, had been picked up by her from the floor of my room; the letter written by Mr. Clavering to my uncle was found in my fire;

196

and the handkerchief which she had seen me take from the basket of clean clothes, was produced at the inquest stained with pistol grease. I could not account for these things. A web seemed tangled about my feet. I could not stir without encountering some new toil. I knew I was innocent; but if I failed to satisfy my cousin of this, how could I hope to convince the general public, if once called upon to do so. Worse still, if Eleanore, with every apparent motive for desiring long life to our uncle, was held in such suspicion because of a few circumstantial evidences against her, what would I not have to fear if these evidences were turned against me, the heiress! The tone and manner of the juryman at the inquest that asked who would be most benefited by my uncle's will showed but too plainly. When, therefore, Eleanore, true to her heart's generous instincts, closed her lips and refused to speak when speech would have been my ruin, I let her do it, justifying myself with the thought that she had deemed me capable of crime, and so must bear the consequences. Nor, when I saw how dreadful these were likely to prove, did I relent. Fear of the ignominy, suspense, and danger which confession would entail sealed my lips. Only once did I hesitate. That was when, in the last conversation we had, I saw that, notwithstanding appearances, you believed in Eleanore's innocence, and the thought crossed me you might be induced to believe in mine if I threw myself upon your mercy. But just then Mr. Clavering came; and as in a flash I seemed to realize what my future life would be, stained by suspicion, and, instead of yielding to my impulse, went so far in the other direction as to threaten Mr. Clavering with a denial of our marriage if he approached me again till all danger was over.

"Yes, he will tell you that was my welcome to him when, with heart and brain racked by long suspense, he came to my door for one word of assurance that the peril I was in was not of my own making. That was the greeting I gave him after a year of silence every moment of which was torture to him. But he forgives me; I see it in his eyes; I hear it in his accents; and you—oh, if in the long years to come you can forget what I have made Eleanore suffer by my selfish fears; if with the shadow of her wrong before you, you can by the grace of some sweet hope think a little less hardly of me, do. As for this man—torture could not be worse to me than this standing with him in the same room—let him come forward and declare if I by look or word have given him reason to believe I understood his passion, much less returned it."

"Why ask!" he gasped. "Don't you see it was your indifference which drove me mad? To stand before you, to agonize after you, to follow you with thoughts in every move you made; to know my soul was welded to yours with bands of steel no fire could melt, no force destroy, no strain dissever; to sleep under the same roof, sit at the same table, and yet meet not so much as one look to show me you understood! It was that which made my life a hell. I was determined you should understand. If I had to leap into a pit of flame, you should know what I was, and what my passion for you was. And you do. You comprehend it all now. Shrink as you will from my presence, cower as you may to the weak man you call husband, you can never forget the love of Trueman Harwell; never forget that love, love, love, was the force which led me down into your uncle's room that night, and lent

197

me will to pull the trigger which poured all the wealth you hold this day into your lap. Yes," he went on, towering in his preternatural despair till even the noble form of Henry Clavering looked dwarfed beside him, "every dollar that chinks from your purse shall talk of me. Every gew-gaw which flashes on that haughty head, too haughty to bend to me, shall shriek my name into your ears. Fashion, pomp, luxury,—you will have them all; but till gold loses its glitter and ease its attraction you will never forget the hand that gave them to you!"

With a look whose evil triumph I cannot describe, he put his hand into the arm of the waiting detective, and in another moment would have been led from the room; when Mary, crushing down the swell of emotions that was seething in her breast, lifted her head and said:

"No, Trueman Harwell; I cannot give you even that thought for your comfort. Wealth so laden would bring nothing but torture. I cannot accept the torture, so must release the wealth. From this day, Mary Clavering owns nothing but what comes to her from the husband she has so long and so basely wronged." And raising her hands to her ears, she tore out the diamonds which hung there, and flung them at the feet of the unfortunate man.

It was the final wrench of the rack. With a yell such as I never thought to listen to from the lips of a man, he flung up his arms, while all the lurid light of madness glared on his face. "And I have given my soul to hell for a shadow!" he moaned, "for a shadow!"

"Well, that is the best day's work I ever did! Your congratulations, Mr. Raymond, upon the success of the most daring game ever played in a detective's office."

I looked at the triumphant countenance of Mr. Gryce in amazement. "What do you mean?" I cried; "did you plan all this?"

"Did I plan it?" he repeated. "Could I stand here, seeing how things have turned out, if I had not? Mr. Raymond, let us be comfortable. You are a gentleman, but we can well shake hands over this. I have never known such a satisfactory conclusion to a bad piece of business in all my professional career."

We did shake hands, long and fervently, and then I asked him to explain himself.

"Well," said he, "there has always been one thing that plagued me, even in the very moment of my strongest suspicion against this woman, and that was, the pistol-cleaning business. I could not reconcile it with what I knew of womankind. I could not make it seem the act of a woman. Did you ever know a woman who cleaned a pistol? No. They can fire them, and do; but after firing them, they do not clean them. Now it is a principle which every detective recognizes, that if of a hundred leading circumstances connected with a crime, ninety-nine of these are acts pointing to the suspected party with unerring certainty, but the hundredth equally important act one which that person could not have performed, the whole fabric of suspicion is destroyed. Recognizing this principle, then, as I have said, I hesitated when it came to the point of arrest. The chain was complete; the links were fastened; but one link was of a different size and material from the rest; and in this argued a break in the chain. I resolved to give her a final chance. Summoning Mr. Clavering, and Mr. Harwell, two persons whom I had no reason to suspect, but who were the only persons beside herself who could have

198

committed this crime, being the only persons of intellect who were in the house or believed to be, at the time of the murder, I notified them separately that the assassin of Mr. Leavenworth was not only found, but was about to be arrested in my house, and that if they wished to hear the confession which would be sure to follow, they might have the opportunity of doing so by coming here at such an hour. They were both too much interested, though for very different reasons, to refuse; and I succeeded in inducing them to conceal themselves in the two rooms from which you saw them issue, knowing that if either of them had committed this deed, he had done it for the love of Mary Leavenworth, and consequently could not hear her charged with crime, and threatened with arrest, without betraying himself. I did not hope much from the experiment; least of all did I anticipate that Mr. Harwell would prove to be the guilty man—but live and learn, Mr. Raymond, live and learn."

XXXVIII. A FULL CONFESSION

"Between the acting of a dreadful thing,
And the first motion, all the interim is
Like a phantasma or a hideous dream;
The genius and the mortal instruments
Are then in council; and the state of a man,
Like to a little Kingdom, suffers then
The nature of an insurrection."
　　—Julius Caesar.

I AM not a bad man; I am only an intense one. Ambition, love, jealousy, hatred, revenge—transitory emotions with some, are terrific passions with me. To be sure, they are quiet and concealed ones, coiled serpents that make no stir till aroused; but then, deadly in their spring and relentless in their action. Those who have known me best have not known this. My own mother was ignorant of it. Often and often have I heard her say: "If Trueman only had more sensibility! If Trueman were not so indifferent to everything! In short, if Trueman had more power in him!"

It was the same at school. No one understood me. They thought me meek; called me Dough-face. For three years they called me this, then I turned upon them. Choosing out their ringleader, I felled him to the ground, laid him on his back, and stamped upon him. He was handsome before my foot came down; afterwards—Well, it is enough he never called me Dough-face again. In the store I entered soon after, I met with even less appreciation. Regular at my work and exact in my performance of it, they thought me a good machine and nothing more. What heart, soul, and feeling could a man have who never sported, never smoked, and never laughed? I could reckon up figures correctly, but one scarcely needed heart or soul for that. I could even write day by day and month by month without showing a flaw in my copy; but that only argued I was no more than they intimated, a regular automaton. I let them think so, with the certainty before me

199

that they would one day change their minds as others had done. The fact was, I loved nobody well enough, not even myself, to care for any man's opinion. Life was well-nigh a blank to me; a dead level plain that had to be traversed whether I would or not. And such it might have continued to this day if I had never met Mary Leavenworth. But when, some nine months since, I left my desk in the counting-house for a seat in Mr. Leavenworth's library, a blazing torch fell into my soul whose flame has never gone out, and never will, till the doom before me is accomplished.

She was so beautiful! When, on that first evening, I followed my new employer into the parlor, and saw this woman standing up before me in her half-alluring, half-appalling charm, I knew, as by a lightning flash, what my future would be if I remained in that house. She was in one of her haughty moods, and bestowed upon me little more than a passing glance. But her indifference made slight impression upon me then. It was enough that I was allowed to stand in her presence and look unrebuked upon her loveliness. To be sure, it was like gazing into the flower-wreathed crater of an awakening volcano. Fear and fascination were in each moment I lingered there; but fear and fascination made the moment what it was, and I could not have withdrawn if I would.

And so it was always. Unspeakable pain as well as pleasure was in the emotion with which I regarded her. Yet for all that I did not cease to study her hour by hour and day by day; her smiles, her movement, her way of turning her head or lifting her eyelids. I had a purpose in this. I wished to knit her beauty so firmly into the warp and woof of my being that nothing could ever serve to tear it away. For I saw then as plainly as now that, coquette though she was, she would never stoop to me. No; I might lie down at her feet and let her trample over me; she would not even turn to see what it was she had stepped upon. I might spend days, months, years, learning the alphabet of her wishes; she would not thank me for my pains or even raise the lashes from her cheek to look at me as I passed. I was nothing to her, could not be anything unless—and this thought came slowly—I could in some way become her master.

Meantime I wrote at Mr. Leavenworth's dictation and pleased him. My methodical ways were just to his taste. As for the other member of the family, Miss Eleanore Leavenworth—she treated me just as one of her proud but sympathetic nature might be expected to do. Not familiarly, but kindly; not as a friend, but as a member of the household whom she met every day at table, and who, as she or any one else could see, was none too happy or hopeful.

Six months went by. I had learned two things; first, that Mary Leavenworth loved her position as prospective heiress to a large fortune above every other earthly consideration; and secondly, that she was in the possession of a secret which endangered that position. What this was, I had for some time no means of knowing. But when later I became convinced it was one of love, I grew hopeful, strange as it may seem. For by this time I had learned Mr. Leavenworth's disposition almost as perfectly as that of his niece, and knew that in a matter of this kind he would be uncompromising; and that in the clashing of these two wills something might occur which would give me a hold upon her. The only thing that troubled me was the fact that I did not know the name of the man in whom she was interested. But chance soon favored me here. One day—a month ago now—I sat down to open Mr. Leavenworth's mail as usual. One letter—shall I ever forget it? ran thus:

"HOFFMAN HOUSE,

"March 1, 1876."

MR. HORATIO LEAVENWORTH:

"DEAR SIR,—You have a niece whom you love and trust, one, too, who seems worthy of all the love and trust that you or any other man can give her; so beautiful, so charming, so tender is she in face, form, manner, and conversation. But, dear sir, every rose has its thorn, and your rose is no exception to this rule. Lovely as she is, charming as she is, tender as she is, she is not only capable of trampling on the rights of one who trusted her, but of bruising the heart and breaking the spirit of him to whom she owes all duty, honor, and observance.

"If you don't believe this, ask her to her cruel, bewitching face, who and what is her humble servant, and yours.

"Henry Ritchie Clavering."

If a bombshell had exploded at my feet, or the evil one himself appeared at my call, I would not have been more astounded. Not only was the name signed to these remarkable words unknown to me, but the epistle itself was that of one who felt himself to be her master: a position which, as you know, I was myself aspiring to occupy. For a few minutes, then, I stood a prey to feelings of the bitterest wrath and despair; then I grew calm, realizing that with this letter in my possession I was virtually the arbitrator of her destiny. Some men would have sought her there and then and, by threatening to place it in her uncle's hand, won from her a look of entreaty, if no more; but I—well, my plans went deeper than that. I knew she would have to be in extremity before I could hope to win her. She must feel herself slipping over the edge of the precipice before she would clutch at the first thing offering succor. I decided to allow the letter to pass into my employer's hands. But it had been opened! How could I manage to give it to him in this condition without exciting his suspicion? I knew of but one way; to let him see me open it for what he would consider the first time. So, waiting till he came into the room, I approached him with the letter, tearing off the end of the envelope as I came. Opening it, I gave a cursory glance at its contents and tossed it down on the table before him.

"That appears to be of a private character," said I, "though there is no sign to that effect on the envelope."

He took it up while I stood there. At the first word he started, looked at me, seemed satisfied from my expression that I had not read far enough to realize its nature, and, whirling slowly around in his chair, devoured the remainder in silence. I waited a moment, then withdrew to my own desk. One minute, two minutes passed in silence; he was evidently rereading the letter; then he hurriedly rose and left the room. As he passed me I caught a glimpse of his face in the mirror. The expression I saw there did not tend to lessen the hope that was rising in my breast.

201

By following him almost immediately up-stairs I ascertained that he went directly to Mary's room, and when in a few hours later the family collected around the dinner table, I perceived, almost without looking up, that a great and insurmountable barrier had been raised between him and his favorite niece.

Two days passed; days that were for me one long and unrelieved suspense. Had Mr. Leavenworth answered that letter? Would it all end as it had begun, without the appearance of the mysterious Clavering on the scene? I could not tell.

Meanwhile my monotonous work went on, grinding my heart beneath its relentless wheel. I wrote and wrote and wrote, till it seemed as if my life blood went from me with every drop of ink I used. Always alert and listening, I dared not lift my head or turn my eyes at any unusual sound, lest I should seem to be watching. The third night I had a dream; I have already told Mr. Raymond what it was, and hence will not repeat it here. One correction, however, I wish to make in regard to it. In my statement to him I declared that the face of the man whom I saw lift his hand against my employer was that of Mr. Clavering. I lied when I said this. The face seen by me in my dream was my own. It was that fact which made it so horrible to me. In the crouching figure stealing warily down-stairs, I saw as in a glass the vision of my own form. Otherwise my account of the matter was true.

This vision had a tremendous effect upon me. Was it a premonition? a forewarning of the way in which I was to win this coveted creature for my own? Was the death of her uncle the bridge by which the impassable gulf between us might be spanned? I began to think it might be; to consider the possibilities which could make this the only path to my elysium; even went so far as to picture her lovely face bending gratefully towards me through the glare of a sudden release from some emergency in which she stood. One thing was sure; if that was the way I must go, I had at least been taught how to tread it; and all through the dizzy, blurred day that followed, I saw, as I sat at my work, repeated visions of that stealthy, purposeful figure stealing down the stairs and entering with uplifted pistol into the unconscious presence of my employer. I even found myself a dozen times that day turning my eyes upon the door through which it was to come, wondering how long it would be before my actual form would pause there. That the moment was at hand I did not imagine. Even when I left him that night after drinking with him the glass of sherry mentioned at the inquest, I had no idea the hour of action was so near. But when, not three minutes after going upstairs, I caught the sound of a lady's dress rustling through the hall, and listening, heard Mary Leavenworth pass my door on her way to the library, I realized that the fatal hour was come; that something was going to be said or done in that room which would make this deed necessary. What? I determined to ascertain. Casting about in my mind for the means of doing so, I remembered that the ventilator running up through the house opened first into the passage-way connecting Mr. Leavenworth's bedroom and library, and, secondly, into the closet of the large spare room adjoining mine. Hastily unlocking the door of the communication between the rooms, I took my position in the closet. Instantly the sound of voices reached my ears; all was open below, and standing there, I was as much an auditor of what went on between Mary and her uncle as if I were in the library itself. And what did I hear? Enough to assure me my suspicions were correct; that it was a moment of vital interest to her; that Mr. Leavenworth, in pursuance of a threat evidently made some time since, was in the act of taking steps to change his will, and that she had come to make an appeal to be forgiven her fault and restored to his favor. What that fault was, I did not learn. No mention was made of Mr. Clavering as her husband. I only heard her declare that her action had been the result of impulse, rather than love; that she regretted it, and desired nothing more than to be free from all obligations to one she would fain forget, and be again to her uncle what she was before she ever saw this man. I thought, fool that I was, it was a mere engagement she was alluding to, and took the insanest hope from these words; and when, in a moment later I heard her uncle reply, in his sternest tone, that she had irreparably forfeited her claims to his regard and favor, I did not need her short and bitter cry of shame and disappointment, or that low moan for some one to help her, for me to sound his death-knell in my heart. Creeping back to my own room, I waited till I heard her reascend, then I stole forth. Calm as I had ever been in my life, I went down the stairs just as I had seen myself do in my dream, and knocking lightly at the library door, went in. Mr. Leavenworth was sitting in his usual place writing.

"Excuse me," said I as he looked up, "I have lost my memorandum-book, and think it possible I may have dropped it in the passage-way when I went for the wine." He bowed, and I hurried past him into the closet. Once there, I proceeded rapidly into the room beyond, procured the pistol, returned, and almost before I realized what I was doing, had taken up my position behind him, aimed, and fired. The result was what you know. Without a groan his head fell forward on his hands, and Mary Leavenworth was the virtual possessor of the thousands she coveted.

My first thought was to procure the letter he was writing. Approaching the table, I tore it out from under his hands, looked at it, saw that it was, as I expected, a summons to his lawyer, and thrust it into my pocket, together with the letter from Mr. Clavering, which I perceived lying spattered with blood on the table before me. Not till this was done did I think of myself, or remember the echo which that low, sharp report must have made in the house. Dropping the pistol at the side of the murdered man, I stood ready to shriek to any one who entered that Mr. Leavenworth had killed himself. But I was saved from committing such a folly. The report had not been heard, or if so, had evidently failed to create an alarm. No one came, and I was left to contemplate my work undisturbed and decide upon the best course to be taken to avoid detection. A moment's study of the wound made in his head by the bullet convinced me of the impossibility of passing the affair off as a suicide, or even the work of a burglar. To any one versed in such matters it was manifestly a murder, and a most deliberate one. My one hope, then, lay in making it as mysterious as it was deliberate, by destroying all due to the motive and manner of the deed. Picking up the pistol, I carried it into the other room with the intention of cleaning it, but finding nothing there to do it with, came back for the handkerchief I had seen lying on the floor at Mr. Leavenworth's feet. It was Miss Eleanore's, but I did not know it till I had used it

203

to clean the barrel; then the sight of her initials in one corner so shocked me I forgot to clean the cylinder, and only thought of how I could do away with this evidence of her handkerchief having been employed for a purpose so suspicious. Not daring to carry it from the room, I sought for means to destroy it; but finding none, compromised the matter by thrusting it deep down behind the cushion of one of the chairs, in the hope of being able to recover and burn it the next day. This done, I reloaded the pistol, locked it up, and prepared to leave the room. But here the horror which usually follows such deeds struck me like a thunderbolt and made me for the first time uncertain in my action. I locked the door on going out, something I should never have done. Not till I reached the top of the stairs did I realize my folly; and then it was too late, for there before me, candle in hand, and surprise written on every feature of her face, stood Hannah, one of the servants, looking at me.

"Lor, sir, where have you been?" she cried, but strange to say, in a low tone. "You look as if you had seen a ghost." And her eyes turned suspiciously to the key which I held in my hand.

I felt as if some one had clutched me round the throat. Thrusting the key into my pocket, I took a step towards her. "I will tell you what I have seen if you will come down-stairs," I whispered; "the ladies will be disturbed if we talk here," and smoothing my brow as best I could, I put out my hand and drew her towards me. What my motive was I hardly knew; the action was probably instinctive; but when I saw the look which came into her face as I touched her, and the alacrity with which she prepared to follow me, I took courage, remembering the one or two previous tokens I had had of this girl's unreasonable susceptibility to my influence; a susceptibility which I now felt could be utilized and made to serve my purpose.

Taking her down to the parlor floor, I drew her into the depths of the great drawing-room, and there told her in the least alarming way possible what had happened to Mr. Leavenworth. She was of course intensely agitated, but she did not scream;—the novelty of her position evidently bewildering her—and, greatly relieved, I went on to say that I did not know who committed the deed, but that folks would declare it was I if they knew I had been seen by her on the stairs with the library key in my hand. "But I won't tell," she whispered, trembling violently in her fright and eagerness. "I will keep it to myself. I will say I didn't see anybody." But I soon convinced her that she could never keep her secret if the police once began to question her, and, following up my argument with a little cajolery, succeeded after a long while in winning her consent to leave the house till the storm should be blown over. But that given, it was some little time before I could make her comprehend that she must depart at once and without going back after her things. Not till I brightened up her wits by a promise to marry her some day if she only obeyed me now, did she begin to look the thing in the face and show any evidence of the real mother wit she evidently possessed. "Mrs. Belden would take me in," said she, "if I could only get to R——. She takes everybody in who asks, her; and she would keep me, too, if I told her Miss Mary sent me. But I can't get there to-night."

I immediately set to work to convince her that she could. The midnight train did not leave the city for a half-hour yet, and the distance to the depot could be easily walked by her in fifteen minutes. But she had no money! I easily supplied that. And she was afraid she couldn't find her way! I entered into minutest directions. She still hesitated, but at length consented to go, and with some further understanding of the method I was to employ in communicating with her, we went down-stairs. There we found a hat and shawl of the cook's which I put on her, and in another moment we were in the carriage yard. "Remember, you are to say nothing of what has occurred, no matter what happens," I whispered in parting injunction as she turned to leave me. "Remember, you are to come and marry me some day," she murmured in reply, throwing her arms about my neck. The movement was sudden, and it was probably at this time she dropped the candle she had unconsciously held clenched in her hand till now. I promised her, and she glided out of the gate.

Of the dreadful agitation that followed the disappearance of this girl I can give no better idea than by saying I not only committed the additional error of locking up the house on my re-entrance, but omitted to dispose of the key then in my pocket by flinging it into the street or dropping it in the hall as I went up. The fact is, I was so absorbed by the thought of the danger I stood in from this girl, I forgot everything else. Hannah's pale face, Hannah's look of terror, as she turned from my side and flitted down the street, were continually before me. I could not escape them; the form of the dead man lying below was less vivid. It was as though I were tied in fancy to this woman of the white face fluttering down the midnight streets. That she would fail in something—come back or be brought back—that I should find her standing white and horror-stricken on the front steps when I went down in the morning, was like a nightmare to me. I began to think no other result possible; that she never would or could win her way unchallenged to that little cottage in a distant village; that I had but sent a trailing flag of danger out into the world with this wretched girl;—danger that would come back to me with the first burst of morning light!

But even those thoughts faded after a while before the realization of the peril I was in as long as the key and papers remained in my possession. How to get rid of them! I dared not leave my room again, or open my window. Some one might see me and remember it. Indeed I was afraid to move about in my room. Mr. Leavenworth might hear me. Yes, my morbid terror had reached that point—I was fearful of one whose ears I myself had forever closed, imagined him in his bed beneath and wakeful to the least sound.

But the necessity of doing something with these evidences of guilt finally overcame this morbid anxiety, and drawing the two letters from my pocket—I had not yet undressed—I chose out the most dangerous of the two, that written by Mr. Leavenworth himself, and, chewing it till it was mere pulp, threw it into a corner; but the other had blood on it, and nothing, not even the hope of safety, could induce me to put it to my lips. I was forced to lie with it clenched in my hand, and the flitting image of Hannah before my eyes, till the slow morning broke. I have heard it said that a year in heaven seems like a day; I can easily

205

believe it. I know that an hour in hell seems an eternity!

But with daylight came hope. Whether it was that the sunshine glancing on the wall made me think of Mary and all I was ready to do for her sake, or whether it was the mere return of my natural stoicism in the presence of actual necessity, I cannot say. I only know that I arose calm and master of myself. The problem of the letter and key had solved itself also. Hide them? I would not try to! Instead of that I would put them in plain sight, trusting to that very fact for their being overlooked. Making the letter up into lighters, I carried them into the spare room and placed them in a vase. Then, taking the key in my hand, went down-stairs, intending to insert it in the lock of the library door as I went by. But Miss Eleanore descending almost immediately behind me made this impossible. I succeeded, however, in thrusting it, without her knowledge, among the filagree work of the gas-fixture in the second hall, and thus relieved, went down into the breakfast room as self-possessed a man as ever crossed its threshold. Mary was there, looking exceedingly pale and disheartened, and as I met her eye, which for a wonder turned upon me as I entered, I could almost have laughed, thinking of the deliverance that had come to her, and of the time when I should proclaim myself to be the man who had accomplished it.

Of the alarm that speedily followed, and my action at that time and afterwards, I need not speak in detail. I behaved just as I would have done if I had had no hand in the murder. I even forbore to touch the key or go to the spare room, or make any movement which I was not willing all the world should see. For as things stood, there was not a shadow of evidence against me in the house; neither was I, a hard-working, uncomplaining secretary, whose passion for one of his employer's nieces was not even mistrusted by the lady herself, a person to be suspected of the crime which threw him out of a fair situation. So I performed all the duties of my position, summoning the police, and going for Mr. Veeley, just as I would have done if those hours between me leaving Mr. Leavenworth for the first time and going down to breakfast in the morning had been blotted from my consciousness.

And this was the principle upon which I based my action at the inquest. Leaving that half-hour and its occurrences out of the question, I resolved to answer such questions as might be put me as truthfully as I could; the great fault with men situated as I was usually being that they lied too much, thus committing themselves on unessential matters. But alas, in thus planning for my own safety, I forgot one thing, and that was the dangerous position in which I should thus place Mary Leavenworth as the one benefited by the crime. Not till the inference was drawn by a juror, from the amount of wine found in Mr. Leavenworth's glass in the morning, that he had come to his death shortly after my leaving him, did I realize what an opening I had made for suspicion in her direction by admitting that I had heard a rustle on the stair a few minutes after going up. That all present believed it to have been made by Eleanore, did not reassure me. She was so completely disconnected with the crime I could not imagine suspicion holding to her for an instant. But Mary—If a curtain had been let down before me, pictured with the future as it has since developed, I could not have seen more plainly what her position would be, if attention were once directed towards her. So, in the vain endeavor to cover up my blunder, I began to lie. Forced to admit that a shadow of disagreement had been lately visible between Mr. Leavenworth and one of his nieces, I threw the burden of it upon Eleanore, as the one best able to bear it. The consequences were more serious than I anticipated. Direction had been given to suspicion which every additional evidence that now came up seemed by some strange fatality to strengthen. Not only was it proved that Mr. Leavenworth's own pistol had been used in the assassination, and that too by a person then in the house, but I myself was brought to acknowledge that Eleanore had learned from me, only a little while before, how to load, aim, and fire this very pistol—a coincidence mischievous enough to have been of the devil's own making.

Seeing all this, my fear of what the ladies would admit when questioned became very great. Let them in their innocence acknowledge that, upon my ascent, Mary had gone to her uncle's room for the purpose of persuading him not to carry into effect the action he contemplated, and what consequences might not ensue! I was in a torment of apprehension. But events of which I had at that time no knowledge had occurred to influence them. Eleanore, with some show of reason, as it seems, not only suspected her cousin of the crime, but had informed her of the fact, and Mary, overcome with terror at finding there was more or less circumstantial evidence supporting the suspicion, decided to deny whatever told against herself, trusting to Eleanore's generosity not to be contradicted. Nor was her confidence misplaced. Though, by the course she took, Eleanore was forced to deepen the prejudice already rife against herself, she not only forbore to contradict her cousin, but when a true answer would have injured her, actually refused to return any, a lie being something she could not utter, even to save one especially endeared to her.

This conduct of hers had one effect upon me. It aroused my admiration and made me feel that here was a woman worth helping if assistance could be given without danger to myself. Yet I doubt if my sympathy would have led me into doing anything, if I had not perceived, by the stress laid upon certain well-known matters, that actual danger hovered about us all while the letter and key remained in the house. Even before the handkerchief was produced, I had made up my mind to attempt their destruction; but when that was brought up and shown, I became so alarmed I immediately rose and, making my way under some pretence or other to the floors above, snatched the key from the gas-fixture, the lighters from the vase, and hastening with them down the hall to Mary Leavenworth's room, went in under the expectation of finding a fire there in which to destroy them. But, to my heavy disappointment, there were only a few smoldering ashes in the grate, and, thwarted in my design, I stood hesitating what to do, when I heard some one coming up-stairs. Alive to the consequences of being found in that room at that time, I cast the lighters into the grate and started for the door. But in the quick move I made, the key flew from my hand and slid under a chair. Aghast at the mischance, I paused, but the sound of approaching steps increasing, I lost all control over myself and fled from the room. And indeed I had no time to lose. I had barely reached my own door when Eleanore Leavenworth, followed by two servants, appeared at the top of the staircase and proceeded towards the room I had just left. The sight reassured me; she would see the key, and take some means of disposing of it; and indeed I always supposed her to have done so, for no further word of key or letter ever came to my ears. This may explain why the questionable position in which Eleanore soon found herself awakened in me no greater anxiety. I thought the suspicions of the police rested upon nothing more tangible than the peculiarity of her manner at the inquest and the discovery of her handkerchief on the scene of the tragedy. I did not know they possessed what might be called absolute proof of her connection with the crime. But if I had, I doubt if my course would have been any different. Mary's peril was the one thing capable of influencing me, and she did not appear to be in peril. On the contrary, every one, by common consent, seemed to ignore all appearance of guilt on her part. If Mr. Gryce, whom I soon learned to fear, had given one sign of suspicion, or Mr. Raymond, whom I speedily recognized as my most persistent though unconscious foe, had betrayed the least distrust of her, I should have taken warning. But they did not, and, lulled into a false security by their manner, I let the days go by without suffering any fears on her account. But not without many anxieties for myself. Hannah's existence precluded all sense of personal security. Knowing the determination of the police to find her, I trod the verge of an awful suspense continually.

Meantime the wretched certainty was forcing itself upon me that I had lost, instead of gained, a hold on Mary Leavenworth. Not only did she evince the utmost horror of the deed which had made her mistress of her uncle's wealth, but, owing, as I believed, to the influence of Mr. Raymond, soon gave evidence that she was losing, to a certain extent, the characteristics of mind and heart which had made me hopeful of winning her by this deed of blood. This revelation drove me almost insane. Under the terrible restraint forced upon me, I walked my weary round in a state of mind bordering on frenzy. Many and many a time have I stopped in my work, wiped my pen and laid it down with the idea that I could not repress myself another moment, but I have always taken it up again and gone on with my task. Mr. Raymond has sometimes shown his wonder at my sitting in my dead employer's chair. Great heaven! it was my only safeguard. By keeping the murder constantly before my mind, I was enabled to restrain myself from any inconsiderate action.

At last there came a time when my agony could be no longer suppressed. Going down the stairs one evening with Mr. Raymond, I saw a strange gentleman standing in the reception room, looking at Mary Leavenworth in a way that would have made my blood boil, even if I had not heard him whisper these words: "But you are my wife, and know it, whatever you may say or do!"

It was the lightning-stroke of my life. After what I had done to make her mine, to hear another claim her as already his own, was stunning, maddening! It forced a demonstration from me. I had either to yell in my fury or deal the man beneath some tremendous blow in my hatred. I did not dare to shriek, so I struck the blow. Demanding his name from Mr. Raymond, and hearing that it was, as I expected, Clavering, I flung caution, reason, common sense, all to the winds, and

208

in a moment of fury denounced him as the murderer of Mr. Leavenworth.

The next instant I would have given worlds to recall my words. What had I done but drawn attention to myself in thus accusing a man against whom nothing could of course be proved! But recall now was impossible. So, after a night of thought, I did the next best thing: gave a superstitious reason for my action, and so restored myself to my former position without eradicating from the mind of Mr. Raymond that vague doubt of the man which my own safety demanded. But I had no intention of going any further, nor should I have done so if I had not observed that for some reason Mr. Raymond was willing to suspect Mr. Clavering. But that once seen, revenge took possession of me, and I asked myself if the burden of this crime could be thrown on this man. Still I do not believe that any active results would have followed this self-questioning if I had not overheard a whispered conversation between two of the servants, in which I learned that Mr. Clavering had been seen to enter the house on the night of the murder, but was not seen to leave it. That determined me. With such a fact for a starting-point, what might I not hope to accomplish? Hannah alone stood in my way. While she remained alive I saw nothing but ruin before me. I made up my mind to destroy her and satisfy my hatred of Mr. Clavering at one blow. But how? By what means could I reach her without deserting my post, or make away with her without exciting fresh suspicion? The problem seemed insolvable; but Trueman Harwell had not played the part of a machine so long without result. Before I had studied the question a day, light broke upon it, and I saw that the only way to accomplish my plans was to inveigle her into destroying herself.

No sooner had this thought matured than I hastened to act upon it. Knowing the tremendous risk I ran, I took every precaution. Locking myself up in my room, I wrote her a letter in printed characters—she having distinctly told me she could not read writing—in which I played upon her ignorance, foolish fondness, and Irish superstition, by telling her I dreamed of her every night and wondered if she did of me; was afraid she didn't, so enclosed her a little charm, which, if she would use according to directions, would give her the most beautiful visions. These directions were for her first to destroy my letter by burning it, next to take in her hand the packet I was careful to enclose, swallow the powder accompanying it, and go to bed. The powder was a deadly dose of poison and the packet was, as you know, a forged confession falsely criminating Henry Clavering. Enclosing all these in an envelope in the corner of which I had marked a cross, I directed it, according to agreement, to Mrs. Belden, and sent it.

Then followed the greatest period of suspense I had yet endured. Though I had purposely refrained from putting my name to the letter, I felt that the chances of detection were very great. Let her depart in the least particular from the course I had marked out for her, and fatal results must ensue. If she opened the enclosed packet, mistrusted the powder, took Mrs. Belden into her confidence, or even failed to burn my letter, all would be lost. I could not be sure of her or know the result of my scheme except through the newspapers. Do you think I kept watch of the countenances about me? devoured the telegraphic news, or started when the bell rang? And when, a few days since, I read that short paragraph in the paper which assured me that my efforts had at least produced the death of the woman I feared, do you think I experienced any sense of relief?

But of that why speak? In six hours had come the summons from Mr. Gryce, and—let these prison walls, this confession itself, tell the rest. I am no longer capable of speech or action.

XXXIX. THE OUTCOME OF A GREAT CRIME

"Leave her to Heaven
And to those thorns that
In her bosom lodge
To prick and sting her."
    —Hamlet

"For she is wise, if I can judge of her;
And fair she is, if that mine eyes be true;
And true she is, as she has proved herself;
And therefore like herself, wise, fair, and true,
Shall she be placed in my constant soul."
    —Merchant of Venice.

"OH, ELEANORE!" I cried, as I made my way into her presence, "are you prepared for very good news? News that will brighten these pale cheeks and give the light back to these eyes, and make life hopeful and sweet to you once more? Tell me," I urged, stooping over her where she sat, for she looked ready to faint.

"I don't know," she faltered; "I fear your idea of good news and mine may differ. No news can be good but——"

"What?" I asked, taking her hands in mine with a smile that ought to have reassured her, it was one of such profound happiness. "Tell me; do not be afraid."

But she was. Her dreadful burden had lain upon her so long it had become a part of her being. How could she realize it was founded on a mistake; that she had no cause to fear the past, present, or future?

But when the truth was made known to her; when, with all the fervor and gentle tact of which I was capable, I showed her that her suspicions had been groundless, and that Trueman Harwell, and not Mary, was accountable for the evidences of crime which had led her into attributing to her cousin the guilt of her uncle's death, her first words were a prayer to be taken to the one she had so wronged. "Take me to her! Oh, take me to her! I cannot breathe or think till I have begged pardon of her on my knees. Oh, my unjust accusation! My unjust accusation!"

Seeing the state she was in, I deemed it wise to humor her. So, procuring a carriage, I drove with her to her cousin's home.

"Mary will spurn me; she will not even look at me; and she will be right!" she cried, as we rolled away up the avenue. "An outrage like this can never be forgiven. But God knows I thought myself justified in my suspicions. If you knew

210

—"

"I do know," I interposed. "Mary acknowledges that the circumstantial evidence against her was so overwhelming, she was almost staggered herself, asking if she could be guiltless with such proofs against her. But——"

"Wait, oh, wait; did Mary say that?"

"Yes."

"To-day?"

"Yes."

"Mary must be changed."

I did not answer; I wanted her to see for herself the extent of that change. But when, in a few minutes later, the carriage stopped and I hurried with her into the house which had been the scene of so much misery, I was hardly prepared for the difference in her own countenance which the hall light revealed. Her eyes were bright, her cheeks were brilliant, her brow lifted and free from shadow; so quickly does the ice of despair melt in the sunshine of hope.

Thomas, who had opened the door, was sombrely glad to see his mistress again. "Miss Leavenworth is in the drawing-room," said he.

I nodded, then seeing that Eleanore could scarcely move for agitation, asked her whether she would go in at once, or wait till she was more composed.

"I will go in at once; I cannot wait." And slipping from my grasp, she crossed the hall and laid her hand upon the drawing-room curtain, when it was suddenly lifted from within and Mary stepped out.

"Mary!"

"Eleanore!"

The ring of those voices told everything. I did not need to glance their way to know that Eleanore had fallen at her cousin's feet, and that her cousin had affrightedly lifted her. I did not need to hear: "My sin against you is too great; you cannot forgive me!" followed by the low: "My shame is great enough to lead me to forgive anything!" to know that the lifelong shadow between these two had dissolved like a cloud, and that, for the future, bright days of mutual confidence and sympathy were in store.

Yet when, a half-hour or so later, I heard the door of the reception room, into which I had retired, softly open, and looking up, saw Mary standing on the threshold, with the light of true humility on her face, I own that I was surprised at the softening which had taken place in her haughty beauty. "Blessed is the shame that purifies," I inwardly murmured, and advancing, held out my hand with a respect and sympathy I never thought to feel for her again.

The action seemed to touch her. Blushing deeply, she came and stood by my side. "I thank you," said she. "I have much to be grateful for; how much I never realized till to-night; but I cannot speak of it now. What I wish is for you to come in and help me persuade Eleanore to accept this fortune from my hands. It is hers, you know; was willed to her, or would have been if—"

"Wait," said I, in the trepidation which this appeal to me on such a subject somehow awakened. "Have you weighed this matter well? Is it your determined purpose to transfer your fortune into your cousin's hands?"

211

Her look was enough without the low, "Ah, how can you ask me?" that followed it.

Mr. Clavering was sitting by the side of Eleanore when we entered the drawing-room. He immediately rose, and drawing me to one side, earnestly said:

"Before the courtesies of the hour pass between us, Mr. Raymond, allow me to tender you my apology. You have in your possession a document which ought never to have been forced upon you. Founded upon a mistake, the act was an insult which I bitterly regret. If, in consideration of my mental misery at that time, you can pardon it, I shall feel forever indebted to you; if not——"

"Mr. Clavering, say no more. The occurrences of that day belong to a past which I, for one, have made up my mind to forget as soon as possible. The future promises too richly for us to dwell on bygone miseries."

And with a look of mutual understanding and friendship we hastened to rejoin the ladies.

Of the conversation that followed, it is only necessary to state the result. Eleanore, remaining firm in her refusal to accept property so stained by guilt, it was finally agreed upon that it should be devoted to the erection and sustainment of some charitable institution of magnitude sufficient to be a recognized benefit to the city and its unfortunate poor. This settled, our thoughts returned to our friends, especially to Mr. Veeley.

"He ought to know," said Mary. "He has grieved like a father over us." And, in her spirit of penitence, she would have undertaken the unhappy task of telling him the truth.

But Eleanore, with her accustomed generosity, would not hear of this. "No, Mary," said she; "you have suffered enough. Mr. Raymond and I will go."

And leaving them there, with the light of growing hope and confidence on their faces, we went out again into the night, and so into a dream from which I have never waked, though the shine of her dear eyes have been now the load-star of my life for many happy, happy months.

212

Made in United States
North Haven, CT
29 April 2024

51876836R00117